KENOBI

STAR WARS

KENOBI

JOHN JACKSON MILLER

DEL REY • NEW YORK

ACKNOWLEDGMENTS

I began developing the story that is *Kenobi* in 2006, when Jeremy Barlow, then my comics editor at Dark Horse, challenged me to write something that hadn't been done as yet: *Star Wars* as a western. Fifty pages of notes later, I had a story better suited for a prose novel than a graphic novel, and so I shelved the project until the opportunity arose. It did in 2012, thanks to editors Shelly Shapiro and Frank Parisi.

Much has been written about life on Tatooine; somewhat less about Ben Kenobi's time of exile. All those works were helpful, and I am appreciative to their authors.

My appreciation goes to Erich Schoeneweiss, Keith Clayton, and everyone at Del Rey, and to Jennifer Heddle, Pablo Hidalgo, and Leland Chee at Lucasfilm.

Finally, my thanks go to my wife and proofreader Meredith Miller, proofreader Brent Frankenhoff, and equestrian adviser Beth Kinnane. (There aren't any horses on Tatooine, but there are saddles!)

THE STAR WARS LEGENDS NOVELS TIMELINE

BEFORE THE REPUBLIC
37,000-25,000 YEARS BEFORE
STAR WARS: A New Hope

 c. 25,793 *YEARS BEFORE STAR WARS: A New Hope*

Dawn of the Jedi: Into the Void

OLD REPUBLIC
5000-67 YEARS BEFORE
STAR WARS: A New Hope

Lost Tribe of the Sith: The Collected
Stories

3954 *YEARS BEFORE STAR WARS: A New Hope*

The Old Republic: Revan

3650 *YEARS BEFORE STAR WARS: A New Hope*

The Old Republic: Deceived
Red Harvest
The Old Republic: Fatal Alliance
The Old Republic: Annihilation

1032 *YEARS BEFORE STAR WARS: A New Hope*

Knight Errant
Darth Bane: Path of Destruction
Darth Bane: Rule of Two
Darth Bane: Dynasty of Evil

RISE OF THE EMPIRE
67-0 YEARS BEFORE
STAR WARS: A New Hope

67 *YEARS BEFORE STAR WARS: A New Hope*

Darth Plagueis

33 *YEARS BEFORE STAR WARS: A New Hope*

Cloak of Deception
Darth Maul: Shadow Hunter
Maul: Lockdown

32 *YEARS BEFORE STAR WARS: A New Hope*

STAR WARS: EPISODE I
THE PHANTOM MENACE

Rogue Planet
Outbound Flight
The Approaching Storm

---

22 *YEARS BEFORE STAR WARS: A New Hope*

STAR WARS: EPISODE II
ATTACK OF THE CLONES

22-19 *YEARS BEFORE STAR WARS: A New Hope*

STAR WARS: THE CLONE
WARS

The Clone Wars: Wild Space
The Clone Wars: No Prisoners

Clone Wars Gambit
Stealth
Siege

Republic Commando
Hard Contact
Triple Zero
True Colors
Order 66

Shatterpoint
The Cestus Deception
MedStar I: Battle Surgeons
MedStar II: Jedi Healer
Jedi Trial
Yoda: Dark Rendezvous
Labyrinth of Evil

19 *YEARS BEFORE STAR WARS: A New Hope*

STAR WARS: EPISODE III
REVENGE OF THE SITH

Kenobi
Dark Lord: The Rise of Darth Vader
Imperial Commando 501st

Coruscant Nights
Jedi Twilight
Street of Shadows
Patterns of Force

The Last Jedi

10 *YEARS BEFORE STAR WARS: A New Hope*

The Han Solo Trilogy
The Paradise Snare
The Hutt Gambit
Rebel Dawn

The Adventures of Lando Calrissian
The Force Unleashed
The Han Solo Adventures
Death Troopers
The Force Unleashed II

REBELLION
0–5 YEARS AFTER
STAR WARS: A New Hope

Death Star
Shadow Games

0

STAR WARS: EPISODE IV
A NEW HOPE

Tales from the Mos Eisley Cantina
Tales from the Empire
Tales from the New Republic
Scoundrels
Allegiance
Choices of One
Honor Among Thieves
Galaxies: The Ruins of Dantooine
Splinter of the Mind's Eye
Razor's Edge

3 YEARS AFTER *STAR WARS: A New Hope*

STAR WARS: EPISODE V
THE EMPIRE STRIKES BACK

Tales of the Bounty Hunters
Shadows of the Empire

4 YEARS AFTER *STAR WARS: A New Hope*

STAR WARS: EPISODE VI
THE RETURN OF THE JEDI

Tales from Jabba's Palace

The Bounty Hunter Wars
  The Mandalorian Armor
  Slave Ship
  Hard Merchandise

The Truce at Bakura
Luke Skywalker and the Shadows of Mindor

NEW REPUBLIC
5–25 YEARS AFTER
STAR WARS: A New Hope

X-Wing
  Rogue Squadron
  Wedge's Gamble
  The Krytos Trap
  The Bacta War
  Wraith Squadron
  Iron Fist
  Solo Command

The Courtship of Princess Leia
Tatooine Ghost

The Thrawn Trilogy
  Heir to the Empire
  Dark Force Rising
  The Last Command

X-Wing: Isard's Revenge

The Jedi Academy Trilogy
  Jedi Search
  Dark Apprentice
  Champions of the Force

I, Jedi
Children of the Jedi
Darksaber
Planet of Twilight
X-Wing: Starfighters of Adumar
The Crystal Star

The Black Fleet Crisis Trilogy
  Before the Storm
  Shield of Lies
  Tyrant's Test

The New Rebellion

The Corellian Trilogy
  Ambush at Corellia
  Assault at Selonia
  Showdown at Centerpoint

The Hand of Thrawn Duology
  Specter of the Past
  Vision of the Future

Scourge
Survivor's Quest

THE **STAR WARS** LEGENDS NOVELS TIMELINE

DRAMATIS PERSONAE

Annileen Calwell, storekeeper
Orrin Gault, moisture farmer and entrepreneur
A'Yark, Tusken war leader
Kallie Calwell, Annileen's daughter
Jabe Calwell, Annileen's son
Mullen Gault, Orrin's son
Veeka Gault, Orrin's daughter
Wyle Ulbreck, moisture farmer
Leelee Pace, Zeltron artisan
Ben Kenobi, recent arrival

A long time ago in a galaxy far, far away. . . .

KENOBI

Until the time is right, disappear we will.

—YODA

Darkness has fallen on the galaxy. The Emperor has taken control of the Galactic Republic, aided by Anakin Skywalker, once one of the brightest of the Jedi Knights, charged with protecting the helpless. Having fallen to the dark side of the mystical Force, Anakin lives on as the Emperor's ruthless enforcer, Darth Vader.

But hope also lives in the form of Anakin's infant son—protected by Anakin's friend and former mentor, Obi-Wan Kenobi. Kenobi flees with the baby to the remote world of Tatooine, where years earlier Anakin's fall truly began when he vengefully massacred a native clan of Tusken Raiders.

Unaware of that event—and still believing that he killed Anakin in their desperate duel—Kenobi settles into a new role, watching over the child and his adoptive family, the Larses, from a distance. But hiding is difficult for one accustomed to action, and even desert Tatooine has those who require the help of a Jedi . . .

PROLOGUE

"IT'S TIME FOR YOU TO GO HOME, SIR."

Wyle Ulbreck woke up and looked at his empty glass. "What's that you say?"

The green-skinned bartender prodded the old human on the shoulder. "I said it's time for you to go home, Master Ulbreck. You've had enough."

"That ain't what I meant," Ulbreck said, rubbing the crust from his bloodshot eyes. "You called me 'sir.' And then 'Master.'" He leered suspiciously at the barkeep. "Are you an organic—or a *droid*?"

The bartender sighed and shrugged. "*This* again? I told you when you asked earlier. My eyes are large and red because I'm a Duros. I called you what I did because I'm polite. And I'm polite because I'm not some old moisture farmer, deranged from too many years out in the—"

"Because," the white-whiskered man interrupted, "I don't do business with no droids. Droids are thieves, the lot of them."

"Why would a droid steal?"

"T'give to other droids," Ulbreck said. He shook his head. The bartender was clearly an idiot.

"What would—" the bartender started to ask. "Never mind," he said instead. He reached for a bottle and refilled the old farmer's glass. "I'm going to stop talking to you now. Drink up."

Ulbreck did exactly that.

To Ulbreck's mind, there was one thing wrong with the galaxy: people. People and droids. Well, those were two things—but then again, wasn't it wrong to limit what was wrong with the galaxy to just one thing? How fair was that? That was how the old farmer's thinking tended to go, even when he was sober. In sixty standard years of moisture farming, Ulbreck had formed one theory about life after another. But he'd spent enough of the early years working alone—odd, how not even his farmhands wanted to be around him—that all his notions had piled up, unspoken.

That was what visits to town were for: opportunities for Ulbreck to share the wisdom of a lifetime. When he wasn't getting robbed by diabolical droids pretending to be green bartenders.

They weren't supposed to allow droids inside Junix's Joint—that was what the ancient sign outside the Anchorhead bar said. Junix, whoever he was, was long since dead and buried in the sands of Tatooine, but his bar still stood: a dimly lit dive where the cigarra smoke barely covered the stink of farmers who'd been in the desert all day. Ulbreck seldom visited the place, preferring an oasis establishment closer to home. But having traveled to Anchorhead to chew out a vaporator parts supplier, he'd stopped in to fill his canteen.

Now, half a dozen lum ales later, Ulbreck began thinking about home. His wife was waiting for him there, and he knew he had better go. Then again, his wife was waiting for him there, and that was reason enough for him to stay. He and Magda had had a horrible fight that morning over whatever it was they'd fought about the night before. Ulbreck couldn't remember what that was now, and it pleased him.

Still, he was an important man, with many underlings who would steal him blind if he was away too long. Through a haze, Ulbreck looked to the chrono on the wall. There were numbers there, and some of them were upside down. And dancing. Ulbreck scowled. He was no fan of dancing. Ears buzzing, he slid off the bar stool, intent on giving the digits a piece of his mind.

That was when the floor attacked him. Swiftly and scurrilously, intent on striking him in the head when he wasn't looking.

It would have succeeded, had the hand not caught him.

"Careful, there," said the hand's owner.

Bleary-eyed, Ulbreck looked up the arm and into the hooded face of his rescuer. Blue eyes looked back at him from beneath sandy-colored eyebrows.

"I don't know you," Ulbreck said.

"Yes," the bearded human responded, helping the old farmer back onto the stool. Then he moved a few paces away to get the bartender's attention.

The brown-cloaked man had something in his other arm, Ulbreck now saw—a bundle of some kind. Alerted, Ulbreck looked around to see whether his own bundle was missing before remembering that he never had a bundle.

"This isn't a nursery," the bartender told the new-comer, although Ulbreck couldn't figure out why.

"I just need some directions," the hooded man responded.

Ulbreck knew many directions. He'd lived long enough on Tatooine to visit lots of places, and while he hated most of them and would never go back, he prided himself on knowing the best shortcuts to them. Certain that his directions would be better than those provided by a droid pretending to be a Duros, Ulbreck moved to intervene.

This time, he caught the railing himself.

Ulbreck looked back warily at the glass on the bar. "That drink ain't right," he said to the bartender. "You're—you're . . ."

The newcomer interjected cautiously, "You mean to say they're watering the ale?"

The bartender looked at the hooded guest and smirked. "Sure, we *always* add the scarcest thing on Tatooine to our drinks. We rake in the credits that way."

"Ain't what I mean," Ulbreck said, trying to focus. "You've done slipped somethin' in this drink to put me out. So you can take my money. I know you city types."

The bartender shook his bald head and looked behind him to his similarly hairless wife, who was washing up at the sink. "Close it up, Yoona. We've been found out." He looked to the hooded stranger. "We've been piling customers' bodies in the back room for years— but I guess that's all over now," he said jokingly.

"I won't tell a soul," the newcomer said, smiling. "In exchange for directions. And a bit of blue milk, if you have it."

Ulbreck was puzzling through that exchange when the bartender's expression turned to one of concern. The old farmer turned to see several young humans entering through the arched doorway, cursing and laughing. Through his haze, Ulbreck recognized the drunken rowdies.

The two in their twenties were brother and sister Mullen and Veeka Gault, hellion spawn of Ulbreck's greatest competitor out west, Orrin Gault. And their cronies were here, too. Zedd Grobbo, the big menace who could outlift a loader droid; and, at just a little over half his size, young Jabe Calwell, son of one of Ulbreck's neighbors.

"Get that kid out of here," the bartender yelled when he saw the teenage tagalong. "Like I told the other guy, the day care's around the block."

At the reference, Ulbreck heard catcalls from the young punks—and he noticed his savior turning to face the wall with his bundle, away from the troublemakers. Veeka Gault shoved past Ulbreck and grabbed a bottle from behind the bar. She paid the Duros with an obscene gesture.

Her fellow hooligans had moved on to a helpless victim: Yoona, the bartender's wife. Catching the startled Duros woman with a pile of empties on her tray, Zedd spun her around for sport, causing mugs to fly in all directions. One struck the shaggy head of a patron at a nearby table.

The Wookiee rose to register his towering disapproval. So did Ulbreck, who had disliked several generations of Gaults, and didn't mind helping to put this generation in its place. He staggered to a table near the group and prepared to raise his objections. But the Wookiee had precedence, and Ulbreck felt the table he was leaning against falling anyway, so he decided to check things out from the floor. He heard a scuffling sound and only vaguely registered the arrival of the bartender's wife, who scuttled into cover beside him.

The Wookiee backhanded Zedd, sending him across the room—and into the table of some people Ulbreck was pretty sure *were* thieves, even though they weren't droids. He'd eyed the green-skinned, long-snouted Rodians all afternoon and evening, wondering when they'd harass him. He knew henchmen for Jabba the Hutt when he saw them. Now, their table upended, the thugs moved—chairs overturning as they shot to their feet and reached for their guns.

"No blasters!" Ulbreck heard the bartender yell as customers stampeded for the exit. The call didn't do a bit of good. Trapped between advancing attackers, the Gaults, who had drawn their pistols when the Wookiee struck their comrade, began firing back at the Rodians. Young Jabe might have fired his weapon, too, Ulbreck saw, had the Wookiee not lifted him from the ground. The titan held the howling boy aloft, about to hurl him into a wall.

The bearded newcomer knelt beside Ulbreck against the bar and leaned across him toward the bartender's wife. "Take care of this," the man said, placing his bundle in her hands. Then he dashed into the fray.

Ulbreck returned his attention to the bar fight. Above him, the Wookiee threw Jabe at the wall. But somehow, boy and wall never met; as Ulbreck craned his neck to see, Jabe's flailing body flew in an unnatural curve through the air and landed behind the bar.

Stunned, Ulbreck looked to see if Yoona had seen the same thing. But she was frozen in terror, eyes squeezed shut. Then a blaster shot struck the floor near them. She opened her eyes. With a scream, she shoved the bundle into Ulbreck's hands and crawled away.

Ulbreck turned his own frightened eyes back to the brawl, expecting to see the Wookiee beating Jabe to a pulp. He saw, instead, the hooded man—holding Jabe's blaster and pointing it at the ceiling. The man fired once at the lightglobe suspended overhead. A second later, Junix's Joint was in darkness.

But not silence. There was the Wookiee's howl. The blaster shots. The shattered glass. And then there was the strange humming sound, even louder than the one in Ulbreck's ears. Ulbreck feared to peer around the edge of the table shielding his body. But when he did, he could make out the silhouette of the hooded man, lit by a wash of blue light—and stray blaster bolts of orange, ricocheting harmlessly into the wall. Dark figures surged forward—the criminal Rodians?—but they fell away, screaming, as the human advanced.

Ulbreck slid back behind the table, trembling.

When quiet finally came, all Ulbreck could hear was a gentle rustling inside the blanket on his lap. Fumbling for the utility light he carried in his pocket, Ulbreck activated it and looked down at the bundle he was holding.

A tiny baby with a wisp of blond hair gurgled at him.

"Hello," Ulbreck said, not knowing what else to say.

The infant cooed.

The bearded man appeared at Ulbreck's side. Lit from below by the portable light, he looked kindly—and not at all fatigued by whatever he had just done. "Thank you," he said, taking the child back. Starting to rise, he paused. "Excuse me. Do you know the way to the Lars homestead?"

Ulbreck scratched his beard. "Well, now, there's four or five ways to get there. Let me think of the best way to describe it—"

"Never mind," the man replied. "I'll find it myself." He and the child disappeared into the darkness.

Ulbreck rose now, turning the light onto the room around him.

There was no-good Mullen Gault, being revived by his no-good sister, as Jabe limped toward the open doorway. Ulbreck could just make out the Wookiee outside, evidently chasing after Zedd. The bartender was in the back, consoling his wife.

Jabba's thugs lay dead on the floor.

The old farmer slumped back down again. What had happened in here? Had the stranger really taken on the toughs alone? Ulbreck didn't remember seeing him with a weapon. And what about Jabe, who'd seemed to hang in the air before he dropped behind the bar? And what was that blasted flashing blue light?

Ulbreck shook his aching head, and the room spun a

little. No, truth was, he just couldn't trust his besotted eyes. No one would risk his neck against Jabba's toughs. And no one would bring a baby to a bar fight. No decent person, anyway. Certainly not some hero type.

"People are just no good," Ulbreck said to no one. Then he went to sleep.

Meditation

The package is delivered.

I hope you can read my thoughts, Master Qui-Gon: I haven't heard your voice since that day on Polis Massa, when Master Yoda told me I could commune with you through the Force. You'll remember that we decided I should take Anakin's son to his relatives for safekeeping. That mission is now accomplished.

It feels so strange, being here, at this place and in this circumstance. Years ago, we removed one child from Tatooine, thinking him to be the galaxy's greatest hope. Now I have returned one—with the same goal in mind. I hope it goes better this time. Because the path to this moment has been filled with pain. For the whole galaxy, for my friends— and for me.

I still can't believe the Jedi Order is gone—and the Republic, corrupted and in the hands of Palpatine. And Anakin, corrupted as well. The holovids I saw of him slaughtering the Jedi younglings in the Temple still haunt my dreams . . . and shatter my heart into pieces, over and over again.

But after the horror of children's deaths, a child may bring hope, as well. It's as I said: the delivery is made. I'm standing on a ridge with my riding beast—a Tatooine eopie—looking back at the Lars homestead. Owen and Beru Lars are outside, holding the child. The last chapter is finished: a new one has begun.

I'll look for a place nearby, though if I hang around too long, I half expect Owen will want me to move someplace else, farther away. There may be wisdom in that. I seem to attract trouble, even in such a remote place as this. There was some mischief yesterday at Anchorhead—and before that, some trouble in one of the spaceports I passed through. None of it was really about me, thankfully, or why I'm here. But I can't afford to react to things as Obi-Wan Kenobi anymore. I won't be able to turn on my lightsaber without screaming "Jedi Knight" to everyone around. Even on Tatooine, I expect someone knows what that is!

So this will be it. From here on out, as long as it takes, I'm minding my own business and staying out of trouble. I can't play Jedi for this world and help save the other worlds at the same time. Isolation is the answer.

The city—even a village like Anchorhead—runs at too fast a pace. Out on the periphery, though, should be another story. I can already feel time moving differently—to the rhythm of the desert.

Yes, I expect things will be slower. I'll be far from anywhere, and alone, with nothing but my regrets to keep me company.

If only there were a place to hide from those.

PART ONE

THE
OASIS

CHAPTER ONE

EVERYTHING CASTS TWO SHADOWS.

The suns had determined this at the dawn of creation. Brothers, they were, until the younger sun showed his true face to the tribe. It was a sin. The elder sun attempted to kill his brother, as was only proper.

But he failed.

Burning, bleeding, the younger sun pursued his sibling across the sky. The wily old star fled for the hills and safety, but it was his fate never to rest again. For the younger brother had only exposed his face. The elder had exposed his failure.

And others had seen it—to their everlasting sorrow.

The first Sand People had watched the battle in the sky. The suns, dually covered in shame, turned their wrath on the witnesses. The skybrothers' gaze tore at the mortals, burning through flesh to reveal their secret selves. The Sand People saw their shadows on the sands of Tatooine, and listened. The younger spirit urged attack. The elder told them to hide. Counsels, from the condemned.

The Sand People were condemned, as well. Always walking with the twin shadows of sacrilege and failure beside them, they would hide their faces. They would fight. They would raid. And they would run.

Most Sand People struck at night, when neither sky-brother could whisper to them. A'Yark preferred to hunt at dawn. The voices of the shadows were quieter then—and the settlers who infested the land could see their doom clearly. That was important. The elder sun had failed by not killing his brother. A'Yark would not fail, had never failed, in killing settlers. The elder sun would see the example, and learn . . .

. . . *now.*

"Tuskens!"

A'Yark charged toward the old farmer who had given the cry. The raider's metal gaderffii smashed into the human's naked chin, shattering bone. A'Yark surged forward, knocking the victim to the ground. The settler struggled, coughing as he tried to repeat the cry. "Tuskens!"

Years earlier, other settlers had given that name to the Sand People who obliterated Fort Tusken. The raiders back then had welcomed the name into their tongue; it was proof the walking parasites had nothing the Sand People could not take. But A'Yark couldn't stand to hear the proud name in the mouths of the appalling creatures—and few were as ugly as the bloody settler now writhing on the sand. The human was ancient. Apart from a bandage from a recent head injury, his whitish hairs and withered flesh were exposed to the sky. It was horrible to see.

A'Yark plunged the hefty gaderffii downward, its metal flanges crushing against the settler's rib cage. Bones snapped. The weapon's point went fully through, grinding against the stone surface beneath. The old settler choked his last. The Tusken name again belonged only to the Sand People.

Immediately A'Yark charged toward the low building, a short distance ahead. There was no thought to it.

No predator of Tatooine ever stopped to reflect on killing. A Tusken could be no different.

To think too long was to die.

The human nest was a wretched thing, something like a sketto hive: scum molded and shaped into a disgusting half bulb, buried in the sand. This one was formed from that false rock of theirs, the "synstone." A'Yark had seen it before.

Another shout. A pasty white biped with a bulging cranium appeared in the doorway of the building, brandishing a blaster rifle. A'Yark discarded the gaderffii and lunged, ripping the gun from the startled settler's hands. A'Yark did not understand *how* a blaster rifle tore its victim apart, but understanding wasn't necessary. The thing had a use. The marauder put it to work on the settler, who had no use.

Well, that wasn't exactly true. The settlers *did* have a use: to provide more rifles for the Tuskens to take. It might have been a funny thought, if A'Yark ever laughed. But that concept was as alien as the white-skinned corpse now on the floor.

So many strange things had come to live in the desert. And to die.

Behind, two more raiders entered the structure. A'Yark did not know them. The days of going into battle flanked by cousins were long since past. The newcomers began flipping crates in the storage area, spilling contents. More metal things. The settlers were obsessed with them.

The warriors were, too—but it wasn't time for that. A'Yark barked at them. *"N'gaaaiih! N'gaaaiih!"*

The youths didn't listen. They were not A'Yark's sons. A'Yark had but one son, now, not quite old enough to fight. Nor did these warriors have fathers. It was the way, these days. Mighty tribes had become mere war parties, their ranks constantly evolving as survivors of one group melted into another.

That A'Yark led this raid at all bespoke their misery. No one on the attack had lived half as long as A'Yark had, or seen so much. The best warriors had fallen years before; these youths certainly wouldn't live to vie for leadership. They were fools, and if A'Yark did not kill them for their foolishness, they would die some other way.

Not this morning, though. A'Yark had chosen the target carefully. This farm was close to the jagged Jundland Wastes, far from the other villages—and it had few of the vile structures by which the residents wrenched water from a sky none could own. The fewer spires— vaporators, the farmers called them—the fewer settlers. Now, it would seem, there were none. Except for the young warriors fumbling, all was quiet.

But A'Yark, who had lived to see forty cycles of the starry sky, was not fooled. A weapon stood beside the doorway leading outside. The old human's, left by accident? Rifle to silvery mouthpiece, A'Yark sniffed.

No. With one swift motion, A'Yark smashed the weapon against the doorjamb. The rifle had been used to kill a Tusken. The smell of sweat from another day still clung to the stock. It differed from the old human's scent, and that of the white creature the settlers called a Bith. Someone else was here. But the rifle could not be used now, nor ever again.

A weapon that killed a Tusken had no more power than any other, so far as A'Yark was concerned; such superstitions were for weaker minds. But just as Tuskens prized their banthas, the settlers seemed to prize individual rifles, etching symbols on their stocks. The human that carried this one was more formidable than the old man and the Bith creature, but he would have to resort

to something new and unfamiliar next time. If he survived the day.

A'Yark would see that he didn't.

The war leader reclaimed the gaderffii from the floor
and shoved past the looting youths. Footsteps in the
sand led around back, where three soulless vaporators
hummed and defiled. A small hut for servicing the foul
machines sat behind them.

Fitting. A'Yark would make the inhabitants bleed for
using the vaporators. Slowly, and so the suns would see.
What the settlers had stolen would return to the sand, a
drop at a time.

"Ru rah ru rah!" A'Yark called, straining to remember the old words. "We is here in peace."

No answer. Of course, there would be none—but
someone was surely inside and had heard the words.
The warrior was proud of remembering them. A human
sister had joined A'Yark's family years ago; the Tuskens
often replenished their numbers by kidnapping. The band
needed reinforcements now, but would not take anyone
here. The settlers' presence so near the wastes was too
great an offense. They would die, and others would see,
and the Jundland would be left alone.

The other warriors filed from the house and surrounded the service hut. The Tuskens numbered eight;
none could challenge them. Cloth-wrapped hands curled
around the shaft of an ancient gaderffii, A'Yark inserted
the *traang*—the curved end of the weapon—into the door
handle.

The metal door creaked open. Inside, a quivering trio
of humans huddled amid spare parts for the thirst machines. A black-haired woman clutched a swaddled infant, while a brown-haired male held them both. He
also held a blaster pistol.

It was the owner of the busted rifle—and A'Yark
could tell he was missing the weapon now. Swallowing

his fear, the young man looked right into A'Yark's good eye. "You—*go!* We're not afraid."

"Settlers lie," A'Yark said, the strange words startling the humans almost as much as they startled the other Tuskens. "*Settler* lies."

Eight gaderffii lifted to the sky, their spear-points glinting in the morning light. A'Yark knew some would land true. And the old skybrother above would see again what *real* bravery was—

"*Ayooooo-eh-EH-EHH!*"

The sound echoed over the horizon. As one, the war party looked north. The sound came again, louder this time. Its meaning was unmistakable.

The youngest Tusken in the party said it first: krayt dragon!

The warrior-child spun—and stumbled over his own booted feet, landing mouthpiece-first in the sand. The others looked to A'Yark, who turned back toward the hut. The war leader had seen enough human faces to read expressions—but even to a seasoned marauder, the visages were startling.

The farmer and his wife didn't just appear relieved. They looked *defiant.*

In the presence of a krayt? The greatest predator Tatooine knew, after the Tuskens? Yes, A'Yark saw. And that wasn't all. The young mother was clutching something, beside the baby, in her free hand.

A'Yark barked a command to the warriors, but it was too late. With the horrific sound in the air, none would stand. The two looters from earlier nearly trampled the fallen youth as they darted away, trying to remember where they'd set their stolen goods. The others clutched their gaderffii to their chests and fled behind the main hut.

Wrong. Wrong! This wasn't what A'Yark had taught them. Not at all! But they scattered before they even knew where the dragon was, leaving their leader alone with the settlers. The young farmer kept his blaster pointed at A'Yark, but did not fire. Perhaps he'd calculated the risk, deciding the unfired weapon was more of a deterrent than a shot by a shaky hand.

It didn't matter. If the settlers had hoped for a distraction, they had gotten one. A'Yark snorted and stepped backward, tan robes swirling.

The warriors were running this way and that. A'Yark yelled, but no one could be heard over the din. There was something unnatural about the sound. But what? No one would pretend to be a krayt dragon! If any could, it would never sound so—

—mechanical?

"AYOOOO-EEEEEEEEEE!"

No mistaking that, A'Yark thought. The moan of the dragon had resolved itself into a head-splitting shrill, far beyond the capacity of any lungs. It was coming loudest from a new source, immediately apparent: a horn attached to one of the silver spires in the middle of the farm. And there were similar sounds, emanating from over the hills to the north and east.

A'Yark stood in the middle of the yard, gaderffii raised aloft. *"Prodorra! Prodorra! Prodorra!"*

Fake!

The young looters appeared again, running over a crest back toward the farm. A'Yark exhaled through rotten teeth. At least someone had heard, over the racket. Now, at least, maybe they could—

Blasterfire! An orange blaze enveloped one of the runners from behind. The other turned in panic, only to be incinerated as well. A'Yark crouched instinctively, seeking cover behind the accursed vaporator.

"Wa-hooo!" A metallic wave, copper and green, swept over the dune. A'Yark recognized it right away. It was the landspeeder that had haunted them before at

the Tall Rock. And now, as then, several settler youths clustered in its open interior, hooting and firing wildly.

A'Yark darted behind a second vaporator, suddenly more confident. There *was* no dragon, only settlers. The Tuskens could be rallied against them, if they stood true.

But they weren't standing. One fled toward the nothingness of the east, and A'Yark could see two more landspeeders racing after him. And the clumsy young warrior—who had barely survived the rites of adulthood days before—hid behind the hut, clutching at the sands in cowardice. Only the suns knew where the others had gone.

No good.

The first speeder circled the settlement, its riders showering fire on nothing in particular. And now another hovercraft arrived. Fancier, with sloping curves, the silver vehicle carried two humans in an open compartment protected by a windshield. A grim, hairy-faced human steered the vessel as his older passenger stood brazenly up in his seat.

A'Yark had seen the passenger before, at a greater distance. Clean-shaven, older than most Tuskens ever got—and always wearing the same senseless expression. *The Smiling One.*

"More to the south, folks!" the standing human said, macrobinoculars in hand. "Keep after 'em!"

A'Yark didn't need to know all of the words. The meaning was clear. The missing warriors weren't nearby, ready to strike. The band, routed, had taken flight.

Seeing the tall human's landspeeder, the cowering young Tusken from earlier squealed and stood. Leaving his gaderffii on the ground, he bolted.

"Urrak!" A'Yark yelled. Wait!

Too late. Another landspeeder banked—and the hollering riders aboard chopped the fleeing Sand Person down with blast after blast. Not six days a warrior, and dead in seconds.

This was too much. A'Yark rose, weapon in hand, and dashed behind the hut. Away from where the laughing settlers, aware only of their killing, could see. Ragged fabric flew as the warrior tumbled over a dune into a dusty ravine. Another dune followed, and another.

At last, A'Yark fell to the ground, gasping. Three had been lost—maybe more. And the Sand People couldn't afford to lose anyone.

Worse, they'd lost to settlers using a low trick no Tusken four years earlier would've fallen for. The settlers would know now: the mighty Tuskens were not what they once were.

Struggling to stand, A'Yark looked down at the ground. The elder shadow lengthened. Like the older brother sun, the band had struck—and failed.

It was time for the Tuskens to hide. Again.

CHAPTER TWO

ORRIN GAULT TOWERED OVER the farm, a lofty witness as some Tuskens ran for their lives—and others ran to their deaths. Clinging to the side of the vaporator tower, he watched the last landspeeder disappear over the horizon.

"Okay, Call Control, that's got it," he said into his comlink. "Shut it down."

He released the comlink button and listened. His ears still rang from the alarm atop the tower, which he had just deactivated by hand. Peering out from beneath the canvas brim of his range hat, he scanned the landscape. One by one, the sirens kilometers away went quiet—and silence returned to the desert.

He looked at the comlink and cracked a grin. *Orrin, son—that's some pull you've got there.* It was nice to reach a point in life where people did what you said. And on Tatooine, where the people were born cussed and nobody took orders from anyone else, it meant even more.

The danger was past. For the first time since receiving the distress signal, Orrin took a deep breath and pondered the barren land below. He'd been born on a farm just like this, far from the nearest way station, nearly fifty standard years earlier. And even now, there was no place he'd rather be in the morning than on the range.

People thought he was crazy for that. Everyone he'd ever met preferred the evening, with its relief from the heat. But once the suns were gone, and the air settled on you like something dead and heavy, you had to get underground. Nothing good happened after dark, with Tuskens and who-knows-what-else on the prowl. Mornings, meanwhile, were like getting out of jail—or so Orrin imagined. On Tatooine you might overnight no better than a womp rat in a hole, but you'd become human the second you stepped outside.

And then there was that little stretch between first and second sun, when the cold night wind would kick its last and the planet itself would sigh. Good water prospectors lived for those moments, when the precious drops that had birthed in the night suddenly realized you were on to them, and fled. A smart farmer like Orrin could smell them, and follow them. And it was *possible* to follow them—because in daylight, nothing could stop you. Not in this region. Not anymore.

Those were the rules. The new rules, maybe—but *his* rules, made possible by his hard work and guidance.

Guess I forgot to tell this batch of Tuskens, he thought, climbing down the ladder. The raiders had ruined more than the morning for these poor people. Orrin winced. The guts of half a dozen maintenance and sentry droids marked the Tuskens' path into the camp. Two vaporators sparked, maintenance doors at their bases bashed open. And then there were the strike points, scattered randomly around the yard. A couple smoked still, where blasterfire had flash-fused the sand into lightning glass. His posse had left those, not the Tuskens. Orrin had never known Plug-eye to use blasters on the way in.

Plug-eye. This raid could have been the work of no other. No other Tusken in this part of the Jundland

Wastes would dare attack at dawn. No one had ever caught more than half a glance at Plug-eye and lived to describe it. If they'd lived, Orrin always said, then they didn't meet Plug-eye, but some other Tusken, with a more amiable disposition. Descriptions of the notorious raider varied. Skinny or fat? Male or female? Short and stubby, or a Wookiee in a robe?

The tales had only two things in common. Plug-eye was as fierce as fire—and where other Sand People had metal turrets for their eyeholes, something must have happened to one of the warrior's eyes. Rather than simply removing the eyepiece, Plug-eye had jammed a crimson stone into the opening.

Or something. The stories didn't even agree on which eye it was. This time, though, things might be different. They'd arrived quickly enough to save some witnesses.

Orrin had already been dressed and in the fields for an hour when the call—or more correctly, the *Call*—came. That fact, and his work team's proximity, had saved the Bezzard family from a horrific end. But what had come before was tragic enough. Two of Orrin's neighbors— cousins, on his ex-wife's side of the family—exited the back door of the house, carrying the body of the Bith farmhand. Orrin looked down as they passed. The posse would handle the burial—just as, over the dune to the east, more volunteers were burning the dead Tuskens. They had to make this as easy for the Bezzards as possible.

He'd lived through it before. When his youngest had died, just as senselessly.

Orrin heard motion in the house. "Mullen, you in there?" he asked.

"Yep."

Orrin's older son—he couldn't bring himself to think of him as the *only* son, yet—sauntered from the building, holding two halves of a blaster rifle. "Looks like Plug-eye was here," Mullen said.

"Figured."

Inscrutable behind his black goggles, Mullen Gault could have been a clone of his father at twenty-five— if the younger man weren't trying so hard to look like someone else. Both were tall and powerfully built, with the ruddy skin of farmers born and raised. There the similarities ended. Blue-eyed Orrin's hair was dark and elegantly graying. He tried to look nice even on the range; you never knew who might happen by. Mullen, meanwhile, had woken in his clothes from the previous night's carousing. That was typical. He'd sacrificed several teeth years earlier to a tangle with a gambler in Anchorhead—and he'd lost another in the same town just recently.

People said that was why Mullen frowned as often as his father smiled, but Orrin knew that wasn't so. The boy had been scowling in the crib.

Orrin took the rifle pieces. Most Tuskens wouldn't leave anything that might be useful. Plug-eye seemed pickier. "How many were there?"

Mullen picked at his beard and stood against the doorway, scratching his back against the jamb. "Three Tuskens dead in the yard. Then those that took off into the hills. Veeka just called—she lost 'em up at the Roiya Rift." Mullen looked keenly at his father. "I figured you'd want me to call off the hunt. They're on their way back."

Orrin snorted. "Well, don't miss ol' Pluggy too much. Next time breakfast rolls around—"

He stopped. A woman's anguished sobs echoed through the house. "The owner. Is she all right?"

"She's out front with the old man," Mullen said. "She's pretty shook up."

"Imagine so." Orrin looked up. "Who's with her now?"

"I said. The old man."

Orrin gawked. "The *dead* old man?" He threw the fragments to the ground. "I told you to make sure someone was with her, Mullen. And you thought I meant *her dead father*?"

Mullen simply stared.

"Mullen, I swear!" Orrin grimaced and jabbed two fingers at the bridge of his son's goggles, clonking his son's head against the door. *"Really."*

The young man said nothing as his father marched back to the landspeeder. Finding his twill half-cape behind the passenger seat, Orrin draped it over his shoulders and turned to face the house. *This isn't going to be easy.*

The sight of dark-haired Tyla Bezzard cradling the old man on the stoop took his breath away. It was grisly, what the raiders had done—it *had* to be Plug-eye. But what chilled him more was how the young woman seemed not to care about the state of her father's body.

Without looking up, she sensed Orrin's approach. "Someone's come, Daddy."

Orrin took off his hat and instinctively knelt beside her. He'd known the woman when she was a child. Her father, Lotho Pelhane, had been a hand on Orrin's family ranch for twenty years. Before Lotho struck out on his own, Tyla and Orrin's kids used to play together. Orrin placed his cloak over Tyla's shoulders. As he did, she buried her head in his chest and bawled.

"I know, Tyla, I know," he said, embracing her. "It's a blasted thing, all right." He looked down at the corpse, still awkwardly slumped against her lap. Lotho Pelhane still had a weeks-old bandage around his head, a surreal sight given the mess that was made of the rest of him. Orrin looked away.

Tyla whimpered. "I—I tried to remember, Master Gault—"

"Orrin."

"I tried to remember. You sold us the alarm and the activator," she said, showing him the remote control device in her hand. She was clutching it almost hard enough to crush it. "I was so scared," she gasped. "I couldn't remember how to turn on the local alarm at first—"

"It's all right," he said. "The Settlers' Call worked just fine. We got your signal. And we came right here." Gently, Orrin pulled her away from the stoop, allowing Lotho's body to almost imperceptibly slip away from her. "You did just fine. Your husband and your boy are safe. We got the Tuskens."

"I don't care!" She looked down at her dead father. "I don't want to stay here! Not anymore!"

Orrin pulled back from Tyla and brought her upright, squeezing her shoulders in his firm hands. "Now, listen. I knew your father. You know Lotho wouldn't want to hear this. He wasn't any more scared of Tuskens than he was of his own shadows."

She looked down at the bandage on her father's head and sniffled. "They nearly got him last month, you know—knocked him down one night at his place. It's why he came to stay with us. But he was getting better. He said he'd gotten away once, so he thought he was safe—"

"That's right. And you made this place safe with the Call. You did the right thing—"

She wept again. Orrin just waited. He'd been here too many times before—though less often, lately. "This was bad, no accounting for it. But we got a bunch of them, and we'll get the rest of them. And it'll get better. You understand?"

She pulled away, suddenly angry. "What do they *want*? They're monsters—"

"Tatooine's got sand and it's got monsters," Orrin said. He looked over to see Mullen standing with the burial detail. "Now, I'm going to check on that husband and son of yours. These folks will take care of your dad, until we get you back to the oasis. Annileen Calwell will put you up there tonight."

Tyla nodded weakly and began walking, still oblivious to the bloody mess her tunic had become.

Orrin looked skeptically at his son as she went out of earshot. "Can I trust you to take care of this woman for five minutes without sending her into another conniption?"

Mullen spoke in a low voice. "Sure, sure. But weren't you gonna ask her about Plug-eye? You said you—"

"Where's my hat?" Orrin looked around on the ground. "I need something to hit you with. Now go!"

Orrin found Tellico Bezzard, the young owner of the homestead, at the machine shed, surrounded by a buzz of activity. The rest of the posse had returned. The grown-ups in the group—a distinction defined more by good sense than age—had tackled without delay the list of things that always had to be addressed in these cases. Though the posse was officially leaderless, Orrin had always been the one to take charge in the past; he was glad now to see that so much of his advice had stuck. Some folks were in the house cleaning up. Others were fixing the vaporators. Still others were gathering the goods the Bezzards would want for their stay at the Pika Oasis. They were working, even knowing they were missing out on important hours in their own fields.

And then there was his daughter, Veeka, and her junior satellite Jabe Calwell, sitting on crates with a flask out, drinking under the morning suns. Orrin knew it wasn't water; after all, Veeka was drinking it. Since her twin brother's death, the twenty-one-year-old had decided to do all the living he'd missed out on. And Jabe, at sixteen Orrin's newest farmhand, was doing his best to keep up with her. They were in the middle of describing how they'd killed one of the Sand People to Tellico, who sat numbly as he bobbled his unknowing baby on his knee. The farmer's blaster sat on the sand, nearby, unfired.

When Veeka noticed her father's approach and grim expression, she grinned awkwardly. "Whoops. Sorry," she said, quickly passing the flask to Tellico. "Here, buddy. Drink up." The frazzled young farmer looked blankly at the container.

Orrin rolled his eyes and barged in. "Sorry is right." He snatched the flask and threw it behind the shed. He glared at Veeka. "Get these people some water. Now."

Smirking, Veeka ambled off, Jabe in tow. Orrin sighed. His daughter had the amiable attitude that Mullen lacked, but her interest in others was a centimeter deep. Both his children had missed the empathy ship.

It fell to him, as usual. Orrin knelt before the young farmer and his infant. "You all right?"

Tellico spoke quickly and excitedly. "Yeah. I'm amazed you got here so fast."

"There was some luck. My hands and I were working the towers on the west range when you activated the Settlers' Call. We were halfway here before the folks at the oasis even got to their speeders."

Orrin knew there was luck, true—but also good design. This was how it was *supposed* to work. When a homestead activated the Call, everyone in this part of the desert moved. If settlers were armed and had a ride, they followed the sirens to trouble. If not, they mustered at the Pika Oasis, where guns and vehicles were garaged behind Dannar's Claim, the area's general store. The alarm at the activating location had a different sound from the others, but all started with something calculated to spook any Tusken: the recorded howl of a krayt dragon. That had been Orrin's favorite touch.

"Well, it's a wonderful thing, sir. Worth every credit."

Orrin smiled humbly. "Tell your friends. It's for all of us, really."

"Her dad—Lotho—never wanted us to buy into it. But—" The young man broke off, and looked away. He clutched the baby tighter.

"You forget about all that," Orrin said. "But I want you to remember something for me, if you can. The Tuskens. What can you tell me?"

Tellico looked to him urgently. "Oh, it was Plug-eye, all right. No mistaking it. Where the right eye was—"

"Right from where you're lookin'?"

Tellico pointed to his right eye. "No, this eye. It *shines*."

Orrin started. "What, like a cybernetic?" That sounded absolutely crazy.

"No, sir. More like a crystal. It caught the light when I looked—and I couldn't take my eyes off it." He shivered in the suns. "Scared the life out of me."

"I don't doubt it." Orrin scratched his chin. "Anything else?"

The young farmer paused. "The robes were different, I guess. No bandolier. But really, I was so focused on the *eye*—"

Orrin stood and patted Tellico on the back. "Forget it, son. Now let's get you and Tyla taken care of. Annileen will put you up at the Claim as long as you need."

Orrin watched as the farmer and child departed. Mullen stepped to his father's side. "Any help?"

"Nope."

Mullen sneered. "And he had a shot at Plug-eye and didn't take it."

"I don't think that boy would know his blaster from his spanner." Orrin looked behind him and chuckled. "Now where's that flask?"

Veeka and Jabe walked up from the house. "I thought you didn't want me to drink this early," Veeka said.

"You *make* me drink," Orrin said. He turned to look at Jabe, fresh-faced and thrilled to be here. The boy was the age his Varan—Veeka's twin—had been five years earlier, when tragedy struck. It was one reason Orrin had taken him onto his maintenance crew: Jabe was a sunny presence.

But Orrin knew what awaited the kid at home. "Boy, when your mother finds out I let you go out with the posse, they'll need to make room for me on the pyre beside the Tuskens."

Veeka opened the maintenance hatch of her sporty landspeeder. "You want to hide back here, runt? You'll just fit."

Jabe blushed at the teasing. "It won't be that bad," he said.

"Oh, yes it will." Orrin stared at the kid. "You'll be begging the Jawas to adopt you."

He stepped forward and clapped his hands twice loudly. "That's it, people. Good job, here. Back to the oasis. Drinks at Dannar's Claim!"

CHAPTER THREE

THE OLD NIKTO WOMAN plopped a bolt of cloth on the counter. "Do you work here?"

Standing behind the counter, Annileen Calwell didn't look up from her datapad. "No, I come in here and do inventory in my spare time."

A moment passed before Annileen suddenly froze. "Wait," she said, eyes widening as she took in her surroundings. "Counter. Cashbox. Title deed." With a look of alarm, Annileen turned abruptly to the alabaster-skinned customer. "I'm sorry, I guess I *do* work here."

It was a game they'd played every day since Erbaly Nap'tee's first visit to the store. Except that for the Nikto woman, it wasn't a game: Erbaly had never once remembered who Annileen was. For a while, Annileen had thought the alien simply couldn't distinguish among humans. Eventually, she figured out that Erbaly just didn't care—and so their game began.

That had been eleven standard years ago.

The shrivel-faced alien clicked her tongue with impatience. "Now, see this?" Her withered white finger jabbed at the fabric. "Do you know why this costs so much?"

"No," Annileen said, smiling primly. "Why?"

The Nikto's cracked lips pursed. She started to say something more, but Annileen stopped her.

"Just a second. They need me in the cantina." Her apron whirled as Annileen spun and walked the meter and a half to where her sundries counter turned into a bar. She picked up a glass that a sleeping prospector had knocked over and then returned to Erbaly. "I'm back," she said.

The Nikto woman tapped her foot. "Is there someone *else* here I can talk to?"

"Now *there*, I can help you," Annileen said. After setting the glass in a basin, she stepped out through a gap in the long counter and walked to one of the back tables, where a green-snouted Rodian huddled silently over his morning caf. Annileen clapped her hand on his shoulder—an act that he seemed not to notice in the least. "This is Bohmer," she said.

Erbaly studied him. "Does he work here?"

"We don't know," Annileen said. "But he's here an awful lot."

"Thank you just the same." The elderly Nikto sniffed disdainfully and headed for the front door.

Annileen picked up the bolt of cloth from the counter and called after her. "I'll set this aside for when you're here tomorrow, Erbaly. Have a nice day!"

Erbaly said nothing as she stormed past Leelee Pace, Annileen's best friend, who was preparing a parcel for mailing—another of the store's many services. The crimson-skinned Zeltron laughed heartily as the Nikto slammed the door behind her. "That's our Annie," Leelee said. "Retailer of the year. Customers can't stay away!"

"Sure they can, Leelee." Annileen orbited one of the luncheonette tables, cleaning it off without looking at it. "See, Dannar had it figured. Anyone can stay away for a while. Until they remember that it's thirty kilometers to the nearest working keg. Then they never want to leave."

"I've noticed," Leelee said, stacking packages. "That was shorter than your usual go-around with Erbaly. Something biting you?"

"No."

Carting the breakfast dishes behind the counter, Annileen knew that wasn't true. But what she'd told her friend about Dannar's Claim certainly was. The place was the largest facility of any kind in the Pika Oasis. Two of the domes had been there since before anyone could remember, part of some ancient farm. Annileen's late husband Dannar had added on, connecting one of the domes with a new oblong sales area beneath a rounded roof. The dome behind now constituted her family's living quarters and guesthouse.

The main building had been Annileen's domain for the majority of her thirty-seven years—and in that time she'd crammed an amount of commerce that defied all geometry into the limited space. Visitors encountered rows of shelves as they entered, all angled so Annileen could see down the aisles from behind her counter, which ran nearly the length of the eastern wall. But most patrons usually headed past the sundries for the rear of the main room. There, near where the far end of Annileen's counter terminated in a bar, a food preparation area sat close to eight cramped dining tables. Every day, Annileen fed and fortified half the workers living near the oasis, not necessarily in that order.

This was her roost, but the complex went on from there. Northwest of the main store was the first garage Dannar had built to service the vehicles of oasis prospectors; it had been expanded many times since, as local mechanics rented bays. To the north and east sat a livestock area, where the few surviving animals from Annileen's father's failed ranch had formed the basis for a thriving livery, serving those daring fools who preferred the reptilian dewbacks to landspeeders.

And all around: the oasis, a wide clearing shielded from the wind by gently rolling sand hills. Once a basin for a prehistoric lake, the area and its clumpy soil gave rise to flowering pika plants and a few hardy deb-deb trees—and something else. Orrin Gault's newfangled cylindrical vaporators rose all around, producing water for delivery in the vast tankers that sat parked outside the Claim's garages. Most of the harvest was bound for faraway parts; the locals drank what they needed and little more. They knew what they had, and its value.

Though gifted at water prospecting, Dannar had never taken much interest in moisture farming. He'd reasoned that a store would weather the bad-harvest years better, and that had mostly turned out to be true. But he'd left his widow with so many secondary businesses under one roof that Annileen feared taking a day off, lest Tatooine's rural economy collapse.

She'd held up okay, or so she thought every once in a while, when she caught her reflection in the glassware in the sink. Annileen could even recognize herself on occasion. The auburn hair of her youth, which she wore tied back, was going to brown, not gray; so far so good. Inside work had never fully met with her approval, but it had kept her skin rosy rather than roasted.

And Annileen's eyes were about the only truly green thing on the whole planet, if you didn't count dewbacks or Rodian barflies. Counting dewbacks was now her daughter's job, anyway. Looking out the square window, Annileen could see Kallie, blond and determined, trying to teach the dewback yearlings some manners before they realized they had the muscle to tear the fencing apart at will.

At least Kallie wasn't messing with Snit, Annileen saw to her relief. The creature wasn't of the cannibal breed;

Annileen wouldn't have let one of those near the compound. But Snit had been bitten by a kreetle as a hatchling, and had been snapping at everything in sight since. Annileen assumed her daughter had the sense to stay away—but she never knew. Breaking dewbacks wasn't a safe job for an assassin droid, much less a seventeen-year-old girl. But Dannar Calwell had never accepted limits, and his oldest child wasn't about to, either. Stubbornness bred true.

Annileen had hoped her son, Jabe, would be different. But it wasn't turning out that way. And between the emergency siren, her kids, and the customers today, Annileen had just about had it. She glared out the window and winced. In pain. *"Ow!"*

"That's new," Leelee said, depositing her parcel and some credits on the counter. She pointed to Annileen's hands. "You have literally cut off your own circulation with your apron strings. Appropriate. A little on the nose, though."

Looking down, Annileen quickly unwound the fabric from her reddened palm. "You're the range psychiatrist now?"

"No, but I've got five children of my own. And I know if you keep staring at Kallie and those animals, she's just gonna try to ride the crazy one."

Annileen turned away from the window. "Now, that's where you're wrong," she said, collecting the money. "It's always the kid I *can't* see that I'm worried about."

Jabe had already been long gone with the prospectors when the Settlers' Call had sounded. Her son knew very well what Annileen thought about him getting anywhere near Orrin's business. But as far as she could tell, the boy didn't care at all. She just didn't understand him anymore. Jabe had something everyone on Tatooine dreamed of: a guaranteed life of safe, indoor work, filling his father's shoes. Instead, the stubborn teen kept sneaking away with Orrin's work crew. Sure, Annileen knew the boy had eyes for Orrin's daughter, Veeka. But he had no more chance with that hellion than he had of becoming Chancellor of the Republic—or whatever they called it these days.

No, Annileen concluded, he'd gone with the crew this morning in retaliation for having been made to clean the cookers before dawn. And if he followed them into danger, that'd be spite, too. That irritated her beyond measure. Spite was stupid. Even Kallie was too smart to ride Snit just to make a point. And Annileen had always figured Jabe had sense . . . *her* sense. He'd give the Tuskens the same berth, wouldn't he?

She was afraid she knew the answer. She found her inventory datapad and returned to staring at it. She couldn't read a word, of course. She only saw Jabe—and Orrin.

Orrin. The Claim had thrived long after Dannar's death because Annileen had one steadfast rule: she never let anyone have anything on account. There was only one exception: Orrin, Dannar's best friend and sometime business partner. Orrin and Dannar's friendship had gone back years, long before Annileen had come to work at Dannar's store as a teenager. The two men had so many side deals that she'd always felt awkward trying to set limits. But Orrin was sorely testing her patience now, dangling the possibility of range work for her son.

Orrin's family was a mess. Why did he meddle with hers? Aggravated, she tried to focus again on the datapad.

"You're holding it upside down," Leelee said from behind.

Annileen didn't look up. "Are *you* still here?"

"I'm waiting for my change."

"You're out of luck. Change is the one thing Tatooine

doesn't have." Taking a deep breath, she looked back at Leelee and smiled wanly. "How much was it?"

Leelee waved her hand. "Keep it. Maybe you can pay Dr. Mell to give you something to help you relax."

"Yeah," Annileen said. "Like a ticket to Alderaan."

As if Leelee's words had summoned him, the local physician, a Mon Calamari man, popped his head in the side door.

"Annileen, are they back yet?" Mell wore a special cowl supplying his tendriled head with moisture, but he was flushed red nonetheless. "The posse. I heard the Call go off!"

"They heard it on Suurja, Doc," Annileen said. "And Suurjans don't have ears." She didn't know if Mon Calamari had ears, either, but she knew Doc Mell wouldn't mind the joke. The Call was a gaudy display of decibels. Half the breakables in the store had fallen to the first test of the system, years earlier. Annileen had learned to tune it out—a talent perfected during a lifetime in retail.

"They still might need a medic. I should meet them on the way back," the doctor said, before cracking the door and pushing his young son inside.

Annileen started. "Hey, wait. Don't leave your kid here!"

"I'll be back!" The door slammed.

Annileen pitched the datapad over her shoulder and felt her forehead. Yes, she was still here—and so were the four other younglings that had already been dropped off when their parents left with the posse. Two were at a table, eating food plucked from the shelf; two more were hiding somewhere. Babysitting wasn't her job, but with people rushing out to help someone in need, she'd found it hard to argue.

Except people frequently left their children when there was no emergency, too.

Annileen looked down on the sniffling pink ragamuffin and rolled her eyes. She sighed. "Oh, all right." She took the boy by the shoulders and pointed him to a rack near the wall. "Take a broom, kid. And nothing else."

"Yes, ma'am." The child began to dutifully sweep the floor near the table where the other children were sitting.

From inside the front door, Leelee laughed. "Good luck, Annie."

Annileen scowled, playfully. "Just go. You're letting the tepid air out."

A low whine sounded from the west, slowly increasing in volume and crescendo. Annileen dashed to the counter to check the video feed from the southern hillside security cam. She saw what she expected to see: landspeeders, coming back from the Bezzard farm.

And she also saw what she had feared to see. Jabe, perched precariously on the back of Veeka Gault's snazzy landspeeder.

Annileen opened the window and called out to her daughter. "Kallie! Bring me a bantha prod."

The girl looked up from her work. "You want the training prod or the big one?"

Dark eyebrows made an angry vee. "Doesn't matter."

CHAPTER FOUR

FOR ORRIN, RETURNING TO the Claim was always like coming home. It wasn't *his* home, of course; it was Dannar's. And then Dannar's and Annileen's, and for the last several years Annileen's alone. But Orrin felt a tie to the compound that went beyond the law, or such law as there was on Tatooine. Orrin had laid the first bricks for the store, driven in the first landspeeder for repair, and eaten the first meal at the lunch counter.

A place was a thing, and you weren't supposed to get sentimental about things. But it was also his last link to the best friend he'd ever had, and that wasn't something he'd ever be able to ignore.

The Claim had been Dannar's big idea. He was good with ideas, even better than Orrin was. Together they'd made great things happen in the oasis; one day, they'd imagined, Orrin's farms and Dannar's market would turn it into a second Anchorhead. Or even Bestine—Orrin could see that happening. The Pika had that much potential.

But Dannar had changed after marrying his salesclerk. He'd always kept a foot in the store after that, never willing to risk more than he could afford at one time. And after Kallie was born? Forget it.

Fatherhood had the opposite effect on Orrin; he

couldn't wait to hit the range each day, searching for treasure in the air. But Dannar's bets were ever smaller, and on surer things. That had made Dannar's Claim a strong operation, to be sure: a good earner, even by Orrin's current standards. But it had meant that only one of them was able to go for the main chance, when opportunity came. By the time Jabe was in the cradle, Orrin's holdings had almost completely enveloped the store property.

Not that Dannar had ever begrudged Orrin success. Dannar had been happy to see someone making use of his ideas—and the fact that it was a friend profiting made it even better. The Calwell and Gault operations were as close as they could be without a legal partnership—which the friends never contemplated, given their mutual contempt for the legal clerks in Bestine. No tax collector had any right to either man's work. And if Orrin wanted to store his vaporator construction speeders in Dannar's garages, or if Dannar wanted to range his dewbacks on Orrin's land, well, they didn't need a document for that.

The policy had continued under Annileen, more or less, in the nearly eight years since Dannar passed. The Claim's spare garages now held the entire Gault work fleet. And when Orrin took administrative control of the Settlers' Call Fund he had co-founded with his neighbors, it made perfect sense that the Claim should serve as its operational base. The facility had plenty of room to house the emergency response vehicles owned by the Fund—and if the responders needed an arsenal, they only had to walk next door to find Annileen's gun racks.

There was one more thing the Claim had to offer, Orrin knew: the reward for a dangerous job well done. As manager of the Call Fund, Orrin had seen the need and made the provision long ago, and no one had ever argued.

His was a vigilante organization with a liquor tab.

"Good stuff here, folks!" Orrin climbed out of his prized USV-5 landspeeder and slapped the hood. The other vehicles were arriving, one by one. "Park the loaners by the garage—we'll take care of them. And you can drink your fill before the lunch rush!"

A cheer rose from the growing crowd. Some quickly headed into Dannar's Claim, but more lingered outside, sharing their stories and trophies. Reminded, Orrin reached into the landspeeder to find his new gaffi stick—or gaderffii, or whatever the savages called the bizarre hunks of metal. The young Tusken cut to pieces in the crossfire had carried this one. Now, with one boot on the bobbing hood of his parked hovercraft, Orrin hoisted the weapon over his head. He gave a war whoop and smiled broadly. Another cheer went up.

"Let's hear it for the king of the Jundland!"

Orrin's head snapped back at the sound of the feminine voice. Veeka was there, having parked her vehicle behind the others. Young Jabe and a couple of other settlers' kids were piling off the back of the speeder, rifles in hand. Veeka grinned at her father and shouted again. *"Hail to the king!"*

"Don't call me that," Orrin growled. He hated the name—and Veeka knew better than to use it. But he heard it again from here and there in the swelling crowd.

"All hail, king of the Jundland!"

"No, no. Don't do that," Orrin said. He laughed, loudly enough so they could hear him. He knew not to take it seriously. These people weren't looking for a ruler; it was why half of them were on Tatooine! They needed to know *he* knew that, too. Orrin leaned the gaderffii against the hood of his landspeeder and raised his hands in humility. "It's a team effort," he said, quieting the crowd. "Always. You folks . . . *you* saved that farm."

His voice rose. "And never, ever forget *why* we're doing this. Remember the people that the Tuskens have killed, for no reason at all. People who were just trying to make an honest living. Farmer after farmer—we've lost more prospecting knowledge than we can ever appreciate. It's why we all came together to set up the Settlers' Call, years ago—to help us take back our lives."

He pointed to a tall vaporator tower, rising from the slope to the south of the store. "Up there on top is the very first siren, erected on Dannar Calwell's Old Number One vaporator. Some of you new folks didn't know Dannar, but he was the best friend a man—and this oasis—could have. The Tuskens took him from us, too, but the siren remains—one of many. That's part of his legacy to us. Dannar's gone, but the call still goes out. And it's our job to answer it!"

Orrin softened his voice. "That's the key, folks. I know you're not fighters. I know you have your own fields you should be working right now. And it's not always easy to find the extra credits that keep the Settlers' Call going. I've sure put plenty into it myself. And not just money." He choked up for a moment, and paused to clear his throat. "But that's just it. Many of you know my younger son died a few years ago, answering the Call. He did it to save a neighbor. There's not a day that I don't miss him—but I don't regret at all what he went to do. A community's a living thing—and our actions together keep it alive."

Orrin looked up. The settlers were watching him, spellbound. As usual.

"That's all," he said, breaking the solemnity. "And before you drink up, a reminder—any of you who haven't paid your subscription for this season, the Settlers' Call Fund office is in the back, behind the secondhand clothing. You might need us at your place one day. These speeders don't run on goodwill!"

Orrin smiled as several of the posse members rushed to shake his hand. He glanced up at the climbing suns. His crews had lost most of a morning in the fields, but this was important, too. Without camaraderie, there was no community—the oxygen that the Settlers' Call needed to function. Subscriptions always went up after a Tusken attack, but that was nothing compared with what happened after a successful defense and retaliation. He nodded to Mullen, who opened the door to the store for the settlers.

Annileen stormed through it, nearly knocking Mullen down. Orrin spotted something long and black in her hands a second before she found her son in the crowd. Jabe, in the middle of being ribbed by Veeka about something, suddenly noticed Annileen. "Mom, I—"

Brzzaappt! A golden electric flash struck the ground not far from the teenager's feet. Startled, the boy jumped backward, tripping over his boots and landing on his rear.

Mullen and Orrin stood back. "Yikes," Mullen said.

Orrin nodded. "Yep."

Jabe looked up from the sand to see his mother holding a bantha prod. "What the—" Realizing what had happened, his immediate reaction was incredulity. "You almost shocked me!"

"Oh, did I miss?" Annileen snarled. "Maybe I should try again!"

"Mom!"

Behind Orrin, Kallie appeared in the store doorway holding a shorter staff. "Mom, do you want to switch to the training prod?"

"This is training him just fine," Annileen growled. Taking a breath, she looked at the bantha prod for a moment before rolling her eyes and tossing it away. She turned and loomed over Jabe. "Now, you listen to me! You did *not* have my permission to skip out on the breakfast prep. You did *not* have permission to go working in the suns with these roughnecks." Her voice climbed. "And you sure as blazes don't have my permission to go out with the posse!"

Jabe coughed, more embarrassed than hurt. "Mom, people were in danger!"

"*You* were in danger!"

Smirking, Orrin gestured to the amused vigilantes, who had forgotten about the free spirits. "A wide berth, gentle creatures, if you please. Annileen Calwell is parenting again."

Hearing his voice, Annileen turned abruptly and sputtered. "And—and *you*!"

Orrin outweighed his best friend's widow by thirty kilos—and yet as she started toward him, he took a step backward. Self-preservation came before public image. Spying the gaderffii resting against the hood of his landspeeder, he playfully picked it up and held it with both hands, in simulated defense. But Annileen kept coming. "Easy there!" he said.

She grabbed at the midsection of the gaderffii and used it to pull him toward her. "I'm telling you for the last time, Orrin. If you ever let Jabe go out on one of your posses again, you better wrap your head in bandages and stay with the Tuskens!"

"Now, Annie—"

"Don't you 'Now, Annie' me!" she cut in, livid. "I mean it, Orrin. You can get your speeders out of my garages and park 'em under a tarp," she said, pushing at the gaffi stick. "You want somebody to feed your crew, you go to Bestine. You want guns, you talk to Jabba!"

"Hey, now," Orrin said, defensively, aware again of the rapt crowd. Even the drinkers had come out of the Claim to watch. "This isn't some eastern town," he said. "This is the Pika Oasis. Nobody here messes with Jabba!"

"You cross me again, and you'll feel like a Hutt landed on you!" Green eyes blazed at him. "Understood?"

"You get the wildest ideas. Now, calm down, or you'll leave your boy an orphan—" With a heave, Orrin tugged at the weapon. He expected resistance, but she let go suddenly and his arm, overbalanced, swung the gaderffii in a wide arc . . .

. . . right into the windshield of his landspeeder. Shards flew everywhere.

Orrin eyed the mess. "Great," he said. "Just great." He looked back at Annileen. "See what you made me do?"

"Me? *You* were holding it." Annileen barely glanced at the shattered windshield. "I hope you took a lot better care of my son out there!"

"Jabe takes care of himself just fine," Orrin said, growing aggravated. "You're treating him like a droid with a restraining bolt!"

"Oh, really?"

"Really!" He and Annileen were in each other's faces, now. "And maybe you should look at yourself," Orrin said. "Ask yourself just why he feels the need to get out from under—"

A husky voice came from the crowd. "Ah, just kiss her already!"

"Who said that?" Annileen's eyes darted around the spectators. "*Who said that?*"

"We *all* did," Leelee said, crossing her arms and shaking her head.

Annileen snorted at her friend. "I thought you left."

"What, and miss the entertainment?"

The settlers to either side of the Zeltron laughed.

While Annileen smoldered, Orrin quickly passed the Tusken weapon to his son. Half the oasis had been trying to set Annileen up with Orrin since his last wife left. The other half assumed they were already together. But

Orrin knew better than to react in the slightest. There wasn't a more dangerous subject in the galaxy.

Annileen pivoted and returned to her son. Kallie was helping Jabe stand: he seemed flustered and a little tipsy to Orrin, but undamaged.

"Leelee's right, Mom," the farmer heard Kallie whisper. "You and Orrin have been doing this dance for years—"

"*You* can be replaced," Annileen told her daughter, ire returning. "Go do something."

Kallie looked at her, offended. "Okay." She turned on her heel and left—abandoning Jabe, who immediately fell back to the ground.

As Annileen collected her son, Orrin directed Mullen to take his landspeeder back to the garage. "It's no big deal. Just have Gloamer put the repair on the account," he said. Remembering some of the debts he had coming due, Orrin lowered his voice and added to Mullen: "The store's account."

The show over, the crowd filtered into the Claim. Annileen brushed herself off; she would have a lot of people to serve. Orrin chanced a conversation with her before he followed the others. "Did you get the Bezzards put up?"

Annileen expelled a deep breath. "They're in the guest quarters now. They came in just as I was heading out to meet Jabe."

"Blessed reason, I hope you at least put down the bantha prod," Orrin said. "Those people have been scared enough!"

Orrin watched as Annileen tried—and failed—to suppress a smile. "No," she said, "they're okay. The doc's in with them."

"That's good."

Before he could enter the store, Annileen pulled at his

sleeve and looked at him with concern. "They said it was Plug-eye."

Orrin spoke softly. "Yeah. They got old Lotho and the Bith farmhand. But we took out a few." He paused. "Our people didn't chase far."

She stared keenly at him. "And Jabe was never in danger?"

"Everyone lives with danger here. You know that. But if you try to turn that boy into a clerk like his daddy, you're gonna lose him altogether. You need to trust me." Orrin tapped her on the shoulder. "Now, if both your children are accounted for, I think we've got about thirty heroes waiting for their drinks in there."

"On the Fund's tab," she said, with what he took for mock sternness. Then she nearly smiled.

Yes, we'll be all right. Orrin grinned as he held the door open for her. This would turn out to be a good day after—

A loud crack resonated from the other side of the building, followed by a feral yelp. A young woman's indecipherable yell came a second later.

Now what? Puzzled, Orrin rounded the building. There, in the side yard, he saw smashed corral fencing—and a cloud of dust heading toward the dunes to the southwest. He could just make out the blond figure amid the whirlwind, hanging on for dear life.

Annileen appeared beside him. "Tell me it isn't!"

"Can't lie to you," Orrin said, peering into the distance. "That would be your Kallie running off on a crazy dewback."

"*Snit!*"

Orrin sighed and shrugged. "Well, you *did* tell her to go *do* something . . ."

CHAPTER FIVE

A'YARK JABBED THE KNIFE again into the warrior's arm. Black streamed from the cut, fouling the young Tusken's wrappings. The shrapnel was buried deep, too deep for A'Yark to reach.

The survivors of the raiding party had been glad to reach The Pillars, a jagged cleave into the Jundland where the settlers and their vehicles could not follow. But the wastes had taken offense at being used for cowardice— and the young Tusken had paid. The injured warrior had evaded the settlers' gunfire, but not the accursed grenade they had thrown before leaving, and what it had done to the rock wall. The arm would grow diseased, the hand unusable. If something happened beyond that, the Tuskens never knew. It wasn't a thing worth knowing.

A'Yark gave the blade to the warrior and spoke the words. They were the words known to all of them, the words that separated a Tusken from the other creatures that lived in the dust.

Whoever has two hands can hold a gaderffii.

The warrior stared at the weapon but did not question his duty. Another would take his bantha; the band could no longer afford to lose warrior and beast both.

A'Yark gave the warrior his solitude and made a mental note to send someone over for the body. The important work was with the others, now. The morning's raid had been a risk—perhaps too great a risk when their numbers were so small. And yet A'Yark had been certain that it was necessary. The settlers had grown too bold. The Tuskens needed to be bolder.

What remained of the clan now hid, like the coward sun, among The Pillars. Legend held that a giant had repeatedly struck the mountains with a dagger here; some said it was the younger sun himself, flailing against his brother. Whatever the explanation, the landscape was unreal. Natural stone columns and crumbling obelisks climbed to the sky, some topped by precariously perched boulders. A maze of narrow passageways crisscrossed among the towers. Some led to caverns, some led nowhere. A clearing amid the tall rocks provided enough room for a cramped campground around a sacred well; banthas and Sand People alike clumped in the craggy stomach of the Jundland.

No one said anything as A'Yark passed through the camp. The dozens who had remained here during the raid knew that many weaklings had fallen. There was no time to mourn the unworthiness of kin. Those names, those voices, belonged to the past. The Sand People had to survive today.

The Tuskens had a word for "tomorrow," but it was seldom used. What good would it be? Death rode behind the Tusken, as the shadows to the bantha. The settlers seemed not to know that. Erecting shelters to protect their precious futures, the settlers became things fat and fleshy—no better than Hutts. Perhaps that was how the Hutts had come to be? A'Yark had never really wondered about it, or much else.

No, only today mattered. Each day's survival was a trophy that could be carried into the tales of the past— a stroke against the damnation cast upon them by the suns. It was a thing to be proud of. But who would tell the stories if all fell?

At the well, the thirsty war leader dismissed the idle thoughts and pulled the rope. The noons were coming. Younglings needed feeding, gaderffii points sharpening—and a new target would need to be chosen. A'Yark would select it, as always.

The container reached the top of the well. For the third time in as many days, it held only damp sand. Others had called it an ill omen. A'Yark simply wanted to kill something.

A cloth-bound youngling ran up and bleated a message from the watch. A'Yark listened with rising anger. There was someone riding an animal through the dunes. Again.

There had been other encroachments near the wastes, recently. A'Yark had even heard of a single hooded human, riding a heavily laden eopie across the desert from east to west, untouched by the Tusken scouts who espied him. A'Yark had flown into a rage over that one. A settler might take a machine across the dunes, or attempt to. But this was the act of one whose wits were lost—or of a being so powerful he felt none could harm him. A'Yark didn't care what the answer was. Such impudence should have been dealt with, no matter what their current state.

The others hearing the youngling took up their weapons right away. *Good,* A'Yark thought. Even after this morning, some spirit remained. But much needed doing here. They would stay, while A'Yark went to investigate and punish the intruder. And if they argued the point, someone else would lose an arm.

This kill would belong to A'Yark.

*   *   *

"Yaah!"

Annileen yanked again at the reins. Vilas heard and rumbled forward, nimbly crawling over the rocky outcrop. He was over it in a few seconds. Another call from Annileen and he was off again, barreling across the floor of the dusty bowl valley.

Kicks from a rider meant nothing to the dewback, whose brownish red scales could protect it against any spur. But Vilas seemed to understand where he was going, and what he had to do.

It was why Annileen had headed directly for him when she'd seen the busted fence. Her landspeeder would have been faster, but Kallie and Snit had lit off in the direction of The Rumbles, a lightly rocky stretch known mostly for the turbulent ride it gave hovercraft. That was no problem, but it also made for more difficult tracking at speed. Vilas, on the other hand, knew right where to go—she hoped.

"That's the one," she said, picking out the right cloud from several dust devils in the distance. Vilas knew it, too. She clung to him. Annileen hadn't ridden in three years, but it wasn't something she was likely to forget. Half the dewbacks in Bestine today had descended from Caelum Thaney's herd. She'd be working on her father's ranch still, if the animals hadn't gotten the Parch, a wasting disease that prevented their cells from utilizing water.

By the end, there had been little left of the herd—or of Caelum, who'd watched as all his farmhands left. After Annileen was forced to take a job working for Dannar, her father became unreachable. Four years later, after she and her mother relocated to a hut nearer the oasis, he finally took a blaster to his sorrows. Annileen had found him at home just three days after her announced engagement. He'd relocated the dozen remaining dewback eggs to what had once been her nursery, years before.

The livery stables and corral at the Claim had been Dannar's surprise wedding present to Annileen; the Thaney legacy lived on outside her store window, providing her distraction and solace. And when Dannar had died, Kallie—then nine—had found that same peace in tending the creatures. Annileen had ceded all care of the animals to her then. Kallie needed it, and there was something else: the girl wouldn't have to spend her teen years debating the price of blankets with people who couldn't remember her name.

It felt good to be on a dewback again, though—even given the danger. Snit had been a temptation, a challenge sitting there for Kallie for far too long. Annileen suspected now that Snit had mountain dewback blood in him; one of Orrin's crews had brought a batch of eggs after digging them up in a field. Mountain dewbacks were just shy of the cannibal breed for craziness. Annileen cursed herself for not doing a proper genetic workup before. She knew how, and the stable had simple diagnostic tools. But she'd been too busy. And neither of her kids was proving much good against temptation.

Kallie was in sight now, half a kilometer ahead. Snit didn't show any signs of stopping. Annileen and her mount cut directly across the flats toward them. Kallie was still out of earshot, but Annileen could see the girl was no longer in control of the beast, if she ever had been.

The Calwell livery beat all others for safety: three mighty girth straps went around each dewback's midsection, securing saddles. But those only worked well if the dewback sat still for the fitting, and she couldn't imagine Snit had. The resultant loose straps, she now saw, had caused the saddle to start sliding off Snit's back to the right. Kallie, her foot tangled in a stirrup, was hanging over the animal's side, desperately clinging to the reins. With every futile attempt to climb back atop Snit, the girl was driving him crazier. He wouldn't stop until he'd shaken her.

Snit topped a rise and vanished. Annileen reached it long seconds later. What she saw on the other side took her breath away. She'd known the eastern reaches were prone to sinkholes, but this place was a geologic minefield. Worse, it was the kind of pockmarked landform favored by—and often caused by—creatures so horrific they nearly defied description.

Sarlaccs. Big underground appetites that preyed on anything foolish enough to wander along. Monsters that could swallow a landspeeder whole, but were often impossible to see until they had you.

And Snit was running straight into the place.

Annileen doubled up on the reins and pushed ahead. Vilas snorted, straining against her. He didn't like the look of the area, she could tell—and she couldn't blame him. But she had to play the odds. Sarlaccs were rare. There was a particularly large one at Carkoon; another near some of Tatooine's many ancient ruins, she'd heard tell. Even a tiny one of their spawn could be a fatal discovery—but there was no other choice now. She prodded the animal into a bounding run, keeping as far away from the mini craters as possible.

"Help!" Annileen's eyes left the pitted ground and darted a hundred meters ahead. Snit was going places fast, and Kallie was still stuck. *"Mom, help!"*

Annileen's heart caught in her throat—but she realized it meant that Kallie had seen her. She gritted her teeth and pushed forward, her senses overloading. There was sand flying everywhere in Snit's wake; Annileen's hair, now unbound, blew openly and violently behind her. The desert floor rose and fell below, present here, absent there. And there was the constant *thrum-thrum-*

thrum of Vilas's feet slamming against the surface, reverberating through her body. Yet she was still gaining.

Vilas got his legs tangled up for a moment, but recovered quickly. Facing away from the chase for that second, Annileen thought she saw a Tusken Raider, peering at her from over a far distant dune. A moment later she was back on track, and sure she was hallucinating. Too much adrenaline. Snit, up ahead, didn't seem to care about anything.

Annileen's voice cracked as she yelled into the wind. "Stop! Stop!"

Snit was only a dozen meters ahead of her—and Annileen could see clearly how Kallie was tangled in the stirrup. The terrified girl was half sliding off Snit's right side now, and in imminent danger of shaking free and landing beneath the beast's massive rear legs. Annileen had to move.

"Sorry, boy," she called to Vilas. "Gotta do this!" She pushed the dewback harder, bringing him within nipping distance of Snit's left hind shank. There was no question of riding up on the right; Kallie would be doubly in danger then, if she fell. Annileen would have to bring the monster under control herself.

Vilas moderated his pace; fearful, Annileen figured, of Snit turning on him. But she was close enough. She released the reins, threw her weight forward, and scrambled up onto Vilas's massive neck, the dewback's scales skinning her gloveless hands.

She looked down at the narrowing space between the two dewbacks. Grit exploded from the ground, each pounding step of Snit's a sandy geyser. If Snit knew Vilas was alongside, he hadn't reacted—yet. But he surely would. What would he do then?

Annileen had mounted a trotting dewback before, but never an angry one running at full speed, from atop an-

other animal. Snit could do anything. It was too dangerous to try.

But she could hear Kallie, too, crying out with every
bump.

Now!

Annileen reached into space, clutching for Snit's rear-
most girth strap. It was the only part of the rigging that
looked at all secure—and it was. The second she had a
firm grasp on it, she heaved herself from Vilas to Snit.

This Snit *did* notice—and he wasn't the least bit happy
about it. He snapped his mighty tail forward, trying
to swat away the woman hugging his back. Annileen
hung on, pulling herself ahead, handhold by tenuous
handhold. Vilas was gone now, having angled off to
the north; Annileen was committed. Still clinging, she
grabbed Kallie's arm and tried to pull her up.

No good. The load was too much, her hold too awkward. Annileen feared toppling them both off. But better they go on or go off the creature together. Annileen
reached over to grab a handful of shirt . . .

. . . and saw something off to the right.

It appeared just at the edge of her peripheral vision.
For a split second, she thought it was the imagined
Tusken. But jerking her head backward for a moment,
she saw the reality was more unbelievable. Another
rider had joined the chase, angling in from the faraway
rise to the southeast. A figure clad in brown, racing at a
diagonal to catch up with them. Running at full tilt—

—on an *eopie*?

Annileen looked down at Kallie, whose face was frozen in terror—and then back at the newcomer. She'd
seen it all right: an eopie. A fraction the size of the dewback, four-legged and tan. An eopie could sprint, but its
legs were no match for those of the dewback. And yet
the hooded figure guided it quickly along, with no more
effort than one would exhibit driving a speeder bike.

Annileen gawked. The rider couldn't possibly catch up to them, but he was certainly trying. Not all desert brigands were Tuskens, she knew—but a smart scavenger wouldn't chase anyone down in this terrain. He'd wait for the women to break their necks. Did this one actually want to help them? she wondered.

He answered that himself. "Hold on!"

The eopie nimbly danced along the edges of the sandpits, making no more imprint with its hooves than if it had been riderless. The man—close enough now that Annileen could make out a human nose and an auburn beard and mustache under the flapping hood—rode the creature expertly, approaching Snit without seeming regard for his own safety. Snit's tail whipped back and forth wildly, forcing the eopie rider to weave and dodge. But he continued to accelerate.

A second later he was alongside the deranged reptilian. Annileen looked ahead at the tortured terrain, worse than anything behind. Snit's massive hind feet might punch through the crusty sand and catch anywhere. When Annileen looked back, she could tell the mystery rider saw the danger, too. His eyes locked with hers. *"Give me the girl!"*

Without thinking, Annileen repositioned her arm under Kallie's chest and pushed. Her daughter, unaware of the new arrival, screamed as she lost her last handhold on the reins. But less than a breath separated the eopie and the dewback now—and a long arm reached from the billowing cloak to grab her. Annileen transferred Kallie's other arm to his and shoved.

Annileen slammed across the monster's back as the weight fell away. She saw Kallie and the rider atop the eopie, which was slowing now from the additional burden. No way would it carry two for long, nor three for a second. Snit was her problem. Recovering, she looked forward. It was just a matter of finding the—

Krakkk! Snit's rear foot struck a hole. Annileen went somersaulting forward, even as the impossible mass of the dewback went aloft underneath her. She saw light as the suns flashed before her eyes—and then darkness as the bulk of the dewback eclipsed them.

And then, nothing.

CHAPTER SIX

"MOM!"

Annileen opened her eyes and swiftly shut them. "I can't see."

"Wait," Kallie said, brushing the grains of sand from her mother's eyelashes. "Try now."

Annileen tried again. She saw a young face stained by saddle grease hovering over her, lit from above by the high suns. Annileen tried to speak, but her voice cracked. "K-kallie. You . . . you—"

"It's okay, Mom. I'm okay."

"—you're grounded," Annileen said. "For life."

Kallie grinned. "She's going to be all right."

"Yes," replied someone else. "She is."

Annileen couldn't hear where the voice was coming from, but she didn't want to sit up to look, either, not when the sand was nice and soft and warm.

Kallie vanished from her view, and another face replaced hers. It was the rider from before. His hood was removed, now. He had reddish blond hair, lighter than his beard and mustache. His blue-gray eyes looked on her with what Annileen interpreted as bemusement. "Hello, there," he said, in an accent she couldn't place. "You've taken a nasty spill."

"You might be on to something," Annileen said, coughing.

He smiled. A pleasant smile, she thought; not one of Orrin's winning ones, to be sure. But understated, and inflected with well-meaning. As was his voice.

"You're in one piece," he said. "You'll be picking sand out of your clothes for a while, but nothing appears broken." The man produced a canteen from the folds of his cloak. It was an old garment, she saw, its deep brown turned tawny in places from wear. Beneath, she could see he wore a blousy tan tunic. The stranger paused as he knelt close. "May I?"

Annileen tried to nod.

He lifted her head gently so she could take a drink. Annileen drank desperately, half realizing that seventeen years of her teachings about strangers in the desert were vanishing before her daughter's eyes. Annileen didn't know what to think about the newcomer, other than that he seemed to be dressed out of her seconds bin at the store.

Annileen gasped as she finished swallowing. She nodded her thanks to the stranger and then narrowed her eyes. "Kallie?"

The stranger stepped away, and her daughter reappeared. "Yes, Mom?"

Annileen's hand shot up, grabbing at the girl's collar. "What were you *doing*?"

A guilty look crossed Kallie's face. "Well, you had half the galaxy showing up at the Claim to get drunk—and before lunch, even. I figured if I didn't get out and work the animals on the range, I'd be stuck in there helping."

"Yes—but why *that* animal?"

"I—I don't know." Kallie shrugged. "Besides, I didn't think you'd care. You were busy with Jabe, *as always*—"

Behind the girl, the stranger fastened the lid on his

canteen and chuckled. "If you were trying to get your mother's attention, my young friend—you succeeded." He flashed that disarming smile again.

Kallie's brown eyes lit up, and she beamed at him. "Oh, please—you can call me Kallie!"

He smiled politely—and Annileen glared at her daughter. "Grounded *for life,*" she said, and tried to sit up. A second later she realized the futility of the attempt and surrendered to gravity.

The stranger was back down in a flash, catching her. His riding gloves exposed his bare fingers, and she could feel them in her hair. "Don't do anything rash," he said. "We just got you back to the world."

"Right." With the help of the two of them, Annileen sat up.

"I was heading home from Bestine when I saw you were having troubles," he said. "That was some masterful riding, you catching up to your daughter. I hope I didn't offend you by getting involved."

"No, no offense," Annileen deadpanned. Turning her head, she saw what had become of Snit. The dewback drooled on the sand, his once-crazed eyes staring mindlessly at her. Looking along the animal's length, Annileen thought his rear leg looked like a half-deflated balloon. The bones, deep inside, had shattered badly from the misstep.

But more remarkable was *where* Snit was: only a couple of meters behind her. The creature had just missed her when he landed.

"It was a lucky thing," the man said.

"Lucky," Annileen said, rubbing the side of her head. There'd be a knot there, for sure. "I was afraid we'd run into a sarlacc."

"A healthy fear to have."

Annileen forced herself to stand. Once sure of her

bearings, she wiped her hand on her shirt and presented it. "Annileen Calwell."

"*Annileen.*" The man seemed reluctant at first to shake her hand, but soon did so amiably. "I haven't heard that one. Family name?"

"Not any longer, if I have anything to say about it," she said, smiling. "Most just call me Annie."

The rescuer paused, and for a moment she thought she saw his eyes fix, as if looking somewhere else. But the gentle smile quickly returned. "No, Annileen is just fine."

"And you've met the tornado," Annileen said.

"Kallie," the girl repeated, going for a handshake of her own.

The man nodded. "Ben."

Before Annileen could ask more, he stepped past her to examine Snit. The animal seemed catatonic. "I don't know much about this species," he said. "But he doesn't look good."

"He's in shock."

Ben appeared concerned. "Can he make a go of it on three legs?"

"Let me ask the livery manager." Annileen looked over at Kallie, who was adjusting the saddle on Vilas. "What do *you* think?"

Her daughter splayed her arms and whined, "I didn't mean for this to happen!" Kallie hated to lose any creatures at all. But even if Snit could somehow go on, Annileen had half a mind to shoot the nasty thing anyway.

Which was when Annileen realized she had no weapon at all, out here on the desert with a vagrant. But as before, Ben somehow seemed to sense her unease. He whistled once, and his eopie scampered back toward him. The animal was spry, despite being heavily laden with gear.

Kallie smiled. "What's her name?"

"Rooh. Or that's what they told me when I bought her." Ben patted the eopie's snout. "Good job, Rooh," he said reassuringly.

It reassured Annileen, anyway. One thing about the lowlifes of Tatooine: they were seldom nice to children and animals. Ben had saved her child *from* an animal.

And with that, her judgment was made.

"Well, good job to you, too, Ben," she said, dusting herself off. "Why were you coming this way again?"

Scratching the eopie's neck, he nodded to the southwest. "I've . . . set up house near the wastes. Just running some errands. Things to do, you know."

Annileen brightened. "No need to go to Bestine." She looked at some of the gear jutting from Rooh's saddlebags. "You're closer to the oasis."

"The Pika Oasis?" He scratched his beard. "I heard there was a shop there."

"Dannar's Claim. Best store in the oasis."

"*Only* store in the oasis," Kallie piped in from behind.

Annileen spoke without looking over her shoulder. "Girl, I hope you're not talking again. Because if you are, you should be apologizing to me and to this man. And to the dewback you nearly killed."

Ben chuckled, and then stifled it. Annileen calculated he had kids of his own, or that he'd at least worked with them. He looked down at the eopie's load. "This store. It has vaporator parts?"

"Wouldn't be much of a store without. And besides, you're looking at the—"

Before Annileen could continue, Ben's expression changed. Suddenly alert, he held up his hand. "Wait," he said, turning.

All three fixed their eyes on Snit's motionless body— and watched, as it began to descend, sinking in the sand. A groan came from beneath, and a tremor rocked the place they were standing.

"I'm afraid that's your sarlacc," Ben said. Tendrils snaked upward, lashing around the huge form of the dewback.

Annileen saw Ben reach for an object beneath his cloak, only to stop when he noticed her watching. She waved him off. "There's no blasting at a sarlacc," she said.

"Perhaps you're right." The tentacles began straining at the dewback, pulling it downward. Ben grabbed at the lead on his startled eopie. Annileen hustled her daughter toward Vilas.

Kallie looked back in anguish. "Snit—"

"Comes out of your earnings," Annileen said, shoving the girl onto Vilas's saddle. She climbed in front. "And you hang on this time."

From atop Rooh, Ben paused to look in amazement at the disappearing beast. The appetite of a sarlacc was something no traveler could see and forget, Annileen knew.

She wanted to ask where he was from, but it clearly wasn't the time. "Thanks again! Maybe we'll see you in the oasis!"

Ben smiled mildly and nodded. "Maybe." He pulled his cowl back over his head.

"See you soon, Ben!" Kallie yelled, waving.

Annileen rolled her eyes. So much for remorse over Snit. Beneath them, Vilas started walking, eager to get away from the new sarlacc pit.

Remembering something, Annileen looked back at Ben, poised to head off to the southwest. "Hey!"

"Yes?"

"I'm sorry," she said. "I didn't catch your last name!"

"Oh," he said, only to tilt backward as Rooh broke into a sudden trot. "Sorry," he said with an apologetic wave as the eopie ran. "I think she wants to get home!"

No doubt, Annileen thought. *She's not alone!*

* * *

From behind a dune, A'Yark watched the trio part company.

The warrior's one good eye was very good, indeed, and the lens in the eyepiece could see far, when adjusted. Whoever had crafted it had done a useful thing with his or her existence. But A'Yark now doubted the work, because the eyepiece had seen something that made no sense at all.

Just after the eopie-riding male had plucked the young female from the racing dewback—an impressive feat, to be certain—the out-of-control creature had tripped in a hole and flipped over, throwing the woman who was riding it. She should have been crushed by the dewback—but instead of falling on her, the beast had been caught by the air itself and actually hovered there, bobbing, for a second. It was as if the world itself had rejected the mad thing. Then it tumbled once in midair and fell away at an angle, coming to rest just shy of the woman's body.

The younger woman, partly hanging over the eopie's saddle in the wrong direction, had not seen it. But the male rider *had* seen it happen—and was unfazed by it. Surprise was the one human expression all Tuskens learned to recognize. This man had not displayed any at all—not even when a giant dewback floated on air.

The Tuskens were well aware of the powers the settlers had at their disposal. They used lesser magics, their spells all relying upon physical components linked together in a certain way. A landspeeder was a conglomeration of trinkets. If the ordering of the pieces was in any way disturbed, it lost its powers. An unreliable magic, to be sure.

But there was no metal, no unnatural material, no mechanism present here. Just humans. That was when A'Yark had slipped back behind the dune, to think.

This was no false dragon call. What did it portend? Things were already bad for the Sand People. If the settlers had now added to their capabilities, then caution was demanded. A'Yark needed to know what the Sand People were facing. What was this power?

And which one of the humans had it?

As far as A'Yark was concerned, there was no reason for the human male to put himself at risk for either of the women. What had brought them onto the desert floor was apparent. The women had obviously tried, as so many settlers had, to tame the very spirit of life on Tatooine—in this case, the dewbacks who belonged in the mountains. It was right that they had failed. They should have died, and the hairy-faced male should have let them.

Living beings helped only themselves—that was the Tusken way. And it suggested that the *woman* had the sorcery in her, to land so gently, and to brush the dewback aside. The man must have known she was in no danger—that she had the power to save herself. Yes. *That* made sense.

While the woman recovered from her feat, A'Yark had sat, contemplating the right path. The conclusion was now clear. The settler woman had to be killed—and quickly, before she taught her skill to another. Now, while her dewback carried two—

A'Yark felt another tremor in the sand. It was gentle, and would have gone unnoticed by another. A'Yark knew it for what it was. The accursed sarlacc had many children in locations unknown to the Tuskens. Most sat inert, starving, never becoming. But the feast of the dewback by one had awakened others. This was no time to find out how many more existed.

No, the information A'Yark had just learned needed to reach the clan. The humans could be found again without difficulty. Then the Tuskens would all move as one, knowing they were doing a truly important thing. It would be the victory they needed to regain their defiant spirit once and for all.

A'Yark left the hiding spot and departed for the hills. Not as the cowardly sun—but as the hunter.

It felt good.

Meditation

Let's try this again.

I'm afraid I haven't had any success with this means of communication, Master Qui-Gon. Perhaps you haven't had anything to say? That's fine. I've tried speaking to you mentally; I'll try speaking aloud for a while, and see if that makes a difference.

Since I last tried speaking to you, I've made some tactical moves. Owen Lars didn't want me hanging about near his home anymore. He had a point, believe it or not. Creeping on hillsides every morning and evening might not be the best way to avoid drawing attention to his farm.

So I've found another place. You might be alarmed when you hear how far away it is. It certainly unnerves me. You remember the Xelric Draw, where we landed the ship from Naboo years ago? This is due south of that, up against the northern wall of the highlands—the Jundland Wastes. Only we're at the far end of the formation from where Owen lives—maybe a hundred kilometers.

It's a funny way to keep watch over someone, I know. I can't get there and back in a day on Rooh— and I'm reluctant to get so much as a speeder bike, for fear of the attention I'd attract. The Tusken natives seem to follow anything shiny they find; I could lead them to the Lars farm if I'm not careful.

And anyone watching from satellite might notice a pattern to my travels.

I've also ruled out leaving surveillance equipment. Access to the galactic mainframe is spotty everywhere here, but regardless, I don't want to own anything that taps into it. I haven't even used the secret one-way message drop Bail Organa provided to tell him I've settled in. The fewer signals coming from my home, the better. What if Palpatine has eyes all the way out here, looking for Jedi Knights he failed to kill? It could happen.

The other Jedi. How I hope others have survived. I couldn't bear to be the only one left. It seems impossible to imagine.

I wish you could tell me—

In any case, with regard to the Lars farm, it's probably okay if I just go over there once in a while, on foot or on Rooh. I can hide better that way, and camp if I need. There won't be a pattern to my movements, or when I choose to go. I won't be able to respond quickly if someone troubles the boy— or even know about it. But at least I won't be the trouble.

Still, I wish there was someone I could rely on, closer to them. I've been hearing some sirens to the north; there was another this morning. I worried it involved the Empire, but I think now it might be a warning system of some kind. Maybe that could be of help, I don't—

This would be easier if you said something. Never mind. I'll be briefer.

This house. It's in worse shape than I thought. I rode into Bestine to make sure it was unoccupied, but I hardly needed confirmation. The Jawas picked the place over long ago. There's a shell of a vaporator, if I can ever get it working right—it needs parts, still. And the place should have a low profile, if I can remove the trash from the yard. You can imagine what kind of junk even a Jawa would pass up.

I was worried it was going to require more trips to Bestine—that's forty kilometers or so—but maybe there's another option. Annileen—

That's Annileen Calwell, a woman from the Pika Oasis, and her daughter. The oasis is closer, and from what she says it has more of what I need to set up housekeeping here.

Meeting her gave me a chance to finally use the name I chose. You'll like this: Ben. I had seen it on the map at the property office in Bestine—there's some mesa by that name. Satine used to call me that—it was a private thing. I like the sound of it.

I'm . . . afraid I drew some attention to myself when I met Annileen. I won't get into details, but she was in trouble, and I helped her. It felt good to be doing something, after all this hiding. And good to be talking to someone again, when I'm feeling so alone and—

Ah, well.

I don't know. I'm closer to the oasis, but it's closer to me, too. Maybe it's not a good idea to become too familiar a sight with the locals.

I probably won't go.

CHAPTER SEVEN

"HOW EEET LOOK, Master Gault?"

"Real pretty, Gloamer." Orrin ran his hand across the new windshield on the landspeeder. "Like new. I don't know how you do it."

Orrin wasn't surprised. Of all the mechanics in the Calwell garages, Gloamer, a green-skinned Phindian whose dangly arms nearly reached his ankles, was by far the best. Starting from a single rented bay five years earlier, Gloamer now ran a vibrant trade taking up a building and a half. That made him the garages' third largest occupant, after the Gault vaporator installation fleet and the storage space for the Settlers' Fund vehicles. Since Gloamer worked on all of those, too, he and his assistants were seen almost everywhere.

"Eees best speeeder in oh-aaay-sees," the mechanic said, his golden eyes alight in their white cavities. "Eees *maaaarvel.*"

Orrin grinned. Phindians could never let go of a vowel, it seemed—and few beings he had met had more appreciation for a fine vehicle. On this one, Gloamer was right: the USV-5 looked as if it belonged on a nicer planet. Orrin had dithered over buying it; a farmer shouldn't put on airs. But selling water was as much a part of the job as finding it, and the high-volume city accounts didn't want to buy from someone who looked like he worked for a living.

Well, that was fine. He could play that game.

Gloamer's lead assistant skittered past, carrying part of a metal airfoil. Something called a Vuvrian, the assistant was easily the most macabre thing in the garage, to Orrin's thinking. Bipedal, but with an insect's head—and apparently a talent for thruster control systems. Orrin didn't have a problem with nonhumans; compared with his parochial grandfather, his opinions were cosmopolitan. Any being willing to put its back into hard work was fine with him. Diligence knew no species. And neither did sloth: there were more than enough human bums around the Anchorhead cantina to give his own kind a bad name.

But Pappy Gault had been right on one thing. Business success was about taking the other's measure. Between any two people, a point existed where what one wanted intersected with what the other had. That point was price, and to get the best possible one, high or low, you had to see things the other person's way. But who knew what a Vuvrian or a Bith was really thinking?

You can't look a fellow in the eye when he's all eye.

Orrin had left Tatooine once, as a teenager. His grandfather had dispatched the hands to Rodia, to fetch a vaporator; even a secondhand device from one of the more technologically advanced planets was far better than anything most Tatooine farmers had in their fields. Left at home, Dannar had joked that Orrin would never be heard from again, once he'd seen the stars.

But if anything, Orrin's brief sojourn told him Tatooine was the real home of opportunity. The galaxy was full of hustlers, all scratching for a credit—and Rodia, a humid place where people clustered under domes, jammed them together in one spot like the jar he used to trap sandflies in. Keep 'em in there long enough, and they'd eat one another. No, Tatooine was much better. Mos Eisley might seem like a menagerie, but you could at least drive away. Tatooine had land—and Orrin had his share.

Thanking Gloamer, he walked along the bays and looked back at his repulsortrucks in the garage. Too many were in the shop, as usual: three more, this morning. It was due not to any fault in Gloamer's work, but to the boneheads that operated them. Orrin's ostensible reason for going into the fields each day was to fine-tune the vaporators for better performance. But in fact, most of that time was spent checking up on his remote teams, who confounded him daily by inventing new ways to damage his machinery, his vehicles, or themselves. They were far behind on getting the fields ready for the harvest, and expenses had soared.

He'd hoped the next generation would take some pressure off him. But Mullen and Veeka had both somehow managed to reach their twenties without really growing up. Mullen's talent seemed to be ticking people off, not leading them—and Veeka was . . . well, Veeka. Jabe Calwell, though, had some of his late father's industry about him. Orrin saw him playing a big role in things, if his mother would let him. But Orrin would have to wear down Annileen first. *Can't have a foreman whose mama won't let him work.*

Things had been quiet on the Tusken front in the days since the Bezzard incident; it would be a while before Plug-eye would get up the nerve, or the warriors, to try another dawn raid. But hostilities were still continuing between mother and son, Orrin heard, as he opened the door onto the sales floor of the Claim.

"It's not fair, Mom!" The voice was male, young, newly deep, and indignant. "It's not fair and you know it!"

"Fair?" Annileen replied. "What's fair got to do with the price of water?"

Jabe was on his knees and surrounded by multi-kilo pouches, a puzzle that in no way seemed likely to fit together on the shelves. He was not happy to be there. "Why don't you get Kallie to do this?"

Annileen looked sternly down the aisle from her counter. "Kallie has her own job, and you know it."

"This stuff's feed. Animals are her department!"

"That's outside the store. This is inside the store. You want me to play back a recording from the last ten times we've had this conversation?" Annileen spotted Orrin's approach. "You better not be here for a piece of this."

Orrin plucked his good cape from the rack by the door and smirked. "No, Annie, I know when I'm beat." He looked down at Jabe. "Sorry, kid. Maybe next career."

Seeing Jabe's shoulders droop, Orrin winked to reassure him. The boy had to know he had an advocate in him. It was just a matter of time.

Orrin tied the cape around his neck as he made his way around the castle of feed sacks. "How's Kallie today?"

Annileen rolled her eyes. "You'll have to ask her when she lands." She pointed down the counter to the luncheonette. There Kallie, recovered from her ordeal several days earlier, was in the midst of retelling the story of her rescue—this time, to some teenage friends in from the fields.

"... and he just appeared, like he rode down out of the sky. And there were sarlaccs everywhere, but he plowed straight through to try to catch up with me ..."

Orrin had heard this one twice in the past two days. He raised an eyebrow to Annileen. "Sarlaccs everywhere?"

"Today, yes." Annileen looked up from scrubbing the counter. "Wait a while. She's added a giant cliff."

"I'm not hearing her mention *your* role in things," Orrin said.

"Oh, I wasn't there," Annileen said, a wry twist to her mouth. "I haven't been in the story for a long time."

"*. . . of course, I'm a great rider, and I could've handled it. But Ben's the type of guy who can't look the other way when he sees someone—sees a woman—in trouble. And he knew he had to save me from certain . . .*"

"When do I meet this deity?" Orrin said.

"No idea." Annileen scraped at a stain with frustration. "You know these drifters out on the wastes. He's probably gotten lost and eaten his eopie by now."

Orrin chuckled. This response was pure Annie, but he could tell she was disappointed their rescuer hadn't paid a call. Orrin was glad she'd found help out there; since she'd left without her communicator, they would have had no way to find her. But the man's absence was probably just as well. Kindly nomads had a way of moving in once they knew you owed them something.

The talk had spread to another table, he heard, as Leelee and the older locals tried to identify the Ben in question.

"There's that Ben Gaddink who sells the sand sculptures out of the back of his repulsortruck," Leelee said.

"You're thinking Ben Moordriver," corrected Doc Mell. "Ben Gaddink runs the apothecary in Bestine."

"Maybe Ben Krissle, the card cheat," a young farmer said.

"*Ben Surrep!*" proclaimed an old one. "No, wait, he's an Ithorian . . ."

In under two minutes they had expanded the list of local Bens to double digits—and completely exhausted Orrin's interest. He stepped to the counter and found

his lunch box and fresh canteen in their usual place. Annileen noticed his cape. "Going somewhere?"

"Subscription drive again."

"Again? I thought the Settlers' Fund met the annual
goal weeks ago."

"Well, safety's something you can never have enough
of," he said. "And the response to the Bezzard raid
shows the Call's working as it's supposed to."

Annileen lowered her voice. "Not counting a couple
of dead people." The Bezzard husband had moved back
home, but Tyla and the baby were still in her guest quarters. "I can't believe there's anyone left around here to
sign up."

"You know the main holdouts," he said. "But I think
we can start offering protection to farms a little farther
away."

"They'll be able to disband the militia in Mos Eisley
before you know it," Annileen said, stepping out from
behind the counter with an armload of batteries. "Good
luck, champ."

Orrin clicked his tongue happily and turned toward
the door to the garage. That meant walking past Jabe
and Mount Feed. The boy was as sad as Orrin had ever
seen him.

"I'm never going to get back on the range with you
guys." Jabe looked up at Orrin forlornly.

"You might be able to help us out in other ways,"
Orrin said. "And give her a week. She'll have forgotten
all about the other day."

"She should have kept Tar around," Jabe said.

Annileen's voice sounded from over the shelves in the
next aisle. "Tar wouldn't have stayed, and you know it!
You're family. This is a family business."

Orrin smirked. "Better learn now, boy. Woman knows
all, hears all." But he happened to agree. Tar Lup was a
hairy-faced Shistavanen that Dannar had brought in to

clerk when Annileen's pregnancy with Jabe turned diffi-cult. Amiable and ambitious, Tar had left for big-city retail, where he was doing well. Orrin had prevailed upon him to return to help out for a few months after Dannar's death, which he did gladly; you could take someone out of the oasis, Orrin liked to say, but that sense of community was always there. But Tar wasn't likely to come back as a stocker, and they all knew it. Jabe shook his head sadly and returned to his chore.

Walking back to the garage, Orrin found his children huddled over the back of a repulsortruck, poring over the goods inside. "That the stuff?"

"Yep," Mullen said, moving aside to let Orrin ap-proach. "It's the last batch of Tusken junk from the Bez-zard raid."

Orrin looked into the back of the vehicle. A couple of bandoliers, another gaffi stick, some putrid-smelling pouches. The Tuskens never had anything they didn't steal from someone else, but it was interesting to try to see the world through their eyes.

"No clothes?"

Mullen snorted. "You want to strip those stinking things down?"

"Not hardly." It was an experience you didn't repeat. Whatever the Tuskens were born as, a lifetime in the suns, under wraps, turned them into something fright-ful. They *smelled* frightful, anyway.

Pulling a spanner from the folds of his cloak, he used it to gently lift a pair of goggles. Tusken eyewear was strange. Some wore normal goggles, sheathed in wrap-ping; others wore independent eyepieces, tightly rooted in their masks. But all terminated in the same nonsensi-cal turrets. Whatever shielding the dull metal tubes pro-vided to Tusken eyes against the suns couldn't have been worth the peripheral vision they took away—and if there was a way to use the lens inside to see farther, he hadn't figured it out.

"Not much here," Orrin said. "Well, you know what to—"

"Got it," Mullen said, wrapping the bundle up.

Orrin backed away from the repulsortruck—and right into another of Gloamer's aides. The female mechanic—this one a proper human, not much older than Jabe—grew red-faced. "I'm so sorry, Master Gault!"

Orrin dusted himself off. "It's all right," he said. "Busy trumps standing around in my world."

"It's an emergency," the dark-haired girl said. She reached for a jug of blue liquid on a shelving unit. "It's Old Ulbreck. His engine overheated again, on the way here from his place."

Orrin knew Ulbreck well. The cheap character probably bought coolant by the spoonful. "He's just sitting out there in the dunes?"

"Of course," the girl said. Looking around, she lowered her voice. "He's afraid someone will steal his vehicle if he leaves. It's no problem—happens all the time. Today it's my turn to go out."

Orrin calculated for a moment. He reached out and stopped the aide. "Look, I'm heading out, anyway. I'll take care of him." He reached for the jug of coolant. "It's the least I can do for the work you've done for me."

"That's wonderful, sir! I'll let Gloamer know."

The girl dashed off, leaving the Gaults alone. Mullen looked to his father. "You figuring on trying to sell Ulbreck on joining the Call again?"

"I'm the king of lost causes," Orrin said, snorting. "As well as the Jundland." He laughed. "Besides, who knows? Maybe saving the old man will put us over the top. Or maybe I'll give Kallie Calwell's hero a run for his money."

"I wish," Mullen said, glaring in the direction of the

door to the store. "I'm sick of hearing that little idiot babble about the heroic drifter."

Veeka chortled. "Give the girl a break. He's the first male she's seen outside of a dewback pen."

Orrin found his landspeeder and settled into the driver's seat. "Be nice. Bored people imagine things," he said. "But if any bronze gods three meters tall come riding up, page me on the comlink. That, I'll want to see . . ."

The red comlink by the till went off. It was Annileen's dedicated connection to Orrin. Communications were always iffy on Tatooine, but Orrin still did his best to stay in touch. She picked it up. "You can't have run out of customers already!"

"That's not it," Orrin's crackling voice replied. "Saw something on my way out. You're about to have a visitor."

Annileen inhaled for a moment.

"No, not *that* visitor," Orrin said, somehow reading her silence correctly. "Someone else."

Annileen listened as he explained. "Right," she said, clicking the comlink off. "Kallie! Jabe! Come on!"

Her daughter looked over to see Annileen picking up the blaster rifle from behind the counter. Jabe, suddenly aware, dropped his broom. "Do you need to activate the Settlers' Call?"

"No," she said, passing him another rifle. "This is a Calwell Call. Get your gun, Kallie. We're about to have company."

CHAPTER EIGHT

THE SANDCRAWLER HAD STARTED its journey in the south, far beyond the great pass. There, the Jundland high country separated to allow entry into the Western Dune Sea, for anyone daft enough to go there. The land between the pass and the oasis was almost featureless, making it easy to spot the metal behemoth rumbling toward the store.

Still, Annileen was thankful for Orrin's early warning. The machines made decent time, for their size, and the alert had given her time to lock away the cash. By the time the rolling rummage sale trundled to a stop in the south yard, Annileen and her children were there waiting for it.

Wearing her gray-brimmed safari hat, Annileen stood in the sandcrawler's shadows. The suns blazed high over the angled nose of the vehicle; if there was anyone up in the control cabin, she couldn't see them. It didn't matter. There was something she had to do now, something she'd done for twenty years of prior impromptu visits by the Jawas. Something she'd seen Dannar do during her first year clerking—a thing that told her then that he wasn't just another grubber who'd go broke in a year.

"Let's do this," Annileen said, snapping the power cartridge into her rifle.

"Aw, Annie," Leelee said. She and the other customers had emerged when they heard the sandcrawler approach. "You're not gonna shoot 'em?"

Annileen said nothing, instead leading her children to the side of the vehicle. Foul steam emanated from the behemoth's overheating engines. "You know the drill," she said. Jabe and Kallie nodded, even as the mighty ramp began to creak open. The ramp end hit the ground with a muted clang. The Calwells raised their weapons—

—and turned them on their crowd of customers. "Now hear this," Annileen said. "This land is *my* property. If there's any trading to be done with the Jawas, *I'm* going to do it. If you don't want to pay my markup, you get on your dewback and head on up to the Mospic Range, or wherever they're going next."

A low, agitated rumble came from the crowd. Annileen responded by firing once into the air.

"I'm serious," she growled. She glared at the gathering. "Any one of you tries to buy a *rivet* from these guys, know this: I'm not gonna shoot the Jawas. Selling's what they do. They're never going to comprehend property lines. *You*, on the other hand, know very well where you are, and what the rules are. So you might as well go back inside. If there's anything worth having, we'll put it on sale—after we've wiped it down."

Her point was made. Grumbling patrons of the Claim started to wander back into the building. Annileen hadn't had to shoot anyone in a long time. One stun blast every few years was usually enough to convince people that this was her commercial terrain. She would let Gloamer come out from the garages and deal directly; in slower years, he'd supplemented his business by buying defunct equipment from the Jawas and refurbishing it. But the store already took a percentage on his trades, so that was in the family.

A tiny figure in a brown cloak and hood appeared on the ramp. Half her height, the Jawa's glowing eyes met hers. He gave a wave. She nodded back. "Keep an eye on them," she told her children, still on guard. "Make sure they don't steal anything."

Kallie laughed. "Who? The Jawas or our customers?"

"Both. Kallie, you watch the Jawas. Jabe, you get back inside and mind the place before they start drinking straight from the taps."

Jabe moaned. "I've been in there all day!"

"Fine. Then you stay out here and Kallie goes inside."

Kallie gave her mother an anguished look. "That's not fair, either. My job is outside, remember?"

Annileen looked coyly at the young woman. "Ah, yes. That *was* you outside earlier, telling all my diners about how Ben saved you from killing yourself." She struck her forehead with her palm in mock surprise. "Oh, wait. That was *inside,* wasn't it? Now scoot!"

Kallie stomped back into the Claim. Jabe gave a triumphant hoot and marched to where Mullen and Veeka were standing with several of the other Gault farmhands, bemused by the whole scene.

Annileen watched Jabe join them and sighed. Her kids were sixteen and seventeen. Would they ever be done competing with each other? Whichever child won each battle, the prize was always one more headache for her.

And she wasn't any happier with Jabe's choice in friends. Mullen Gault had been a grump of a kid and hadn't improved, and Veeka had been a mess ever since her twin brother died. Annileen wouldn't let Kallie near the older girl. She wasn't having the same luck keeping Jabe away.

Someone tugged at her sleeve from behind. Annileen thought for a second it might be a Jawa. Instead, she turned to see Erbaly Nap'tee standing there. "Do you work here, young person? There was no one inside at the counter."

Annileen sighed aloud. Slinging the rifle over her

shoulder, she grasped the Nikto woman gently by the shoulders and turned her to face the lead Jawa. "Here. Ma'am, you have my personal permission to buy from the Jawas. Courtesy of Dannar's Claim."

The lead Jawa chirped at Annileen in puzzlement as the elderly customer approached him. Annileen shrugged. "She's for sale, if you want her," she said, darting quickly away to look at the wares coming down the ramp.

It took less than five minutes for the Jawas to bring down everything worth owning; they were well practiced at this. Annileen surveyed the lot. Too many droids, as usual. She didn't carry them. Dannar had never liked selling things he didn't know how to fix, and it was a good policy. You didn't want to guarantee a machine just to have it start a killing spree in someone's kitchen. The small appliances, however, she could put out as-is. Walking down the line, she was struck by remorse, as always: every one of these things was scavenged from the home of some prospector family in the hills that couldn't make a go of it. One cooker she recognized on sight; she'd sold it three times.

"Togo togu! Togo togu!"

Annileen's eyes turned back toward the ramp. Two tiny Jawas were clawing quickly up it, leaving a third wailing creature behind. Veeka and several of the Gault farmhands had formed a circle and were tossing the terrified Jawa as if it were a throw-toy.

"Lose the Jawa, buy the drinks!" Veeka rasped, having already laughed herself hoarse.

"Hey!" Annileen yelled. "Quit that!" She rushed toward the group—stopping only when she saw that Jabe was part of the circle. Annileen's eyes bulged. *"Jabe!"*

Jabe looked up at the voice. It was enough distraction to cause him to drop the toss heading his way. The Jawa squealed and scampered loose, heading for the ramp.

Jabe had heard his mother's voice—but the farmhands were closer, egging him on.

"Buy the drinks! Buy the drinks!"

"No, you don't," Jabe said, bursting through the circle to chase the meter-tall creature. Annileen reached the foot of the ramp just as Jabe dashed up it. Jabe vanished inside the darkness of the doorway. "I've got you, you little—"

"—yaaaghh!"

Jabe reappeared, eyes wide and the blood drained from his face. Behind him in the doorway loomed someone else. A hooded figure all in brown, just like the Jawa who had escaped—but twice the height. Desperate to escape the giant, Jabe tripped and tumbled down the ramp, even as Veeka and the other hands went for their blasters.

Annileen laughed as her son landed at her feet. "Blasters down, folks. It's not the Giant Jawa Avenger." She smiled as her rescuer looked down at her and saluted. "Hello, Ben," she said. "Welcome to the Claim!"

Ben removed his cowl. "Good afternoon—er, noons." He looked up and took a breath, clearly pleased to be out of the wretched air of the sandcrawler. "I hope I didn't frighten anyone. The Jawas were kind enough to give us a ride in."

He whistled, and Rooh appeared in the doorway, behind him. He fished around and found her lead. "I'd have stepped out earlier, but she got a bit tangled up in there." Ben's eyes turned back down the ramp, to where Annileen stood over Jabe. "Is the boy all right?"

"He hasn't been right for a while," Annileen said, lifting Jabe to his feet by his collar. She glared at him. "I told you to watch the Jawas, not use them for sport. Now get back over there!"

Jabe meekly recovered his rifle and trudged to the far

side of the product display line, eager to avoid eye contact with his friends.

Ben and his eopie stepped down onto the surface. "Your son?"

"I'm ashamed to admit it," Annileen said, chuckling. "He must have thought you were a giant Jawa."

"Ah," Ben said. "Must be the eyes."

"Ha!"

Scratching Rooh's neck, Ben looked up at the store building ahead of him. "Nice place."

"For out here in the wastelands," Annileen said.

"I didn't say that."

"It's okay," she said, trying in vain to remember the last time someone worried about offending her. "It should be nice. It's mine."

Ben stood and walked his animal toward the building. He read the block letters carved in the sign out front. Sand had collected in some of the indentations. "Dannar's Claim."

"He founded it, I came along later," Annileen said, finding a morsel in her pocket for the eopie. It was such a docile creature. It took after its owner, she thought. "Dannar's my husband."

"Your husband," Ben repeated. His eyes scanned the crowd outside the sandcrawler.

Annileen rubbed Rooh's face, lovingly. "It's just me now—and the two kids you've already met." She smiled. "What brings you here?"

"Your invitation," he said, nodding toward the animal. "I could use some feed for Rooh."

Annileen stood. "You've come to the right place." She looked back toward the sandcrawler, where her son stood limply against the gargantuan vehicle, guarding nothing in particular. "Jabe! Get this man some eopie feed! *Now!*"

The boy looked up. "But I thought you wanted me to watch the Jawas."

"Forget it," she said. The Jawas were clustered around Erbaly now, occasionally chattering to each other as they listened to the elderly Nikto woman's questions. *They're probably all trying to figure out how to end the conversation,* Annileen thought. She looked to Ben. "First bag's on the house."

Ben lowered his eyes. He did that a lot, she'd noticed. "Please, you don't have to give me anything. I can pay—"

"It's for saving me the burial expenses for my daughter. Besides, one meal and Rooh will have you back here every week. Only the best, here."

"Just let me tie her up," Ben said, spotting the livery yard. "I knew the feed would be a big load for her on the way back, so I asked the Jawas for a ride in."

Annileen watched him lead the animal away. Jabe stepped back from the doorway long enough to whisper to her. "Did you say 'Ben'? Is that the guy?"

"Unh-huh." She repositioned her hat and exhaled. "He's only a few days late."

"Ben!"

Jabe had entered the store less than twenty seconds before his mother and the visitor passed through the door. But it had been enough time for him to inform his sister of Ben's arrival—and for her to inform the two dozen patrons in the place.

Ben nodded as the girl met him at the entrance. He'd already placed the cowl back over his head, Annileen saw. She didn't blame him at all.

"Hello, Kallie," Ben said.

"Hey, you remembered!" Kallie beamed. "Welcome to our store. Let me show you around the place—"

"Your place is the dewback pens," Annileen said.

Kallie pointed at her mother. "Yes, but *you* told me to

work inside. Come on," she said, grabbing at Ben's sleeve. "What do you need? Because you know we've got it."

"Yes, well, I've got a broken bridle—"

"Tack room!" The girl led him toward the back of the sales floor, between tables of curious diners. Annileen followed, fearful for the man's dignity. If Ben acknowledged the stares at all, she didn't notice. But she wasn't going to have a new customer scared off. Particularly a customer to whom she owed a debt.

Ben stood in the doorway of a tiny room, looking at the array of gear. "It was a closet," Kallie said, suppressing a blush. "But it's the one part of the store that's mine."

Annileen reached past them for a rack of bridles. "I thought it would give her something to do."

Ben looked back into the store, alive with shoppers and diners, drinkers and postal patrons. "You seem to do a great many things already."

"Except stop raging dewbacks." Annileen passed a bridle to Kallie and pointed her outside. "Get that fitted up for him."

Miffed at having been dismissed, the girl smiled at Ben and dashed for the exit. "I'll be back!"

"She'll be back," Ben said drily.

Annileen led Ben back through the dining area—an obstacle course of diners with questions about his earlier rescue. Who was he? Where was he from? Didn't he know no one with good sense went out onto The Rumbles? Where did he live, and would he like to know how to adjust his vaporator? Would he like to buy a landspeeder, so he didn't have to hitchhike with Jawas? Had he come from offworld, and if so, what was really going on with the Republic? Seeing the man blanch a little at the barrage, Annileen hustled him toward the front of the store. "Press conference *after* he's done shopping."

"Sure, sure." Leelee stood, arms crossed, surveying

Ben as only a lusty Zeltron could. "Keep the new arrival to yourself."

Annileen turned her head and whispered, "You have a husband and five kids!"

"And a pulse," Leelee said, a hand on her own red-skinned wrist. She smiled. "Bring him back soon."

The newcomer's head sank a little lower. Annileen looked up the aisle, alarmed. More patrons were looking at them—and now the Gaults were inside, studying the new arrival. She had to do something.

"Excuse me," she said, leaving Ben by a rack of shirts. She walked to her counter and hopped up on it. Standing, she cupped her hands together and shouted in her best last-call voice, "Now hear this! This is a one-time-only event. The Jawa embargo is off. *Shop!*"

It took a moment for the words to register—and then bedlam. Ben stood back, startled, as a flood of customers rushed for the exit. Some at the bar remained, but all the gawkers left.

Ben looked up, obvious thanks on his face. "A special occasion, I take it."

"I always said the Jawas might be good for something someday," she said.

"You never know what role someone will play," he murmured. He watched her thoughtfully as he helped her down off the counter.

CHAPTER NINE

THE METAL TUB WAS FULL. Overfull, in fact. Annileen had taken advantage of the calm to walk Ben through every aisle of the store, helping him find the items on his list—and many things that weren't. She'd even pointed out which cheaper imported products were just as good as the more expensive local ones. Had any of her regulars overheard her, she'd have been mortified.

Nobody got this kind of service.

And he'd responded to it, Annileen thought. "This store is a living thing to you," he had remarked. A strange observation, to be sure. Almost poetic, coming from a—a what? She didn't know. Ben hadn't told her anything substantive about himself.

"Where are you from, Ben?"

"All about, really."

"Why are you here?"

"On Tatooine, or here at the store?"

"What do you do?"

"This and that. Nothing important."

That last answer described two-thirds of her patrons. She'd gotten more substance out of some of her discussions with Bohmer, the Rodian who spoke no Basic. But while Ben's non-answers were frustrating, they neither surprised nor offended her. None of her customers told her much on the first visit. Not verbally, anyway.

What they bought, however, spoke volumes. And Ben's tub—a portable washbasin now doubling as a shopping basket—brimmed with clues for the retail eye.

The curtain rod told her he wasn't camping. The basic tools told her he hadn't been there long. The tins of food paste told her he intended to stay for a while—and that he lived too far away to shop often. The containers of industrial-strength solvent told her he had a big cleaning job ahead.

And rags. Who bought *rags*? Someone who traveled light, who'd arrived without old clothing to spare for cleaning.

Finally, there was that other little tidbit, which she had very nearly overlooked: a bed pillow. Just one.

She casually strolled the aisles, finding out a little more from him in between Kallie's periodic interruptions to report her progress. When the supply room failed to yield packing accessories sized for Ben's eopie, the girl had taken it upon herself to invent something with spare parts. She'd lashed two smaller feed sacks to a third to create a saddle pannier, and had spent the last half hour working on increasing the load. Only twice did Annileen and Ben hear the surprised bleat of a tipped-over animal from outside.

"Kallie means well," Annileen had said.

Ben hadn't seemed concerned.

And while he'd sounded knowledgeable about life in the desert, Annileen had grown to believe he didn't know much about Tatooine. All desert worlds were the same—except in the ways they weren't. Many an over-confident transplant had learned the hard way. A foolish Geonosian had gone broke protecting his house here against flash floods that existed only in his homeworld memories.

But as customers reentered, one by one, Ben grew anxious for the tour to end. "This should be sufficient," he said.

"Are you sure? I'm not trying to up-sell you."

"I'm just afraid I'll need a second eopie before we're through."

Annileen chuckled. "We sell those, too." She placed the armload of goods she was carrying on the counter, while Ben set the metal tub on the synstone floor. "All right. One cashier, no waiting."

He shuffled on his feet and reached in his pocket. "Are, uh, Republic credits still good here?"

"As good as they ever were," she said, stepping behind the counter. "We don't pay politics much mind. Let me deal with the loose things first, and then we'll get to what's in the tub." She began adding the items to his already lengthy sales tab—and as she did, she could see him counting along, keeping a running tally to himself. It wasn't the nervous watchfulness of her more strapped customers, but he was still keeping track. *So he can afford all this,* she thought. *But money still matters.*

"Look there," a gruff voice said. "Someone's done some shopping!"

Annileen looked toward the exit to see Mullen standing in the doorway with his sister, Veeka. Behind them loomed Zedd, one of their Jawa-tossing accomplices. Zedd was human, but only just: muscle-bound and, currently, black-eyed. She had heard that a social misstep involving a Wookiee in Anchorhead had caused the latter condition, as well as the departure of several of Zedd's teeth. It was Zedd's incapacitation that had given Jabe his chance to fill in on the lead Gault service crew; Annileen was happy to see Zedd return to work.

But she wasn't happy to see him here, now. Mullen's bad attitude only grew more toxic when he had his pet mountain shadowing him. The doors slammed shut behind the trio, who started walking purposefully toward the counter.

"Surprised you're buying here, 'stead of from your *little friends,*" Mullen said, approaching Ben from behind. "Decent people don't take rides from Jawas."

"It won't replace shuttle service, that's true," Ben said. He didn't look up from folding and sorting his cloth goods on the counter.

Annileen paused her own counting. "Be nice, Mullen."

"That's right. Remember—he's the big hero!" Veeka strutted up to the counter beside Ben. She hoisted herself onto it, nearly knocking his neat stack of cloth goods onto the floor.

"Get off there," Annileen said, shoving at the young woman. Veeka didn't budge.

Ben slipped his folded purchases inside his new pillowcase. "It's all right," he said, quietly. "It's just high spirits."

"Spirits is right," Annileen said, sniffing at Veeka. "And not even an hour past lunchtime. Well done." She wished again that Dannar had never decided to keep the bar open all day long. A look at Mullen and Zedd said they were similarly lubricated. "Don't you people have vaporators to get back to?"

Mullen belched. "Our machines. Our schedule."

"I don't think your father would agree with you," Annileen said.

Mullen knelt by the washbasin at Ben's feet. "That's a lot of junk he's buying. Is his money good?" Mullen grabbed the handle of the tub with one hand and slid it closer. If Ben took offense—or even noticed—as the dark-haired man pawed through his purchases, Annileen didn't see. "I wouldn't trust him," Mullen finally pronounced.

Annileen slammed her datapad on the counter. "That's

enough, all of you! Last I checked, Mullen Gault, your name wasn't on the deed—or anything else, except maybe that arrest warrant in Mos Entha. Why don't you go back there?" she said.

Veeka sidled closer to Ben, reached out, and put her thumb underneath his chin. "He's a nice one," she said, tilting his face upward like livestock under study. "Looks hungry, though."

"Another grubber starving on the range." Mullen looked up from where he crouched, to Ben's left. "He wasn't saving Kallie—he probably wanted the dewback for a meal!" Behind, Zedd guffawed.

Veeka gripped Ben's hairy chin between her thumb and forefinger. "I don't know. I'd be fine with him saving *me*." She lifted his face toward hers and leered at him. "How about it, Bennie? You want to save a *grown-up* for a change?"

"Fine," Ben said, politely. "Do tell me when one comes in."

Annileen laughed loudly.

At the sound of laughter at Veeka's expense, Zedd surged forward. Like half the Gault farmhands, the bruiser thought the boss's daughter lit the stars in the sky. With Mullen still at Ben's feet with the tub, Zedd grabbed at the shopper's shoulder in righteous indignation.

That was when it began.

Kallie entered through from the livery yard, to the right of the group. She carried the bantha prod from the Jabe incident, the latest in a series of items she was returning to the tack room in her ongoing effort to see Ben. She saw her dashing hero, all right—standing uneasily, with Veeka perched lasciviously on the counter with a leg on either side of him.

Stunned, infuriated, and long possessed of the view that the wrong Gault twin had died years earlier, Kallie raised the bantha prod. Seeing the hate in Kallie's eyes, Annileen hurriedly grabbed Veeka's collar. As her mother attempted to pull the young woman back from danger, Kallie snapped the prod in the direction of Veeka's dangling right foot.

The next second passed quickly. Annileen saw Ben turn to avoid the prod, raising his right hand ever so slightly. It was at that moment that the prod, which had a patented never-slip grip, flew from Kallie's hand. Its electrified tip glanced harmlessly against the counter, missing Veeka's boot—and somehow, also, Ben's torso. He turned ninety degrees as the implement fell past his knees to where it finally came to rest: planted, vertically, into the metal tub that held the rest of Ben's shopping.

A metal tub still being held by the hand of Mullen Gault.

Skraakkkt! With a crackling discharge, the device expended its entire energy supply in one tumultuous flash. Mullen screeched louder than the Settlers' Call siren had ever sounded. Startled, Veeka fell backward into Annileen. The sudden weight of Veeka knocked her feet out from under her, and the two landed in a tangle on the floor behind the counter.

Annileen scrambled to extricate herself and rise. The first thing she saw across the counter was Zedd looking stupidly down at Mullen, writhing in agony on the floor. Snarling, Zedd charged Ben. The older, smaller man stepped lithely out of the way, sending the lumbering Zedd into a display of cans of whitewash. The collision wasn't as loud as Mullen's scream, but it was quite a bit messier.

Without a word, Ben turned, bowed slightly to Annileen and Kallie—the only others still standing—and slapped a pile of credits on the counter. He grabbed the loaded pillowcase and fled through the door to the livery yard.

Bewildered, Annileen hopped onto the counter and jumped to the other side, her boots just missing the writhing, weeping Mullen. Ben's tub of purchases was still there, abandoned. She ran to the doorway, where Kallie was calling out after him.

But more chaos waited outside. Mullen's electric screech seconds earlier had evidently placed the Jawas under the impression that a logra—a burrowing predator with a taste for the short merchants—had surfaced inside the store. Now they were ending all transactions and moving their goods back into the sandcrawler, to the frantic yells of dissatisfied customers. Two unrelated brawls had broken out.

And beyond, past the revving sandcrawler, Ben and Rooh rode off toward the desert. Flummoxed, Annileen started to follow, to alert him to his forgotten goods.

But Erbaly Nap'tee confronted her in the doorway first. "The little glow-eyed man told me to come talk to you," the Nikto woman said. "Do you work here?"

CHAPTER TEN

ORRIN SPUTTERED AT THE COMLINK. "I told you not to call me with this garbage!"

He tilted his head back toward his landspeeder, trying to make the glance casual. The old man hadn't over-heard him. Wyle Ulbreck was still inside the USV-5, en-joying the blast of the air-conditioning.

Orrin doubted that the old skinflint enjoyed anything except counting his money, but that wasn't important. He hadn't come to the farmer's rescue out of friendship, or even benevolence. This was a sales call. And Veeka had just interrupted it with a strange, disconnected story of chaos in the Claim, damage to the store and his son, and some nonsense about Kallie's hero.

"I don't care who did what," he said into the device, aggravated. The last thing he needed was trouble with Annileen. Once, she had barred the entire Gault em-ployee base from dining at the Claim. After a week of lunch box living, Orrin had a mutiny on his hands. There was only one response. "You'll clean up the store, apologize to Annie, and then get out here and finish your shift!" He deactivated the comlink.

Standing in the suns, Orrin looked back at the old man in the landspeeder and smiled weakly. Ulbreck still wasn't paying him any mind. The old man had more hair on his face than his head—and, yes, Ulbreck was using Orrin's comb to straighten his beard. *Lovely*, Orrin thought, closing the bonnet on Ulbreck's stalled repulsortruck. The battered ST-101 would be able to make it to the Claim using the coolant Orrin had brought. Now he had to make the favor pay off.

"You're ready, Master Ulbreck," Orrin said, opening the passenger-side door to his landspeeder. "Sorry about the delay—I had to take a call." The old man grunted. Orrin gave a rumpled smile. "It was just trouble at home. Do you—uh, plan on having children, Wyle?"

"I'm seventy-five."

"Take my advice," Orrin said, grimacing. "Don't. It's safer that way." He offered his hand to help Ulbreck stand up, but the old man ignored it.

Ulbreck was still in good shape for his age. He had recently sworn off liquor, after some event Orrin knew little about. But Orrin attributed Ulbreck's condition more to his having delegated most of the work on his sprawling ranch to an army of farmhands in recent years, instead of toiling in the hot suns himself. Spreading to the south and east of Orrin's holdings, Ulbreck's property was more than twice the size—and Orrin doubted the man had visited a single one of his vaporators in a decade. It hadn't hurt their production at all. Ulbreck was rolling in wealth he never spent.

All the more reason to protect it. "Speaking of safety," Orrin said, conscious of the awkward transition, "I was wondering if you'd thought about joining the Settlers' Call Fund."

"Here we go again," Ulbreck said, derision evident in his gravelly voice. "Knew that coolant wasn't free." He threw Orrin's comb back inside the landspeeder.

"I'm not trying to sell you anything. The Fund helps the community protect people. Farmers, just like you—"

"I got my own security." Ulbreck tromped across the

sand toward his vehicle. "I don't need to be paying for your people to sit around getting soused."

"They're not mine," Orrin said. "The Fund belongs to the whole oasis community—I just administer it." He closed the passenger door to his landspeeder and followed Ulbreck. "Look, you run a business—and you expect results. So do I. I respect that. If you want results, just look at the other day, and what happened at the Bezzard place—"

"I saw you didn't save half of 'em!"

Orrin stepped back. "That's not fair, Wyle. Those people died before the Call was activated. But the farmer and his wife and child, though—we *saved* those people." He tried a different tack. "Look, yours is the largest spread around here not part of the Fund. If you came in, we'd be able to upgrade our equipment. Maybe even put out some patrols to cover your place, as well as some others. Proactive, like."

The old farmer stopped at the open door to his repulsortruck and turned his head. Orrin stepped forward, expectantly—only to see the old man spit on the sand.

"Not interested in anywhere else," Ulbreck said. "My people watch my place. If Plug-eye comes around, you'll see a Tusken dance." Ulbreck climbed up into the cab of the tall vehicle. As he started the engines, he looked down at Orrin, almost as an afterthought. "Eh—thanks for the coolant."

Orrin shook his head. Some people you just couldn't help.

The repulsortruck gone, Orrin kicked the empty coolant container across the sand. He'd made most reluctant farmers come around, one way or another. Not Ulbreck. The old man knew the Fund based its fee on the amount of land to be protected. Ulbreck balked at paying more than anyone else on pure principle.

Well, he'll figure it out . . . one day, Orrin thought.

There were more potential members to sign up; he'd need to check his map. He opened the door to his landspeeder, its engine still running as it pumped out frigid air. He slipped into the driver's seat, only to find the oily comb underneath his backside. Blanching, Orrin chucked it out the window—

—and saw the pair of figures topping a dune to the northeast, approaching him. Finding his electrobinoculars, Orrin studied the sight.

"Well, what do you know," he said aloud. "One chance lost, another found." He put the hovercraft into motion.

The USV-5 coasted to a stop just short of the new arrivals. As caravans went, Orrin thought it pretty meager: a hooded man, walking alongside a heavily laden eopie. Neither reacted as Orrin triggered the landspeeder's open-topped mode.

Orrin smiled. "Hello, there!"

"Greetings."

"That's a big load you've got."

The sandy-haired nomad eyed him warily. "It's mine, if that's what you're wondering. I've come from the store."

Orrin chuckled. "Oh, I know. You don't have the wardrobe for a Tusken." The farmer deactivated the engine and climbed out. "I'm Orrin Gault. This is my land here—"

"My apologies," the traveler said, looking back at the horizon. "Is it possible to get to the Calwell store without crossing the Gault land?"

"Not really, no." Orrin grinned. He offered his hand. "I think I know who you are. You're that Ben I've heard so much about."

Ben took Orrin's hand and shook it, tentatively. "Heard . . . about *me*?"

"From Kallie Calwell. The Calwells and the Gaults—we're close. And I owe you a debt of thanks. It sounds like you saved her from herself."

Ben lowered his eyes. "I think Kallie embellished some. I was passing through and lent a hand. Anyone else would do the same."

Orrin liked the sound of that. "Quite right. But still, let me get you a drink." He turned back to the landspeeder.

"We're a ways from a cantina," Ben said, puzzled.

"But not from the canteen." Orrin produced a gleaming silver flask and offered it to Ben. "Enjoy."

Ben nodded and opened the vial. He drank—and did an immediate double take. Gasping, he mouthed, *"Wow."*

"And that's lukewarm," Orrin said, smiling broadly. He slapped the windshield of the landspeeder. "I know you're on your way somewhere, Ben, but the least I can do is show you around. For a new neighbor."

Ben looked up, cautious. "How . . . do you know I'm a neighbor?"

Orrin laughed. Something about wearing hoods made half the newcomers on Tatooine think they were on a secret mission. "I doubt you're making supply runs for the Jawas. They went the other direction, anyway." He gestured toward the landspeeder. "Come on—just for a few minutes. You trespass, you get the guided tour. You might say it's the penalty."

CHAPTER ELEVEN

THE USV-5 ROCKETED across the dunes. Hill after hill bristled with shining new vaporators, metal stalagmites stabbing into the sky. Ben sat quietly in the passenger seat, taking it in. He'd resisted the tour, at first. But Orrin had brought out an emergency canvas shelter from the landspeeder, and within moments the eopie was inside, munching on the feed it had been carrying.

Orrin watched Ben out of the corner of his eye as he drove. The man seemed quiet—and, thankfully, unmarked by whatever had happened at the Claim. Orrin felt bad about that. The oasis regulars, his kids included, could be rough on newcomers.

"I'll tell you," Orrin said again, "I'm sorry about whatever happened back in the Claim. When my kid called—I knew in a second who was to blame. You got any little ones, Ben?"

"Just the eopie," Ben said.

The farmer laughed. "I'll tell you, if kids were as teachable as eopies, this hair would still be black. Annileen's are something, too—but you already saw that with Kallie."

"Energetic," Ben allowed.

"And all trouble."

Ben looked at him. "But worth it?"

"Don't put words in my mouth," Orrin said, feigning seriousness—before breaking out into laughter again. "No, most days I work out here with Mullen and Veeka—and sometimes Jabe, Annileen's boy. You met him?"

"At the sandcrawler," Ben said simply.

"Lot to keep track of, I know. Sometimes it's hard for me to tell where Annie's family stops and mine begins." He elaborated briefly on his friendship with Dannar, and how Annileen had been running the shop since Dannar's death. "That Annileen—she's a tower of power."

Ben nodded, and returned to idly staring out the window.

Orrin smirked. If Ben were interested in Annileen, that should have registered a response. But he seemed detached, or at least respectful of Orrin's territory. Which was silly, of course. Orrin and Annileen had never been like that—or, at least, she'd never been like that with him. Orrin was married when Dannar hired Annileen; by the time Orrin's union started going wrong, the Calwells were married themselves, with Kallie on the way. Orrin wondered sometimes what would have happened if Liselle had taken off earlier—but no. The Pika Oasis wouldn't be what it was today if he and Dannar had been romantic rivals.

Ben broke the silence. "How did Dannar Calwell die?"

It was a puzzling turn, Orrin thought. "I'll get to that," he said, applying the brakes. "We're here."

The landspeeder came to rest atop a hill overlooking a wide expanse empty, but for vaporators, as far as the eye could see. The men disembarked and studied the scene. Some devices were clustered together, others separated by hundreds of meters.

"Pretty, isn't it?"

"Unusual patterns. The way they're placed, it's almost—"

"An art? Not far from it," Orrin said. "This is Field Number Seven—but I call it the Symphony." He pointed toward the nearest vaporator, halfway up the rise they were standing on. "Follow me."

At the device, Orrin turned a key in a lock, opening a small door on the vaporator. Inside sat a vial, sealed beneath a tap. Orrin removed it. "You're the guest, Ben. You do the honors."

Ben took the vial and examined it.

Orrin nodded. "Go ahead. It's what you had a while ago."

Ben raised it to his lips and drank thirstily. A split second later his face showed that had been a mistake. *"It's freezing!"*

"It's this new Pretormin vaporator model—comes off the compressors like that," Orrin said, taking the vial back. "But have you ever tasted sweeter water in your life?"

"I'll let you know when my tongue thaws out," Ben said, shaking his head to clear it. "The vial wasn't that cold—"

"Things aren't always what they seem." Orrin sealed the door on the vaporator and gestured to the horizon. "See, Ben, it's taken me six years. But we've finally brought Tatooine into the new era. All those towers I started with eons ago—they're gone. Rubbish for Jawas. These Pretormins are gonna change this world, and the oasis will be at the center of it."

Ben squinted up at the tower. "I admit I never really understood—I thought water was the simplest thing in the universe to produce."

"Maybe in the universe," Orrin said, "but not on Tatooine. Lots of reasons. Fuel cells make water, but they also make heat, something we've got enough of. That's just for starters."

Ben listened, interested. "And you're too remote to ship anything in."

"Right. But who'd want to?" Orrin walked back to the top of the rise. "You see, that's the secret to this dead old planet. She's hiding her water. But what she's got is the tastiest anyone's ever had. It's so good, I could see Tatooine being a net exporter of water—if we can just get at it." His voice grew solemn. "*And I can.*"

He traced his hands in the air, connecting the dots that were the faraway towers. "Those little drops can run, but they can't hide. These machines in the right place, tuned the right way—they knead that sky like clay. They play the notes—and the music comes."

"The Symphony," Ben said, respectfully.

Orrin nodded. "A lot of pieces have to work together at once. We're still working at it."

"I'm impressed."

Ben wasn't a farmer—or anything else, as far as Orrin had been able to learn. But he seemed to have a feel for what Orrin was trying to do. Maybe, if Ben turned out to have a skill, he could even be a decent farmhand once Orrin started hiring again.

Orrin returned to the landspeeder, suddenly weary. Farming, he loved. The rest of his life was just *necessary.* But he wasn't out today to farm. So first things first.

"You asked about Dannar," he said, gravely. "The Tuskens killed him, eight years ago. He'd stopped to help a rider in the desert—like you did with Kallie. Tuskens killed them both."

"I'm sorry," Ben said.

"Well, it's been a while," Orrin said. He turned back toward the younger man. "Annileen said you were riding in from the east, the other day. I don't guess you've ever heard of the Lars family?"

Ben cleared his throat. "The *Lars*, you say?"

"Cliegg Lars. Everyone heard about it." Orrin pointed to the east. "Moisture farmer over on the other side of Jawa Heights. If you're new, you wouldn't know. The Tuskens—same band that got Dannar, I've always thought—kidnapped Cliegg's wife."

Ben started to say something, but stopped.

Orrin continued. "Anyway, folks over there mounted a rescue mission—a bunch of farmers that didn't know one end of a rifle from another. They didn't have experience chasing Tuskens. They didn't have the equipment. They didn't have vehicles conditioned for more than a trip to check the vaporators."

"It . . . went badly?"

"Son, that's the understatement of the year. Thirty went out. Four came back." Orrin remembered that horrible day, and the days that had followed. Several victims had been longtime acquaintances. A lot of moisture-farming wisdom had died at once. "Twenty-six, gone," he said.

Orrin went silent to let the man take it in. Ben was troubled by the story, he could tell. It helped to paint a picture for people, sometimes—and the Larses' experience was as close to a worst-case scenario as it got. Orrin had never met Cliegg—he'd heard the poor soul was dead now. But his tale of torment almost always had an impact.

Ben looked up from the ground. "And what happened next?"

"Funerals, mostly." Orrin didn't add that he'd picked up a few tracts of land from the estates; someone had to work them. He leaned on the hood of the floating landspeeder. "Funerals and recriminations. You see, those people didn't have what we've got in the oasis. The Call."

Orrin quickly explained the Settlers' Call system. Ben listened intently, noting that he'd heard the alarm echoing over the desert once before. Orrin grinned, pausing to take credit for the krayt dragon idea. "Nothing sends a chill through their bandages like a krayt yowl."

He continued the sales pitch, well practiced by now. "If the Lars raid had happened here, things would have gone a lot differently. A posse is a business. It's people coming together for a goal. You've got to invest, and prepare. And when the Call comes," he said, pointing to one of the vaporator towers, "you know you've got a chance."

Ben noticed the siren mounted atop the machine. He seemed impressed. "So it's a militia, then?"

"Nothin' like that. Oh, sure, there's a militia out of Mos Eisley—three or four full-timers, all afraid of their shadows. They never range this far out. Anyone with a mind for that kind of fighting would've headed offworld and made better money at it. This thing, it's just the people. They're not in it for the money. They just want to help."

Ben nodded.

Orrin coasted into his wrap-up. "We respond. We rescue. And if we can't make a defense in time, it's our policy that every attack on a household rates a counterstrike. It's what the Tuskens understand, and it works."

Ben looked to the east. "How far out do you cover?"

"As far as our subscribers live," Orrin said. He walked to the side of the vehicle. "I've got a map here."

Ben approached. "As far as where—what did you call them, the Lars family lived?"

"No, but anything's possible if we get enough people on board," Orrin replied as they both climbed into the speeder. "But I thought you and your eopie were headed southwest."

Ben shook his head and studied the map. "Just curious."

The eopie was sleeping beneath the canvas when Orrin returned with Ben. Orrin was sure he'd gotten Ben's interest in the Settlers' Call, but he hadn't coaxed much information out of him.

Ben had a place against the northern outcrops of the western Jundland Wastes, and he'd come from somewhere else, probably the Republic. The Republic had never really paid much attention to Tatooine, and locals here usually responded in kind. Orrin had heard something about a big change that had recently taken place in the Republic, but Ben seemed to know less about it than he did. Ben had asked *him* for news, in fact.

But while Orrin still didn't know what Ben did for money, he was confident that he had some. Otherwise, Annileen wouldn't have sold him all the goods the eopie was carrying. Her gratitude seldom went that far.

"So," Orrin said, watching the man repack the beast. "You want to sign up with the Fund? You don't have to fight with the posses—your credits pay for them to do it."

Ben finished tightening the load and looked at him. "I . . . don't know, yet. I'm still getting settled in."

"Understood. But that's more reason to join. One less thing to worry about."

"You'll have to let me get back to you. I'm still not sure—" Ben paused, seeming to hear something far away. Orrin followed Ben's gaze to the hills, but couldn't hear anything for several seconds. Then, he heard and saw the familiar whir of his daughter's Selanikio Sportster landspeeder, heading toward them from the oasis.

"Good ear," Orrin said. "That'd be Mullen and Veeka. I guess they're dried out and ready to get back to work."

Ben looked warily in that direction and turned to take the eopie by the bit. "I'd better go—our first meeting didn't end well."

The eopie started to trot, and Ben jogged along with it. He passed Orrin, who leaned against his landspeeder, frustrated. *Now* his kids decided to get back to work. *Terrific.*

"Listen, remember the offer," Orrin said. "The price I cited during our ride is good only while the subscription drive is on. It goes up next week."

"I'll consider it," Ben said, waving behind him. "And thanks for the drink."

"Sure you won't—"

"No, no, I must be on my way. Far to go and all."

"All right, then. But come back around when you decide."

"I will."

Orrin's shoulders slumped. Zero-for-two today. And two more troubles had arrived and were walking up to him. Veeka looked her usual self, for this afternoon hour. But Mullen had a frazzled appearance that gave him pause. What had his son gotten into at the Claim?

"Where's Zedd?" Orrin asked.

"Hurt again," Mullen said, glaring at the figures departing to the southwest. "Was that *him*?"

"Who?" Orrin looked in the same direction. "You mean the guy with no job and no past, heading into the middle of nowhere like someone with no sense? That's Ben, all right." He glared at his daughter. "You marry a man like that, and I'll feed you to a sarlacc. Now get to work. I'm behind schedule already."

Meditation

Today was . . . interesting.

I took a chance and went to the Pika Oasis. Dannar's Claim, the big compound up there. They have just about everything I need—except, maybe, an army to free the Republic.

But I didn't stay. That's part of the problem. There are too many people there—but not quite enough, either. The bigger places like Mos Eisley, I can lose myself in. So many travelers come in and out. This place is busy, too, but the oasis also has a lot of regulars, who do nothing but watch the comings and goings all day. My arrival was, I'm ashamed to say, something of a spectacle. And, uh, my departure, too.

I can't let that happen again.

I also met one of the big landowners on the way out—Orrin Gault, something of a local institution. I was reluctant to talk to him too long, and I tried to say nothing of substance. But he's nice enough, and I sense that he feels better if he knows everyone who's around. Trying to hide from a man like him might not be wise. He seems to mean well.

And this Settlers' Call system of his could be the answer to my problems keeping an eye on the Lars family, if their service could be extended that far to the east. I know—it would be better not to involve them. But if Anakin's mother was taken, it could happen again.

I'm here to protect the child. When it comes to the Tuskens, the locals' help might come in handy. It's a threat they're familiar with. I had a brush with the Sand People years earlier, when you and I brought Padmé here; they're formidable warriors. If something happens such that I can't continue my watch—

—well, let's not think about that. But it's nice to have options.

Orrin—again, he's very much a hail-fellow-well-met. I like him. Quite the salesman, to be sure. And while he's obviously very proud of what he's built out here, he also seems a little self-conscious about it—enough so that he tries to put on an air of humility. Even if it's just a sales ploy, I think it's a little endearing.

Anakin could have used a bit of that. We were all impressed with what he could do. But he was impressed, too—and not in the least thankful for it. No, not near the end.

I have his lightsaber, you know. It's right here, sitting in my hands. Some nights, like this, I just sit and stare at it, wondering what I could have done to help him.

I look, and I look, for answers. Then I put it away in the trunk, and try to forget.

It's impossible, of course.

Maybe if he'd grown older—had been able to grow older—he'd have gotten some perspective. But that just wasn't to be.

If only he'd listened to reason, hadn't forced me to do what I had to do, then I wouldn't be here, now, feeling like a—

No.

Good night, Qui-Gon.

PART TWO

THE KILLING GROUND

CHAPTER TWELVE

A LARGE HOVERCRAFT LEFT THE COMPOUND, heading to the east. There was a dark-haired human male driving it, not much more than a youngling. A'Yark had seen this one before, and kept silent count as the vehicle made for the horizon.

Once it had left, A'Yark slipped back behind the dune and brought out the black rock. A smudged mark was made on the wrappings of the warrior's left arm, while another was rubbed off the tally on the right arm. Too many marks remained there, each one representing a settler present in the oasis compound. Dozens arrived before the suns rose each morning, and the place remained in motion until well after night fell. Keeping count had tested A'Yark's wits. And the total didn't even include the people who lived in the buildings.

Only one of them mattered, of course.

A'Yark checked the stock of the blaster rifle, where more counting could be found. Ten whittled notches. Ten days since the raid on the human farm had gone wrong. Ten days since the human woman had avoided death by dewback by mystical means. The Sand People, hearing A'Yark tell of her, had chosen to call her *Ena'grosh*, the Airshaper. A'Yark had not had to convince them of what her existence meant. Settlers so empowered would threaten them all.

A'Yark had known one person to have such powers: another Tusken, long since dead. That raider had come to join the Sand People willingly, an exceptionally rare thing—and had survived the welcome and trials that followed, which was almost unheard of. That warrior had the ability to shape the air, too, a fact that had certainly helped during the initiation.

But that recruit had ultimately proved mortal—and that gave A'Yark hope now. It meant an Airshaper could die. This woman must, before she taught her skills to the other settlers.

A'Yark had found the Airshaper's home easily; she'd made no efforts to conceal the path of her surviving dewback. Settlers might have found tracking difficult on the rocky ground between the pitted area and the oasis, but they were not Tuskens. A'Yark had crept up to the compound for a simple reconnaissance—only to realize the scope of the challenge.

It was more than the sheer number of arrivals and departures. This place was the fortress of the Smiling One.

It had to be. The war leader recognized from afar the vehicles the settlers had used in the defense of the farm. These and many more were stored in the huge garages. How large an army did the Smiling One have? A'Yark hesitated to find out.

A'Yark had also seen the fuzzy-faced eopie rider from earlier—but only once, seven days ago, departing the compound quickly with his mount. The human's presence had been puzzling, as A'Yark had never seen him arrive; he had to have traveled with the Jawas. That fact alone was offensive. Jawas were no better than the parasites the Sand People plucked off their banthas. They were the children of the coward sun, to be sure. The eopie rider even dressed like one of them, in his brown robe. Perhaps Hairy Face—that seemed a good name for the man—was a shaman to the Jawas, able to command the chattering things.

The watchful raider had thought to follow the man as he journeyed toward the wastes. But the Airshaper had appeared in the yard, calling vainly after Hairy Face—alongside her foolish dewback-riding child. A'Yark had realized something else, that day: the Airshaper also had a son. He was the one who had just driven away in the repulsorcraft. The boy wasn't much older than A'Yark's own son.

Young A'Deen was back with the others today, going through the rites of adulthood. A'Yark didn't want to be there. It would mean seeing what had become of the ritual. By tradition, the tested youth was to have hunted and killed a krayt dragon. But krayts were few in The Pillars where the tribe hid, and so were eligible Tusken youths. So the elders had decreed that some other creature might suffice, such as a logra. Still dangerous, but nothing like a krayt.

A'Yark thought the choice was cowardly and had said so. It described a clan so weakened that it could no longer keep to its principles. If A'Deen fell to a krayt, fine. The child would have been adjudged a weakling and would have deserved death. It didn't matter that the boy was the last of A'Yark's children. The warrior would have taken a blade to A'Deen personally rather than see him live as a failure. But no one would know A'Deen's worthiness now.

They would be killing womp rats next and pretending it was bravery.

More movement at the garages. The Smiling One was out there again, babbling to the freakish thing that tended the vehicles. A'Yark kept watching the place.

This was it, the center of all the Tuskens' problems. The Airshaper had shown A'Yark the way.

And soon, A'Yark would lead the rest of the Sand People to her.

"Keep going, I'm listening."

Annileen wasn't listening, but it hardly mattered. Wyle Ulbreck spent far more money at the store than any other visitor to the Pika Oasis—and far more time, too. Ulbreck had a platoon of farmhands to run his spread; he knew in his heart that droids were thieves, programmed by Jawas to steal from their masters. The old moisture farmer had first pontificated on that subject when Annileen was running the counter at seventeen. Twenty years later, he was still talking about it—among countless other topics.

At the moment, Ulbreck was on another classic: the four times he had seen rain.

". . . and the second drop was right in my eye, let me tell you. I felt it, and I was lookin' up, too. You'd think rain would be like the mists some see on the ground, steaming up. But no, it comes right down at you just like it fell out of a freighter . . ."

"Unh-huh. Right."

Annileen nodded as she dusted the merchandise on the shelves behind the counter. Ulbreck's ramblings were like recordings of familiar songs, arranged in a different medley each day—because while the old farmer remembered a lot, he often forgot his place. An engineer who visited the Dune Sea years earlier once described Ulbreck's stories as transcendental loops, defying the laws of physics—and storytelling.

She didn't know about that. But she did suspect the cause of her pain: Ulbreck's wife, Magda. Annileen had never seen the woman. But it was clear she dispatched her husband to the store at the crack of dawn every morning, to torment someone else for a change. This made Magda both a wise woman in Annileen's ledger— and deserving of a smack in the face, should they ever meet.

". . . but you know, I swear I seen a freighter take off once and go right through a flock of neebray. And the things just hit the ground like sacks of spanners. Which is why I don't go near that Mos Eisley no more, 'cause they're always tryin' to kill people and take their money . . ."

"Unh-huh. Right."

Annileen looked around, plaintively, for different company. It was futile. The breakfast rush was over; the workers would be in the vaporator fields for hours. The Bezzards had left her guest quarters early that morning to return home, anxious to pick up the pieces of their lives. The settlers around the oasis were resilient, as they had to be. Annileen didn't miss the extra burden, but she did miss the baby.

Her babies were at work. Jabe had taken the store's LiteVan speeder truck to the dry goods distribution center in Bestine; Kallie was out back with the animals. That left her alone with Bohmer, the slow-motion Rodian, sitting at the luncheonette table, considering his caf. She wondered what he saw there, sometimes.

She slouched against the cabinets and sighed. FIND WHAT YOU NEED AT DANNAR'S CLAIM, the sign outside read. What she needed was a month away on a lush green forest planet.

". . . but back then the first time I was workin' for real money, on a vaporator, I just started crossin' circuits. Beginner's luck, they called it. That was the second time I seen rain—or maybe it was the first. I've spent the rest of my days tryin' to figger out just what I did . . ."

Annileen looked up. Orrin entered through the back

of the store, whistling and wearing the natty dress browns she'd picked out for him from the high-end catalog. Clicking his leather boots together, he smiled broadly at her. "How do I look?"

"Like you just landed from Coruscant," she said, smiling wanly back.

"Thanks to my fashion coordinator." Orrin's expression hardened when he glanced at Ulbreck. Realizing the old man was in mid-rainfall, Orrin rolled his eyes and plunked down his satchel. "Got a meeting in Mos Eisley. That new hotel is taking bids for a water supplier."

Annileen nodded. Since the last commodity bust, Orrin had redoubled his efforts to lock in regular purchasers at preset prices.

"I'll talk to a couple of farms on the way back about joining the Settlers' Call. Folks who actually *care* about protecting their assets." Orrin shot a pointed look at Ulbreck, but the old man paid him no mind. Annileen knew that Orrin had tried again—and failed again—to sign Ulbreck up a week earlier.

Turning his attention to the counter space, Orrin patted his vest pockets. "Blast!"

"Forgot your credit pouch again?" Annileen knew this story, too. Orrin raised the hinged section of the counter and stepped to the cashbox—sealed, as it had been in her husband's day, with the barrel of a blaster pistol inserted into a pair of metal rings. Annileen watched as Orrin removed the blaster and pulled out a handful of credits.

He looked at her, abruptly. "Oh, I'll leave a—"

"Forget it."

Money in one hand, he placed the other on her cheek and smirked. "Thanks, Annie. Nobody loves me like you do."

"You're probably right."

She watched the man leave. Nobody had ever kept accounts between the two families when it came to the small things. But lately, Annileen had increasingly gotten the sense that whatever she owed Orrin for protection and helping to rear her son paled next to the meals, supplies, and petty cash he'd taken out of the store.

Still, a sunny nature counted for a lot, and if she wasn't going to begrudge Wyle Ulbreck his audience, it was hard to refuse Orrin his little liberties—especially now that he was in his "big business" phase. Drunk divorcé Orrin had been a trial, years before. The new model verged on blowhard—especially now, as he seemed to be selling in overdrive lately. But that was a definite improvement.

Ulbreck plopped down a bottle of Fizzzz and a credit on the counter. "Say, did I tell you about the first time I saw a krayt dragon?"

Enough! Annileen's eyes scanned beneath the side counter. There it was—the tub of goods Ben had left behind the week before. She'd gone back and forth for days about restocking the shelves with the material. Now, opening the window behind her, she decided to do something else.

"Kallie!" Annileen leaned out the window. Her daughter was behind the store, in the livestock yard. "Kallie, can you hear me?"

"No!"

"Can you watch the counter for a couple of hours?"

"No!"

"Great. Come on in."

Annileen shut the window and pulled the tub from beneath the counter. She was looking in the little mirror behind the kitchen door when Kallie appeared from the back, a sodden, sullen mess. Annileen threw her daughter a rag. "Clean up. I need you to work the till."

"Do I have to?" Kallie glared at her mother.

"You have something better to do?"

"I'm mucking out the dewback pen." The girl peered in at Ulbreck, who was now nattering away to the hapless Rodian. "So the answer is yes."

"Sorry, sweetie." Annileen stepped out from behind the door. Her hair was pulled back in a bun, and she was wearing her light cloak and hood. "I need to run to Arnthout to see a man about some dricklefruit."

"Dricklefruit, my eye. I know where you're going." Stepping behind the counter, the girl watched her mother pick up the tub of goods. "You're the one that said nothing good ever comes from the Jundland Wastes!"

"Hush," Annileen said, already to the exit. "I'll be back before lunch."

Kallie's voice went up two octaves. "Tell Ben I said hello!"

The whir of a landspeeder sounded outside—and Ulbreck reappeared at the counter before Kallie, continuing his winding tale. He didn't even seem to notice that he'd switched Calwells.

CHAPTER THIRTEEN

THOOM! THOOM! THOOM!

If not for the sound, she would've driven past it. White-on-white under the climbing suns, the squarish hut with its pourstone dome neatly blended with the Jundland Wastes. Only when Annileen banked the X-31 along the desert floor did she see the glint from the vaporator out back. The hut squatted low on a southwestern bluff—likely, she figured, situated over a cave. *Another Last-Ditch Lodge.*

The term was fully pejorative, referring to frontier dwellings built on the theory—never proven—that the uplands of the wastes yielded more condensation at night. No one knew for sure, because even the hardiest farmers seldom lasted more than a season. These were places for grubbers on their last chance and would-be wizards who just knew they had magical combinations of vaporator settings no one had ever thought of before. The whole thing was ludicrous to Annileen. Assuming anyone hit it lucky, what investor in his right mind would build an industrial farm out here? Crazy.

She wasn't crazy, though, to pick this direction. Anni-leen had seen Ben head out from the oasis days earlier, and Orrin had reported meeting him out this way. After the past airless week, a hint of a trail still existed. Now she spotted Ben's eopie quivering out front, less worried about her approach than the noise from out back.

Thoom! Thoom!

Annileen parked the speeder and reached into the rumble seat. That had been an invention of Dannar's: ripping out the back of the middle console to make room for the younglings—or, in this case, Ben's tub of supplies. Realizing what the sound was, she suppressed a laugh as she walked the goods up the hill.

"All right," Ben called out from behind the house. "I take your meaning. You're upset. You can stop now!"

Thoom! A mountain of hair, easily his match for height, backed up and charged again, horns-first, into the side of Ben's hut. *THOOM!*

Annileen propped the tub on her hip and watched with a barely concealed smile. "Having a problem with your bantha?"

"No, no. Why do you ask?" Ben gripped a rope and tried to get the calf's attention. He'd been at this a while, Annileen saw. His blousy white shirt was dingy, and sweat dripped from dark blond hair exposed to the sky. The animal snorted angrily and returned to its mission.

She pointed to the rope. "What are you planning to do with that?"

"I'm considering hanging myself." He looked up at her, exasperated. "I don't know what I did to set it off. Normally, I'm good with animals."

"Well, as you saw with Kallie the other day, they're still animals," she said, setting down the tub. "Forget the rope. Let me have a try."

He gestured indifferently. "Be my guest."

Annileen removed her gloves and strolled toward the massive creature. "Raising animals isn't like raising teenagers. Kids don't know what they want, and they want it now. Animals, on the other hand, usually *do* know what they want. Like this guy," she said, edging toward the bantha calf. "He thinks your house is his mother."

"His *mother*?"

"Yep." Feeling the steaming breath of the wild behemoth, Annileen reached out gently and touched the calf's face. The bantha stamped its feet impatiently. "Mama's probably wandered farther up into the wastes."

"He can't find her?"

"If *you* had this much hair over your face, you might lose your way, too. To a bantha calf, everything that's bigger than food is probably Mom."

"A good rule of thumb." Ben crossed his arms and watched with concern as Annileen inserted herself fully between the animal and the battered wall. "What do we—I mean, what do *I* do?"

"*Shhh.*" Annileen traced the calf's eye sockets with her fingers. Leaning forward, she nuzzled its face. The bantha's hooves stilled. The woman whispered to Ben. "*You* are going to watch me point him somewhere else."

Ben stood back as Annileen strode forward, pushing the young bantha by the horns. It outweighed her by a metric ton, at least—and yet it was backing down the hill. At the foot of the bluff, she turned it to one side and gave it a swat. Long, shaggy hair swaying, it moseyed off.

"Won't he die out there?"

"Nah." Annileen pulled a handkerchief from inside her boot and rubbed her hands. "He won't be alone that long. If he doesn't find his herd, he'll find a Tusken to adopt," she said.

Ben nodded. "My house thanks you. I did try—well, to *calm* it."

"It's all right. You were probably its first human."

Annileen caught a trace of a smile before the man turned and started back up the hill to his house.

Ben's expressions in the store had been happier, she thought; here, he seemed a little downcast. *It must be depressing, living alone so far out here.*

He looked back at her. "Why are you here, Annileen?"

"Special delivery." Walking with him, she pointed to the tub of goods. "Most of our thieves take things without paying. You're the only person I've met who paid and left his stuff."

"I'm a very poor thief, then." Ben moved the bin into the dubious shade of the vaporator. He scratched his head. "I'm sorry for the trouble the other day. I hope there weren't any damages—"

"I should be apologizing to you. It's a friendlier store than that," she said. "When I didn't see you again, I was afraid they'd scared you off."

"Ah." Ben looked around. "No, I've been busy."

To Annileen, this side of the house looked like bazaar day for the Jawas—lots of gear sitting around and gathering sand. And while the doorway to the house was here, the door was not. The burlap curtain she'd sold him hung across the entrance.

"The former residents left me with a work in progress," Ben said.

"A while ago, it looks like."

"Yes. I'd thought to build my own home, but that's more involved than I'd expected," he said. "But there seems to be no shortage of abandoned buildings."

"You should at least get a door."

Ben looked amused. "Are you trying to sell me something else?"

"Just afraid you're gonna freeze at night. A lot of this stuff needs to be inside, in fact." She walked toward the eopie pen. "And you need to get a tarp over this feed, or it'll be baked in an hour."

"Will the eopie care?"

"No, but you might, if you have to live around her."

"Ah." Ben craned his neck. "I was just putting a tarp over my funnel plants."

"No, those need to breathe. They won't get drier than they already are."

"Then everything balances out," he said, lifting the cover from the gritty foliage. "I was afraid of a sand-storm."

"Then you've seen one before. Anyone who has would be afraid. But no—if you see the rock hornets start to swarm, then you can worry. They beat the forecast half the time."

Ben nodded. "Home delivery *and* the weather report. This is fine service."

"It's how I maintain my monopoly. I keep my custom-ers alive." She pointed to the hood sewn to the collar of his shirt. "For example, if you're going to keep working out here, I'd put that up before double noon."

He laughed. "I did survive before I met you, you know." But he dutifully donned the cowl.

Annileen smiled. "Just looking out for you. Ever hear of Jellion Broon?"

"No."

"There's a reason for that." She reached for the can-teen strapped around her shoulder and offered it to him. When Ben declined, she took a swig and continued. "Broon was a great holovid actor when I was a kid. My mother loved him. Anyway, he came to Mos Espa for some race story he was acting in, and he caught the bug. Fell in love with the desert. The guy was raised in total privilege, and he sets eyes on the Jundland Wastes and becomes obsessed." Annileen cocked her head over her shoulder toward the rocky hills and snorted. "I can't imagine why."

"Continue."

"So Broon buys a dump out here—no offense—and tells people he's doing research on his own production, a desert epic. And off he goes."

"Ah. And no one ever saw him again."

"Yes and no."

"Hmm?"

"He survived all right. Showed up in Bestine six months later—looking *twenty years older*. The suns and the wind ripped him up something awful. It looked like someone'd taken a plastorch to his face. His own agent didn't recognize him, and his studio wanted nothing to do with him." She pointed to the eopie, munching away, its head under the tarp now covering the trough. "Take it from Rooh. Keep your hood on, or you'll dry out like a sack of gorrmillet."

They said nothing for a moment. Finally, Ben picked up his tub of goods and started toward his doorway.

"So are you an actor?" she asked.

Ben chortled. "No."

"Not out here painting pictures? Not writing about life in the desert?"

"Or in general." Ben drew back the curtain just enough to set the supplies inside. He closed it before she could see anything. "No, there is nothing to tell. I am really quite uninteresting—except to wayward banthas."

"Right."

"Thanks for the supplies. I won't put you to such trouble again." Ben turned toward the debris-laden yard. "Now, if you'll excuse me, I have much to do."

"How long are you staying?"

Ben stopped in his tracks and gave her a look. A

look, she thought, that said in the most pleasant but firm way that the interview was over.

Annileen backed down the slope toward her land-speeder. "Well, you know where we are if you need anything. And I almost forgot—four days from now there's a big race at Mos Espa. If you'd like to see what the store looks like without so many rude idiots around, that's your chance." She looked keenly at him. "People depend on one another around here. It's no place to live alone."

Atop the rise, Ben cracked a small smile. "To hear you talk, anyone in my care would be dead in five minutes."

"We'll see," she said, turning back to her speeder. "See you, Ben."

If he's hiding, he's new at it, she thought, settling into the driver's seat. In her years of running the store, Annileen had seen her share of people trying to disappear. From spouses, from Republic justice, from the Hutts—there had even been one runaway from a traveling circus. One thing she'd noticed: in an area where everyone knew everyone else's business, the more nondescript someone tried to seem, the more curious the neighbors became. You needed a label, so people could forget about you. She'd always joked that when her kids finally drove her to run to the hills, she'd become known as the crazy lady who stewed mynocks for dinner.

Maybe Ben would figure that out, she thought as the engine revved. But he was certainly failing at shooing away interest. The man looked . . . well, *sad* whenever he thought she wasn't looking. Anyone like that just had to have a story.

Pulling away, Annileen circled a rock and looked back up the bluff. She saw Ben looking up at the suns—and removing his hood.

Strange.

*   *   *

Back at Dannar's Claim, the hands from the Gault fields were in and gorging. Jabe was among them, back from Bestine. He didn't look up when his mother walked in. She stepped past the diners to the tap to refill her canteen.

Two trays balanced on each arm, Kallie paused to study her. "You forgot the dricklefruit."

"*You're* the dricklefruit," Annileen said, walking toward the back. "Any messages?"

"One from your daughter, wanting to know what Ben said."

"He said thanks for the groceries."

Kallie rolled her eyes impatiently. "Wanting to know what Ben said about *her*."

Annileen emerged wearing an apron and looked primly back at Kallie. "He said he's happy to know I have a daughter who's such a good and loyal worker—and who minds her own business."

Kallie swore. Annileen didn't bother to scold her. Seeing Ulbreck in mid-conversation, she stepped in to clear his table. "So, Wyle. Where were we?"

A'Yark returned to The Pillars exhausted. Having seen the Airshaper depart the compound before double noon, the marauder had raced to a waiting bantha. But there was no hope of catching up with the landspeeder. The Airshaper's route appeared to match her hairy-faced rescuer's path from days earlier; it was a reasonable assumption that she had gone to see him. Perhaps they were spouses, after all.

More useful information. A'Yark had intended to tell the others on returning. The Tuskens did not have war councils; it was not the way of Sand People to discuss and connive. Tuskens were so single-minded of goal, so similarly driven, that little coordination was necessary. They moved as a single entity. The only need for words was in sharing information about a target. With that, they would all know what to do.

But a surprise waited in the shadows beneath the towering rocks. A gathering was under way—without A'Yark.

A'Yark recognized the low grunts of Gr'Karr, oldest remaining member of the tribe. "The omen is good," the old fighter was saying, clutching the horn of a young bantha calf. "Bounty comes to us. The time is right."

"What animal is this?" an incensed A'Yark demanded, barging into the circle. "And who told you to speak without me?"

"I did," barked another Tusken, huge and dominating. H'Raak was a recent addition, the last mighty survivor of another tribe. "No one needs to hear the words of A'Yark to know what to do."

The one-eyed Tusken ignored the brute. H'Raak had never accepted A'Yark's role in the group, convinced his own size and strength meant all—a foolish belief. The dewback the Airshaper rode had been huge, and yet it yielded to the sarlacc. Sometimes it was better to lie in wait. "The calf. It wandered here?"

Old Gr'Karr measured the beast's hair. "The calf should be given to your son, wily one. A'Deen is Tusken now."

"No," A'Yark said, paying no mind to the reference to the boy. "Not this bantha." There was something wrong about it. A'Yark could tell. Tuskens and their banthas were one being, some said; A'Yark thought that was idle nonsense. But a warrior who did not understand his mount would not live long.

A'Yark stepped closer. The calf stamped nervously.
There was something familiar about the animal. *No, not
the animal,* the warrior thought, reaching out and grasping a clump of its hair. The creature squealed, but did
not move.

"The Airshaper has touched it," A'Yark said, releasing the bantha. The scent of the woman was plainly
there, just as it had been on the wind that day on the
pitted field.

A murmur went through the circle. "Then it should
die," H'Raak said, lifting his gaderffii.

"No." A'Yark stood between the bantha calf and the
others. "The human touched this calf today. She might
have a bond with it."

The statement disquieted the group. Gr'Karr spoke
haltingly. "A Tusken bond?"

"The Airshaper rode a dewback. It died. She may
have come here, seeking a new mount." A'Yark paused,
working it out. "The Airshaper may think as we do."

"Enough," H'Raak said, pounding his weapon against
the stony wall. "Enough foolishness! We should ride.
A'Yark says the settlers strike at us from the compound.
The compound must be destroyed—and the Airshaper
slain!"

"No." A'Yark slapped the bantha, sending it on its
way from the circle. "Kill the Smiling One who leads the
posses, yes. Even Hairy Face, should he appear. But if
the Airshaper respects the bantha, then perhaps she is
no settler. She may join us."

A louder rumble emanated from the gathering. H'Raak
laughed. "*Join* us?"

"The Airshaper has great powers, and may also have
a Tusken heart. How many settlers know the ways of
the bantha?" A'Yark looked through the rocky towers
to the north. "If no one else at the compound has the

power of the Airshaper, then yes, certainly, we seize her. She learns our ways, she lives. If not, we will learn her powers—one way or another. And she dies."

"You make a mistake," H'Raak said, the hulking warrior's voice booming. "You think of the *ootman,* the Outlander who once joined your clan. That was long ago—and the Outlander is dead. His gods failed him."

"All gods fail," A'Yark said, arms crossed. "The shadows of failure follow every living thing. Gods are no different."

"You do not lead," H'Raak said, voice dripping with disdain. Both hands on his weapon, the behemoth threatened the smaller warrior.

Enough of this. A'Yark looked coolly up at H'Raak and called out. "A'Deen!"

From the caves where the younglings carved the dinner meats, A'Yark's son appeared. "Yes, honored parent?"

"You *did* pass the test, child?"

"I am Tusken." The shrouded youth lifted his gaderffii proudly.

"That is well," A'Yark said. A moment later, the one-eyed warrior's arm shot upward, catching H'Raak beneath the chin. Another moment later, the others saw the knife, lodged in H'Raak's throat.

H'Raak dropped his gaderffii and stumbled backward, gagging. A'Yark kicked the warrior in the groin, knocking him to the ground. A few seconds' more work and A'Yark rose, blackened blade in hand.

Gr'Karr looked at the body and fretted. "We cannot spare any warriors, A'Yark."

"One was born, another died. All is equal." A'Yark looked back. "A'Deen. You will need a bantha. Take H'Raak's."

The old raider objected. "But the bantha should die with its rider. It's our tradition—"

"Many traditions are dying," A'Yark said, wandering off into the darkness of The Pillars. Night was falling. There was much to plan.

Meditation

Good morning, Qui-Gon.

Quiet here, as always. I know there are seasons on this planet, but I'm still not sure which one I'm in. But it is peaceful.

You know, we trained ourselves to be able to find solace even in the busiest places. Coruscant teemed with souls, and we meditated right at the center of it. By comparison, you'd think this place would be ideal for meditation.

I can't tell you why it isn't.

You used to say that in cases like this the problem wasn't the place; it was the person. I'm not sure what I'm supposed to do about that. It's not as though I'm going to be any less worried about things after I've been here six months. Or six years, or however long it takes for hope to return to the galaxy. It's not like I'm going to suddenly get my friends back. It's not like I'm going to feel any better about what I had to do to poor Anakin. It's not like—

No.

No, no. I'm sorry. I don't feel like doing this right now.

CHAPTER FOURTEEN

THE REPUBLIC. For a thousand generations, it had been out there. The bright center of the galaxy, shining light into the imaginations of everyone who lived on the Outer Rim. The Republic had seen tumult and change, invaders and oppressors. It had resisted the incursions of armored nomads and crazed cultists. It had even turned its back on the rest of the galaxy for a time, protecting itself against a dark age of fear and plague. But light had always returned.

Weeks earlier, someone in the store had told Annileen that the Republic had changed yet again. She hadn't paid much mind. The bright center for her meant Mos Eisley, the large spaceport in the distant east—a bustling metropolis that made the capital, Bestine, look like the farming community it really was. Annileen liked visiting Mos Eisley, despite its well-deserved reputation as a den of criminal activity—and on a day as slow as today, she would have found some business excuse to go.

But Jabe and Kallie were both in Mos Espa, as was practically everyone else. The Comet Run Podrace was no Boonta Eve Classic, but it emptied the Pika Oasis as efficiently as the plague. Gloamer had shut down the garages and left with his crews; most of the independent mechanics, normally willing to profit from his absence, had followed suit. Kallie had rented half the livery animals to racegoers. And naturally, Orrin had given his vaporator crews the day off. His workers already spent so much time in the Claim that Annileen wondered if any of them could tell the difference between workdays and holidays anymore. Dannar's one criticism of his best friend had been that Orrin confused popularity with profit. He made money, but he also spent a lot to look like a big man, too.

Annileen would never be accused of making that mistake. She gave no thought to closing the store. The revelers would return in a spending mood, whether they'd won their bets or not. The evenings following races were the most lucrative in the store's year. She'd cover her month's expenses before last call.

But the race days themselves were quiet. Annileen had shared a quiet breakfast with Leelee; Annileen had actually sat at a table for a change. Afterward, the Zeltron woman headed home, where she planned to lie in a luxurious coma all day until her family's return. Annileen gave Old Ulbreck unlimited access to the bantha jerky jar with instructions to tell Erbaly Nap'tee, should she come by, that the store's owner had emigrated to Heptooine. Finally, after supplying Bohmer with a full carafe of caf, she grabbed her floppy hat and satchel and stole into the southwestern yard.

There she sat on a blanket in the shade of the store's mammoth vaporator, her back against the machine's frosty base, feeling every puff of cool air that wafted off the compressor. Datapad on her lap, she looked at the images and imagined. In seconds she was sitting on the coast of Baroonda, a place alive and teeming with nature. Or Capital Cay on Aquilaris, watching the seacroppers bring in their catch. Or on the Gold Beaches of Corellia—or some other locale.

It was an old datapad, one she hadn't looked at in

STAR WARS: KENOBI   135

years. She thumbed again through the pictures. More
faraway places—distant both physically and into the
past. The holo-emitter on the device didn't work anymore, but she didn't care. The collection of pictures was
a hopeless wish list collated by a much younger person.
The planets still existed, for sure; she doubted Chancellor Palpa-whoosit or anyone he was fighting had the
power to change that. But the places were impossibly
beyond her reach.

She'd brought the datapad outside to refresh her
memory about those distant places. Ben had gotten her
thinking again about the galaxy—well-traveled company always did. She'd hoped to ask him if he had been
to any of the worlds in her pictures. But the morning
had passed with no Ben.

It had been silly to expect him to come, Annileen
thought. The man had already bought most of what he
needed, and a lot of the prospector types could stay out
for weeks at a time. Or perhaps he'd forgotten her mention of the day. Or maybe he was at the races, himself.

She rejected the last possibility. That would make Ben
like everyone else here—and thus far, he hadn't seemed
like that. But she had to admit she had no idea what he
might do. Once again, she mentally calculated the time
to traverse the distance from Ben's house to the oasis on
eopie-back. Why didn't the man have a landspeeder?
Just another mystery—but little puzzles were all that
separated one day from another at the Claim.

Sadly, this puzzle seemed doomed to have only three
or four pieces.

Doomed. This was the right datapad for thoughts like
that. Annileen shifted back to another document and
read. She had written it such a long time ago; it almost
seemed scripted by another person.

*"My name is Annileen Thaney, and I would like to tell
you about myself . . ."*

She hadn't been Annileen Thaney in nearly twenty years. It had been that long since she'd written anything but a bill of sale. And what she read now aggravated her. The words were written by a child, about a child. Or rather, about a grown-up who would never exist.

Annileen grew increasingly disgusted with each paragraph—until finally, she reached her breaking point. She stood and turned to the right, where a sand berm had piled up behind the vaporator. Grasping the datapad in one hand, she twisted her torso and hurled the device. The datapad spun like a discus, sailing over the dune and out of sight.

Annileen plopped back down on the blanket, satisfied and ashamed in equal parts. It *was* an old device, rarely used—and what was on it was of no use to anyone. Let the Jawas have it.

But suddenly she realized she'd never heard it land.

"Lose something?" Ben said. The cloaked man stood atop the dune, with the suns high behind him and the eopie at his side. In his right hand, he held the datapad.

Annileen stumbled as she tried to get up. "Sorry," she said, quickly recovering her composure. "I hope I didn't hit you with that."

Ben held up the datapad, amused. "Obsolete model?"

"Obsolete life," Annileen said, grinning. "And I can sell you ten better datapads than that."

"I wouldn't have use for them, I'm afraid." Ben smiled politely as he stepped into the shade behind the vaporator. Out of the glare, he glanced at the screen. What he saw made him look again, more closely. He scanned the words. *"Educational opportunities . . . offworld . . . swift placement."* He looked to her, eyes widening. "Why, this is a university application!"

Annileen felt flushed. "Look at the date on it," she said.

"Oh." Ben's eyes narrowed. "More than twenty years ago," he said.

"It's from after my father lost most of his ranch—not long after I had to go to work for Dannar. Back then I still had my sights set on working with animals."

"A zoological expedition authorized by the University of Alderaan," Ben read aloud. *"Travel ten worlds in a two-year exobiology program."* He looked up at her. "It sounds nice."

"For someone." She took off her hat and ran her fingers through her hair. "Twenty years ago, maybe."

Ben studied it further. "I don't know about that— it looks like they've been offering this program for centuries." He looked up at her. "I'm sure they're still running expeditions—"

She winced. No, she didn't want to go over this again, and certainly not with him. Seeming to sense her unease, he deactivated the gadget and offered it. "Don't you want this?"

"I threw it away." She changed the subject. "So why are you here?"

He straightened and cleared his throat. "I have actually come for a drink," he said, lowering the datapad.

Annileen's eyebrows rose. "Really."

"Yes," he said. "I've been having trouble getting my old vaporator into service. But I met Orrin Gault the other day, and he had the best water I've ever tasted. I was wondering—"

She smiled. "By the keg, my friend, by the keg. But first," she said, "you should try *this*." She reached out and took his hand.

Her touch startled him, but as she turned him to face the vaporator he saw what she had in mind. A key sat lodged in a lock. "Ah," he said, watching her open the door. "This is one of Orrin's—what did he call them, his Pretormins?"

"Yes," Annileen said, rotating the tap outward to become a spigot. "And it's not Orrin's. It's mine. Dannar put up the first GX-9 in the oasis here, before he died. Your canteen, sir?"

Ben reached into his cloak for his canteen and gave it to her. He watched as she filled and returned it. He steeled himself before drinking the cold water. He gasped nonetheless. "Amazing," he said, rubbing icy lips with the back of his hand. "It's even better than Orrin's, if that's possible."

"Thank my husband."

"I thought—" Ben capped his canteen. "I thought he had passed?"

"He did." Annileen gestured to the blinking controls inside the open panel. "Dannar adjusted this vaporator once, years ago—just fooling around. He got what you're drinking there. We've never changed the settings. Orrin's been trying to replicate them all over the valley."

"He took the idea and ran with it."

"I guess so." She turned back and gestured to the store. "Dannar didn't mind. We had enough worries without getting into the farming business. You know what they say—don't dig for treasure. Sell the shovels."

She turned back toward the store, suddenly downcast. "I guess I've been out here long enough," she said. She beckoned to Rooh. "Let's get you fed and watered, girl." The animal trotted toward her. Ben watched them for a moment before kneeling to gather her blanket.

"I'm sorry to have reminded you about Dannar," he said, walking along behind her. "Orrin said he'd stopped to help people in the desert?"

"It was just like him," Annileen said, leading Rooh to the troughs near the livery. She knelt to tie the eopie's lead to a post—and stayed down, lost in thought.

Ben studied her in silence.

"Wait a moment," he said. "It wasn't just eight years ago, was it?" He looked at her. "It was eight years ago *today*."

"You're good." She looked up at him. "One of our locals was in the Comet Run. We were going to have a big celebration here. Dannar had gone to Mos Eisley for something special." She shook her head. "That's crazy, isn't it? Send someone out for fleek eels, and they never come back."

Ben stood back, respectful of her moment. "I'm sorry, Annileen. I won't patronize you by saying I know how you feel—every tragedy is different, and personal. But you can take some solace in that he *was* committing a selfless act—"

"Well, Ben, that's just it," she said, eyes glistening. "It's fine to sacrifice yourself—if no one else has claim to you. Dannar belonged to us—and we never gave him permission to die." Her forehead crinkled, and she tightened the knot on Rooh's lead.

Ben seemed taken aback. Noticing, she stood and offered a weak smile. It wasn't good business to depress the customers. "Sorry. It's just the day," she said.

"I could leave if it's—"

"No, no," she said, taking the blanket from his hands. "I've usually been alone on this day. Used to think it was better." *And yet I invited you,* she did not say. "Maybe it's time for a change."

He regarded her for a moment and then brightened, the clever smile reappearing. "You know, why not? I think, perhaps, we both could use a change of pace for a day."

"You have a pace?" She laughed. "I don't even know what you do!"

"I solve problems." Ben prodded her toward the side door of the store. "And for this problem, I propose a strategy of mutual distraction—in which you regale me with an expert discourse on the flora and fauna of Tatooine, over lunch. I know just the place, nearby. I've heard a lot about it."

"I'd better not have to cook."

He held the door open. "Never fear. I do amazing things with survival rations."

CHAPTER FIFTEEN

"**WELL, WE'VE DETERMINED ONE THING,** Ben. Whatever job you had before you came here—you weren't a cook. But you tried."

"I didn't try. I *did*," he said, grinning as he took the dishes. "It's just what I *did* wasn't very good. I have a friend who's quite militant on the subject of trying." He looked at the remains on the platter with remorse. "Gartro omelets are supposed to be much better than that."

Annileen laughed. "It wasn't that bad."

"I have another friend who owns a diner," he said, disappearing into the alcove. "He'd have fired me on the spot." Dishes clattered.

Annileen rocked back in the chair and laughed again. *Well, Ben has friends, whoever he is.* It wasn't hard to see why. He played the quiet one. But scraping the surface, she found an infectious enthusiasm for all things. Their lunch had lasted an hour and a half, as they'd shopped from the shelves to find what he was looking for—and the repast had spread across two tables. He'd listened intently to her stories of life on the ranch and at the oasis—and now he was doing the dishes.

And he was living as a hermit?

"Don't feel bad," she said as Ben reappeared. "We didn't exactly have all the ingredients."

"You came close," he said, wiping his hands on a towel. "As frontier stores go, this is a supermarket on Coruscant."

"You've been there?"

Ben looked at her for a second—and then over at Old Ulbreck, who let loose with an angry snort. The farmer had been snoring loudly in his chair for hours, after having gorged on jerky. Annileen had joked that Magda Ulbreck—or his heart doctor—would send over a bounty hunter for him any minute. Ben had laughed, but she'd noticed his slight tension at first meeting Ulbreck, and for a moment, she could've sworn Ulbreck recognized Ben. But the old man had obviously dismissed the thought, because after that he paid Ben no mind. Which was, Annileen thought, a lucky stroke for Ben: to Ulbreck, strangers were either potential thieves, or audiences for his stories. Now Ben nodded toward the farmer. "He looks happy," he said.

"I'm happier when he's asleep," she said, rising. "But don't change the subject."

"What do you mean?"

"I mean you've done it again. You've managed to let me talk all through lunch, and you've hardly gotten a word in edgewise."

"It's called being a polite guest," he said.

"Are you sure you're not wanted for something? No price on your head on Duro for running illicit omelets?"

"No, nothing like that," he said, leaning against the counter. He looked around, taking everything in. "I just—I guess you could say now I just *watch*. And this is a peaceful enough place for it." He looked out the window toward the livery yard.

"What do you think so far?"

"It might seem that there's not much here," he said. "But what there is, there's plenty of."

There was something uncertain in his voice, Annileen

thought, as if Ben couldn't yet decide whether he liked Tatooine or not.

He turned back to her. "Sorry—no offense to your home. Far be it from me to judge something from one part." He walked back to the table for more dishes.

"No, you're perfectly safe in judging one part of Tatooine from another," Annileen said, surveying the room. "Grains of sand, settlements, *settlers*—we're all pretty much the same. It's always been like this, and it's never going to change."

"I try to avoid the words *always* and *never*," Ben said, taking the cloth to a plate that was already clean. His tone grew solemn. "Things that seem permanent, a given, have a way of changing quickly, to something you don't recognize. And not all change is for the better."

She studied him closely. Pleasant on the outside, torn up on the inside? Many of the people in her life were the opposite—you had to get through layers of abrasiveness to find the niceness in them, if it existed at all. Maybe this was the key to the man. "Did . . . something happen to you, Ben?"

"No," he said, looking at the dish. Almost under his breath he added: "Not to me."

Abruptly, he turned away—and began wiping off the tables they'd sat at. He stepped gently past Bohmer, who still sat motionless at his solitary table with his beverage. Brightening, Ben regarded him with admiration. "Now, *here's* someone who knows how to watch."

Bohmer's focus hadn't changed, still on the steaming cup.

"I never know what he sees there," she said. "I don't even know why he comes in every day." She wondered, sometimes, what sadness was in the Rodian's life.

"Do you speak any Rodian?" Ben asked.

"I'm not sure *he* does. All these years, and I don't

know anything about him." She cocked an eyebrow at Ben. "I guess it's contagious."

Ben looked at the chrono on the wall. "Well, I should buy my keg of water and go," he said. "Your race fans will be back soon." He walked to the stack of transparent drums in the corner. Lugging one of the large containers down, he turned and fished for credits in his cloak.

Watching him count, Annileen spoke up. "Hey, wait," she said. She started toward the door to the garage. "Meet me outside, okay?"

Ben looked back at her, puzzled. "I should really be getting—"

"Just trust me. I'll be just a second."

Ben stood with his keg on the stoop outside the store. A garage door opened, and Annileen's old X-31 emerged, with her at the controls. She parked it next to him and debarked. "Everyone's not due back for a couple of hours," she said, reaching for the water container. "I'll drive you."

"That's not necessary!"

"No, it'll be fine," she said, lifting. "We'll go around to the livery and put Rooh in the rumble seat."

"Will she ride there?"

"My kids did. So we know it holds wild animals."

Ben looked back, seemingly troubled. "Really, you don't have to do this. It's been a fun afternoon—something I didn't know I needed. But you can't leave the store empty."

"It's just Ulbreck and Bohmer in there. I think it's safe." Annileen gave Ben a look that exuded confidence. She'd gotten him to relax; she wasn't about to let him ice up again. She reached out with her hand, only barely aware of a high, distant whine on the air. "It's all right, Ben. I'm just saving you some time. Come on—"

The sound grew louder—and Ben's eyes widened, suddenly serious. He grabbed her arm. "*Annileen, look out!*"

She saw it just for an instant, out of the corner of her eye. A copper-colored shape rocketed around the corner of the garage. The vehicle clipped her parked landspeeder where it hovered, sending it spiraling.

In the same second, Ben threw his body into hers, knocking her off her feet. The two of them hit the sandy ground together. The world above went black as the underside of the careening X-31 whipped over them. The landspeeder slammed into the synstone outer wall of the building with a colossal crack.

Ben rolled free, wary and alert. Annileen sat up, bewildered. Her landspeeder sat on the ground a short distance from the garage entrance. The vehicle's right side was dented. Its left engine hung off, lopsided. And behind Ben, she could now see the cause: Veeka Gault's Sportster, its nose smashed and half buried in the sand. Behind the controls, dazed, sat the young woman herself.

And in the passenger seat: Jabe!

Annileen sprang up, overcome with worry, but on reaching the wreck, her expression changed. Her son looked up at her—and giggled uncontrollably. "Hi, Mom. We're home!"

She could smell the cheap lum ale the Hutts served at the raceway. "Are you *kidding* me?" Her eyes darted to Veeka, similarly inebriated. Annileen scrambled across the crushed hood of the vehicle to reach her. "*Veeka!*"

The young woman looked at the shopkeeper lunging toward her and burst into giggles herself. "Mama's Jabey is all right," she said in a syrupy voice. "But you shoulda parked somewhere else. It's race day—"

"Where's your father?"

On cue, two more landspeeders arrived, hurtling around the corner of the garage building. The first, driven by Zedd and Mullen, nearly caused another collision. Behind it, Orrin's silver landspeeder arrived in a more orderly way. Kallie was driving, as Orrin chatted over the seat to a trio of horn-headed Devaronian males. Annileen recognized them as the business contacts from Mos Eisley he'd been desperate to impress.

"We're in the holy compound now, folks," Annileen heard Orrin say to them as they stopped. "Kick the sand off your shoes, and genuflect as you enter." Stepping out of the vehicle, he saw Annileen's wrecked speeder first—and then her, charging toward him. "Uh-oh."

"*Look!*" Annileen sputtered, arms waving. "Look what they did!"

Orrin walked up to the Sportster. Veeka and Jabe tumbled out, rocky on their feet but otherwise unharmed. He looked them over and then glanced at the battered wall of the garage. He whistled. "Looks like another lap at Mos Espa," he said loudly. The Devaronians laughed.

Annileen wasn't amused. "Your daughter was drunk! And driving my son!"

"The race ended early," Orrin said.

"This one did! Is that your idea of an explanation?"

Orrin closed the distance with her. "The race was flagged to a stop halfway through. Two of the Hutts' teams got into a brawl. Big disappointment." He shifted to a quieter voice and gestured toward the store. "Everyone's going to want drinks, Annie—"

"Everyone's *been* drinking—or hadn't you noticed?" She turned to see Jabe trying to edge his way toward the store. She pointed at him with a force that could have knocked him down. "And don't you think of moving!"

Annileen turned back on Orrin, who was clearly uncomfortable with the scene playing out before his wealthy customers. She didn't care. "Orrin, Jabe is not an adult. I said he could go to the races if you watched him. You call this watching?"

Orrin put his hands up before her. "Annie, you know these trips are a rite of passage for these kids. And besides, this is Tatooine. A body that works all the time is pretty grown up, no matter what the age. Isn't that right—"

Before Orrin could get whatever support he was expecting for his argument, a high female voice carried over all the others. Kallie, who at first had been spellbound by the wreck scene, had suddenly noticed someone at the periphery. *"Ben!"*

Forgotten by Annileen since the crash, Ben had stepped up to check on Jabe, earning a bad look from the boy. Which made four, as Ben was getting them now from Veeka, Mullen, and Zedd, as well. Kallie's greeting was as enthusiastic as theirs was hostile—and Orrin's was different altogether.

"Oh. Hello, Ben," Orrin said mildly, after the surprise registered. He looked back at Annileen, eyebrow raised. "You two were here all day?"

Ben stepped backward toward the wreck of the landspeeder. "Really, I just stopped by for water—"

Orrin saw the bashed keg, its precious contents on the ground and evaporating. He saw his ranch's label there and smiled. "You liked it, then?" Suddenly elated, Orrin pushed past Kallie and took Ben by the shoulder. "This is wonderful! Ben, there's folks I'd like you to meet."

As Orrin pushed him toward the Devaronians, a squirming Ben looked back at Annileen in near panic. She merely shrugged. No force in nature could protect someone once Orrin was in salesman mode. And especially not when he had a celebrity endorsement in the making.

"Ben, these people run the Lucky Despot, a hotel, ca-

sino, and conference center going in at Mos Eisley."
Orrin turned to his guests. "This man—a big hero
around here, by the way—rode all the way in from the
wastes, just for a drink of Gault's Sparkling Seven. The
best-tasting water in any tap from Tatooine to Taanab!"

Ben nodded meekly as the Devaronians enthusiasti-
cally shook his hand and chattered about their trip—
and him. They had many questions:

> Did you really come so far just for the water?
> Would you go to Mos Eisley for it?
> How much would you pay, by the glass, in a
>   posh metropolitan setting?
> Did you really save the store owner's daughter
>   from a rampaging stampede of banthas, as
>   she told us in the landspeeder?

Hearing that, Annileen looked at Kallie, whose shoulders sank in embarrassment. But Kallie's imagination
and crush were relatively important. At least Kallie was
sober, as she always was. Jabe seemed to be steadying,
but he wouldn't be for long if he followed Veeka inside.
"The bar is closed!" Annileen yelled.

Orrin stepped back, waving his hands. "Now, don't
say that too loudly. I'm supposed to be showing these
people a good time. And they only got to see half a
race!"

"They'll see a murder if your kids get within a light-
year of my son again."

Orrin grasped for her hand. "You know I'll make
good on the landspeeder. Just more work for Gloamer.
But I really need this. Okay?"

Annileen groaned, disgusted. "Fine. I'll serve the
Devaronians—only. But let me go extricate Ben before
he decides to never visit this—"

She stopped speaking as she noticed Ben's expression,

from amid the group of visitors. Orrin noticed it, too. "Something wrong, friend?"

The man looked back at the store, eyes narrowing. He started to speak—when the side door burst open. Bohmer appeared in the doorway of the Claim, his big, dark eyes bulging. He tripped on the stoop and fell forward—

—revealing the dagger protruding from his back.

And the giant Tusken Raider standing behind him.

CHAPTER SIXTEEN

THEY HAD APPROACHED THE OASIS from the northeast. The passage had been difficult, but A'Yark had studied the problem closely. There was no other way. The warriors had spent three days on a long, looping approach from The Pillars, stopping only to overnight in quickly erected—and just as quickly dismantled—huts constructed of canvas and bantha ribs.

A'Yark had made a gambit based on the suns themselves. Whatever their failings, the skybrothers' movements were reliable. The accursed shadows told the wise Tusken much: not just the time of day, but also the time of year with great accuracy. And near this day in past years A'Yark had seen travelers making pilgrimages to the northwest, like kreetles drawn to a corpse.

Was it some sort of rite? A curious raider had followed once, reporting back a great gathering where settlers paid homage to their bloated Hutt gods with games and spirits. It was vile foolishness to A'Yark, who nonetheless saw an opportunity. As larger vehicles began traversing the desert, taking supplies northwest, A'Yark had inferred that the next fête day was near. An opportunity to find the oasis lightly defended.

The Tuskens had infiltrated the compound in pairs, hiding behind the barn buildings. The structures were large enough to screen the movements of many. And A'Yark had brought many, indeed. *All* the warriors had come: the aged, the injured—even son A'Deen, on his first hunt. Only the women and children tending the banthas had remained behind.

From a surveillance perch atop one of the barns, A'Yark had seen the Airshaper and Hairy Face in the main building. Alone, or close enough. It was perfect.

Perfect—until the first landspeeder had appeared from the northwest, early and unbidden. A'Yark had recognized the newcomer as the settler vehicle that had arrived first during the assault on the farm, days earlier. Two landspeeders followed behind, including the shining vehicle of the Smiling One. Undeterred, A'Yark had leapt from the rooftop and started the charge. The Tuskens still had superior numbers and surprise.

They had caught all their enemies at once. Warriors streamed across the livestock yard toward—and into—the buildings. A'Yark hooted. There was no need for a command. The others knew.

Find the Airshaper—and kill the rest!

"Tusken!" Orrin pulled his blaster from his shoulder holster. He'd only worn it to impress the Devaronian investors. Now he fired it into the doorway of the Claim. The rifle-toting warrior ducked back inside and began returning fire.

The Devaronians stood mystified, perhaps thinking the event was a frontier entertainment staged by Orrin. That ended when one of them took a rifle blast to the chest. Orrin screamed for the others to get down with him, using his vehicle for cover. To his right, Zedd and Mullen drew their blasters; to his left, Veeka and Jabe hid behind the wrecked Sportster. A savage in the compound was a sobering sight, to be sure. Orange fire painted the approach to the building.

"Hold your fire!" From his position along the outside wall near the doorway, Ben pointed at Bohmer. The Rodian, knife still in his back, was clawing at the dust, trying to pull himself forward, even as the blaster bolts blazed above him.

Orrin gawked at Ben. *Hold fire, now?*

But Ben was already on the move. Whipping off his cape, the man spread it like a net and hurled it toward the doorway in one swirling motion. The Tusken's rifle bolts followed it upward. Ben dived downward, tumbling across the narrow field of fire. Reaching Bohmer's side, Ben took hold of the Rodian and heaved. A second later, both figures were huddled against the synstone wall, just to the left of the open doorway. The Tusken blazed away again, raking the place where Bohmer had fallen.

Hiding behind her downed landspeeder with Kallie, Annileen yelled to Orrin, "Don't shoot! You'll hit Ben!"

Orrin sent her a plaintive look. Veeka and Jabe had retrieved their weapons from her vehicle and were firing wildly. It was clear from the ruckus that the Tusken in the store was definitely not alone. There was no telling anyone to cease fire, not now. Ben seemed to know he was on his own, too, as he struggled to drag the bleeding Rodian back away from the firing zone and toward the nearest garage bay.

"There's more!" Mullen yelled, pointing southeast. More Tuskens appeared around the corner of the store, gaderffii raised. One charged Zedd, smashing the massive farmhand in the rib cage. Orrin brought the exposed attacker down with a blaster bolt and yelled for Mullen and Zedd to fall back. They'd been successfully outflanked. The Sand People were striking from inside the store and from around it.

Mullen reached his father's position, gasping. "The Call! Activate the Call!"

"I left the activator at home," he said, swearing. "We were going to the races!" He looked back to Annileen, behind the nearby X-31. "Do you have your activator?"

She couldn't hear him. Annileen had found a moment to fish her rifle from her backseat—and was angrily blasting away at her uninvited guests. Orrin repeated his question, straining to be heard. She looked at him, flustered. "I don't carry the thing around! This is your home base. It's supposed to be safe!"

Ben dashed forward from the garage where he'd left Bohmer. He slid to a grinding stop behind Orrin's landspeeder. Between shots, Mullen looked at him and snarled, "Next time, bring a blaster. You ain't getting mine!"

Ben ignored him. "Another wave!" he yelled, and pointed to a new group of Tuskens. Screened by their attacking companions, the newcomers charged across the Claim's southern yard toward the giant vaporator.

Orrin looked through the chaos at them, momentarily confused. That was Old Number One, the first Pretormin tower in the oasis. The Tuskens were attacking it, clubbing its base with their gaffi sticks.

Annileen pointed at the tower's tip. "It's the Call! They're after the Call!"

Of course. Orrin understood right away. The Settlers' Call used a standard transmitter to connect the subscribing farms and the vigilantes. But there was also the siren—and here, as at the Bezzard farm, it sat at the highest point in the area: atop the vaporator.

Which also happened to be where the transmitter was located.

A daylight raid—and now this! It added up. *"Plug-eye's here!"* The crafty Tusken had figured it out somehow, and was trying to gag the oasis before any cry for help could be raised.

Ben yanked at Orrin's sleeve. "They're not in the garage complex yet."

Orrin looked back. Only one bay was open—the one Annileen's landspeeder had exited earlier. What Ben said was true, but it didn't make sense. "There's a pass-through between the store and the garages," Orrin yelled. "If they're in the store, why haven't they come through there yet?" Tuskens attacking from the garages would effectively envelop them.

"I don't know," Ben said. "Something's stopping them. Let's take advantage. Get people to safety!"

It made sense. Orrin gestured for the surviving Devaronians, both scared witless, to make a break for the open garage. They did, and the others followed, one by one. After Ben helped Zedd, in agony since his attack, stagger in, Mullen and Orrin followed. Now their cover became the Tuskens' cover, as the warriors crouched behind the landspeeders and fired into the garage bay.

Orrin looked back at the work floor. If they could avoid the Tuskens' blasterfire, they could reach the hallways leading to the rest of the bays, including those with the Settlers' Call vehicles. There would be more weapons there, and a chance of escape—and he and Annileen both had the codes to open the doors. But Ben, crouching with poor Bohmer, kept looking at the doorway leading back to the store.

"There's a reason they haven't come through," Ben said.

He seemed to be concentrating. How anyone could concentrate in this situation was beyond Orrin. "What difference does it make?"

"No," Ben said. "Listen!"

Orrin stood as close to the doorway as he dared, fearing Plug-eye and friends would charge in at any second.

But all he could hear was blasterfire and the horrific screams of Tuskens.

"What in—" Orrin looked back at the people in the garage, hiding behind equipment and firing out at the Tuskens. His kids and Zedd. Annileen and her kids.

Who were the Tuskens inside fighting?

"Was anyone else coming from Mos Espa?" Annileen asked from cover.

"We left early to beat the rush," Orrin said, scratching the side of his head with the handle of his blaster. "Was anyone else in the store?"

Annileen's eyes widened. "Ben!" she said. "The surveillance cams!"

Ben looked to his side. There was a flickering screen, a monitoring station for all the locations within the garage. Orrin watched as Ben quickly cycled through them. The man seemed to know his way around a security system, the farmer noticed. The garage bays all seemed empty of Tuskens. The only activity was in the store, which came up as the final image.

"That's what I thought," Ben said, turning. A determined look on his face, he left Orrin's side and reached for one of Gloamer's big fire extinguisher canisters. "Hold the fort," he said as he disappeared around the corner into the pass-through.

Orrin's jaw dropped. *Is the man crazy?*

"Ben!" Annileen yelled. Heedless of the incoming blasterfire, she dived across the garage floor to Orrin's side. "Ben's unarmed," she yelled to Orrin. "We've got to follow him!"

"No," Orrin said, clutching at her sleeve. "Wait. Look here!"

Annileen glanced for an instant at the security monitor—and then looked again at it, gawking alongside Orrin. There, in the overhead view of the retail store, they saw what was occupying the Sand People.

Old Ulbreck had wedged himself behind the collapsed rifle racks and the weapons counter and was using the full arsenal at hand to keep the Tuskens at bay!

"Well, I'll be," Orrin said, bringing the cam into focus on the old man. "I'll be blasted!"

"So will he," Annileen said. "He can't hold out much longer!" More Tuskens were entering the store from the front entrance and the livery yard. She tugged at Orrin. "We've got to—"

At that moment the scene on the monitor began to cloud up. The blasterfire could still be seen—and then just light. *Blue* light, flashing around in a haze. Orrin shook his head, unbelieving. *What's happening in there?*

Annileen broke loose from his hold and dashed into the hallway. Orrin looked back at the others in the garage. "Hold 'em off! I'll be back!" he shouted.

Orrin ran through the short hallway. He skidded to a stop when he saw Annileen ahead, just standing there, her ankles lost in a lowering cloud of chemical retardant. The haze inside was still thick, but the flashing blue lights had stopped. And in place of the many combatants seen on the monitor earlier, only one figure stood now amid the smashed tables of the luncheonette: Ben. Standing over the bodies of a dozen or more Sand People, his hand slipped inside his tunic, as casually as if he were putting away his credit pouch.

A familiar old and now very weary voice came through the mist from Orrin and Annileen's right. Wyle Ulbreck popped out from behind the gun counter, repeating blaster rifle in hand. "Die, you wretched—"

Ben stepped quickly between the old farmer and the newcomers. "It's all right, Master Ulbreck. It's just friends here." He gestured to the fallen Sand People. "You got them all."

Orrin looked at the bodies, stunned, and then up at

Ben. The man had a canny look on his face. "Wyle did all this?"

Suddenly self-conscious, Ben stammered. "I, uh—saw what he was up against." He gestured to the spent canister, nearby. "He just needed a little distraction so he could finish the job."

Annileen looked dumbfounded. At Ben, then at Ulbreck, and finally at the mess of the store. "I'm speechless," she said.

Orrin looked at the old man, coughing as he staggered out from behind his makeshift fortress. "I woke up and these characters were coming in," Ulbreck said, eyes wandering in tired amazement. "I don't rightly know how I got 'em all—"

"But you did," Ben quickly offered. "Every one. All on your own."

Orrin shook his head. Old Ulbreck would be telling this story for years. Orrin stepped over to try to help the frazzled man stand—only to have his effort rebuffed.

"Lemme go, Gault!" Ulbreck snarled at him, suddenly fully aware again. "And you wanted to provide security for me? You can't even keep your own spread safe!"

Orrin's breath caught in his throat. Yes, this surely looked bad. But the blasterfire was still going outside, and the other Tuskens might reenter at any minute. He prodded Ulbreck toward the center of the store, and the old man didn't object.

Annileen was in motion now. Stepping over bodies, she reached her counter.

Ben saw her kneel and start to dig around. "What are you looking for?"

"The cashbox!"

Orrin raised an eyebrow. "I don't think the Tuskens care much for credits."

Annileen ignored him. Finding the box beneath a

smashed shelf, she slipped Dannar's old pistol from its position in the lock. "Here," she said, tossing the weapon to Ben.

Orrin darted from one shelf to another, trying to stay out of sight of the doorways. There were Tuskens everywhere outside, and with the screen of the chemical fog dissipating, every entrance was vulnerable. Reaching Ben, Orrin saw the man holding the pistol, contemplating it. "I hope you learned to use that, where you came from."

Ben had started to respond when figures loomed in the doorways on every side of the store. Tuskens, all— carrying gaderffii and blaster rifles. Orrin began to raise his rifle, only to have Ben place his hand on his the farmer's wrist. "Not now," Ben said.

The Tuskens at the front of the store parted to allow another to enter. Orrin strained to see through the haze. Shorter than the others, this one wore looser-fitting robes, with no bandolier. And only a single eyepiece, on the left. A red gem glinted where the right eye should be.

"*Plug-eye,*" Orrin whispered, gravely. This was it. He hoped his kids had made it out.

But the lead Tusken wasn't interested in Orrin. A wrapped hand thrust forward, pointing at Annileen. "*Ena'grosh,*" a low voice said, less guttural than other Tuskens whom Orrin had heard. And he heard many, now, as the others repeated the same word. "*Ena'grosh.*"

"They mean you," Ben said, watching Annileen walk around from behind the counter, cashbox in hand.

Orrin moved to stop her, but Ben again held his arm. "I think she's got this," he said confidently.

Annileen stood bravely before the Tuskens, opened the cashbox, and pressed the button of the small device inside. A device Orrin recognized as the remote control activator for the Settlers' Call—a call which now went out from the oasis, both over the airwaves, and as a roaring scream from a siren outside. A siren that still worked.

The recorded krayt dragon screeched, and behind Plug-eye, the Sand People responded as Sand People usually did.

"We're closed," Annileen said coldly. "Get the hell out of my store!"

CHAPTER SEVENTEEN

FOR THE SECOND TIME in a month, A'Yark stood before a human settlement, yelling after fleeing cowards.

"Prodorra! Prodorra!"

Hoax!

It was no use. Despite the war leader's efforts to teach the others, it was the morning raid at the farm all over again. A'Yark had explained that the krayt dragon call was a deceit. They even knew how to silence it, by attacking the towering water-leech with the sound-maker atop it. Their minds understood, and their bodies had followed the initial plan. But their attacks had failed to squelch the siren, and now their spirits betrayed them. Even A'Deen had fled the Airshaper's home, ignoring his "honored parent."

A'Yark looked back over the rise at the structure. The Airshaper was still in there, as were the bodies of the first wave of Tusken attackers. So many slain! Had the Airshaper somehow struck them down? This was her sanctuary. It made sense she would call upon all her powers to defend it. But A'Yark still knew the numbers favored the Tuskens, if they could be compelled to fight.

Young A'Deen skittered up the dune. "We must go," the youth said, rushed breaths whistling through his mouthpiece.

"No!"

A'Deen was A'Yark's only surviving child—yet the warrior struggled to resist the urge to smash the youth's face in. Such fear in A'Yark's bloodline? Unthinkable!

So A'Yark chose not to think on it. "No. Recall the others. We get what we came for, or—"

The warrior's head turned. The siren was still blaring, its scream having resolved into a long monotone. But there was another sound there, too.

"Landspeeders," A'Yark spat. Responding to the alarm, or arriving by chance? It didn't matter. A'Yark looked south. The retreat of the others had turned into a mad dash, all of them heedless of their leader and without any care for their camping gear, abandoned in the staging area.

A'Deen bowed his head, looking suddenly quite small. "Honored parent. *We must go.*"

"All my offspring were born under the cowardly sun," A'Yark said, stomping past the child warrior. "We must catch up to the others."

"It is right. They go to safety."

"No." A'Yark said, hardly believing what was happening. "We must catch them—*because they're heading the wrong way!*"

The ground quaked beneath Orrin's dress boots. A dozen meters above, the Settlers' Call siren screamed its ear-piercing warning to the oasis and beyond. But neither sound waves nor retreating Tuskens could distract the farmer from the sorry sight in front of him.

The base of Old Number One sparked, the vaporator's control panels bashed to bits. Dannar's secret formula was gone. Orrin had recorded the settings many times over the years, with the Calwells' permission, but the water from his Pretormins had never been as sweet.

Old Number One was unique. Some flaw, some short circuit, perhaps even some rewiring Dannar had never told him about. Orrin had feared to pry further into the device, so as not to destroy its magic.

Now it was gone.

But the siren had done its job, safe on its mount. It had been Dannar's notion to place it up there; Orrin would have preferred to see it located anywhere else, in case the thing upset the prized vaporator's performance. Dannar had safeguarded against that by powering the alarm independently from the vaporator's grid. That decision by a dead friend had saved them all. Short of climbing to the top or knocking the column over, the brutes had no chance of disabling the clarion.

Dannar had saved them. And now, the siren would avenge him and his home. Settlers arrived by landspeeder and dewback, eopie and speeder bike. All had been returning from Mos Espa, already bound for the Claim; the siren and digital signal had sped them along.

Orrin turned to the gathering group. Settlers thronged outside the garages and store. The Tuskens hadn't caused the initial landspeeder wreck, but the vehicles, scorched by blaster bolts, gave the impression that they were in a war zone. Jabe and Veeka were inside the store, relaying rifles uncovered from the collapsed racks out to the would-be vigilantes.

Outside, Mullen held up his hands, directing the settlers to form a perimeter. The Tuskens had withdrawn, but they could return at any time. Anyone as crazy as Plug-eye could do anything. Orrin shook his head at his recollection of the vaunted warrior. No vengeful demon, just a Tusken, short and a bit stocky; unafraid of the siren, but unable to calm the others. Well, maybe that would protect the Claim now.

He looked to where Ben was kneeling with the Rodian. Doc Mell, who had returned from the races with his youngling, approached Orrin. "Bohmer's alive," the Mon Calamari said.

"Alive!"

"I can't figure out how. You said that human was tending to him?"

"As soon as the Tuskens left. I saw . . . no, I *didn't* see what Ben was doing. But he must have dressed the wound." Orrin breathed a sigh of relief, his first real one in an hour. "Rodian skin must be tough."

Doc Mell looked back in wonder. "We'll still need to get him to Bestine in my speeder right away."

Orrin nodded. "We'll clear a path." The place had become a traffic jam. Drills prepared farmers to arrive in an orderly manner to arm themselves, departing in the Call Fund's war-ready vehicles. But everyone had come from one direction this time, and the parking area was a mess.

"Sir!"

It was an alien voice, one Orrin had momentarily forgotten all about. The two Devaronian executives appeared next to him, carrying their colleague on a litter. He was dead.

"We've paid someone to return us to Mos Eisley," the older of the pair said, his voice somber. "There is a funeral to prepare."

Orrin lowered his head. "If you'll wait, I'll—"

"No waiting." The Devaronians moved the corpse toward one of the newly arrived landspeeders.

"I recognize your loss," Orrin said, struggling to sound respectful while making himself heard amid the growing commotion. "But after a while, we can discuss things again? You still have a hotel, and I still have—"

"No," the younger Devaronian replied gravely. "You brought us to see the Gault farms. We saw a barbaric place. One you can't defend, even for a day." He looked down sadly at his dead companion. "Poor Jervett feared this trip was a fool's errand. It seems, in death, he was right."

Orrin raised his hands. "Please, understand—"

"*Excuse us!*"

Orrin watched, plaintively, as his would-be business partners proceeded with their unhappy chore. His mind raced. There still might be some way to salvage the deal. But so much was happening, and now he was aware of a grating voice nearby. Ulbreck was outside, recovered and telling his tale of heroism to anyone who'd listen.

And people *were* listening, amazed. There were a dozen dead Tuskens in the shop; everyone near an entrance was taking a look as Annileen and others tried to move the bodies. Blaster bolts had killed some, but others looked seared and scarred. What had Ulbreck found beneath the counter to shoot them with? The old man hadn't seemed to know himself, earlier. But now he was filling in blanks as quickly as he could imagine them. Ben, the drifter, remained in the story, but he'd arrived after it was all over, the crazy fool bringing a can of fire retardant to a gunfight.

There was something else in Ulbreck's tale, which he repeated every third sentence. "Sure I did it myself—you can't depend on Gault and his little club for nothing. Settlers' Call?" He spat through brown teeth. "*Settlers' Fall* is more like it!"

"That's not fair, Wyle!" Orrin pushed through the crowd toward the old man. "This was a fluke. A festival day—"

"I wouldn't pay another credit to that fund if I were you," Ulbreck shouted. "I'd want a refund!" Around him, several of the listeners nodded and began chattering to one another.

"No!" Orrin could feel his heart thumping. "Listen to me, all of you!" He stepped over to his landspeeder, putting his boot on the hood just as he'd done in his victory celebration, days earlier. It was the same pose, the same crowd—but so different now. "Everyone, the Call *worked*. Annie just didn't have her activator at hand. As soon as the alarm sounded, they all took off like scared womp rats." He raised his voice. "All of 'em—even *Plug-eye*!"

Plug-eye? The dissonant conversations in the crowd suddenly became one. "Plug-eye was here?" asked a farmer.

"Yes—and they all headed that way," Orrin said, pointing toward the south. "We got a report from a sky-hopper. They're headed toward Hanter's Gorge!"

The buzz became silence. Then the party erupted into shouts. Someone said it: *"We go now, we can get them all!"*

Orrin looked around, uncertain, as the clamor rose. Of course, the mob was right, the prospect obvious. Plug-eye had brought out more warriors than had been seen in recent memory. Now they were fleeing toward Hanter's Gorge, a well-mapped part of the Jundland Wastes that sat close to the nearest entrance to the Roiya Rift, the rocky labyrinth where the Tuskens liked to hide. Plug-eye might think they were heading for safety—but in fact, they were moving into a trap. This could be a chance for the Settlers' Call posse to eliminate the Sand People and finish off the threat once and for all.

Orrin glanced at the departing Devaronians and then down at Ulbreck. The old man had lost his audience, but he'd be talking again soon. Orrin had to preempt that.

He looked up at the suns. Seeing lots of daylight left, Orrin made a decision. No, he couldn't let this go unanswered. The Tuskens had struck the heart of the operation, knowingly or not. The locals paid their hard-earned credits to the Settlers' Call Fund. If the Call couldn't protect its own headquarters, it wasn't much good, was it?

He shot a direct look at Mullen. "All right! This is it. Muster drivers to the left, gunners to the right." He smiled darkly and fired his blaster into the air. "We're going hunting!"

"This is disgusting," Leelee said, poking a Tusken corpse with a broom handle. Her crimson nose crinkled. "I don't think I'm eating here again."

"Thanks for your support," Annileen said, pulling at a canvas tarp. A dead Tusken warrior lay facedown on it, the body jostling as she dragged it toward the eastern door of the Claim. She didn't know what Sand People ate, but this one weighed plenty.

Plug-eye's party had barely been gone when Annileen had set to work calculating how to repair her store. It couldn't wait. Too many people had seen the mess in the Claim, and had reacted just as Leelee had. There wasn't any thought of opening again today; the Tuskens had ruined a profitable evening, along with her property. But if there was any hope for the future, the cleanup couldn't wait.

Kallie, her riding kerchief pulled up over her mouth, reentered and pitched a pair of gloves to Leelee. "Ready for another one," the girl said. "Should we start piling them in the dewback pen?"

"Can't," Annileen said. "They stink too much. The dewbacks will never sleep there again." She turned to her daughter. "Tie a hoverpallet to the back of the LiteVan. We'll haul it into The Rumbles as soon as Orrin gives us the all-clear."

"The Rumbles? We'll have corpses rolling off all over the place."

"I really don't care." Annileen glared at the black

smear on the floor where the Tusken had been. Let a sarlacc have what was left.

A total violation of everything she held dear—and on this day, too! Annileen had stepped outside only once, just long enough to see what had happened to Old Number One. It was one of Dannar's last daily presences in her world, and she could tell from twenty meters away that it was damaged beyond repair.

At least her family was fine, although she could think of better ways of sobering Jabe up than a Tusken attack. All her worries from before felt like a relief now. Disciplining her son—what was *wrong* with him?—should be a cinch, after all this.

Ben appeared in the doorway from the garage. "Dr. Mell has left with Bohmer," he said, wiping his hands on a rag. "He'll survive."

"It's a miracle," Annileen said, brightening. "I don't know what you did, Ben, but I'm glad you were here today."

Leelee looked up from her mopping. She pointed at Ben, and then at Annileen. "You. And *you*. You were here together today?"

"All day," Kallie whispered to Leelee, loudly enough so Annileen could hear. "Alone." Leelee looked back at Annileen and raised an eyebrow.

"There were also some Tuskens," Ben said. "I'd better go." He put the hood back over his head and walked swiftly past the Zeltron woman. Leelee smirked as he passed.

Annileen gave an exhausted sigh and nodded. She started toward the stack of water containers, leaning but intact. "You should probably get that water you paid for." She pulled off her gloves and started to walk toward him, but he was already opening the door.

"*Wa-hooo!*" came a call from outside.

Ben paused in the doorway as one landspeeder after

another drove past, full of cheering passengers. Annileen trudged toward the door, wearily. *If those are fans
back from the race,* she thought, *they're going to be disappointed.*

But when she joined Ben outside, she saw the garages
had emptied of Settlers' Fund vehicles—all of which
were now streaming to the south, crammed with hollering, blaster-wielding settlers, young and old. Mostly
young. And Orrin's USV-5 was far in the lead, carrying
several.

"Oh, dear," Ben said. "You don't think—"

"I do think," Annileen said, swearing. She ran back
toward the garages, calling for her son.

She found only Zedd, seated and massaging his injured rib cage in a medicated stupor. It took two tries to
get him to answer. "They've gone after Plug-eye," he
finally said, wincing. "Hanter's Gorge."

"Jabe! Did they take Jabe?"

"He was the first to go," the farmhand said, grinning
through broken teeth. "I hope he fries a few for me."

Furious, Annileen dashed past the injured man into
the garage. Twenty seconds later she emerged astride an
old speeder bike—one of Gloamer's less-used rentals.
Gunning it around the corner of the store, she saw Ben
walking toward his eopie.

"Jabe's gone with them," she said, hovering. "They're
headed for Hanter's Gorge."

Ben looked at her with concern. "I don't know the
place. How bad is it?"

"Bad enough. There's no way out of there," she said.
"The Tuskens will have no choice but to fight!"

Ben's eyes narrowed. "He's with Orrin—but that
didn't mean much earlier."

"I know." Annileen gripped the throttle. "He's sixteen, Ben—and he was drinking. I don't know what
shape he's in right now."

"I'm worried about the shape *you're* in. You're exhausted." He stepped toward her and took hold of one of the handlebars. Even with the bike in pause mode, her hands were shaking. But her eyes blazed with determination and anger.

"This is the day I lost Dannar, and I nearly lost his store today. I'm not losing his son today, too!"

"I'll go instead," Ben said, after a moment. "I'll look after the boy."

"Look after us both, or neither of us," she said, twisting the throttle and scooting forward on the seat. "Because I'm going!"

CHAPTER EIGHTEEN

ANNILEEN'S PULSE HADN'T SLOWED at all as the kilometers sped past, but it felt better to have Ben with her. She felt his arms grip around her stomach as the speeder bike banked. She had chosen to drive; she knew where they were going, and Ben had seemed willing to let her take the lead.

The afternoon suns beat down on her forehead. She'd left without head wear. What had she said to Ben about the suns and aging? *Try having kids,* she thought.

Jabe! What was *wrong* with that kid? So he hated working in the store. She'd been bored, too, at his age but she had to work, and so did he. She could understand his hanging around with the Gaults to let off steam. But the boy was slight—no scrapper like Zedd, no beady-eyed gunslinger like Mullen. Bounty hunting was not in his future. Why risk his neck hunting Tuskens?

She already knew the answer. The Tuskens had killed his father. Today was an anniversary for Jabe, as well.

She just hoped she could reach him in time.

A'Yark screamed in agony.

The warrior had never run so hard for so long. Sand People knew how to run; the cowardly sun had taught them that much. But there was a reason Tuskens seldom strayed far from their camps and banthas. The gaderffii was a fine weapon to hold for a sprint, but after a distance it became cumbersome, and even the nimblest runner risked a bashed kneecap. A'Yark had slammed both in this chase, further aggravating leg muscles that were already on fire.

And without their banthas to guide them, green warriors were likely to lose their way. The group ahead had. The foolishness was theirs, but the failure belonged to A'Yark, who'd calculated for a successful raid and an orderly withdrawal. Unless A'Yark turned the fleeing warriors around, all would perish.

A'Deen had the speed of youth. The newest warrior of the clan had dashed ahead, carrying A'Yark's warning. The Tuskens had passed through the box canyon known as the False Mouth, thinking it led into The Pillars. A path did exist that led up and out, but only A'Yark knew where it was.

A silver landspeeder screeched past. The vehicle of the Smiling One.

I should've killed you when I had the chance, A'Yark thought.

A'Yark dived behind a dark formation on the craggy hillside and watched. More machines followed. Some bore toward the False Mouth. But others parted from the company and headed up the navigable inclines east and west of the gap. A flying machine with angular wings hovered above, just out of rifle range.

So many settlers. So many vehicles. The Smiling Man's forces had thwarted A'Yark's band in the past, killing some and driving the rest away. But this was different. A'Yark had struck at the human in his lair and failed. No quarter would be given.

A'Yark saw the flier pass between the suns. The elder sun had failed to kill, too; his sentence was a lifetime of running. A'Yark could flee now, and live. But not the rest.

And A'Yark had sent A'Deen to join them. The last surviving son. The end of the line.

Many lines are ending. A'Yark cursed the pain and dashed up the hill.

"You got 'em! You got 'em!"

Orrin's face beamed as he clicked off the comlink. The skyhopper had led them well, its operator calling down the locations of the Tuskens below. Further confirmation came from the Tuskens' futile blasterfire into the air, useless attempts to bring the three-winged vessel down.

A volcanic coulee in the foothills of the Jundland Wastes, Hanter's Gorge twisted from its wide opening back around two corners. There, it branched off into a dozen steep staircases, most too tall even for a Wookiee to scale. But the eastern and western walls of the canyon were level on top—and the settlers had something the Tuskens didn't: eyes in the air. The Tuskens had walked into a death chamber.

"Hang back from the edge," Orrin ordered the settlers parked nearby. There was no sense drawing fire. "Wait until they try to climb out. Then take 'em."

It was already happening. Atop an escarpment jutting into the gorge, another group of settlers was already firing downward, picking off Tuskens like insects on a wall. Orange blasts peppered the cliff face around the nomads. One after another, they howled and fell. More settlers—he recognized Jabe and Veeka among them—fired on those who hit the ground.

Cheers went up to Orrin's left as the scene repeated farther up the canyon. Orrin had been reluctant to make a sortie so soon after the oasis attack, but he realized now it was the thing to do. The people needed it. The locals wouldn't feel the same about the Claim or the Settlers' Call without something to cauterize the wound. The attack deserved an answer.

No, this had to happen. And as he casually walked toward the edge, rifle raised, he was surprised how good it felt. He wasn't alone; he saw the same buoyant spirit in the faces of those around him. Several he recognized as neighbors from the east who'd gone to bury the bodies of Cliegg Lars's posse, years earlier. He couldn't imagine what they'd seen that day. Few had ever talked about it since. Some had wanted to retaliate then, but they understood that going on a hunt so far from territory they knew was a recipe for disaster.

Orrin thought it did something to a person to walk away from a scene like that. You could hide and tell yourself you were doing the right thing, but any blood a human had would turn to dust. Or acid. For them, this moment was more than right.

It was *necessary.*

He crouched as he reached the edge. Such caution *wasn't* necessary. No return fire came from the floor of the gorge. Dozens of rag-wrapped warriors ran this way and that, some abandoning their gaffi sticks and guns as they sought pathways out of the death zone.

What a dumb bunch, Orrin thought. He'd been afraid they'd gotten smarter when they attacked the oasis. An improbable concept, to be sure; couldn't be much intelligence attached to bandaging one's head and living in the desert. But Dannar's Claim was the center of defense for all the lands surrounding the Pika Oasis, and hadn't they attacked the tower with the siren? Watching the savages scuffle to survive now, he decided it was random chance. Plug-eye might have some sense, but the rest of the Tuskens were of low quality.

Orrin knelt and set to work lowering their quantity. A

slight-looking raider was high on the far rise, scrambling up a rocky incline toward a gap. Orrin sighted the bandit and fired. The shot struck the Tusken in the center of his back, throwing him across the other side of the crest and out of sight.

"Was that Pluggy?" his neighbor asked.

"Too tall. But we'll sort 'em out later," Orrin said. He clucked. "They're wearing their death-shrouds, folks. Put them in the ground!"

Annileen gasped.

From the western side of the gorge, she and Ben had ridden up a spiraling, pebbled approach to a notch in the hillside. Creeping up the shattered rock incline, she'd heard the shots echoing all throughout the canyon. Now, lying on her stomach, she saw everything.

"They're . . . they're being massacred."

Ben, a few meters behind her, said nothing.

"The Tuskens, I mean," Annileen said, looking back over her shoulder at him. "They're being massacred."

"I know," Ben said. He was kneeling, his eyes closed. He seemed to have a headache. From the suns or the sounds, or the whole day? Annileen didn't know. He seemed to have gone to that dark place again—the place that his trips to the Claim had helped him escape. But she could feel a headache coming herself—especially when she spied Jabe, happily blasting away in the shooting gallery alongside his friends.

She shook her head. There was no reaching Jabe's location from here, but he wasn't in any danger, and neither were she and Ben. She stood, intending to try to yell to her son. But muscles that had been tensed since the Tuskens arrived at the Claim suddenly became jelly. Feeling the wind leaving her, she fell to her knees, eyes still focused on Jabe.

Ben joined her at the lookout point. Kneeling beside her, he spoke, his tones low and measured. "How does this make you feel? Given what the Tuskens did to Dannar. And to your store."

"Bad." Annileen closed her eyes, not realizing why she'd answered that way. And then she said it again. "*Bad.*"

Ben lowered his head. For a moment, she thought she heard him say, *"Good."*

A'Yark leapt, cape blousing as boots hit the ground. Up from the gully, another warrior cowered beneath an overhang. Seeing A'Yark, the terrified warrior crept out, quivering.

Not my son. A'Yark simply pointed to the short rise, behind. Another coward, another lost fool who didn't deserve saving. But there'd be time for recriminations later.

A blaster shot struck the nearby rock face. Throbbing feet again went into motion. A'Yark knew the gorge, and its places to hide. A'Deen would be somewhere. A'Deen, who had listened, and not fled. Listened, and gone to find the others.

A'Yark heard more Tusken voices over the rise. There was still a chance.

"That's a speedy one," Mullen said, watching his father shoot.

"Yep." Orrin couldn't keep a bead on the Tusken, but it hardly mattered. One Sand Person would hop out of his rifle sights, and another would dart back in, begging to be scorched.

Blaster bolts everywhere, all heading in one direction. This was one of the great battles, Orrin thought.

Centuries earlier, Alkhara, a researcher-turned-bandit, had turned on his Tusken allies in the Great Mesra Plateau, wiping them all out. Scores of Tuskens had been slain more than a decade earlier, caught up in a battle between Hutts. No one counted bodies those times; of the former, only the legend existed. Orrin was a farmer, not a general, but he had a feeling the Comet Run Day Battle would be high on the list of Tusken takedowns of all time.

It was dizzying. Lowering his rifle, his eyes went from one corpse to another to another. So many it began to give him pause. "Too much," he said to his son, under his breath.

A fellow farmer overheard him and laughed. "What, are you boys afraid we'll put the Settlers' Call out of business?"

Mullen shot his father an anxious look.

"No," Orrin said, raising his voice. "There'll always be Sandies behind every rock in the Wastes."

He went back to his crouch and scanned the nooks in the opposing rock face. Tracing a tumble-down upward, he saw movement. His finger brushed the trigger for half an instant before his mind registered what he'd seen.

"Annie?"

Mullen stepped up beside him as Orrin stood and pointed. They passed Mullen's macrobinoculars back and forth. It was Annileen, all right, Orrin saw.

And Ben. Again.

"They're just sitting there," Mullen said. "Don't they want a piece of this?"

Orrin looked back and cracked a smile. "Not everyone's a fighter."

Annileen turned back toward the speeder bike, hovering at the foot of the rocky stair. There wasn't much else she could do, she thought. Orrin would get Jabe home. And there was so much to take care of back at the store. Her shoulders sinking, she looked at Ben. "My guests are gone. I'm sure we could use a hand on cleanup if you wanted to stay—"

"I really should fetch Rooh and go home."

"Fine." She didn't try to argue. She started down the hill, past enormous boulders, toward the vehicle.

She didn't get there. A tall Tusken emerged from behind a great rock, gaderffii clutched overhead in both hands. For a moment, she stood motionless, too startled to move.

The Tusken did the same, recognizing her. *"Ena'grosh!"*

Annileen felt Ben's arm touch hers from behind—and then the world went flying around her. In the next second, Ben was standing where she had been, arms raised and grappling with the Tusken for control of the great weapon. Brown and tan capes spiraled in a stumbling dance across the broken ground, boots just missing Annileen where she had fallen.

She reached out, hoping to grab the Tusken's boot and trip him. But in the confusion, she caught Ben instead, sending him off balance. The Tusken surged forward in anger, forcing Ben backward. Knocked to the ground, Ben clung to the gaderffii with both hands, pushing up against the weight of the attacker now trying to crush him.

Scrambling to her knees, Annileen suddenly remembered the one thing she'd brought with her besides Ben and the speeder bike. Ripping the blaster from her holster, she stumbled toward the Tusken, preparing a point-blank shot—

—only to see the raider suddenly go limp, a deadweight. Ben heaved at the gaderffii and the figure rolled over, and over again, tumbling down the incline toward the speeder.

Annileen reached for Ben. "Are you all right?"

"I'm fine," he said, brushing himself off. "But I think our friend was almost dead when he got to me."

Keeping her pistol pointed at the body, Annileen slowly approached. The Tusken's robes were singed, the result of a precision blaster rifle shot. "Dying? But he tried to kill you."

"He made one last effort," Ben said, bringing the warrior's weapon downhill.

Annileen looked back at Ben in disbelief. Calm as usual.

Ben passed her and knelt next to the Tusken's body. "Yes," he said, examining the corpse. "Dead for sure. And young, too. Probably Jabe's age."

Annileen's eyes widened. She had never looked closely at a Sand Person. One didn't want to linger around them too long—as she'd just experienced!—and there wasn't much to see. The wrappings, robes, and cape all hid the figure within. But she could see it now as Ben rolled the Tusken over. The warrior's frame was slight, like her boy's.

"Jabe's age," she said, staring at Ben skeptically. "People, just like us?"

"No, that's not the lesson here." He looked up at her. "You wanted to be an exobiology student. The galaxy is full of creatures that are nothing like us at all. We can try to understand them, and we should. But even if we accept that they're doing what comes naturally, one is not beholden to comply when the sarlacc asks for dinner."

Annileen chuckled for the first time since that afternoon, in the store. But the breath of relief that followed wasn't fully out of her lungs before she saw another figure, peeking over the northern ridge at her. The sight froze her in place.

"Plug-eye," she said, recognizing the face from earlier.

"And company," Ben said, gesturing west and south. All the survivors were here, it seemed, lurking over the hillsides. Heads bobbed up and disappeared—as did gaderffii and blaster rifles.

Annileen started toward the speeder bike. Ben rose and stopped her. "No," he said. "They'll shoot us just as the posse shot at them."

The posse! Annileen looked back at the rise to the east. She and Ben would be targeted for sure trying to scramble up there—and none of Orrin's group knew they were even here.

There was motion beyond the hills. "They're regrouping. Probably making sure we're alone," he said, lowering his voice. "Stay calm and follow my lead."

She looked at him, startled. "To do *what*?"

"A little exobiology experiment," he said, kneeling beside the dead Tusken. "Quick. Give me a hand!"

CHAPTER NINETEEN

THIS IS CRAZY! THIS IS CRAZY!

Annileen shivered in the afternoon suns, oblivious to the heat. Fear had long since turned her blood to ice, her muscles to stone. Still, Ben walked, so she did, too.

They walked on either side of the hovering speeder bike, each holding a handlebar. The dead warrior's gaderffii stick was propped across the bars, in front of them at chest level, as they pushed the vehicle forward. Slumped over the seat lay the body of the Tusken raider, half hanging where Ben had placed it.

She'd thought Ben insane when he'd lifted the stinking corpse from the ground, and had raised her voice to object when he hefted it atop the bike. He'd quickly shushed her. The Tusken survivors were out there, probably looking down at them. The fact they hadn't attacked yet, Ben had whispered, meant they were figuring out whether Ben and Annileen were alone. But it was just a matter of time. So he had started walking the bike toward the northern rise.

Now Annileen saw them all on the other side of the hill. Plug-eye knelt, weapon in hand, above seven Tusken survivors. The warriors had taken refuge in a blowout: a hollow formed by the wind rushing and eddying against the slopes leading toward the gorge. Lying prone in its shallow recesses, their tan capes blended in with the sand, protecting them from the eyes of whoever was in the skyhopper.

Annileen looked up, worried. She hadn't seen the flier in a while. Maybe it needed refueling, or the posse no longer required it. Annileen sure needed it now. The Sand People watched as she and Ben approached—some looking at them, some looking up. *They know it,* she thought, breath catching in her throat. *They know we're alone.*

"You're not alone," Ben said.

In the sandy indentation a dozen meters away, Plug-eye rose. Others stood, too, watchful of their leader. Unconsciously, Annileen slipped her right hand from the handlebar and felt for the blaster, holstered at her hip.

"Don't," Ben said.

A'Yark stared, dumbfounded. Surely the warrior's single remaining good eye was failing now. The humans—Hairy Face and the Airshaper—were walking steadily toward them.

The Airshaper had no sirens here, no trickery. Did she have such power that she could walk brazenly into the Tuskens' midst? Even if she did, such presumption had to be punished. Even hunted, even terrified, the Tuskens would exact revenge—

"A'Yark!" a warrior said. "Look!"

A'Yark looked between the humans and recognized the limp form on the vehicle.

A'Deen.

* * *

Annileen forgot Ben's warning when the one-eyed warrior snarled. She released the handlebar and drew her blaster. The Tusken started toward them. Behind, more Sand People rose from the depression. But before Annileen could shoot, Ben moved in front of the bike and into the line of fire.

Only then did Annileen realize that Ben had the dead boy's weapon in his hands. Ben raised the gaderffii— and then did something that astonished Annileen and the Tuskens both.

He placed it on the ground.

Slowly, so the Tuskens could clearly see what he was doing.

Plug-eye, who had closed half the distance to them in the previous moments, stopped.

Ben kept his eyes on the Tuskens as he released the weapon and backed up. "I'm showing," he said, just above a murmur, "that I haven't taken a trophy."

He took another step back and gave the hoverbike a gentle shove with his hand. Annileen, startled, clutched in vain at the seat as it passed.

The vehicle floated gingerly across the distance to the lead Tusken, who grabbed at it. In a hurried move, Plug-eye yanked the body from the speeder bike and knelt over it, while the other warriors stood behind.

Annileen watched as the hated marauder examined the body. Something was off. The crease of the cloth, the shape of the kneeling figure. But mostly, the way Plug-eye touched the face of the dead youth—

"She's a female," Annileen whispered to Ben. *"She's his mother."*

A'Yark looked up at the sound of the Airshaper's voice and howled.

Who cares if the settlers hear? Fury charged through A'Yark's tired limbs. Many foolish warriors had died this day. But A'Deen had acted as a Tusken!

A'Yark bellowed and lifted her son's gaderffii. Behind her, the others raised their rifles. The Airshaper had caused this. Her existence had compelled A'Yark to lead her people into this great massacre. *Who cares if the Airshaper has a blaster, or great powers? She will pay!*

Before A'Yark could take another step, Hairy Face darted in front of the Airshaper, his brown robe parting as he moved. Metal flashed at the human's waist, catching the afternoon suns.

A weapon? No matter! A'Yark charged—

—and stopped, looking again at the short metal rod hanging from a clip in the folds of the man's cloak. The Airshaper could not see it, but A'Yark could. And A'Yark remembered seeing such a thing before, years earlier.

"Sharad," A'Yark said, pointing at the man's half-hidden weapon. *"Sharad Hett."*

Now it was Ben's turn to look stupefied. Annileen couldn't see what had made the Tusken woman stop her advance. But whatever she had just said had apparently mystified Ben.

"Sharad?" Ben gently closed the folds of his cloak, suddenly seeming to understand. "You knew Sharad Hett."

Behind, a couple of the warriors started to move again. The war leader snarled at them. An argument ensued. Ben listened, keenly interested.

"A'Yark," Ben finally said, daring to interrupt. "That is your name? A'Yark!"

* * *

Hearing her name in a settler's mouth made A'Yark flinch. Names were precious things to Tuskens. The humans gave names to animals, so they would come when called. No settler had the right to call a Tusken anywhere. Not if he wanted to live.

And yet, Hairy Face was something else. He carried the blade that made light, just like Sharad Hett. The wizardly warrior who had come to live with their people, so many years before—a being wielding the same magic powers A'Yark had ascribed to the Airshaper.

One of A'Yark's younger companions started forward again. He had not known Sharad, not understood the human's power. Before A'Yark could say anything, Hairy Face raised his hand.

"You don't want to hurt us," he said, using the strange settler words. A'Yark understood them, barely. She had learned the talk from her adopted sister, K'Sheek—and Hett, whom her sister had married.

The young warrior did not know the human words. And yet, he said them now, in the Tusken tongue. *"I don't want to hurt you."*

"There has been enough killing," Hairy Face said.

"There has been enough killing," the warrior repeated.

A'Yark gawked. Those were words no Tusken had ever said in any language. There was no doubt. A'Yark realized her mistake. The Airshaper hadn't saved herself from being crushed out in the desert that day. It had been Hairy Face with the power, all along.

A'Yark recalled the settler building from earlier, and the bodies on the floor. The blows dealt her kin had not resembled blaster marks—and Sand People surely knew those. A'Yark hadn't thought anything of it then. But now?

"Stay back," A'Yark told her companions. "I will explain later. Stay back—and beware."

The Tuskens shifted anxiously but complied, moving back toward the depression.

"Ben?" the Airshaper asked Hairy Face now, frightened and puzzled.

"*Ben,*" A'Yark said, looking again at the silvery weapon, barely visible within his cloak. "You are Ben."

Annileen had thought she was past the point of shock. But hearing Basic words in the braying voice of a Sand Person was yet another stunner.

Ben simply nodded. "You would know the words, wouldn't you?" he said, carefully. His voice was soothing, as smooth as when he'd spoken earlier to A'Yark's companions. Somehow, they'd understood—and complied.

Annileen gawked. *Who is this guy?*

"Perhaps you can understand this," Ben said, pointing to the body behind A'Yark. "This woman—*Annileen*—did not shoot your son. You know the burns. That mark was from a long-range rifle."

A'Yark did not turn to look. "One settler killed. All settlers killed."

"You are mistaken."

This wasn't something to debate, Annileen thought. She'd certainly shot at plenty of Tuskens earlier, at the Claim. Ben seemed to want to defuse the immediate tension, at least with his words. His body remained poised, ready to act—although Annileen didn't know what an unarmed man could do against the Tusken woman and her band.

The Tusken woman. Annileen looked at A'Yark, seen before through a mist of fire retardant and by others only amid panic. As far as Annileen had ever heard, Tuskens had distinct gender roles. Males fought; women tended the banthas. The few images she'd seen showed Tusken females dressed in even bulkier outfits, their hoods pulled down over large faceplates. But the one-eyed Tusken before them was outfitted as all the others, save for the lack of bandolier.

Ben pointed to the suns, creeping closer to the heights of the western Jundland. He spoke in simple terms, matching the Tusken's. "You struck. The settlers struck. The day ends. We will depart." He nodded to the east, where hooting and hollering had commenced beyond the hillside. "We depart, and you depart," he added ominously, "while you can."

A'Yark looked down at the gaderffii stick in her hands. It had belonged to her father, and it had not saved him. Nor had it saved her son. It was right to plunge its point into humans, to crush them with its bulk, to grind their bones with its flanges. Hairy Face—Ben—might have the power to kill her. She would die, but the others would live, and they would exact a price.

But then A'Yark thought again of the magic weapon the man carried, and the last time she had seen one. She wanted to know more, but knowledge could not come from a dead wizard. And if the human cheers over the ridge meant the rest of the band was gone, then A'Yark and the survivors could not linger.

A'Yark turned back to A'Deen. Handing her gaderffii to another, she heaved the corpse from the ground.

"We depart, and you depart," A'Yark said. "While you can."

"Forty-eight," Mullen said.

"Forty-eight!" Orrin looked down at the canyon

floor as he descended the rocky stair. "That the head count?"

Mullen gave a laugh, a rare guttural thing that had always made his father cringe. "I can't make any guarantees about body parts," Mullen said. "Some of the Tuskies that fell hit pretty hard."

Orrin surveyed the scene. It was truly a mess. The trail of Tusken corpses wound around the corner of the gorge and out of sight. He whistled. "I didn't think this many hit us at the oasis!"

"There were some in camps east of the Claim that Jayla Jee saw," Mullen said, referring to their friend in the skyhopper. "I think they were in reserve to take captives. But when the Tuskens at the Claim fled, they all went."

Most of the vigilantes had already made their way down here, making sure none of the injured Sand People would come back to haunt them. Orrin's daughter was here, too, trying her best to make her way through the organic obstacle course at the foot of the eastern rock face.

"Disgusting," Veeka said, holding her nose. "Let's get out of here."

Before Orrin could respond, a shrill beep resounded from his pocket. "Just a second," he said, pulling out the comlink. "How's our recon, Sky One?"

"All clear, Master Gault," crackled the voice of the skyhopper pilot. Orrin had directed her to complete a wide circle. "And it looks like you were right," Jayla said. "Annie Calwell and that drifter *were* here—but they've ridden off to the west."

The west? Orrin's eyebrow rose. West to Ben's place, maybe? The Claim was back to the north. He thought to go after them, but then an approaching group of celebrants reminded him of what needed to come next.

Rifle-toting Jabe was among them, receiving backslaps from the older settlers. Orrin clicked off the comlink and smiled. "You get any, son?"

"I did, sir. Or I think so."

"Well, pick out a prize so we can go."

Beaming, Jabe stepped toward the twin tangles of metal. The vigilantes had piled the gaffi sticks and rifles separately. The boy looked back at Orrin. "You think the one that got my dad is here?"

"Great suns, boy! I don't know. Just pick your favorite." While Jabe deliberated, Orrin edged back to confer with Mullen. "We need any of this junk?"

"No, we've got plenty."

Jabe reached into the gaderffii pile and found a silvery specimen, shorter than the others and relatively clean. Veeka laughed. "Just your size, runt." The others laughed at the blushing kid before surrounding him, offering congratulations.

Orrin looked back at the killing ground. The Tuskens deserved every bit of this, surely. His boy Varan. Dannar Calwell. Even that Lars woman—all had gotten some justice today. But Orrin understood that squaring accounts here made for a change to the rest of the balance sheet.

"Will Zedd be ready to go again soon?" he whispered to his son.

"I wouldn't count on it," Mullen said. "Doc Mell only had a second with him, but he said he could be out for a month this time. Maybe more." He raised a hairy eyebrow. "Why, are you afraid this thing today will mess us up?"

"I don't know," Orrin said. He turned back to the crowd and locked eyes on Jabe. The boy always looked happy outside the store, but now he was positively over the suns. Jabe spotted Orrin and raised his shiny trophy, earning another cheer from the others.

Orrin smiled back. The boy was really growing up. He joined the applause.

"That's it, folks," he said, stepping into the crowd. "First the racers tried to ruin our good time, and then the Tuskens. Let's get back to the Claim and show 'em we still know how to celebrate!"

CHAPTER TWENTY

WITH CARE, A'YARK PLACED one rock upon another. It was important to select the right mix of stones. The pile had to last for eternity, holding the remains of A'Deen above Tatooine's surface. Tomorrows only mattered to the dead.

A'Yark's clan did not bury their fallen. Nor could they, here in the shadows of The Pillars, where the ground was tough enough to snap off the end of any pick. No, A'Deen would lay atop the bed-altar, protected from wildlife by massiffs, the trained reptilians the Tuskens kept as camp guardians. His battle then would be against the suns—his spirit against theirs.

Eventually, even the most defiant warrior's body would succumb to the wind. Then a new level would be built over his remains, the growing mound providing a tower to support the body of that warrior's sons, or grandsons. But the graves of A'Deen's ancestors were far away, in a different part of the wastes.

So here, in the evening shadows of this misbegotten place, A'Yark silently built a solitary bier for a boy who had been warrior for less than a week. No descendants would join his tower, but his spirit would last as long as the stones of his resting place did. A'Yark chose carefully. It was the work of a mother.

A'Yark was that, and a warrior, as well. The traditional divided roles of the past were a luxury the clan could not afford. There simply weren't enough to fill them. All that had changed after a single dread day thirteen cycles earlier. Today's losses had been bad, but they were nothing compared with what had happened the day the clan battled the Hutts.

The day Sharad Hett died.

A'Yark stopped sorting and wondered. It was safe, now, to pause and reflect—as safe as it was going to get. She thought about Ben's weapon, and visualized the owner of the other she'd seen. Sharad Hett was the *ootman*, the Outlander of local legend—but to A'Yark, he was a real being. He was, in fact, family, because of a different human A'Yark had met first: K'Sheek.

A'Yark had been born as K'Yark, the youngest of six children. When three of her siblings died from plague, her father Yark repopulated his household through a time-honored practice: abduction. K'Sheek, so named by the Tuskens who kidnapped her from a local settlement, was nearly an adult when she came to live with A'Yark's family. A'Yark, still a child, was granted the privilege—too often, a chore—of bestowing on K'Sheek the ways and words of the Tuskens.

In so doing, A'Yark learned some of the soulless breathings the settlers called words. She remembered them well, evidently, as the one called Ben had understood her today. K'Sheek had spoken many human words, most of them sad. Over time, A'Yark realized her new sister had been living as a slave of the humans. Life with the Tuskens was not freedom, because the Tuskens were not free—bound and cursed, as they were, to inhabit the blasted lands. To K'Sheek, pale and miserable, it was almost more horrible than death. A'Yark often expected her to vanish into the wind.

But as a long chain of Tusken torturers had found,

where humans were concerned, fragile bodies often contained durable spirits. Yark allowed both A'Yark and K'Sheek to learn the ways of the warriors. He had assumed, correctly, that K'Sheek would learn their ways faster—and had defended his daughters against all criticism. *There will come a day when all must fight,* he had told the elders. *We are too few.*

While K'Sheek learned the Tusken words, both sisters learned combat. A'Yark saw that humans had great potential, as K'Sheek's talent continually amazed. But something more startling was to come over the horizon from the cities and into the Tusken camp.

A volunteer.

Sharad Hett had ventured willingly into the wastes, bent on suicide—or, rather, on joining the Tuskens, which was much the same thing. A settler taken by force could enter the tribe, as K'Sheek had; but there was an important difference. The Tuskens had chosen K'Sheek. Sharad Hett had presumed much, and had to be broken.

A'Yark's people certainly tried.

But Sharad had survived the punishments and emerged stronger. The elders whispered he had been part of some ancient and foreign army, suffused with powers from angry spirits. And Sharad carried a great and magical weapon, something no common settler carried. A shining green blade of energy.

In time, Sharad earned the garb and gaderffii of a Tusken, showing his face to the sky for the last time. He took fellow human K'Sheek as his mate—a match not of convenience, but affection—and together, they had a son, A'Sharad. But K'Sheek had not lived to see their child grow. Might against the enemy was one thing, but Tatooine posed threats of its own. Not long after her son's birth, K'Sheek disappeared into a sandstorm.

Vanished into the wind—but A'Yark had not grieved over the loss of her sister. The presence of the child had bound Sharad to the Tuskens for life. Freely using the terrible powers and weapon at his disposal, Sharad became a war leader, training his son alongside him.

A'Yark saw little of the humans in those times. With her permissive father dead, her lot became that of any other female in the tribe. She took a spouse; she bore children. The group swelled as survivors of other clans joined, and for a time the Tuskens were strong. Under Sharad, structure had replaced chaos. Leadership, something every Tusken defied on principle, seeped into practice as Sharad could have his sway on any issue.

They feared him, yes. But they also followed. Sharad had never believed the Tuskens were a cursed people. With such a warrior—a *wizard,* really—the Tuskens could escape their fate and become mighty indeed.

But that, too, was presumption. For other forces existed on Tatooine, more powerful than any single warrior. The greatest of the Hutts, Jabba, had for some reason manipulated Tusken tribes across the Jundland into an all-out war with the settlers—a fight that had claimed the life of A'Yark's oldest son, just six cycles old. An answer had to be given, and Sharad had led her clan and others into battle against the Hutts. But Jabba brought many thralls to battle that day, and countless Tusken warriors died, including her spouse, Deen. Sharad had died, too. Even Sharad's son vanished, although no Tusken ever found the body.

A bad omen, and it told true. The makeshift Tusken alliance forged by Sharad collapsed, with the surviving clans melting away into the hillsides. A'Yark, a mother holding two little children, found herself forced to hold together what remained of her tribe. The few warriors that had survived were damaged, physically and spiritually; able to carry gaderffii, but unable to command others. Sharad had left no successor.

A'Yark hadn't sought the role of war leader. There

was enough to do, simply making sure the clan ate. But when no one rose, she did. It had once been her father's tribe, after all; they had seen her ride with warriors before. And more than ever, her decimated people understood the meaning of their creed: *Whoever has two hands can hold a gaderffii.*

Losses continued in the decade after Sharad's death. A'Yark had shared in them, losing another son—and later an eye, taken by infection after a wound. The crystal that now sat in its place had been a gift from Sharad. But the greater blow was to the clan's spirit. When a mightier band of Tuskens vanished literally overnight several years earlier, leaving just the remnants of their camp behind, her group grew increasingly timid. A'Yark had tried to revive their spirits by example and, later, by daring exploits like the morning raids. After today, though, such things wouldn't be possible. The shaper had no more clay to spare.

A'Yark stared back between the stone towers to the tents. Her people wandered, wraithlike, as if waiting for a final blow. There was no way to prevent such a stroke. Only seven males of warrior age remained: those she had brought from the gorge. And they lived only because their cowardice had driven them to run the fastest.

Of all Sand People, A'Yark had no objections to arming the rest of the clan. But even with a rifle placed in the hands of every mother, elder, and youngling, the prospects were poor. The Tuskens didn't train; all experience came from combat. They would die before they learned anything.

No, it was pointless to resist. The clan would dissolve, its members drifting into bands where they would have no station or standing. Unless—

A'Yark looked up, startled. *Yes.* When her people had been desperate before, Sharad had used his powers to give them purpose. In fact, he had brought larger groups to his side. With a similar leader, the Yark clan might become more than the rump of a once-mighty tribe. A'Yark's group could become the nucleus of a second united front, crushing the settlers once and for all—with another Sharad.

With "Ben."

If Ben was another Sharad, the Tuskens couldn't afford to see him allied with the settlers, to be sure. But what if he could be made to join the Tuskens? He would have to be compelled; he'd already shown violence to her people inside the oasis store. But compelled how?

Ben seemed to want to protect the storekeeper, but there was no chance of using the woman for leverage. Another foray against the compound was out of the question. Humans were odd creatures, forming attachments to irrelevant beings and things. Perhaps there was someone else Ben cared for on Tatooine that he would do anything to protect.

Even if it meant becoming a Tusken, himself.

Eye wide open, A'Yark resolved to find out. Her exhausted body coursed again with energy and will. If a pressure point existed, A'Yark would discover it—and exploit it.

But first, her youngest child had to be put to bed.

CHAPTER TWENTY-ONE

BEN HAD SAID LITTLE on the way home from the gorge. Annileen had been the opposite, asking one question after another as their speeder bike moved into the lengthening shadows of the western Jundland.

> *What happened in the store with Ulbreck?*
> *What was the name that Plug-eye—A'Yark—*
> *said to you?*
> *And how did you recognize it, especially when*
> *you're new to Tatooine?*

He'd never answered, acting as if he couldn't hear over the whine of the bike. And maybe he couldn't. Annileen had driven slower and slower, hoping to disarm him of that excuse. It hadn't worked. "You're losing altitude," he'd said.

Well, I won't argue that. Annileen felt the weight of the day on her shoulders as she coasted toward Ben's hovel.

"Here we are," she said, activating the brakes. Earlier, near the gorge, they'd briefly debated going back to the Claim so he could pick up his eopie. But night was falling, and even with the local Tuskens seemingly at bay, it was still Tatooine. Other predators moved in the dark.

"Thank you," he said, climbing off the hovering bike. She looked up at his house. He'd made a little headway in cleaning up the surrounding area, but not much. "I'll run in at dawn tomorrow to fetch Rooh," he said. "You won't even know I'm there."

Annileen climbed off the vehicle and followed. "You know, my offer still stands if you want to save yourself a walk. My guest room's empty tonight. I'd love to have you—"

"*No!*" Then, seemingly embarrassed, he adopted a calmer expression. "I mean, I'm sure your family and store will need all your attention after today. You don't need company underfoot."

"I'll have it, whether I want it or not," she said, remembering the usual after-action routine of the vigilantes. Would they really expect to party in a Tusken-ravaged store?

Yeah, probably, she thought.

"I'll leave you to it, then," Ben said. He began walking toward his house. "I hope your patron is doing better."

Annileen blanched as she recalled the sight of the injured Rodian. "Poor Bohmer," she said. "I was thinking about him earlier, too. He always sat there, staring. I never knew why. But I just imagined such *sadness* in his life, to make him sit there. For him to get hurt like that—"

Ben stopped and looked back. "It wasn't sadness."

"What do you mean?"

"Well, I saw him today—and on my first trip, there, as well." Ben clasped his hands together. "I could tell. That wasn't sadness. That was *contentment*."

Annileen stared. "How do you know?"

"It's just a feeling," he said, blue eyes looking off into the setting suns. "But I've seen sadness before, in all kinds of faces. Bohmer was content. The drink you brought him in the morning, the table he sat at—it was his place in the universe."

"But he got hurt there—"

"Protecting the place he loved. I think he'll be okay with that." Ben turned and began walking again up the hill in silence.

Annileen thought back to Ben talking about loss, earlier in the day. He was struggling with something, she could tell—something pretty bad. But at the same time, he seemed so centered. Centered, in the middle of nowhere.

She fumbled for words before finally settling on three. "Who *are* you?"

He laughed. "Ben. We've been over this."

No joke. Annileen shook her head. "Freelance philosopher of the desert, doctoring and rescuing!"

"I don't think it happened that way. You'll remember it differently, later."

Annileen stood at the foot of the hill and put her hands on her hips. "Well, you're wasting your talent out here. Someone like you—you ought to be *doing* something." She paused, before going ahead with the impetuous addition: "Or you ought to have a family to watch over."

Ben paused. He looked over his shoulder at her, the little smile back on his face. "Well, you never know. Perhaps I already *have* a family to watch over."

Annileen rolled her eyes. She turned and climbed onto her speeder bike.

"Oh," Ben called suddenly. He reached into the folds of his cloak and retrieved something rectangular from his pocket. "I just realized, in the commotion—I still have your datapad."

"Keep it," Annileen said, grinding the throttle. "Souvenir of a crazy day."

"But the safari. Your application—"

"I'm not going anywhere," she said. "There's a new species to study right here." She released the brake and soared away.

As stressful days for Annileen went, this one already ranked only behind Jabe's difficult breech birth. And it wasn't over.

After Ben's, she stopped by Doc Mell's place. Learning that Bohmer was sedated and resting in Bestine, she returned home, anticipating a mess of a store—and another war, when she found Jabe. He'd skipped out on work, taken up with trashy friends, and defied her by going after Tuskens. Twice! It was one thing to arrive butt-first into the world, but Jabe was going for the endurance record.

She wasn't surprised to see lights on inside the Claim, with landspeeders scattered about. What did surprise her was the Claim itself, once she stepped through the door.

Yes, there were drunkards celebrating; more than she'd ever seen in the place before. But the store itself was spotless. The gun counter and shelves had been repaired, the nasty smears on the floor were gone, and products were back on their shelves reasonably close to where they belonged. The smell was even gone.

Raising a drink from within a gathering of mostly male revelers, Leelee smiled at her. "Everyone who didn't go with the posse pitched in," she said. "It gave us something to do."

Annileen looked around, suspicious. She didn't trust anyone to be in her store without a Calwell present. "Everything's still here?"

"We might have fed ourselves a little off the shelves—but it's a small price, no?"

Annileen walked up to her friend. Even for a Zeltron,

Leelee looked flushed; the party had been going for a while. Annileen recognized her friend's husband, Waller, in the mix, telling his own tales from the assault on the Tuskens. "Who's with your kids?"

"The guard droids," Waller called out, toasting with an empty mug. "Plug-eye's finished. The droids are all we need!"

"All we need *tonight*," Orrin said, clearing his throat loudly from behind the bar. He was a startling sight, having donned his spare set of fancy city clothes from the office—and an apron over them. Host and bartender, he refilled glasses with a smile. He spotted Annileen and nodded to the empty bottles. "I'm keeping track."

"No, you're not." Annileen approached. "Give me whatever's left," she said, settling wearily on a stool at her own bar.

Orrin was already pouring. "You were out there, weren't you?" He laughed. "Annie, you're a marvel. What was it Dannar said? You can't spell adrenaline without Annileen."

"Dannar never could spell," she said, taking the glass. "That's why he hired me." She downed the drink in three seconds and deposited the glass on the bar in front of him. "Now what did you think you were doing, taking Jabe out there?"

Orrin's smile crumpled for a moment before a young voice saved him. "Don't blame him, Mom. It wasn't his idea!"

Annileen glared as Jabe stepped in from outside. The boy paused before Orrin. "Wyle Ulbreck's gone, sir."

"Blast," Orrin said, shaking his head. "I'd hoped to rub the big victory in his face." He looked around the room and raised his voice. "Everyone knows the Settlers' Call works now, right? This place is the proof!"

A ragged, drunken cheer went up. Annileen ignored it.

She slid off the stool and blocked Jabe from reaching the happy crowd. "Jabe. You have to stop."

"Stop what?"

"I'm too tired for the list," she said, clutching at his shirt. "But let's start with the gorge. You were killing!"

"Killing Tuskens!" The boy waved his hands theatrically. "They're not civilized, Mom. They're not *anything*!"

"You don't know that," Annileen said. "They're not womp rats that you can shoot for fun!"

Jabe wrenched away from her grasp. "They killed Dad. They tried to kill *all* of us, today!"

"I know, but—"

"But nothing. I at least *did* something." Anger flared in the young man's eyes. "Did *you* do anything after Dad died?"

Annileen froze, staring at her child. He looked more like Dannar every day, even as he acted like someone she'd never met. "I did do something after he died," she said, finally. "I opened the store the next day." In a chillier tone, she added: "Like he would have wanted."

Jabe pushed past his mother. She didn't stop him. He paused at the bar to speak to Orrin in a loud voice, for the benefit of his mother. "With Zedd laid up, you've got an opening on your lead vaporator team. I'm available."

"No, he's not," Annileen called out from behind him. Drying his hands on a dishtowel, Orrin smiled awkwardly at the boy. "She calls the tune, son. Sorry." Orrin nodded to Annileen, who didn't respond. A moment later, Orrin leaned over and spoke in lower tones. "There's other ways you can help me, I'm sure."

Annileen threw up her hands. "You can help him by cleaning up whatever's left of this place tonight. I'm done." Grabbing a pre-packed meal from behind the counter—and an open bottle—she pushed past her son and trudged through the crowd to her living quarters.

The sound from the celebration continued to reverberate throughout the Claim and into her household most of the night, but she didn't hear much of it. She ate wearily and dragged herself to bed. As her head hit the pillow, Annileen had one last thought: that she had not seen Kallie since her return. But her body rejected any further worries for one day, and her mind surrendered itself to sleep.

Meditation

I don't know what you can see from where you are, Qui-Gon, but I doubt you missed today's trip.

No, once again, I wasn't intending for it to be a big production. You don't have to tell me what our mutual teacher used to say. I don't crave excitement or adventure—or rather, I crave them not, as he would have put it. I was going to the store for water, on a day when nobody was supposed to be there. That's all.

I thought my tricky moment for the day was running into the little old man from the incident at Anchorhead—he seems to be a regular at the Claim. When he didn't remember me, I thought I was free.

Instead, I got into a riot and a range war. And I forgot all about the water. And my eopie.

Will there be a galactic incident every time I want to get out of the house? Because I can stay home, in that case. Really, it won't be a problem!

Then again, it was certainly good I was there, given what happened at the store. I'm not so sure about the second part of the afternoon, though— heading off after Jabe. There wasn't any stopping what occurred there. It's so difficult seeing things like that and doing nothing.

But I guess I'd rather see, and do nothing, than not see at all. I'm missing so much of what's going on in other places. I can't live blindfolded. It's not really the Kenobi way.

Speaking of what I saw, I'm not so sure I liked the side I saw of Orrin Gault today. He had to save face after the compound was attacked; that much I understand. But he wields an awful lot of power here. These people listen to him—he must know that. There's responsibility that goes along with that.

Maybe I'm being too harsh. He acted the way he did because his family and friends were in danger. But we both know where that particular excuse can lead.

The Tuskens—well, that was another surprise. But maybe it shouldn't have been. I'd met the man A'Yark knew, long ago, and heard the story about him later on. I'm straining to remember more details about that. Maybe later.

Then there's Annileen.

I was tempted to call her "the Intrepid Annileen" just now—because she seems to be able to deal with whatever horror this planet can imagine. That's what I need to become: absolutely familiar with all the dangers here. She takes them in stride. Not because she's fearless, but because she knows she has to go on, to take care of all the people in her life.

That's not a bad role model to have. I guess I can become "the Intrepid Kenobi" if I must.

If I'm going to go on—and we both know I must—I'm going to have to find a way to stop tear-

ing myself up over what happened. There's pain, yes, but a lot of it lately is self-inflicted.

Like this. You see what I'm holding here—again. A last remembrance, I've told myself. But I'm locking it away now. And I would be a lot better off if I put it away once and for all, and tried to go on.

Like Annileen has had to do. I can learn something from her, I think.

And yet, when I think about her, I have to consider . . .

. . . wait.

Hold on.

. . .

Someone's here!

CHAPTER TWENTY-TWO

"*KENOBI.*"

Annileen rubbed her eyes. "What?"

"Kenobi," Kallie said, beaming across a cup of blue milk. "That's his name."

"What?" Annileen glowered at her daughter. Annileen had risen at the usual deathly hour, remembering Kallie's absence from the night before. But the girl was here, now, at the breakfast table in the family quarters. Wide awake—and positively quivering with excitement.

"It's his name," Kallie said.

"Name? Whose name?"

"Ben's name!"

Annileen stepped forward. "How do you know that?"

Jabe called from the larder. "She went to his house!"

Annileen turned toward the counter, where Jabe had thankfully prepared her high-test meltdown caf. She downed a swig and turned back to the table. "Now. *What?*"

"She went to his house," Jabe repeated, bringing a plate to the table. Bleary-eyed, he looked as if he'd slept in his clothes. "Ben's house."

Annileen gawked. "Before I took him home yesterday?"

"No." Kallie dug into her breakfast as if nothing was

wrong. "It was after he got back—while he was there. After you left."

"Wait. You were there at *night*?" Annileen asked.

"Alone," Jabe added, drawing a glare from his sister.

"At night. Alone." Annileen's whole body shook. "With *Ben*?"

Kallie smirked. "Calm down, Mom. Your eyes are going all Rodian on me."

Annileen fought the urge to go outside and scream. Instead, she refilled her cup and sat down at the table beside a snickering Jabe. "All right," she said, rubbing the back of her hand against her forehead. "From the beginning."

Subdued, Kallie explained. "I took the LiteVan out, like you'd said. To get rid of the bodies."

"I meant we'd get Orrin's hands to help do that—not for you to go alone!"

"It was horrible, Mom. The smell was driving the dewbacks berserk. And it wasn't good for me, either." Kallie's small nose crinkled. "Once I got out there, I just unhooked the hoverpallet and left it. Believe me, you'll never want to use it again."

One more expense. Annileen frowned. "And then?"

"Then I swung past Hanter's Gorge—but it was all over by then. The landspeeders were leaving. And I saw the two of you, heading for Ben's place. I wanted to make sure you were okay—"

"So you followed us?"

"I tried—but your bike was a lot faster than the LiteVan. When I got there, you must've already left."

"If I was already gone, how did you know you were even at the right place?" Annileen asked.

Kallie pointed behind the counter. "You circled his place on the map the other day after you came home."

"I could've been marking a sarlacc pit to avoid!"

"But you weren't," Kallie said. "And you told me about the curtain on his door."

Annileen scowled. "And you talked to him? I can't believe you bothered him at—"

"Oh, he didn't know I was there," Kallie said. "At least, I think he didn't. I was kind of . . . hanging around outside."

Annileen stood up abruptly, her chair squeaking against the stone floor. "You peeked in on him?"

"I couldn't see much—"

"I don't care!" Annileen looked at the ceiling, mortified. "You invaded the man's privacy?"

Jabe shook his head between bites. "Glad it's not me this time."

Kallie sneered. "Shut up."

"Wait," Annileen said, turning. "You thought *I* was in there, didn't you? In this man's house!"

Kallie blushed. "The thought *did* cross my mind."

"So you listened at his door!"

"It's not a door. It's a curtain. And I didn't stay long," her daughter said.

"How long?"

"A couple of hours."

Annileen gawked. *"A couple of hours?"*

"I needed to make sure you weren't in another room," Kallie said, smiling meekly. "And it got interesting—"

"I don't care how interesting it was," Annileen said. "You could have gotten killed out there at night!"

"But I didn't."

Annileen shook her head. There was never any good answer to that where her kids were concerned. They'd had the safety argument again and again. A danger survived was no danger at all, to hear them tell it.

Moreover, intrusion on this scale was an entirely new entry in the portfolio of her children's misdeeds, and that made the episode all the worse. *What made Kallie think that was acceptable?* Annileen found her chair and let gravity take hold.

Kallie took her mother's vacant expression as a signal to go on. "His name's Kenobi."

"Someone called him that?"

"He called himself that," Kallie said. "I couldn't see who he was talking to—but he said it. He was just sitting there, talking about his day, and the people he'd met, and the Tuskens."

Annileen looked at her with skepticism. "You're not just making this up?" She tried the name out. " 'Ben Kenobi.' " She'd known other customers by the surname over the years, and seen it spelled several different ways on her receipts.

Jabe dabbed up the last of the gravy on his plate. "Lot of Kenobis around. There's the couple near Bildor's Canyon."

"There was that podracer pilot," Kallie interjected, excitedly.

"No! He was a Muun!"

"Please don't start this," Annileen said. "I already have a headache. Just tell me what he said. All of it."

Kallie's smirk returned as she wiped off a blue milk mustache. "I thought you wanted to protect his privacy."

"A little late, now. Speak."

Kallie told, as best she could, what she could remember. "Ben Kenobi" was upset about his trip to the Claim, upset that he kept walking into disruptions. He was troubled by what he'd seen at the Gorge—who wouldn't be, Annileen thought—and he wasn't thrilled with how Orrin had led the assault. Jabe rolled his eyes at that. And then he talked about the Intrepid Annileen.

"And then?" Annileen asked.

"And then, nothing," Kallie said. "He heard me—

or heard something. I ran back over the hill to where I'd left the LiteVan."

Jabe snorted. "Did he come out after you with a big metal cleaver?"

"No!" Kallie shrugged. "Well, if he did, I didn't see." She bit her lip. "But now that I think about it, earlier I did see *something* . . ."

Annileen was almost afraid to ask. "What?"

"Well, he was sitting, like I said, with his back to me. And he was in front of this trunk. And I think he was holding something—something special, I think. He talked about putting it away—and then he did."

Jabe stared. "What was it?"

"If I knew that, I would have told you," Kallie said. "Idiot."

Annileen sat, back underneath the spell. " 'And yet, when I think about her, I have to consider—' " She looked up and sputtered. "What in the Great Pit is *that* supposed to mean? You sure he didn't say any more?"

"Any more about *you*, you mean?"

"Kallie!"

"No," Kallie said, leaning dejectedly with her elbow against the table. "And he didn't say anything at all about *me*."

Jabe smirked. "The ingratitude. After you'd let him save you, and all."

Kallie grumbled. "Yeah!"

Annileen struggled to take it all in. "And you say there was no one else there."

"I don't think there was—but I don't know."

Annileen thought. He could have been speaking to someone on a comm system, yes—although transmissions from the Jundland were often problematic. Or he could have been dictating.

Or he could have that secret family he was talking about. Was that what Kallie had seen him holding—

some possession that reminded him of the family he'd left behind? That might explain some of the sadness that seemed to hang over him at times.

Jabe had another explanation. "He sounds deranged," he said, rising with his dishes. "Crazy kook, sitting in the wilderness, talking to himself."

"You don't know that," Annileen said. "And that crazy kook helped save us here—and helped me track you down to the canyon."

"Where I was in no danger at all," Jabe said, wiping his hands. "I'd worry you're in worse trouble being alone with him."

Annileen looked down. "We weren't very alone when the Tuskens showed up."

"I mean besides that," Jabe said. "What do you know about this guy?"

"Not enough, evidently." Annileen stopped to reflect. After a few moments, she laughed. "Don't you see, Kallie? He heard you. He *knew* you were out there. That was all for your benefit!"

Kallie rose from the table. "Think that if you want. But I think Ben Kenobi thinks about you." She patted her mother on the back as she passed.

Annileen put her head in her hands. "I can't believe this. I've raised a sadist and a voyeur! Are both my children insane?"

Standing in the open doorway with his sister, Jabe answered. "I don't know, Mom. You're the one who took off after the Tuskens with the crazy man."

As her kids headed off to work, Annileen sat motionless at the table. "He's *not* crazy," she said, her face twisting into a frown. "He just . . . *talks to himself*." Setting aside her cup, she decided the matter deserved more thought.

Then she promptly fell asleep in the chair.

CHAPTER TWENTY-THREE

"KING OF THE JUNDLAND!"

Orrin just nodded and waved as the family of four cruised past, cheering him as they departed the oasis. There was no use being modest, now. The vigilantes had won a historic battle the day before, and word had spread across the region. Orrin would see that it reached the Devaronians in Mos Eisley, too. They'd know he'd avenged their partner without delay, and there might yet be hope for the hotel contract.

Even after the late-night celebration, Orrin had risen early in anticipation of starting his good day as soon as possible. So far, it had exceeded his hopes. Everyone around knew this was the day of the week he kept his office hours in the Claim, and many had visited him. The plaudits from his neighbors were nice, but—more important—people he'd intended to make calls on were arriving to subscribe to the Fund's protection services.

Success sells.

He hadn't let anything get him down today. Not when Ulbreck had arrived at the Claim after breakfast, armed with a new batch of stories with which to bore the clientele. Orrin would wait to pitch him again on the Settlers' Call after the man had run out of people to torture.

Nor had his expensive meeting with Gloamer the mechanic bothered him. It was funny that, while most of the damage the Tuskens had done to the Claim had already been repaired, the most lasting harm had been caused when his spoiled daughter put Annileen's X-31 into the stone wall. Repairs would park Annileen's landspeeder for weeks. Orrin would happily loan her a vehicle from his work fleet. But he'd let Veeka—whose Sportster was in even worse shape—find her own rides for a while. Maybe slowing down would be good for her.

No, the only thing that had tested his smile was Old Number One. His technicians were finding what he had realized, earlier. The vaporator mechanism had survived— tough things, these Pretormins—but Dannar's precious settings had been lost. The first test vial had produced what Orrin judged an absolutely pedestrian cocktail of two parts hydrogen and one part oxygen. Later tests yielded no better results . . . and sickened his heart.

But sorrow would wait today. Every visitor had brought him something: business, congratulations—even a sugar cake. And now, as he saw another figure approaching on foot from the southwest, he wondered what good tidings this person brought.

Orrin squinted. *Well, I'll be,* he thought. He stood tall and waved. "Hey, Kenobi! *Ben Kenobi!*"

For a moment, the hooded man appeared to disappear back behind the dune. But when Orrin charged up the rise, he found Ben kneeling to adjust his boot. "I thought that was you," Orrin said.

Ben stood. As Orrin shook his hand vigorously, Ben said, "I'm sorry. I thought I heard you say—"

"Ben Kenobi—that's your name, isn't it?"

Ben looked down, around, and back to Orrin. "Yes, but—"

"But what?" Orrin smiled.

"I was just curious how you heard it."

"Oh!" Orrin laughed loudly and slapped Ben on the

back. "You'll find out when you go inside." He turned toward the store, coaxing Ben along.

"Perhaps another day." Ben pointed past the store. "I wasn't going inside. I'm just here for my eopie—"

A high-pitched shout came from the Claim. "Ben!"

The men looked over to see Kallie in the open doorway of the store, waving frenetically. Annileen stood behind her, looking a little embarrassed.

"I think you're going in, brother." Orrin put his hand on Ben's shoulder. "Kenobi. There was a Kenobi down around Arnthout, sold damper coils for repulsorlifts. You any relation?"

"Anything's possible." Ben smiled narrowly, teeth clenched together, as Orrin pushed him toward the doorway.

Kallie stepped outside to greet him. She smiled. "Rooh's been waiting for you, Ben."

Annileen walked up, grabbed her daughter by the shoulder blades, and pivoted her 180 degrees. "You. Elsewhere. Now." Kallie looked back at Ben, flashed her teeth, and dashed happily back inside the store. Orrin laughed.

Ben looked to Annileen. "Really, I'm just here for the eopie . . ."

"Nonsense," Orrin said. Eight Settlers' Call holdouts had wised up and joined up today; maybe Ben was Number Nine. "A drink for our new neighbor!"

Orrin held the door open for Ben. The man stepped forward, only to be stopped by Annileen. She looked up at him. "Before you walk in, I just want to say—I'm sorry."

"I'm not sure what you have to apologize for," Ben said. Then he stepped inside the Claim.

"Kenobi!"

The man's eyes widened at the sound of the name

called out by the clutch of people at the end of the bar. But Orrin guided him inside.

Leelee Pace looked back from her packages and waved. "Hey there, Ben Kenobi!"

By the sundries aisle, Doc Mell told his child, "There's that Ben Kenobi. I think he's a doctor, too!"

And at the bar, Jabe contributed a glare as he wiped down the counter. "Crazy old Ben. Still talking to yourself?"

Ben looked at Annileen—and then back at Orrin. The visitor was slightly bemused, Orrin was glad to see. It happened this way all the time. People came to the oasis wanting to keep to themselves, for whatever reason—not knowing that small-town life made privacy completely impossible. Seeing Wyle Ulbreck approaching, Orrin shot Ben an apologetic look.

"You're the fellow from yesterday," the old man said, tugging at the sleeve of Ben's robe like a tailor droid checking a seam. "You're a Kenobi?"

Ben pulled his sleeve back. "I—"

"Hired a Kenobi once. Gormel, they called him. Thief. Stank of spice all the time. I fired him quicker than you can say your name."

"Well, I didn't say my name—to you, anyway." Ben politely turned away. "Please excuse me."

Ulbreck followed him. "You saw me yesterday when them Sandies was here—you saw how many I put on the floor." Ulbreck gestured to the tables. "Come tell the folks what I did. Some people won't believe an honest man—"

Orrin interceded. "Honestly, Wyle. Another time." He peeled Ben away from the old man and guided him toward the bar. "Sorry," he said, lowering his voice. "Some people will cling to you like mynocks if you let them."

"It's all right," Ben said, his eyes settling on Kallie as

she chattered with some teenage friends. "I think I know what happened now."

"I'm sorry," Annileen said. "Kallie came looking for us and ended up snooping. I'm mortified."

Orrin gestured for others to leave the bar, making room for him and Ben. "Gossip gets around pretty fast where there's not a lot goin' on."

Ben nodded. "I would've thought the invasion and massacre would have kept the circuit going for a while."

Orrin raised an eyebrow. "I wouldn't call it a massacre," he said, his tone more serious. He didn't like that word. "It was *justice*."

Ben looked down, as if aware he'd spoken wrong.

"There aren't innocents among Tuskens, Ben. We know that group was the one that struck us here—but it doesn't really matter. They're predators, same as a krayt."

"Understood."

Orrin waved to Jabe to bring over drinks. He didn't want to make Ben squirm *too* much—not if he might subscribe to the Fund. But he didn't mind taking the man down a bit, either. Orrin knew Ben's kind. Ben would play modest and detached until he had every woman in the oasis interested—and then they'd find out he was trouble. Orrin just hadn't figured out what *kind* of trouble, yet. Kallie's story, blabbed around the bar before lunchtime, added more evidence to the case for crazy. But Ben's actions the day before suggested he might be something else—maybe some kind of Clone Wars veteran who'd lost his nerve for fighting. That would track with a bleeding heart for Tuskens.

Change in tactics, then. Orrin took his glass and toasted. "To keeping people safe."

Ben nodded. "I can live with that."

Orrin started his sales pitch anew. This time, he described the Settlers' Call Fund as the best hope for peace.

If Tuskens were intelligent—as their encounter with Plug-eye seemed to suggest—then maybe they could learn, Orrin said. If they learned every settler household on the desert was under the same shield, they might turn their attentions to the Western Dune Sea, instead. "Let 'em hassle the Jawas for a change."

He started to talk pricing, knowing that if Kenobi's place were close to the Jundland, he could ask for a sizable fee. But Ben interrupted with something that surprised him.

"How much," Ben asked tentatively, "would it cost to extend your protection out even farther?" He affixed his eyes to the drink in his hands. "Say . . . to where that kidnapping you told me about happened?"

"What, the Lars place?"

"Well, around there," Ben said.

Orrin noticed Annileen pause nearby. Since they'd started talking, Annileen had circled back and forth, dealing with matters in the store—and yet, Orrin noted, she kept swooping back cometlike to the bar, catching an earful where she could. "The Lars place. That's way out there. Isn't it, Annie?"

"Past Motesta Oasis," she said, turning back to her shelving.

"Past Jawa Heights, even," Orrin said, calculating. "What kind of business do you have that'd need protecting out that way?"

"Just curious," Ben said casually. "You were describing the potential a minute ago. I was just wondering what was feasible."

Orrin nodded. "Well, let's see," he said, pulling a datapad from his vest pocket.

Ben waited as Orrin pretended to run the numbers. It was impossible, really. Orrin knew there wasn't any prospect of extending patrols to Owen Lars's farm. It was more than a hundred kilometers from the oasis, with a chunk of the eastern highlands in the way; the Settlers' Call would have to install satellite armories farther east before they could even consider it. And they wouldn't—because the Fund was, at its roots, a local collective.

But Kenobi didn't need to know that.

"I would think nineteen hundred credits a year would cover it," Orrin said. The figure was huge. More than anyone was paying currently, except for Ulbreck, if he ever bit. "And we'd need that up front to get weapons caches and patrols set up." He looked Ben in the eye. "I don't know if you can find that."

Ben suppressed a laugh. "I don't know that I can, either!"

Thought so. Orrin nodded and started to put away the datapad. Then Ben said something in a softer voice: "But I don't know that I *can't.*"

Orrin raised an eyebrow. He'd known Kenobi had money enough to buy supplies, but why would anyone of means live and dress as he did? "What kind of work are you—"

He was interrupted by a high whine from outside, syncopated with a *thumm-thumm-thumm* that grew louder every second and rattled cans from the shelves. Annileen looked up. "What the—"

Jabe peered out the window behind the counter. "You're not gonna believe this, Mom!" The screech passed from east to west, heading toward the parking area. Annileen hurried to the side door, Orrin alongside her.

It took Orrin a second to realize what he was looking at. It was a landspeeder, but some fool had modified it to make it look like a snubfighter, with wings mounted on either side and a long, pointed nose grafted onto the front. The vehicle was painted a shocking red, with orange mock flames on the air intakes. And it was currently making violent revolutions in the sand, its fake wingtip cannons nearly clipping several of the vehicles parked nearby.

The *thumm-thumm-thumm* resolved into a musical beat. Orrin saw now that the central turbine for the ridiculous-looking landspeeder was, in fact, a giant speaker, blasting sounds that nearly lifted pebbles from the ground.

Behind Orrin and Annileen, Kallie yelled to be heard. "The animals are going crazy! Did the Call siren break?"

"I don't know *what* it is," Annileen said, gawking.

The canopy of the strange vehicle slid forward to reveal the driver, a spindly thing with a leathery face and a head shaped like a teardrop. His cranium tapered off into a gray curl that pointed to the sky. He wore a black trench coat—in Tatooine heat!—and as he stood up in the driver's compartment, Orrin spied not one, but *three* blaster-bearing shoulder holsters peeking out from underneath. Picking up a jeweled cane, the alien stepped out of the strange speeder.

Half the occupants of the store were at the windows now, watching the driver. Two knees divided each of his legs into thirds, and golden anklets shook back and forth as he kicked the sand with his hooves. Any jangling the rings did was purely theoretical, as the speaker continued to boom away.

"That's a Gossam," Ben said, at the window.

"That's an idiot," Annileen replied from the doorway. "What's he brought with him?"

They soon saw. Crammed into the backseat of the vehicle were two enormous green masses—figures that now struggled with each other. If the driver was a mystery to many of the Claim's patrons, all could recognize Gamorreans, the great porcine warriors who worked for any lowlife that would feed them. The two fought, each trying to squeeze through the small space to exit the vehicle. When one finally won out and clambered out on the right, the entire speeder-thing nearly flipped over. The Gossam driver berated the Gamorreans, cracking at them with his gem-tipped cane.

"What the blazes is he supposed to be?" Annileen said.

Orrin froze. Sudden realization washed over him. *No. No, they wouldn't send anyone here. Would they?*

It took him just a second to answer his own question. Orrin stepped backward into the store, nearly stumbling over his own feet. The good day had taken a turn.

CHAPTER TWENTY-FOUR

"WE'RE HERE TO SEE ORRIN GAULT," the shrivel-faced Gossam said, standing in the doorway to the Claim.

"I can't hear you," Annileen said. "You've deafened us all." She had let the creature enter only after he agreed to turn off the alleged music; that communication had required two minutes of makeshift sign language.

The Gossam clip-clopped on the synstone floor. His sickly yellow eyes traced the shelves around him, as if taking inventory. He reached for a flask inside his jacket, revealing his blasters for Annileen to see clearly. A swig later, his gray lips smacked loudly. "Orry-Orry-Orry," he said, as if trying out a new tongue. "Orrin. Orrin Gaa-*woooolt*. *Orrin Gault.* Is one of these sounds familiar to you, grubber?"

Orrin was missing, but over the shelves Annileen saw that the door to his office was open. He'd likely gone for his blaster. Behind the counter, Jabe had pulled the pistol from the cashbox. Annileen waved him off. If she didn't want Jabe hunting Tuskens, she surely didn't want him killed in a shootout with . . . what? Whatever these people were.

"I'm Bojo Boopa," the Gossam said, surveying Annileen. "But you will call me Master Boopa."

"Not if you don't want me to laugh." Annileen looked to her left. Ben was standing casually at a clothing rack, trying to pay the visitors no mind. But she saw his eyes dart between her and Jabe in a way she found reassuring.

The Gamorreans thundered forward, bumping against shelves. Items clattered to the floor.

"Hey!" Annileen stepped up—only to freeze as one of the titans growled. The other balled his fist and punched a display, knocking packages all across the aisle. At the bar, Jabe began to move.

"There's no need for trouble," Ben said, interposing his body between the Gamorreans and Annileen.

Boopa leered at him and returned the flask inside his coat in a move that displayed his blasters to the watchful customers. "What are you supposed to be? A hero?"

"Not at all," Ben said, kneeling. "I'm the janitor." He began picking up the fallen containers and placing them back on their shelves.

Orrin stepped out from his office in the back. "I'm Orrin Gault," he said, his earlier smile gone. He approached Boopa, eyeing him coolly. "Can we get you something?"

"Hardly." The Gossam sniffed disdainfully as his neck craned. Seeing the room Orrin had emerged from, he pointed. "Is that where you do business, Orry?"

"Some of the time."

"Well, let's go." Twirling his cane, Boopa trotted down the aisle toward the office.

Orrin gave a look to Annileen—and half a glance to Ben—before turning to follow. "This'll be just a minute," he told them. The door closed.

*   *   *

Orrin, you've lied to me, Annileen thought. It wasn't just a minute. It had been closer to fifteen, each one spent in alternating anxiety and annoyance.

Anxiety over what was happening inside the office. The newcomers weren't moisture farmers, to be sure. Orrin had dealt with shady folks before; one almost had to in running a ranch the size of his. Some supplier somewhere was always under the massive thumb of a Hutt. And she'd known Orrin to deal with merchants now and again whose property might not have been legally obtained. But that was about cutting corners. This seemed like something else again.

"Do you think the Devaronians sent them for revenge after their partner died?" she had whispered to Ben.

"I've never known hoteliers to be a vengeful lot," he'd responded.

She'd shooed Kallie and Leelee outside. Several of the customers had left at the sight—and occasional gaseous sound and smell—of the Gamorreans, but some of her regulars of sterner stuff remained, keeping a watchful eye from their tables. Jabe had refused to leave, taking station at the gun counter. If Ulbreck could hold out against a Tusken mob from there, Annileen thought, Jabe should be reasonably safe. She noticed that the old farmer himself had departed, perhaps deciding his adventure the day before was story enough for one week.

And there was Ben, sorting idly through blankets and evaluating spanners. His eyes casually shifted to the Gamorreans and the closed office door. He was curious, to be sure—but not nearly as anxious as Annileen, and his presence had made her feel calmer.

Calm enough that she could feel annoyed. If the Gamorreans had ever been to a store before, Annileen couldn't tell. They grabbed whatever they wanted from the shelves, as if it were their own private pantry. They were making a mess, but as long as they were stuffing their faces, they weren't breaking things—or people.

"That's not good," Ben whispered as he passed her.

"The store's survived Tuskens. It can handle this."

"No, I mean the shorter one just ate a handful of metal bolts. He'll regret that."

Annileen had swept her fifth aisle in the Gamorreans' wake when the office door opened. She strained to hear Boopa's words.

"—not gonna work, Gault. You may be a big man here," the Gossam said, emerging. "But this little kingdom of yours is a dust mote in the boss's eye."

Orrin stepped out and put his hands on his hips. "Well, you can tell your boss—or anyone who wants to know. This oasis is for good people. We don't want you around!" He cast a sideways glance to the dining area, where he saw the wide-eyed customers listening intently. He pointed to the exit. "Now go, and take your muscle with you!"

Boopa beckoned to his fat companions. "Let's go, boys. This place stinks." He looked around, his snout crumpling. "You've had Tuskens here!"

The trio filed out of the building. Orrin followed and stood in the doorway, yelling out after them. "And keep that blasted music off as you go!"

Annileen stepped to the window, watching in amazement. Boopa was back in his ludicrous vehicle, pulling away—quietly. She looked back to Orrin. "What was that all about?"

Orrin turned back to face the occupants of the store. "It's nothing," he said, straightening. "Some gangsters hoping to shake down honest folk for protection money. An old story." He pointed a thumb out the window. "But it turns out that the Settlers' Call has multiple uses.

Once they heard how fast we'd gotten an army here to fight the Tuskens, they lost interest."

The statement was delivered as modestly as any she could recall coming from Orrin's mouth—and it sent a wave of excitement through his audience. Several customers approached, eager to talk to him about joining the Call Fund. Annileen looked at Ben. The man seemed as confused by the experience as she was.

Annileen turned to sweep up the remains of the Gamorreans' dining, but Orrin stepped free from the crowd and tugged at her sleeve. "Oh, Annie. We need to talk—*about your landspeeder.*"

Annileen did a double take. It wasn't the subject she'd expected was on his mind now, not with new business at hand.

"There's a delay," Orrin said, sounding earnest. "Gloamer said so. But you don't have to worry," he said. Releasing her sleeve, he took her hand. "I'm going to get something sorted out. In the meantime, you can use the USV-5."

"*Your* landspeeder?" The offer startled Annileen. Orrin's luxury vehicle was the pride of his existence. She suspected the only reason he let his son behind the controls was to make it look as if Orrin rated a driver.

"I don't mind," Orrin said, bringing his other hand atop hers. He clasped them tightly and looked directly at her. "After all, you're almost *family.*"

Annileen's eyes widened. At the mention of her landspeeder repair, she had expected Orrin's usual excuse-with-a-smile routine. But this was different. He looked serious. A meaningful expression for others, but Orrin looked that way so infrequently she had no index to measure his sincerity against.

"*Family,*" he said again, loudly enough so those around could hear.

Annileen was aware of eyes watching from around the room. Part of her wanted to ask where this was coming from. Instead, she could only stammer. "T-thanks."

She withdrew her hand and stepped back. Orrin turned his head and saw Ben, lingering in the next aisle. "Oh. Kenobi," he said, drily. "Were you ready to talk business about the Fund?"

Ben shrugged. "I'm sorry. I may have been wasting your time—"

Orrin looked back, coolly. "No law against it." He looked over at the mess on the floor. "You know, Ben, stuff keeps happening when you're here. I hate that we keep inconveniencing you."

"Yes, I should be about my business," Ben said mildly. He bowed and turned away.

Orrin walked back toward his office, the exultant customers following. Annileen goggled. *Did Orrin just tell one of my friends to leave?*

Suddenly indignant, she stomped after Orrin, intending to ask exactly that. If it had been a dismissal, it was the lightest, politest she'd ever heard—but no one but she had the right to tell anyone in her store what to do. Just as she reached the back of the crowd, however, something told her to look back.

Ben was gone.

A breathless Kallie met her just outside the door to the livery. "Did Ben leave?" she asked, anxiously. "Rooh's gone!"

"Yep." Sighing, Annileen looked back into the store. "And he never got the water keg we owe him."

"Bizarre. Where do you think he's from, Mom?"

"I don't know. But wherever it is, they sure don't understand the concept of shopping."

Meditation

Enough.

Just three visits—and chaos.

I shouldn't have gone. I'm endangering the mission.

I won't go back there again.

And needless to say, I'll be doing these chats mentally from now on. I expect you understand why.

PART THREE

THE BRIGHT CENTER

CHAPTER TWENTY-FIVE

SAND PEOPLE LIVED WITH sores every day. At birth, every Tusken infant was swaddled tightly in bandages. The nurses worked so fast A'Yark had never seen her children's faces. Channeled through little mouthpieces, her sons' cries had been tinny and agonized. Babies had no way of appreciating the curse that existence represented, nor did they appreciate the shame of exposed flesh. But they quickly became acquainted with the price the coverings exacted on the body.

Numberless in a lifetime, sores simply had to be endured. K'Sheek had been slow to learn that, years earlier; the human abductee had thought her wrappings were something that could be changed for cleanliness or comfort. She was wrong. Sand People added to their birth wrap as they grew, each new patch a testament to their defiance and survival. If a pebble got into the wrappings, it was simply layered over. The carbuncle it caused became a reminder of the past. A funnel plant simply grew new skin over its wounds. A Tusken could do the same.

A'Yark understood that defeat was just another sore Sand People lived with. Defeats had to be felt, each and every one—and remembered. And in the days since the massacre at the gorge, A'Yark had felt it every time she

opened her eye. The survivors in The Pillars were pathetic, clinging to life like lichen. The first few days had
been the worst, with the remaining handful of warriors
making pitiful forays to find hubba gourds. *Proud raids,
indeed!*

The arguments followed. Those posed less danger to
A'Yark, now, since most of her rivals were dead. But
hapless elders walking in circles decrying their fates irritated her greatly.

And finally, the sacred well in The Pillars, usually reliable, was dry most days now. The clan's need hadn't
been reduced much by the massacre; a herd of ownerless
banthas remained, and it made no sense to butcher
them, whatever tradition said. The worriers had blamed
A'Yark and the failed raid for the water problems, too,
despite the fact that word was filtering in of similar issues for other clans, elsewhere. If Tatooine had grown
angry with its tenants, all Sand People were suffering,
not just one tribe.

A'Yark had no time for recriminations. For while
keeping the group from dissolving had taken most of
her time, she had still found spare hours for the important thing: keeping watch on Ben.

The human's lair was close: farther to the west, along
the northern face of the Jundland. A'Yark had found it
easily. The winds had been light, and while Ben had
shown guile in his attempts to hide his footsteps, no one
could track like a Tusken.

Ben had not returned to the oasis in many days.
A'Yark had wondered about that. Didn't he protect the
human woman Annileen? The compound was *her* home.
Had she moved to his? A'Yark didn't know—but wasn't
about to venture to the oasis to find out. That would be
madness now.

One day, however, A'Yark had spotted Ben riding
east. There were cities that way, but he wasn't taking

the fastest route. Rather, he kept to the ridgeline, avoiding contact with settlements. Unable to range far without leaving her defenseless clan behind, A'Yark had lost him.

So instead, she sat with her bantha and waited. And watched.

Ben returned the next day to his home. His only cargo was the camping gear he'd taken with him. Whatever his trip east had been, it wasn't a supply run.

What drove a human? A'Yark wished she had spent more time listening to Sharad Hett. He had been unwilling to talk about his earlier life with the outsiders; that, after all, was what had driven him to join the Tuskens. She hadn't even asked K'Sheek many questions. The Sand People had no interest in understanding their enemies. It was enough to know that they bled and died when attacked.

But now, with the might of her band broken, A'Yark *needed* to understand. This Ben wanted something; all beings did. It governed his habits and movements. Was the thing he wanted to the east?

A'Yark would have to consider that another time. The gourd gatherers were late in returning. *They can't even do that right.* A'Yark finished sharpening the point of her gaderffii and walked down from The Pillars onto the desert floor.

In the distant northeast, she saw a peculiar sight. One bantha after another appeared on the horizon. The eldest member of the foraging group rode the lead beast. The fourth and final bantha had a cable around its neck, and was dragging something like a landspeeder. Except it was three times as long as any A'Yark had ever seen.

"What now?" Gaderffii raised in indignation, A'Yark charged across the sand, trying to get the attention of the makeshift caravan. The hovercraft had a large flatbed surface in back, with something huge lying upon it.

A vaporator tower.

A'Yark skidded to a halt. A young Tusken was operating the vehicle, although certainly not as it was supposed to be operated. The thing lurched forward in fits
and starts, bumping against the rear legs of the irritated
bantha in front of it. The machine was sparking, with
fumes rising from beneath its hood; this would likely be
its last trip, anywhere.

The sight of A'Yark caused the bantha riders to stop.
That, in turn, resulted in the landspeeder again slamming into the rear bantha. The animal screamed and
kicked, its massive foot causing the hovering vehicle to
bob and weave on the air.

A'Yark didn't know which warrior to smack first. She
chose the one in the machine.

"A settler abandoned it," the would-be driver said.

"And you didn't kill him?"

The war leader's tone was enough; the young warrior
bowed his head in shame. "They fled. We thought the
prize was more important."

"The prize!" A'Yark walked along the length of the
flatbed. "What are we to do with this?" She smacked
the vaporator with her gaderffii, producing a loud clang.
"Are you Jawas now? Will you peddle trash for crumbs?"

"It makes water," the warrior sitting atop the lead
bantha said. "Water! We need—"

"I know what it does!" A'Yark leered at the metal
abomination, astonished that any Tusken didn't know
the offense it represented to the natural order. "Settlers
defile the land with vaporators. We destroy them. We
do not—"

A'Yark paused. "Wait," she said, considering. She
faced the driver. "You took this thing from the Smiling
One's farm?"

"The human war leader from the oasis—and the
gorge?" The driver shrank in his seat. The memory of

the massacre was still fresh. "No. You told us to stay away from his lands. This was in a different place."

Well, at least they listened to one thing, A'Yark thought. Her reconnaissance had given her a sense of what territory the Smiling One considered his. Taking something belonging to him might bring his forces out on another hunt. A'Yark never shrank from battle, but the others would not be ready for that meeting. It was best avoided.

Sounds came from within the rock formation. A'Yark turned to see children peeking down, curious about the new arrivals. Others would see the giant device, too, if they left it near the entrance to the rift. A'Yark pointed her gaderffii and grunted a command. "The thing will fit in the cave beneath the overhang. Carry it up there— and try not to break it."

The young warriors looked at one another, puzzled at the reversal. A'Yark's next yell put them into motion.

A'Yark watched it go past and calculated. She wasn't sure what they would do with it, if anything. But circumstances were dire, and even an object that had no meaning to the Tuskens might become important in the clash against the settlers. It only took a pebble to cause a sore.

CHAPTER TWENTY-SIX

"GIVE ME THE BAD NEWS," Orrin said, squinting upward from beneath his farmer's hat.

Veeka shimmied down the scaffold. "Eighty-seven milliliters."

"That's it?" Orrin was stunned. A human on Tatooine could sweat more in five minutes. "The settings have got to be wrong."

The young woman mopped her brow angrily and glared at her father. "You want to go up and see?"

Orrin didn't. It had been like this everywhere in the eastern range. The Gault sweetwater formula had been producing fine at the test towers just a month earlier. Now it was programmed into all the Pretormins during what normally was the most productive time of the year.

And the sky seemed to have given up on them.

"Diagnostic?"

"Not gonna say anything different today than it did yesterday," Veeka said. She wiped her hands on her work pants. "Dad, we've got to do something else."

What? Orrin didn't know. It wasn't normal, this performance. It went against everything he knew about the art *and* the science. Nothing in the atmosphere had changed; everything was well within expected parameters. Yet each of his ten-thousand-credit machines was turning out pedestrian water, half a glass at a time.

Some farmers simply lost the knack. He couldn't believe that was the answer. Everything happened for a reason. But it was almost as if the Tuskens' damaging of Old Number One a couple of weeks earlier had killed the recipe everywhere. There was no connection, of course; the machines were discrete entities, each adjusted by hand. Yet the vaporators acted as if the magic was gone.

Veeka scaled the tower again, preparing to close the maintenance doors, set high above the reach of Sand People or wildlife. Clinging to the side, she called out, "Someone's coming."

Wyle Ulbreck's old repulsortruck puttered across the horizon from the direction of the oasis. Orrin recognized it instantly—as did his son, working nearby. Mullen saw his father straightening his shirt. "Don't tell me you're gonna try again!"

"A farmer lives on hope," Orrin said, waving his hat at the traveler.

Ulbreck's vehicle slowed to a stop near the crew. The old man squinted out the window. "Oh," he said, recognizing Orrin. "It's you."

Orrin smiled. *Who else would it be on my own land, you imbecile?*

"You're leaving early, Wyle." Orrin stepped to the door. "Finally tell everyone how you saved the Claim from the raging horde?"

"That's not it," Ulbreck said. "Got a call. Some blasted Sandies stole one of my new towers before we even put it up!"

Ulbreck launched into a rant about Tuskens, Jawas, and incompetents everywhere. Orrin didn't try to hide his own amusement as he waited for a pause. "Sorry to hear that," he finally interjected. "Anyone hurt?"

"Just my pocket!" Ulbreck pounded his fist against

the dashboard. "What in the suns would Tuskens want with a vaporator, anyway?"

Orrin had no idea. He'd never heard of such a theft before. Some vaporators were not much taller than a human, but his Pretormins and Ulbreck's new industrial machines were gargantuan. For the Tuskens to have stolen one, Ulbreck's vaunted security personnel must've fled their hauler and left the motor running.

The crisis was ready-made. "Maybe time to sack some people—and go with proven professionals," Orrin said.

"Don't start that again!" Ulbreck glared down at Orrin. "You can't even protect the Claim. How are you gonna protect my place?" He turned and spat into a cup he kept handy. "Pests, these Sandies. Wasting time, costing money—"

Orrin was undeterred. "Well, let's see, Wyle. Since the Tuskens attacked the oasis and we answered, nobody's seen Plug-eye or any other Sand People. But you just got attacked. And yours is the biggest patch that isn't protected by the Settlers' Call."

"What are you sayin'?" Angered, Ulbreck stopped his engine, causing the repulsortruck to settle on the sand with a thump.

"I'm saying maybe the few Tuskens we let live have figured out where the weak spots are. And you're it."

Ulbreck swore. "You're crazy. Tusken's got a head like a boulder. They're incapable of thought." He looked back out at Orrin's vaporator tower, looming above. "Besides, say it's true. I can put up my own sirens, same as you."

"Yeah, but will anyone respond to them?" Orrin fished in his pocket and found the remote activator. After the oasis raid, he carried it everywhere now. "It's not just the sound, Wyle. With this, I can get an army here. An army I can send to get your vaporator back— and crack some skulls in the process."

"Those bums aren't an army. They just want the free drinks you—"

"Whatever it takes." Orrin looked at him cannily. "Now, I can't get you in at the old rates. Prices have gone up. And bringing in all your territory is going to incur costs you're gonna have to bear. Last in, you know."

"Make that *never* in!" Ulbreck restarted his engine. "I don't care if Jabba the Hutt signs up. Wyle Ulbreck takes care of his own business!"

Orrin threw up his hands. With a metallic groan, the repulsortruck continued on its way.

Mullen looked at his father. "Told you it was a waste of time."

"Figured it was worth one more shot," Orrin said. "This close to the harvest, nobody but Wyle has any money." He thought for a second and chuckled. "And maybe that Kenobi."

Mullen raised an eyebrow. "Kenobi?"

"Ben. Guy that made a fool out of you, remember? That's his name," Orrin said. Quickly, he recounted Ben's questions about extending protection far to the east.

"Out near Anchorhead?" Veeka asked, climbing down the ladder. "What business has he got out there?"

"No idea." Orrin strained to remember details from the conversation. Ben had mentioned the Lars farm. *Why he would care what happens out that way?*

Veeka chucked her tool kit into the back of their work vehicle. "You really think he has money—that he wasn't just talking?" She grinned. "I thought you said he was an idiot."

"That I did," Orrin said, staring at the Jundland peaks far away. "Man lives on the fringe, babbling to himself and dressing like the Tuskens stole his wardrobe. That's the sort of human driftwood your mother would take in." *And leave with,* he did not have to say. "But crazy people need protecting, too. Some even have money."

Probably not this crazy person, though. Orrin knew it wasn't worth wasting thoughts on the man. Ben hadn't been around in days—and there were bigger problems coming up. He took a last forlorn look at the vaporator. "Let's pack it in. We're not going to fix this by the deadline."

Mullen was startled. "No harvest? But those people who came to see you—"

"Shouldn't have been allowed anywhere near the Claim," Orrin said, aggravated. It had been a sore point in the family. Somebody on the work crews should have stopped "Master Boopa" before he reached the Claim. Or at least alerted Orrin.

Veeka stood beside her brother. She looked serious, for once. "What will you—I mean, what will we do?"

"Your great-granddaddy told me something," Orrin said. "Every problem's got two solutions. You wait until you figure *two* ways out of a problem—and then you try them both at the same time. Because by the time you need a backup plan, it's too late."

Orrin paused and thought about what was scheduled to happen in the next twenty-four hours—and about the plans he had to deal with it all. "You go see if Zedd's ready to work," he said, flashing a reassuring smile as he climbed into his vehicle. "I've got some things to prepare."

CHAPTER TWENTY-SEVEN

LEELEE NEARLY DROPPED her packages when she opened the door. *"Annileen!"*

In the middle of the Claim's dining area, a scaffold sat tipped at an angle, two of its supports wedged against the domed ceiling above. Annileen clung to the top of the structure, dangling precariously. She looked over her shoulder at her visitor. "Hi, Leelee. What's new?"

The Zeltron set her parcels down and rushed over. A bucket lay overturned in the middle of a white, soapy puddle, near where the rickety tower stood. "You're washing the ceiling?"

"Not anymore, no." Annileen's wet hand slipped again. In grabbing hold, she set the whole structure quaking. "I've been calling for Jabe, but I think he's in the stockroom!"

"Asleep, you mean." Leelee pushed a table away to reach the scaffold. She steadied it long enough for Annileen to twist around and reach for one of the vertical supports.

Carefully, Annileen climbed down. "Thanks," she said, breathing deeply. "I was afraid I'd have to wait for the dinner rush."

Leelee looked around. The afternoon crowd was always thinnest during harvesttime. The store was empty, except for old Erbaly Nap'tee, poking through a basket of remnants. "Didn't Erbaly offer to help?"

"No, but she asked me to help her," Annileen said, drying her hands on her overalls. "I'm pleased to say I know what's in inventory even in midair." She turned the fallen bucket upright and searched for the mop, as if nothing had ever happened.

Leelee marveled. "You decided to wash the ceiling—alone."

"Putting up sealant, actually," Annileen said. "You guys did a good job cleaning up after the raid, but I wanted to get at those blaster score marks on the pourstone before they caused cracks."

"What, in thirty years?"

Annileen shrugged. "I have the time now." She started mopping.

Mystified, Leelee walked back to reclaim her packages. "Good thing I came. Though, if you'd kept that activator on you, you could've set off the Settlers' Call."

"That would've gone over well with everyone in the fields, for sure," Annileen said. "I can see the holo now: *Woman Summons Militia to Save Her from Own Stupidity*."

Giving the floor up for later, Annileen walked behind the counter. She looked in wonderment at the stack of packages Leelee had brought to ship. Leelee was a talented sculptor in her spare time, specializing in primitive designs; she had customers on worlds all over the Outer Rim. "How do you find these people?" Annileen asked.

"Ex-boyfriends," the Zeltron said, smiling primly. She ran a crimson finger down a digital list of names on the manifest she was holding. "They're all still fans."

"Of your work—or you?"

"An artist tries not to ask," Leelee said. "You could use a hobby yourself, Annie. You've been a bundle of energy for the last few weeks. What's going on?"

"I don't know," Annileen said, processing the packages. Leelee was right, of course. Just during the last couple of weeks, Annileen had changed the layout of the packaged goods section, helped Kallie re-fence the dewback run, and streamlined the store's accounting procedures. That morning, she had built a new table by hand especially for Bohmer and his new hoverchair, when he finally got the okay to return and resume his caf intake. If the facts of her life hadn't changed in recent days, she'd made sure it felt like a whirl, all the same.

"I know what's wrong," Leelee said.

"No advice requested, Leelee." Annileen stopped transcribing. "Look, I get it. The big things in my world are never going to change. But there's a lot of little stuff I can fix, and I might as well get to it."

"Phooey on that," Leelee said. "I say you haven't seen Ben since he ran out of here that time, and it's driving you up the wall. And onto the ceiling," she added.

Annileen rolled her eyes. "Really," she said icily. "What makes you think that?"

"Because you've just given my latest masterpiece a shipping label for something called the 'Kenobi system.'"

Annileen looked at the letters she'd absentmindedly printed and blushed. "Oops."

"It's okay," Leelee said, gesturing to the mislabeled package. "It *is* a fertility statue."

"That's *all* I need." Annileen laughed. She shook her head and corrected the label. "Okay. I admit it. It bothers me that he never came back."

She'd almost lost track of how long it had been since the Tusken attack—and the crazy, surreal day after. The visit by "Master Boopa." The strange change in Orrin's behavior toward her. And Ben's vanishing act upon becoming the center of attention. He hadn't returned since.

"I guess we scared him off," she said. Newcomers

were like that, sometimes. They didn't know the locals gossiped about every new arrival, just to forget about them when someone else came along. She'd even avoided adding any more fuel to the fire by keeping to herself their desert encounter with the Tusken matriarch. It had worked. Only two people had even mentioned Ben to Annileen recently. Orrin asked occasionally whether he had returned. And Kallie asked the same thing, only every five minutes.

Orrin appeared in the hallway from the garage. Annileen saw him give a moment's glance to the scaffold before disappearing into his office without a word.

"That's another weird one," she whispered to Leelee. Orrin's best behavior around Annileen had been a thing of wonder lately; it was the new story captivating the regulars' attention. "You want to talk to someone, talk to him."

Leelee snorted and made a pronouncement. "Annie, my friend, Ben is exactly what you've needed."

"How do you mean?"

"Because you've kept Orrin at arm's length for years," Leelee said. "And he got used to it. But now that there's another suitor for Princess Annie, he's got to make his move."

Annileen cast a horrified glance at the office door. "I don't *want* him to make his move!"

"Is that so?" Leelee smirked. "I think you *want* Orrin interested—so it'll force your mystery man to do something."

"You're mentally ill," Annileen said. "Seriously, what is it with you Zeltrons? You'd matchmake for droids, if they'd listen."

"They do listen, Annie. That's why there are so many droids."

Annileen groaned. This really wasn't what she needed—or was looking for. Things were fine with Orrin as they were. *Well, no they aren't.* But Orrin was more an older brother—or, sometimes, a third child. He had been Dannar's friend, and that was how she still saw him. Why did he want that to change now?

She started to say something when Leelee shushed her. Orrin emerged from the office, having changed his shirt and neatened his hair after his day in the fields. He saw the women and smiled. "How are my favorite people today?"

"One of us was nearly burying the other," Leelee said, gesturing to the scaffold. "You've got to get Annie out of this place before she starts alphabetizing the oil cans."

Beaming, Orrin strolled behind the counter. "Have no fear. Orrin Gault has the plan, and it's in motion already." He put his arm around Annileen and gave her a half hug. "You're getting tomorrow off." He grinned down at her. "Happy birthday."

Annileen pulled away. "What do you mean?"

"I mean I've just talked with Tar Lup," he said, referring to the Calwells' onetime assistant. "He's got some time off from his place in Eisley, and I've convinced him to spend tomorrow here, watching the store."

"Why can't Jabe—" Green eyes stared, suspicious. "Wait. Where will I be?"

"Mos Eisley. You deserve a day in the city," he said. "And I want you to take the whole family. Kallie can close up the livery—nobody's around right now, anyway." His eyes narrowed. "Take Jabe, too. Maybe if you spend more time together as a family, things will improve."

Stupefied, Annileen looked to Leelee. The Zeltron was wide-eyed, listening with rapt attention. "You're going with us, I suppose?" Annileen asked Orrin.

"Oh, no," he said, fishing around in his pocket. "Not with the harvest!"

"Right." She looked at him, still not fathoming his intent. "Why Mos Eisley?"

Orrin found what he was looking for: a small sealed envelope. "Here," he said. "It's the other part of your surprise, to make sure you go. Open it this evening."

Annileen took the envelope. "What are you up to, Orrin?"

The farmer laughed. "Just make sure I'm around when you open it." He winked at Leelee and stepped out from behind the counter.

"My birthday's the day *after* tomorrow," Annileen said.

"This offer is good for tomorrow only," Orrin proclaimed, walking toward his office. "I've spent all afternoon making the plans. Don't send poor Tar away!" The door closed behind him and locked.

Leelee clutched for the envelope. "Give me that! I want to see!"

"No!" Annileen said, pulling it away. She felt dizzy. *What in the world is going on now?*

Meditation

I had the dream again.

It was like I've described before. I wasn't myself. But I saw the world through—something. A tunnel, a filter. And then I heard a scream.

You're tired of hearing about this dream, I expect—I've had it once a week since coming to Tatooine. I always wake in wonder. I always feel it's about Anakin somehow.

Only the last couple of editions have changed some. The tunnel is narrower, brighter. Normally the view is hazy and red. This time it was almost like seeing through—well, a Tusken's eyes, as strange as that sounds.

And hearing the scream didn't hit me as hard, this time. I felt more apart, aloof. In the past, it's had more of an effect on me.

I don't know what it means.

I'm worried the dream represents the smothering of light in the galaxy, and my own misgivings about being far from the scene. Could I really stay here so long that I no longer feel the cries of those Palpatine harms?

Don't worry, Qui-Gon—I'm not speaking this out loud. I'm still ashamed at what you must think of that horrendous blunder, when I was overheard. You must think I'm a Padawan all over again.

But I know how it happened. I've been focusing too hard on trying to contact you, trying to replicate the feelings I was having that time you spoke to Yoda and me. I was trying to separate myself mentally from my surroundings, and because of that, I didn't sense Kallie's approach.

It doesn't seem that the girl overheard anything too revealing—or saw me holding Anakin's lightsaber. The Force was with me there. And there are apparently a number of people around whose names sound like Kenobi, so nobody's drawn the connection. Yet.

Still, I can't take any more chances. I was getting too drawn into the lives of the people at the oasis. It's ironic. You were the one who always told me to focus more on the living Force—the lives of those around us now, rather than the big picture that Master Yoda ascribed to. Living here, getting involved in this little world, with its little dramas? It's been enlightening.

I missed all this while rushing about to save the galaxy. Seeing that, for many people, the smaller struggles are just as important to them as our larger ones are to us. It was a good lesson for me to learn.

But it has to end there.

So I'm strictly confining my travels to my mission. I checked on the boy earlier this week; the farm seems fine. I managed to steer clear of Owen Lars this time. The man doesn't like me at all.

And I'm going to keep working on the house. I have to do something about this coolant unit, which I think was built in the time of Arca Jeth. But don't worry—there are other stores on Tatooine besides the Claim. Not many, but they exist . . .

CHAPTER TWENTY-EIGHT

"HAPPY BIRTHDAY, ANNIE!"

Annileen waved back from the window of the speeder truck. "Thanks!"

There wasn't any point in telling the farmhand that her birthday was still a day away. Everyone who'd visited the Claim since the night before had heard the reason for her journey. And harvest workers on three previous hillsides had already yelled the same greeting to her, all of them excited for her.

Annileen was excited, too. Dressed nicely, she was heading to Mos Eisley, her daughter in the passenger seat and son in back—and none of them had argued yet at all. It was a birthday miracle.

They were in the LiteVan II today. Dannar had brought the retired SoroSuub model back into service the year they married, and it still handled most of the heavy work for the Claim. Orrin had needed his USV-5 landspeeder back for some reason, but Annileen didn't mind. She was still reeling, not quite believing the contents of the envelope Orrin had given her. Jabe and Kallie were discussing it in the darkened cab, now.

"I've been telling you Orrin's a great guy," Jabe said.

"I guess I was wrong," Kallie said. His older sister, also cleaned up in colorful clothes from off the rack, read from the gold-colored slip in the light from the window. *"To Annie. This certificate good for . . .*

". . . *Ben!"*

Annileen glanced at her daughter, startled. "What?"

"There!" Kallie said, lowering the document and pointing out her window. "To the right! Ben Kenobi!"

Annileen braked and banked the massive machine at the same time. Sure enough, Ben and Rooh came into her field of view.

It was a comical sight, one that reminded her of her first visit to his place, and the angry bantha calf. Ben was on his hands and knees in the middle of a blasted plain, trying to talk to Rooh. The eopie was lying on her belly in the sand, legs folded underneath as she chewed on a lonely patch of desert foliage. Her harness was connected to a makeshift sledge, upon which sat a heavy and ancient coolant pump.

Annileen pulled the LiteVan up alongside. "Going somewhere?" she asked.

"That was the original idea," Ben said. "It isn't working out."

Annileen stopped the engine. Kallie went for her door latch. Jabe leaned over the front seat, aggravated. "Not again, Mom. *This guy*—"

"Helped us, and needs help now," Annileen said. "You just sit here and stay out of the suns."

When Annileen climbed out of the vehicle and onto the desert floor, Kallie was already there, trying her best to get Ben to notice her festive red outfit. But the cloaked man's attention remained on his eopie.

"Rooh just stopped," Ben said. "She's eating this—whatever it is."

"It's desert sage," Annileen said.

"I didn't think anything grew here."

"Something grows everywhere." Annileen knelt next

to him and stroked the lackadaisical eopie's snout. "There, girl. It's all right."

Seemingly discomfited by Annileen's proximity, Ben stood up and gestured to the cargo. "I can't seem to get her to move. I keep thinking I've attached the sledge wrong."

"No, it's fine," Annileen said.

"Then she's just objecting to carrying extra weight," Ben said, standing over the prone animal.

"That's for sure," Kallie said. She tried to stifle a chuckle, and failed. Annileen gestured for her to pipe down, but found herself smiling, too.

Ben stared at them, mildly flustered. "I'm missing something, aren't I?"

"No, you're *getting* something," Annileen said, kneeling beside the animal and touching her abdomen. "In a couple of days, it looks like."

"You can't mean . . ." Ben looked at Rooh's midsection, flabbergasted. "Pregnant?" He stammered. "That's simply not possible. I only *have* one eopie!"

"Not for long," Kallie said, snickering.

Annileen scooted over and felt Rooh's abdomen. "How long have you had her?"

Ben shuffled. "Er—I don't recall. I bought her some time ago." His brow furrowed. "You don't think this— er, *happened* at the oasis, do you?"

Kallie burst out laughing.

Annileen smiled, too, but looked down so as not to embarrass Ben any further. "Eopie gestation times are a *bit* longer than that. It looks like you got two for the price of one on that purchase."

"One cannot cast blame in matters of love," Ben said. "Or whatever." He cracked a smile, in spite of himself, and knelt. He rubbed the animal's face. "You've been keeping secrets, my little friend!"

"Congratulations, Grandpa," Annileen said.

With Kallie's help, Annileen removed the harness from Rooh's back. Freed, the animal stood up and resumed chomping on the weed. Annileen looked at the coolant unit. "Pretty beat up," she said.

"It's seen use," Ben said.

"In the Great Hyperspace War, maybe." Annileen shook her head. "I've never seen a coolant pump this old."

Ben cleared his throat. "Yes, well, I was hoping they've seen one at the repair shop in Bestine." He gestured to the east.

"You're going to *another store*?" Kallie said, eyes filling with dismay.

"People are like that, sweetie," Annileen said. "Give them a discount once and they'll never respect you again."

A snarky voice bellowed from inside the darkened window of the LiteVan. "You won't get that fixed in Bestine!"

Ben looked at Annileen and raised an eyebrow.

Annileen rolled her eyes. "My son. The other hermit." She walked to the speeder truck and slapped the window frame. "How do you know that, Jabe? You haven't even seen it!"

Jabe peeked out at them. "The supply shop in Bestine is closed. The Geelers' son is getting married. They'll be gone for a week."

Ben looked worriedly up at the suns and then down at the damaged unit. He swallowed. "A week, you say?"

"Or more," Jabe said, vanishing back into the darkness of the backseat. "The wedding is on Naboo. They decided to make a vacation of it."

"How wonderful for them," Ben said, deflated.

Kallie grabbed at her mother's arm, nearly knocking her down. "Mom! Ben can come into Mos Eisley with us!"

"Mos Eisley?" Ben's face froze. He looked to the east, his expression apprehensive. "I don't need to go to Mos Eisley!"

Jabe's voice called out again. "Hear that? He doesn't need to go to Mos Eisley."

"You hush," Annileen said. She looked back at the coolant pump. "You can get same-day service there," she said.

Ben waved his hands. "No, no. I'm sure you're on a supply run. You'll need room—"

Kallie bubbled with enthusiasm. "No, it's fine! We're not carrying anything!"

"You're not?"

"No! No!" Annileen's daughter found the document in her pocket and thrust it toward Ben. "Read this!"

Without taking the slip from the girl's hand, Ben read aloud the hand-printed words. *"To Annie: This certificate is good for a SoroSuub JG-8 luxury landspeeder, at Delroix Speeders of Mos Eisley. Ask for Garn. Sorry for all the trouble with your family speeder, hope this makes up for it."* Ben paused before concluding: *"Happy birthday. Love, Orrin."*

Ben looked back at Annileen, his eyebrow slightly raised. He smiled, gently. "Does this mean—"

"I don't know. Orrin's been like this lately. How should I know what it means?"

Kallie clapped her hands, elated. "I know what it means. It means I'm getting a new landspeeder. Mom's old one, as soon as Gloamer fixes it!"

"Like blazes!" Jabe yelled out from the LiteVan. "We haven't settled that!"

Annileen shrugged. "We're still negotiating a distribution of assets. Maybe they'll both get it."

"Is that wise?" Ben asked.

"Oh, yes," Annileen said. "This way, when they finally decide to run away from home, they'll get farther. Now, come along with us."

"No, really, that's not necessary." Ben pointed to a pair of figures by a tower on a distant northern ridge. "I'll just ask the folks whose land this is for help."

Annileen squinted. "Don't bother," she said, recognizing them. "This is Wyle Ulbreck's spread we're on. After the Tuskens ripped him off yesterday, his sentries are probably chained to the vaporators."

"Anything to save the skinflint from joining the Settlers' Call," Jabe said from the van. "He'll learn one day."

Annileen pointed at Ben with mock sternness. "And if you keep fighting serendipity, Master Kenobi, it's going to fight back. Now come on," she said, walking back to the sledge. "Let's get this unit into the truck."

Surrendering, Ben patted Rooh's head. "Should we carry her with us?"

A screech came from the vehicle's interior. "You're not putting that animal in *my truck*!" Jabe yelled.

"Your—" Annileen sighed. "A minute ago you wanted my landspeeder!"

The LiteVan went silent.

"He's sulking," she said to Ben. "But that's okay. I think our expectant mom will be happier at home." She turned Rooh west and gave her a pat on the behind. Promptly, the animal began loping off, retracing the sandy trail left by the sledge. "She'll find her way."

Ben looked after Rooh, concerned. "You know, I really should go with her. To make sure she'll be all right."

Kallie laughed. "I don't know what other trouble she could get into!"

"Don't worry," Annileen said, wiping her hands together. "She'll be home before the happy event. And you'll be living in a cool and comfortable house."

Resigned, Ben turned to help them lift the coolant unit. "I really do hate to prevail upon you to change your plans—"

"You're not changing *these* plans," Kallie gushed. "We're going to Mos Eisley!"

Annileen smiled. Ben's reluctance was almost charming—the man, she suspected, simply didn't want to be in anyone's debt. She'd just have to convince him it wasn't a concern. "The clan has spoken," she said. "You'd better come along."

Ben responded with a pained smile.

The Shistavanen had an evil-looking face, Orrin thought—nothing but fangs, pointy ears, and mud-colored hair. And yet Tar Lup was as cheerful a being as he'd ever known. More cheerful still, standing behind the counter of Dannar's Claim in his neat city-bought jacket.

"Thanks again for this chance, Master Gault," Tar said, the natural growl in his voice somehow sounding amiable. "It's good to be in charge, if even for a day. I don't get that in my regular job."

Standing atop a chair in the dining area, Orrin lowered the holocam he was holding. "That's fine, Tar. Glad you could come back and help out." Snapping the device off, he stepped down. He'd made sure he, too, was looking his best today, in the fineries Annileen had ordered from offworld. He needed to.

Pausing in front of the substitute clerk, Orrin looked down at the holorecorder in his hands. "Oh, this is part of another surprise for Annileen," he said. "Gonna get her some decent flooring in here for a change."

Tar smiled toothily. "That's wonderful. I was always fond of the Calwells."

"Me, too," Orrin said, stepping past Bohmer at his table. The Rodian had picked a day when Annileen was out to make his return, but she wasn't missing much. Patched up but heavily medicated, Bohmer seemed even more catatonic than usual. Orrin walked through the gap in the counter. "Tar, I need to get back in there for another second, if you don't mind."

"Certainly." The Shistavanen stepped out of the way.

That'll do it, Orrin thought, taking another look at the electronic manifest behind the cashbox. He checked the chrono on the wall. He had everything he needed and plenty of time to get to his meetings. All was going according to plan. *Both* plans.

Veeka walked in from the parking area. "Ready when you are, Dad." She walked to the bar and pulled her flask from her vest. Hopping onto the surface, she reached past the startled Tar to grab a bottle.

"No, you don't," Orrin said, before she could start filling. "Not today."

"Whatever." Irritated, Veeka dropped the bottle, which landed back into place with a glassy clank. Orrin passed her the holorecorder.

Tar watched, puzzled, as father and daughter walked toward the exit. "Will you be back for lunch, sir?"

"No, I'll be out most of the day," he said, giving the store a last look. "But, uh . . . tell Annileen I'll have something to talk to her about tonight."

Tar responded, but Orrin didn't hear. He had things to do.

CHAPTER TWENTY-NINE

FOR THE FIRST HALF of Annileen's life, Mos Eisley had been no more than a concept. Her father had feared the place, and clerking gave her few opportunities to travel. But the city was always out there: a magnet drawing the starships she occasionally saw high overhead. It had inspired her young imagination.

Images she had seen depicted Mos Eisley as a knotted web of crowded streets separating dusty domes, used and decaying. She hadn't wanted to believe the pictures. Those vessels in the sky hailed from cosmopolitan places with shining spires. Why would they visit Tatooine at all, if the city weren't something special? She'd looked forward to finding out for herself.

When the day came, it was one that already ran high with expectations: her wedding day. After the raucous sendoff from their friends, Dannar had surprised her by steering Orrin's borrowed landspeeder past Bestine and continuing east. As the kilometers sped by, the young bride's anticipation only grew. Spacecraft that soundlessly soared in the oasis sky rumbled and gleamed here, all heading to or from the steaming mirage on the horizon. For a few wonderful minutes, Annileen had allowed herself to imagine that her surprise honeymoon included a trip on one of those starships. To the Core

Worlds, perhaps. Or better, to one of the wild places shown in the university safari brochure. Reaching the streets of Mos Eisley, which turned out to be as shabby and hectic as the pictures had shown, did nothing to still her hopes. Her sights were set higher.

Dannar had pulled the vehicle up to the Twin Shadows Inn, an acceptably clean—if far from posh—establishment off Kerner Plaza. The stay was the gift, all that a rural shop owner starting out could afford.

But even with her stellar hopes dashed, Annileen soon realized that if she was looking for an exotic locale with strange creatures, Mos Eisley easily sufficed. Kerner Plaza was a relatively upscale neighborhood, with clean showrooms alongside outdoor bazaars. Located near the Republic travelers' aid office, the streets were safe enough to walk at twilight without blaster in hand. And Dannar had even taken her to dinner at the Court of the Fountain, where she had marveled at every sight. Only a Hutt-owned establishment was rich enough to use water for decoration.

Mos Eisley *was* a violent, congested mess, but it was also exciting and surprising, a doorway jammed half open to another dimension of adventure. If Mos Eisley wasn't the next best thing to going to the stars, it was still several steps closer than anything else on Tatooine. To this day, Annileen remembered every moment of the trip.

She and Dannar had never made it back to Mos Eisley together; some store emergency always interfered. But Annileen had returned several times since Dannar's death; usually alone, but once with each child individually. She and Dannar had always talked of bringing the whole family here at some point, but the chance had never come.

Now she walked the streets of the city with both children at once—and, for the first time, with a new companion. Ben walked behind the group, his cowl pulled low over his head. He stepped quickly to keep up with the Calwells, saying little. They looked like any other family, out on the town—only with a son unhappy to have his father along, and a father who wasn't too thrilled, either.

"He could have waited at the repair shop," Jabe said as the group turned a corner.

"It was going to be five hours!" Kallie said.

"I wouldn't have minded," Ben said, pleasantly. "There was a chair there."

"It had an engine manifold sitting on it," Annileen said, shaking her head. Jabe's annoyance at their hooded tagalong hadn't lessened since the testy ride in from the desert. The boy started walking faster through the crowd, ahead of his mother and sister. "Slow down, Jabe," Annileen said. "Stay with the group." She looked back at Ben and smiled. "You, too."

Ben gamely followed, but Annileen could tell wandering a busy city wasn't his first choice for a good time. Strange—he had seemed so well traveled to her. Well, maybe she could change that.

Turning the corner into Kerner Plaza, however, the foursome encountered a different form of traffic. Dozens of hammer-headed Ithorians thronged the open space, stomping their tree-trunk feet and jubilantly waving sound-makers and silver tassels. Within a second, the crowd of brown-skinned giants engulfed the human visitors.

"I think we've wandered into a wedding," Ben yelled, straining to be heard over the din.

"They have a lot of them here," Annileen called back, smiling.

A leather-skinned Ithorian danced past on spindly legs. Spying Annileen, the long-necked creature grabbed her by the shoulders and spun with her into the festive crowd. Whirling, Annileen could see Jabe reaching for his blaster—and then Ben placing his hand on the boy's wrist. Kallie was in the dance, now, too—as was, Annileen saw, just about every poor pedestrian who had wandered past.

The twirling slowed long enough for her to see a panicked Ben in the arms of a tall female Ithorian bedecked in garlands. The mother of the bride? Annileen didn't know. As they both spun, she could only tell that Ben definitely didn't want to dance, and that he just as surely had no choice, as the wave of partygoers surged again.

Finally, the alien released her, centrifugal force whipping her away to the side of the street. She braced herself against a stone column, laughing between gasps for breath. A delighted Kallie broke free next—followed by Ben. His hood down and hair mussed, he looked like a man who'd just finished a podrace.

Reclaiming her hat, Annileen scanned the crowd for Jabe. She found him against the nearest building, leaning standoffishly and clearly prepared to pull his blaster on anyone who came near. "I thought you wanted to get out of the store to have fun," she said.

"Not my idea of fun," her son said. His flustered look vanished a second later, however, as a procession of scantily clad Twi'lek women emerged from the building behind him, carrying trays of multicolored drinks.

Well, we've found your idea of fun, Annileen thought. Another group of servers followed. Twi'lek males, their attire even more unsuited to the dangerous suns, brought silver platters with exotic foodstuffs for anyone and everyone.

"This party is getting better all the time," Kallie said, smiling. "Can we stay here?"

Annileen looked over at Ben. He looked gray. She couldn't imagine he wanted to stay in the festival a second longer. Looking at the building the servers had emerged from, though, she realized where she was. *Serendipity,* she thought, amused.

Gesturing for the beleaguered Ben to wait for a moment, she took her children aside. "You kids can have lunch down here. One hour," she said.

"Two!" Kallie said.

"Three!" Jabe added, gawking at the women.

"An hour and a half," Annileen said. She jabbed her finger against Jabe's sternum. "You're on alert. We're not going to have another Mos Espa. If you leave Kallie's sight for an instant—or get near anything stronger than blue milk—she's going to call me. I'll be here in a flash—and you'll be in a world of hurt." She looked around at the crazed partiers. "And don't either of you get engaged to—well, anyone!"

Kallie laughed. Rolling his eyes, her brother nodded. "Where will *you* be?" he asked.

Annileen looked back at Ben, standing out of earshot. "I have some questions that need answers," she said. "You kids have fun."

Hat in hand, Orrin walked down the steps from the branch office of the Aargau Investment Trust. There wasn't any point in being dejected, as the official had said nothing he hadn't heard once a month for three years. Bankers annoyed Orrin more than lawyers did. What to make of people who had so much money they were willing to drop piles of it on others across the galaxy, just because they had an idea?

Even a good idea, Orrin thought. But at least the banker had confirmed what he'd wanted to know. He removed the holocam from his satchel and tossed it into the open backseat of the USV-5.

Mullen was there, snoring. Orrin looked around. He

didn't know where Veeka had flitted. "Wake up," he said, slapping his sleeping son with his hat.

By reflex, Mullen reached for his shoulder holster—before recognizing his father. "Well?"

"It's going according to plan. Plan One, anyway." Orrin scanned the buildings across from the bank until he found what he was looking for. Locating the cantina, he found Veeka, too—emerging with three scruffy-looking human spacers, all of whom looked quite unable to fly despite the noon hour. Seeing her father, she made her good-byes.

"She sure makes friends fast," Orrin said, resigned.

"That's because she always buys," Mullen said, slipping into the front seat.

Hands on his hips, Orrin glared at Veeka as she approached. "Do you ever listen?"

"I'm fine," Veeka said, knocking the holo-emitter out of the way and sliding into the backseat of the land-speeder. "I'll be ready."

She seemed sober enough, Orrin thought. Well, he couldn't worry about rehabilitating his family now. There'd be a chance for that—after.

He strapped on his blaster and climbed into the passenger seat. The engine started, and the landspeeder moved back into the crowded streets of Mos Eisley. "Set the windshield to opaque," he said. "I don't want to run into Annie today."

CHAPTER THIRTY

ANNILEEN FOUND THE CAFÉ again easily. She and Dannar had discovered it years earlier, just paces from the Twin Shadows Inn and up the street from the building from which the Twi'leks had emerged. Ben didn't resist when Annileen took him by the hand, leading him past the crowd and inside.

"Thank you," he said in the lobby, exhaling. "I owe you a life debt."

"You sure hate crowds," she said, climbing the stairs to the upper level.

"When Ithorians dance, it's best to get off the floor."

The master of the house greeted them warmly. Annileen had always enjoyed Café Tatoo II, including it on her solo trips to the spaceport. The kindly old man led her to the awning-shaded balcony, overlooking the plaza. Ben chose a chair at a table away from other diners. She sat across from Ben, ordered the lunch special for them both, and clasped her hands together, ready to study her subject. She had been waiting forever for another chance to talk to him alone. Now she couldn't figure out which question to ask first—if Ben would let her.

He shifted uncomfortably in his chair. "The clerk at the repair shop did say five hours, no?"

"Five hours," she said. "Take your hood off. You're in a civilized place now."

Ben complied.

"I was worried when you didn't come back to the store," she said. "It's been a long time."

"Ah. Yes, I've been busy," he said, raising his glass to drink.

"With?"

"Things."

"Things," she said, unbelieving. It was amazing how the man could use something as small as a cup to hide behind.

Seemingly sensing her frustration, he set the drink down and grinned. "You've seen the grounds of my palace. I'm still working through the junk that might be toxic."

Annileen nodded. "I was afraid we'd scared you off. With Kallie snooping around, telling everyone your last name."

"Most people have one," Ben said. "Why shouldn't I?"

Annileen put her elbows on the table and leaned over toward him. "I was also worried that maybe Orrin had scared you off," she said in a quieter voice.

"Oh, no." Ben sat casually back in his chair, putting some distance between them. "I like Orrin. And . . . he seems to like you."

"This week," Annileen said. "Usually, that means he wants something."

"The landspeeder's a nice gesture. Perhaps he's in earnest."

Annileen sat up straight, regarding him skeptically. "Really."

Ben shifted again, tracing his finger around the circumference of his glass. "You know, I don't know much about these things. But sometimes people's attitudes can change over the years. They can get closer." He smiled at her, awkwardly.

"Unh-huh." Annileen reached for her glass and drank; now she was the one hiding her expression. Inwardly, she was amused to no end. She didn't know if Ben was trying to palm her off on Orrin or not, but he had just revealed some truth. He might stop runaway dewbacks and talk to Tuskens, but Ben Kenobi was on completely foreign territory when it came to discussing matters of the heart.

A rickety server droid approached from behind Ben, saving him from further embarrassment. Annileen recognized the mechanical. "Hi, Geegee."

The bipedal violet-colored droid set down the food and bowed. "It is nice of you to remember, madam." The droid was an ancient model; its hands quivered slightly as it placed the plates before the couple. "Good appetite to you, patrons."

Annileen smiled as the electronic waiter rattled away. "GG-8 served us when Dannar and I were here on our honeymoon," she told Ben. "It was the first time a droid had ever brought me anything. I felt like the Queen of Alderaan."

Ben took fork in hand. "You could have a droid at the oasis, I'm sure?"

"The farmhands don't like to see them. They take away jobs on the range."

"Well, you seem kind to them," he noted.

"No reason not to be," she said.

Ben smiled and began to eat.

All through lunch, Annileen felt like a tracker losing a trail. Ben still seemed to have that sadness hidden deep within—it came out whether he wanted it to or not. But every attempt to nudge him toward a personal revelation resulted in his nimble escape to another topic. She couldn't become cross with him; even this verbal fencing had the same fun and easiness of their lunch the day of the podraces. Rather, she began to feel sorry for how much work he was putting in, changing subjects.

Fine, she decided as she finished her dessert. If Ben was going to insist on being more interested in her life than in talking about his, well, she'd make the sacrifice. And Ben *did* seem willing to listen to her entire litany of worries. About Kallie, and what future she might find. The livery wasn't yet drudgery for her, but there weren't many options beyond that. Would she really be happy married to some farmhand?

And of course, they talked about Jabe. Annileen had kept closer watch on her son since the Tusken massacre. The boy wasn't out of control, but for some reason Jabe wanted her to think he was. Ben seemed to share her concern. "When people show you signs, it's important to read them," he said.

But mostly, they talked about her. About her childhood, and animals. About her father, and the failed ranch. About her hopes to study, and how that direction had changed. And about the thing that, above and beyond Tusken Raiders, Orrin's antics, or even her children's upbringing, occupied the most territory in her life.

The Claim.

And Ben wasn't having any of her complaints about it. "I know you love it. I've seen you. You enjoy holding court—being the center that holds it all together."

Annileen laughed. "You want the job? It's yours."

"Oh, no," Ben said, picking at his dessert. "I've never been one for the politics of large rooms." He took another bite. "Or smaller ones."

Annileen smiled.

"Consider parties," he said. "They've always struck

me as big uncontrolled experiments in social dynamics. It's as if you're stress-testing every relationship you have at once."

"You're having lots of parties out there on the Jundland?"

"Just me and the eopie—soon to be plural."

"And assorted eavesdroppers," Annileen said. "If you don't mind my saying so, you don't seem cut out for the hermit life."

Mouth full of cake, Ben stopped himself from laughing. "We were talking about *you*."

"Right. Well, life at the store isn't what it's cracked up to be." Annileen looked at the frayed awning above and clenched her fists. *Okay, if you really want to hear it, here goes.*

"I'm listening."

"You see the Claim as a place to come to," she said. "To interact, to get away from the nothingness. Well, everyone else around the oasis sees it the same way. Everyone. They show up before the second sun is up in the morning—and *then they never leave*."

"I have noticed a certain resident status for some."

"For *some*?" Annileen's hands shook on the table, rattling her dinnerware. "Dannar used to joke that the Claim was the tenth largest city on Tatooine, when it was full. And I'm not sure that's far off." She looked down at her empty plate. "I'm barely holding together my own family, and yet I'm keeping all these other people going, too. I'm not just feeding and clothing my own. I've got everyone!"

Catching her breath, she looked up at him. He was still listening intently, but she was embarrassed all the same. "Sorry," she said. "Am I ranting?"

Ben spoke calmly—that stoic reserve in full evidence. "A life that seems small on the outside can be limitless on the inside. Even a person living in the remotest place can be concerned about hundreds. Or the whole galaxy."

Annileen stared at him, mesmerized. "Who *are* you?"

" 'Crazy Ben,' your son says." He grinned. "I actually think I like the sound of—"

Ben stopped suddenly. Annileen followed his gaze across the street and saw a human in a black uniform and hat standing beside a figure fully clad in white armor.

A spacesuit of some kind? "What is *that*?" she asked.

Ben slid back in his chair, away from the balcony railing. "Well, I'm not sure," he said, his voice lower and softer than it had been. He looked again out of the corner of his eye. "I would almost say it looks like a clone trooper. I've . . . seen holos of them." He studied the figure for another second before looking away. "But the uniforms are slightly different."

Annileen watched the strange pair. They weren't looking at her—or even at the festival going on all around them. Instead, they were examining the building they were standing in front of. "That suit's got to be awful in this heat," she said. "I wonder why they're here."

"I don't know," Ben said, head down as he scraped his plate. "Er—what are they doing now?"

Spying the datapad in the hand of the hatted figure, Annileen recognized the behavior instantly. "They're taking inventory," she said. "That used to be the Republic's aid station on Tatooine. I don't know what it is now, given whatever has been going on out there."

"What *has* been going on?" Ben asked.

"You'd know more than I would. I've never left the planet," she said. "But if they're with this New Order or whatever it is, maybe they're still figuring out what it is they own."

"Mmm," Ben said. He glanced around, newly uneasy.

Annileen checked her chrono. "I guess we'd better get down there ourselves and get back to the kids."

"You know what? I think we should wait awhile." Ben stretched and patted his stomach. "To go down to the street."

A little surprised, Annileen nodded. "Sure. More time to talk, I guess."

"And it's the strangest thing. I'm suddenly developing a chill." Ben rubbed at his throat. "I hope I'm not coming down with something." With that, he pulled his hood back over his head and sank lower in his seat.

Annileen shook her head. Obfuscation Kenobi was back.

Across town, Mullen signaled from his post near the round building.

"Nothing yet," Veeka said, speaking into her comlink.

In the passenger seat of the landspeeder, Orrin shook his head. "They said Docking Bay Eighty-Seven." For the third time that minute, he checked to see if his blaster was in its holster. He just felt more comfortable knowing it was there.

Orrin knew the docking bay wasn't where the second of his two Mos Eisley meetings was to take place. He had called the meeting; the other party would take every step to place him at a disadvantage. He knew he didn't need to be worried, given his plans. But still, he wanted Mullen and Veeka nearby, checking things out. Whatever faults his children had, there wasn't much they couldn't handle if things came to a fight.

He was mostly sure things wouldn't—but he still reached down to pat the handle of his blaster again.

"You won't need that," a voice said from behind him.

Orrin turned to see Bojo Boopa sitting in the backseat of the USV-5, pointing a blaster at him. He hadn't heard the Gossam get in, but now he saw the creature's Ga-

morrean companions taking station at either side of the
vehicle, parting only to permit the entry of a character
Orrin had never met before.

"Nice speeder," the scaly-faced Klatooinian said, taking the driver's seat. The bronze-skinned creature then
burst into giggles. "I want one! I want one!"

Orrin looked at the alien—and then back at Boopa
with alarm.

"Just drive, Jorrk," the Gossam said, lowering his gun
and stretching out in the cushy seat. "Our buddy Gault
here has somewhere to be. And he'd better tell us what
we want to hear."

CHAPTER THIRTY-ONE

"NOW, KIDS," ANNILEEN SAID, "you realize this will be *my* landspeeder and not yours, right? Just so we understand each other."

"Huh?" Jabe said, sitting behind the controls.

Equally spellbound, Kallie ran her hand across the hood. "Oh, yeah. Sure, Mom."

Ben grinned at Annileen. "I think you're in trouble."

"I have been," she said. "For seventeen years."

Annileen looked around the Delroix Speeders showroom. There were models here she'd never seen—nor was she likely to, out in the desert. With its open cockpit and ornate steering vanes up front, the JG-8 seemed the least practical of all; she'd need to keep it in the garage to preserve its ruby color.

"It's nice," Ben said, examining the display nearby. The price was there, at the bottom, listed with options and without. Both figures were in the tens of thousands of credits. He looked up at Annileen. "It's a generous gift, to be sure."

"A gift. Right," Kallie said, rolling her eyes. "If you can't win their hearts, buy them. It's the Gault way." She looked back at her mother, who was admiring the interior. "But it's the only way we'd ever get something like this."

"Oh, I could afford to buy it myself," Annileen said. "But I never would."

Ben raised an eyebrow. "I didn't think a frontier merchant did so well."

Annileen smiled. "What, did you think the personal deliveries to new arrivals cut into the profits?"

"I really don't—"

"It's twenty-plus years of scrimping and saving—and avoiding whatever new thing Orrin had for us to invest in." She ran her hand along the rich fabric on the seats. "But this is amazing. I didn't think anything like this existed."

"It *is* amazing, isn't it?" asked a husky voice. The dealer, a happy, squat human in his fifties, patted the rear engine lovingly. He gestured to the backseat. "It's the extended model, ma'am, straight from Sullust. Extra room in the back for light cargo, or for your children." The retailer looked at the teenagers fawning over the vehicle, and then at Ben. "Congratulations, sir, on raising such a fine family."

Ben stammered. "Oh, no, these aren't—"

"—as fine as you think," Annileen finished. She grinned at his unease. *Breathe, Ben.* She turned to the dealer. "But the landspeeder looks wonderful, Garn. What happens next?"

"Master Gault authorized the contract yesterday afternoon, ma'am. She's all yours." The seller passed her a pouch containing the vehicle's maintenance codes. "Be sure to tell Orrin that Garn Delroix provided good service."

"I will." Annileen looked back to see that Kallie was already in the passenger seat, and that Jabe had started the engine. "I'd better go now, if I ever want to see it again. Come on, Ben!"

Ben followed her into the backseat. Annileen gasped

as she sat down. "Have you ever ridden in anything as nice as this?"

"It is nice," he said.

Jabe guided the vehicle out through the wide doorway and into the busy streets of Mos Eisley. The foot traffic was noisier than the landspeeder by far. "Take it easy, now," Annileen warned her son, leaning forward to be heard.

"No problem." Jabe smiled broadly and gripped the control stick—

—and the landspeeder rocketed ahead, accelerating at a sudden rate that pushed three Calwells and a Kenobi back into their luxuriously cushioned seats. Jabe guided the gleaming vehicle through the curved streets at a break-neck pace. The landspeeder drew close to one building and then another, before whipping under the neck of a surprised saurian ronto. By the time the giant bolted, the JG-8 was careening down another street.

"Stop! Stop!"

A second after Annileen yelled her command, Jabe punched the brake—and the world stopped moving outside. Driver and riders were tossed forward into the restraint webbing, which caught them like a mother catching a child.

Annileen was less gentle with her own child. "Jabe, what were you thinking?"

"Sorry! I just touched it," Jabe said, stroking the steering yoke admiringly. "Not as good on the turns as I'd like. But I'd bet Gloamer could really soup it up."

"Not going to happen!" Annileen said. Ben seemed amused.

She looked at her daughter. "Both of you, switch into the back. The grown-ups are taking over."

Kallie opened her door and stepped out of the hover-ing vehicle, while Annileen stood in her seat, wondering where they'd wound up. They were in a bazaar in a part of Mos Eisley she'd never been to before. Standing by her mother's side of the vehicle, Kallie pointed off to the left. "Hey, is that the Bezzards over there?"

Annileen turned to look. It was a young couple, yes—but they were older than her recent houseguests. "Not the Bezzards," she said, squinting. "But I do know them."

Reclining in his seat, Ben smiled mildly. "Annileen knows everyone."

"Yeah, the man came through once looking for parts for something," she said. "That's Cliegg Lars's son, Owen."

Ben's eyes widened—and locked on the couple emerging from behind the fruit stand, a basket of purchases in the man's hands.

"Sad story, the Larses," Annileen said, only half noticing Ben's sudden move to adjust his boot. Across the road from the landspeeder, the brown-haired woman with Owen Lars turned, and Annileen saw what she was carrying. "Hey, they've had a baby!"

Kallie started to wave to the couple. "Let's call them over!"

At once—and quite free from Jabe's grasp—the landspeeder's control stick slammed forward, causing the vehicle to hurtle ahead again. Kallie twirled and fell to the sandy street, buffeted by the jet wash from the twin engines. Aboard, the unrestrained Annileen fell backward into Ben's arms.

The boy grabbed the steering yoke in panic. The vehicle skirted over the top of a wheeled cart and ripped through an intersection, even as its young driver fought the controls. "It's stuck!" he yelled.

Annileen scrambled across the center console and helped him pull back on the stick. All at once it gave way, and the acceleration died. The vehicle floated to a stop in front of an illegally parked starship, whose owner, fearing the arrival of authorities, ran for his loading ramp.

She fell back into the backseat, out of breath. Ben seemed rattled and wary, but otherwise intact. She clutched at her son's sleeve. "Jabe, I told you to knock it off!"

"I didn't do it, Mom! It started on its own!"

"On its own?" Annileen felt as if an artery had ruptured in her head. "You nearly killed your sister!"

Rising cautiously, Ben raised his hand. "No, no. I saw it," he said. "Jabe's telling the truth. I saw the control stick. It slipped forward, on its own, while you weren't looking."

Both Calwells looked at Ben. Annileen looked incredulous. Jabe was absolutely stupefied. "Th-thanks," he said.

"I don't believe this," Annileen railed. "Pricy landspeeders don't just start driving!"

"Still, that's what I saw," Ben said. "Jabe saved us." He bowed his head slightly to Jabe, who looked at him in wonder.

Aggravated, Annileen shook her head. "I'm gonna give that dealer a piece of my mind!"

Ben put up his hand. "I don't think that's necessary—"

Annileen glared at him. "What, you'll save us from wild animals and Tuskens but not defective vehicles?"

Ben was speechless.

It was as harshly as Annileen had ever spoken to him, and she regretted it instantly. She sank back into the seat and tried to calm down.

She looked about. They were in a neighborhood she'd never seen before. "Where are we?"

Placing his hood back over his head, Ben scanned the area. "Nowhere near where we were," he said, with what almost seemed like satisfaction. He was breathing easier now, Annileen saw, and it made her feel better. Until her comlink went off.

"Jabe tried to kill me!" the tinny voice shrieked.

"It's all a dumb mistake," Annileen told her daughter over the comm. "Stay where you are, Kallie. We'll be back for you in—"

Ben grabbed at her sleeve. "Annileen," he said, pointing out of his side of the vehicle. "There!"

She looked out to see a landspeeder that resembled Orrin's, being driven by a Klatooinian. It parked near the Mos Eisley Inn, and Bojo Boopa emerged from the back. The other passenger door opened.

"Orrin!"

Annileen rose in her seat and watched, spellbound, as across the way two armed humans stepped up and frisked Orrin. His holster was empty, she saw, and the man made no move to oppose the search. He looked grim.

"That's the Gossam from the store!" Annileen said.

Jabe reached for his blaster. "They're mugging him!"

"No." Ben reached forward and touched the boy's shoulder firmly. "I don't think that's what's happening."

Then what is *happening?* Annileen wondered as the human and alien toughs conducted Orrin past the hotel and toward an alleyway. She looked at Ben. "Orrin's not even supposed to be in town today!"

Jabe started to move again, only to be stopped this time by Annileen.

"Mom, they're taking him away! We've got to help him!"

"We don't know what's happening," Annileen said. "It could be business. It could be nothing," she added. But she didn't believe it.

She looked plaintively to Ben, who was already out of the vehicle. He walked to the driver's side and spoke quickly. "You two get Kallie and return here. I'll see what I can find out."

"You?" Jabe objected. "You're crazy. You don't even carry a blaster!"

"And if one is necessary," Ben said sternly, "that's more reason you shouldn't go." His expression softened. "Orrin was one of the first people to welcome me here. If he needs help, I'll get it for him."

Reluctantly, Jabe agreed. Ben waved to Annileen. "See you soon."

Orrin marched toward the durasteel doors of the town house. It was an unassuming place—a pourstone blockhouse in the shadows of the Mos Eisley Inn, with a large dome to the left of the front entrance. It wasn't what he'd expected at all. And while he had an escort, there were no guards outside the building. It didn't make sense.

Or maybe it did. Who'd be crazy enough to attack *here*?

Boopa pointed him to the main entrance. Orrin walked up the steps, ready for anything. He nearly fell back down them again when a black sensor orb jabbed out from an iris near the doorway.

It spoke in Huttese, and then again in Basic. *"Identification and purpose!"*

Orrin took a deep breath. "Orrin Gault." He looked at his hands and flexed his fingers. "I have important business to discuss—with Jabba the Hutt!"

CHAPTER THIRTY-TWO

HUMAN SWEAT DRIPPED ONTO finely carved ceramic tiles. Jabba's foyer was as richly appointed as the building's exterior was modest. Orrin wasn't surprised. He'd heard Jabba kept a presence in Mos Eisley, apart from his mountain palace; the Hutt seemed to want to convey a benevolent paternal presence to the locals.

There was nothing benevolent about the place, though. *This* was where the guards were, Orrin realized. Four more Gamorreans stood here, two at either side of the door, large poleaxes in their hands. They looked bored.

Bojo Boopa and Jorrk followed Orrin in, blasters at the ready. As they marched Orrin down a wide hallway, he again felt the empty space in his holster. Boopa had even taken his comlinks; Mullen and Veeka had no idea where he was.

The audience chamber loomed ahead, behind a roll-away blast door. A silvery bipedal droid emerged and scanned Orrin's body, confirming that he was unarmed. Orrin felt like everyone was watching. Why did they put people through this? Was this really necessary?

The droid said in guttural tones, "Jabba will see you now."

Great suns, Orrin thought, pulse racing as he urged his feet to move. *How did it come to this?*

He inhaled deeply and walked through the doors. In the center of the rotunda, atop the long wooden platform built for a Hutt's power sled, Orrin beheld . . .

. . . something else. In place of a sled, a small figure in a light green business suit huddled over a desk. The pink-and-brown creature punched numbers into a datapad. Credits of all colors sat stacked in orderly piles on the desktop. A squat safedroid wobbled on its wheels nearby, its maw open and ready to accept currency.

Orrin didn't recognize the desk worker's species. He had an almost simian face, his cheeks accented by two straight, finely coiffed tufts of quill-like whiskers. Large, studious black eyes remained fixed on the calculations before him as he entered each new figure with zeal. And like the Gamorreans at the gate, he paid no mind to the new arrival.

Jorrk shoved Orrin toward the center of the room. Behind, Orrin saw three more Gamorreans along the room's perimeter—and Boopa, who placed Orrin's comlinks and blaster on a small table.

Orrin looked up into the dome above the room. Slivers of light from vents cut high in the bowl filtered down through heavy wire mesh netting, suspended meters above the floor. The metal web made no sense architecturally; the only break in the pattern was at the focal point of the dome, where a square mass sat over the center of the room. Orrin squinted. Was something up there?

With a cautious last look at the guards, Orrin removed his hat and spoke. "I'm here."

"Indeed you are!" The being at the desk looked up and smiled toothily. "I *like* this human. Observant."

"They told me Jabba was here," Orrin said, feeling

some blood reentering his limbs. "Either they were wrong, or you've lost weight."

"Ha!" The suited alien slapped the desk for emphasis. "Observant, *and* with a sense of humor." He set down his datapad and stood. "Yes, I like this! I want to be in business with such a person, I do!"

"But who are you?"

"Ah. Mosep Binneed, your humble servant," the creature said, bowing. He was a full head shorter than Orrin. "I manage Jabba's portfolio when he's not here."

Clutching at the brim of his hat, Orrin shifted uncomfortably. "Boopa said this was Jabba's place, so I assumed—"

"His Immensity is a busy creature," Mosep said, lifting a small tray of money. Like cleaning crumbs from a plate, he slid the credits into the safedroid's innards. "But Jabba knows the people of Mos Eisley feel better when he's around. So at this office, Jabba is always in. My cousin Lhojugg and I are the joint caretakers."

"Is that so," Orrin said, not caring. *No Jabba?* He was thrilled!

Mosep looked up, a sparkle in his eye. "I also travel under Jabba's name from time to time, representing his interests. It doesn't hurt to confuse the competition. So, yes, for today's purposes—with our master's kind permission—you could say I *am* Jabba."

Jorrk chortled. "Monkey Jabba, Monkey Jabba!"

"That's unkind, Jorrk," Mosep said, casting a sidelong glance at the tough. "You'll have to excuse my associate. He saw a Geniserian sand monkey once, and hasn't failed to find his joke funny since. I am, of course, a Nimbanel." He looked back at Orrin. "A good tactic for Jabba, though, don't you think?"

Orrin felt impatient. "Why are you telling me this?"

"Because you're part of the family, Orrin, my boy. No secrets among us, are there?"

"I'm not part of *your* family!"

Jorrk giggled again.

Mosep bristled his whiskers and reached for his datapad. "If you insist on getting to business—let's see. Yes, here's your record." He read quietly, his hairless lips every so often smacking. "My, this is disturbing."

While Mosep continued the routine, his tongue occasionally clicking, Orrin fought the urge to move, to say something. *This is torture!*

At the thought, Orrin glanced up and saw movement above the netting. A dark, lithe figure moved past the lights, glancing against the mesh and raising a racket. "Something . . . something's up there."

Mosep didn't look up from the datapad. "That would be the Kayven whistlers," he said. "Carnivorous fliers. They live in the rafters—but occasionally we hoist a treat up to them."

Orrin looked up with alarm. The square shape nearly above him, he now saw, was a cage, attached to a pulley system reaching into unseen heights above. "A *treat*?"

Mosep looked at Boopa. "Yes, who was the treat today?"

Boopa lifted a human leg bone from the floor beside him. "Problem gambler, I think."

Mosep smiled at Orrin. "They've had their fill. You can relax."

Orrin could do no such thing. There were more sounds above—and more shadows. For a moment, he almost thought he saw a bipedal figure in motion, soaring from one of the ventilation slits to the cable. Another clatter followed, with more wings slamming the nets.

"I've read enough." The Nimbanel accountant set down the datapad. "You owe us quite a bit of money, my boy."

"I'm not your boy, Binneed!"

"All I know is certain obligations have not been met,"

Mosep said. "But I'm getting ahead of myself. *You* called this meeting." Mosep sat down in his chair and cracked his hairy knuckles. "I suspect it's *not* because you're ready to repay in full."

"I'm working on that," Orrin said, reaching for his courage. "No. I want you out," he said, firmly.

"Out?" Mosep smiled mildly. His long whiskers bristled. "How so?"

"Out of my hair. Your punks have been coming around my ranch, my store—"

"*Your* store?" Suddenly interested, Mosep looked again at the datapad. "No, no. My records show your holdings only include the ranch, the vehicles in the garages, and the barracks for your muscle."

"They're called *farmhands*!" Orrin raged. "Not that you people would know. You haven't done a day's honest work in your lives."

"Oh, they work," Mosep said, idly sorting credits. "It may not be poking around in the sand or sweating the air for water, but it's work. Investments are made. Capital is expended. And a return is expected."

"Yeah, or you sweat *us*!"

"You're the one making this unpleasant, Orrin. Or Master Gault, if you prefer. The fact that you're dealing with me ought to be a sign of respect, I should think. My superior knows there are different kinds of business, and that they must be conducted in different ways." He turned his black eyes on Orrin. "Believe me, if Jabba *wanted* to deal unpleasantly, you'd have known it by now. Still, we must check on our investments—and that means going to the site. Including this store, which you seem to keep offices in."

Another clatter from above. The hoodlums paid it no mind.

"My business depends on my reputation," Orrin said, chastened. "Part of the value in my operation is goodwill. I've worked twenty-odd years to build it. If your thugs start showing up, I lose that."

"Indeed?"

"You bet," Orrin said. "People will start to measure the water coming out of Gault drums, to see if I'm shorting them."

Mosep rose from the desk and began pacing. "It's too late for such concerns. You comprehend that, Orrin—you're a good businessman. Or you *were* one. You know we can't let this continue."

Orrin looked around, wary of any movement. "Look, this year's harvest is going to be big. *Real* big. It's taken a while to get the new vaporators set up right, but it's about to turn around—"

"I don't understand much about agriculture, I'm afraid," the accountant said. "But I know arithmetic. Even if we kept to the payment plan you were on, I don't see any way you could make poor Jabba whole again. Not even," he added, "if you tap your *other* resources."

The comment threw Orrin. "Other resources? What are you talking about?"

Mosep tapped the datapad and smiled knowingly. "Pretty clever, what you boys are doing out there. Even if Jabba thought of it first, more than a decade ago."

"I don't know what you're—"

"Fine. Play innocent." Mosep pitched the datapad to the desk, where it disturbed the credit stacks. "I guess it's so easy, anyone can do it. Though this year's Tuskens aren't much for fighting back."

Another ruckus from above. Orrin shook his head, trying to register everything. "Wait. Did you say you were going to change the payment plan?"

"Yes," Mosep said. "You might say that *we* want out." He fingered his vest buttons. "Double your usual payment for tomorrow—and the full balance in two weeks."

Two weeks? Orrin gulped. Even the first condition was impossible. "I've tried to keep up. You've seen it! It's just this last couple of payments that have been short. Why now?"

Mosep grinned. "I thought you wanted it to be over."

"It'll never be over," Orrin said, enraged. "I know you people! You get your claws into someone and you never let go!"

"In another time," Mosep said, "we'd be perfectly happy to have . . . a long-term *engagement* with your business. We find you to be rather inventive, for a rural. But the truth is Jabba is in need of cash, now, not investments."

"In need of—" Orrin looked around. Apart from the macabre mess of a ceiling, the rest of the room stank of money, right down to the finely woven tapestry hanging behind the platform depicting a scene from Hutt history. "You seem to be doing pretty well!"

Mosep looked at the credits on the desk and chuckled. "No, Jabba needs a good bit more. It's this Galactic Empire the Republic became. It's quite the change. Until we see how it'll deal with the Hutts, Jabba wants as much cash on hand as possible."

"To bribe the new people, you mean!"

"Or whatever is necessary. No business likes uncertainty." Mosep looked at his pocket chrono. "So, twenty-four hours for the penultimate payment, shall we say?"

Orrin slouched, feeling the weight of the galaxy. He stammered. "I—I have some plans. I can get it. But I might need more time. If you could take a little less tomorrow—"

In the center of the room, Mosep snapped his fingers, suddenly reminded. "Yes, that's right. I'd forgotten about that. We've taken a little less already, these last three payments. It's why we sent you Bojo." He looked to the guards. "Well, as you've done us the convenience of coming here, you can be punished for that right away."

Orrin dropped his hat. *"What?"*

"Smash his hands," Jorrk said, cackling. "He won't need that swank drivey-drivey anymore."

"Naw," Boopa said, slapping the Klatooinian in the chest with the back of his hand. "Smash his legs. He spends time in that store. Everything he needs is just a crawl away."

"No, no, no!" Mosep shook his head vigorously, his face disappearing in a blur of whiskers. "This gentle-being still has a day to find payment. We can't allow punitive measures, however just, to impede his mobility." Mosep looked Orrin over. "We'll give him an hour with the nerve disruptor in the basement. Sir, what shape is your heart in?"

Orrin's eyes bulged. "I—I—"

"I suppose we'll find out," Mosep said, nodding to the guards. "One for the show, please." Then he beckoned toward the droid, standing by the doorway. "I'll watch the feed from up here. Can you bring me some caf?"

CHAPTER THIRTY-THREE

ORRIN LUNGED TO THE RIGHT. He'd seen the sealed door there, providing Hutt-sized access to the street. But a Gamorrean waddled in front of the exit, giant blade in giant hand. Another hulking figure lumbered toward Orrin from behind. Bojo Boopa and Jorrk blocked the main entrance and any chance of reaching his comlinks and blaster, still sitting tantalizingly on the table.

"Time to play 'Fry the farmer'!" Boopa said.

"Fry, fry!" Jorrk exclaimed with glee.

Orrin looked around in desperation. All he saw was Mosep, trying to escape the center of the room before the Gamorrean behemoth stepped on him. "Careful, friends!" Mosep said. "There's no need to be hasty. Most accidents happen in the workplace!"

The Gamorrean behind him lunged. Orrin twisted and fat fingers raked at his back. But the movement only brought Orrin into Jorrk's reach. *"Fryfryfry!"*

"No!" Orrin wrested free from the Klatooinian and fell toward the wooden platform. His chest slammed against the tile floor. He tried to wriggle forward, but Jorrk grabbed at his feet. Writhing, the farmer rolled over—and at that instant, he heard a metallic snap. A dark metal shape appeared above the heads of his attackers.

Klaaang! The heavy metal cage from the rafters crashed down, pummeling one of the advancing Gamorreans, caroming off the green brute, and knocking Jorrk off his feet. Startled, another of the Gamorreans stumbled backward and landed on Mosep. The accountant howled in pain.

Boopa pointed up into the dome: a square opening now existed in the mesh where the metal prison had been. Still on his back, Orrin saw what Boopa saw: a tan-clad figure high in the lofty shadows, clinging to what remained of the chain.

"Somebody's up there!" the Gossam shouted. *"Blast him!"*

Forgetting the farmer, Boopa started shooting upward. Jorrk joined him, and then two more guards entered from the hallway, blasters raised. Orrin took a quick look at the figure above; whoever was up there was now in spectacular motion, using the cage's severed lifting chain to bounce from wall to wall. Orrin couldn't wait any longer. On his hands and knees, he quickly scuttled up the platform and behind the desk.

Orrin instantly realized that the Nimbanel's desk was in the safest place in the room. All the gun-toting thugs were firing upward, through the gap and the meshwork. And while the shots seemingly had no effect on the impossibly nimble intruder, they did get the attention of the dozen or so Kayven whistlers in the dome. Annoyed by the blasterfire, the meter-long reptilian fliers soared downward, swooping through the opening toward anything moving.

"Yaaaghh!" Jorrk yelled as a whistler latched onto his shoulder and bit. The Gamorreans were squealing, trying to fend off attacking fliers with their axes.

"The door!" Boopa yelled, cowering behind a statue. "Open the doors to the street!"

"Only Jabba's sled triggers the door!" came a response from somewhere in the room.

Orrin hid under the desk. Now and again, the terrified farmer heard a fleshy thud nearby. He peeked out to search for a weapon but could find only credits, scattered on the floor around him.

"Close the blast door," someone yelled. "They'll get into the house!"

But Orrin did not hear a door being moved. All he heard were screams, the thunder of feet, and the high-pitched whistles of Kayven predators that had evidently gone off their diets. The ruckus finally faded when the parties involved took the fray into the rest of the residence.

The room fell silent. Orrin cowered beneath the desk, which had twisted sideways in the bustle. Before he could emerge, however, he saw Boopa creeping out from behind a bronze statue. Wary and frazzled, the Gossam looked up and around. Spying Orrin, he pulled a blaster from one of his holsters.

"I didn't do this!" Orrin yelled.

"I'm sure you didn't, water man. But somebody's gonna suffer for this," Boopa said, climbing the platform. He pointed the blaster down at Orrin, underneath the desk.

Orrin felt the sudden thump of boots on the desktop above him, out of his sight. He saw Boopa looking up, astonished.

"You?" Boopa yelled. "I've seen you before!" Orrin saw the Gossam raise his blaster—

—and vanish. Boopa rocketed off his feet and flew toward the far wall. He slammed headfirst into the pourstone surface, and then his limp frame dropped to the floor, like an insect falling off a windshield.

Orrin blinked. Had a whistler grabbed Boopa? He couldn't understand how. The creatures weren't large enough. One settled on Boopa's body now and began to feast. Hearing no others, Orrin crept out from beneath the desk. There was no one standing atop it. Who had Boopa seen?

Above, through the square gap in the mesh, the broken chain continued to sway, light from the slit windows glinting off it. One window was open to the outside, but there were no whistlers to escape through it. Apart from the one now busy with Boopa, all were gone.

Stumbling off the edge of the platform, Orrin witnessed the mess the room had become. Two Gamorreans lay dying, as well as two henchmen Orrin hadn't seen before. There was his blaster on the floor near the overturned table, along with his white comlink. He could hear the red one, beeping somewhere in the debris; he didn't bother to look for it. His hat was crushed beneath the cage.

And then there were the credits, scattered everywhere from Mosep's desk. Without thinking, Orrin began stuffing his pockets. Some of it was surely his money, after all. No one here would be the—

"H-hello?"

Orrin stopped dead at the sound of the voice. From underneath a Gamorrean, Mosep moaned. "Is someone out there? I believe I'm fractured."

"I didn't do this, Mosep," Orrin said, forgetting the credits and edging toward the door. "I'm just a businessman!"

Stopping in the doorway, Orrin calculated for a moment, then turned. With a strong heave, he rolled the Gamorrean off Mosep's body. The Nimbanel gasped for air.

Weakly, Mosep turned his head to the right. Seeing the mess, he sighed. "I'm beginning to think this particular trap is ill conceived." He looked back at Orrin.

288 JOHN JACKSON MILLER

"You have my gratitude," the accountant wheezed, still prone.

"And anything else?" Orrin asked, clutching his sides to hide the currency bulging in his pockets.

"Twenty-four hours." Mosep beheld the room. "I expect I'll have some remodeling bills to pay before Jabba returns."

Orrin gave the room a last look and ran.

CHAPTER THIRTY-FOUR

ANNILEEN CLICKED OFF her red comlink. "Orrin's still not answering," she said. What good was having a direct communications link to the man if he never answered?

That is, if he *could* answer. Standing beside her new landspeeder in front of the Mos Eisley Inn, Annileen fought to dispel the thought. Orrin and Ben had been gone for more than an hour. She and Jabe had fetched Kallie, and then she'd dropped Jabe off to retrieve the LiteVan, to give him something to do. Anything to keep the boy from rushing into the town house to save Orrin, if he needed saving.

Tired of waiting, she pocketed the comlink. "I'm just going to go to the door."

Kallie tugged her sleeve. "Wait, Mom. Here comes Jabe!"

The LiteVan hovered to a stop next to the new landspeeder. "Look who I found," Jabe said, hopping out. The side door opened, and Mullen and Veeka disembarked.

"Oh, joy," Kallie said.

"Hush." Annileen walked up to Mullen, who looked more bewildered than usual. "Mullen, have you been able to reach your father?"

The young man mumbled something inaudible. Beside him, Veeka shook her head.

Annileen pressed them. "What are you all doing in Mos Eisley?"

Tongue-tied, Mullen looked at his sister. Veeka shrugged, uncomfortably. "We were just, you know, in town."

Annileen stared at the pair. "You're a wonderful help."

The Gault siblings clearly knew something, which was an unusual enough condition for them in Annileen's eyes. But before she could ask further, a horrific screech pierced the air.

"Look there!" Jabe said, pointing up the street.

The heavy front door to the town house opened. Half a dozen people of various species bolted from it, running for their lives. In the next second, three winged creatures jetted through the doorway, one after another. They soared low over the heads of panicked pedestrians before angling for the rooftops.

"Kayven whistlers," Annileen said, unbelieving. She was on offworld safari, after all, without ever leaving Tatooine!

Last, Orrin emerged from the town house. Flushed, hair mussed, the man looked as if he'd lost an argument with a Wookiee. He started to head one way up the street before changing his mind and turning in a different direction. He was about to turn yet again when Annileen saw him and called out.

"Hey!"

She approached him. "Orrin, what was going on in there? What was that about?"

Flustered, Orrin looked back at the building and started walking. What passed for police in Mos Eisley arrived, while others gathered to watch the fattened whistlers roosting across the way. Orrin charged through the crowd. Annileen had to walk quickly to keep up. Orrin finally slowed when he reached where Boopa had parked the USV-5, some distance from the town house.

There, he caught his breath and flashed a beleaguered grin to Annileen. "Well, I'm not selling any water to *that* place!"

"Are you joking? Who *were* those people?"

"A dead end," he said, pulling a mirror from inside his landspeeder. "Serves me right for trying to follow every lead." He combed his hair with his fingers.

Annileen looked at the others in disbelief.

"Yeah, uh, it was a business deal," Mullen said.

Veeka nodded. "That's it. Er, I mean, that's why . . . we're here." She gulped. "Yeah."

Orrin rolled his eyes. He moved to straighten his collar. But the act of tugging at his shirt caused dozens of credit chips to tumble from his vest pockets.

Calwells and Gaults alike gawked. "Orrin, what is this?" Annileen demanded.

Orrin knelt, red-faced, as he tried to collect the credits from the dusty ground. It was mostly small change, but from a wide variety of systems—and there was a lot of it. "The, uh . . . *client* compensated me for my travel."

Kallie looked at the pile of currency in his hands and laughed. "Did you come here from Coruscant?"

The jittery man didn't answer. He looked up at his son. "Get down here, Mullen, and give me your hat!"

Mullen stared blankly. "Where's *your* hat, Dad?"

"Shut up and give it to me!"

Mullen passed his hat to his father. Orrin resumed his frantic gathering, only looking up when he saw motion from the end of the street, in the opposite direction from the town house.

Orrin dropped the money and stood. "Kenobi," he said, watching Ben approach.

292 JOHN JACKSON MILLER

Annileen turned. "You're back!" She looked at Ben and then at the town house. "I thought you were going to check on Orrin?"

Ben bowed. "It seems you've found him first."

Annileen stared at him searchingly.

Jabe shook his head. "Big help *you* were."

Orrin looked at the ground, puzzling things through. His eyes widened. "You were looking for me? You've . . ." He stopped mid-sentence and looked back at the town house in the distance. He turned back to Ben. "You've been here all the time?"

Ben pointed over his shoulder with his thumb. "I'm having some repair work done. The Calwells were kind enough to direct me where I was going. And, yes. Annileen thought she saw you earlier. But I got sidetracked by a rather insistent street merchant." He clasped his hands together. "Has there been some excitement?"

Orrin glowered at him. "No, none at all." He turned back to Annileen—and saw the glistening new landspeeder behind her. His face brightened. "Hey, you got it!"

"It's what you sent us here for," she said. "It's lovely, Orrin. But it costs so much—"

"It's nothing. I'm good for it!" Orrin gestured to his feet, where Mullen and Veeka collected the remaining credits. He stepped over them to join Annileen next to the new vehicle. Putting his left hand on the JG-8's front steering vane and his right arm around Annileen's midsection, he managed to hug both her and the landspeeder at the same time. "She's a beauty, isn't she?"

Accepting the hug despite her unease, Annileen nodded. "It is."

"And so's my Annie," he announced to the others, his arm grasping her more tightly. "A beauty, I mean."

Orrin released her and turned her to face him. "Annie,

listen. This is important. It's, uh—why I wanted to be here in the city with you now. I knew Mos Eisley was special for you." He took her right hand. "That landspeeder is just the start. I want you to marry me."

"*Marry you!*" Annileen's eyes bulged. *What?*

"The whole oasis has had us married for years. What are we waiting for?"

"We've been waiting?" This was news to Annileen. She looked out at the others. Kallie and Jabe looked as astonished as she was; Mullen and Veeka, attentive. And Ben simply watched, emotionless.

Orrin clutched her hand harder. "I've half raised your kids. You've helped me raise mine—"

"Don't blame *that* on me!" Annileen yanked her hand away. She looked back at Mullen and Veeka. "No offense."

"None taken," Mullen growled. Both Gault siblings held hats full of cash.

Annileen turned on Orrin. "You have to admit this is strange. Until recently, you've never shown the slightest interest in me!"

"Come on," Orrin implored. "You know that's not true!"

"*Serious* interest. You've joked, sure—"

"If I joked, it was only because I was afraid," Orrin said. "Afraid you wouldn't think I was worthy of taking Dannar's place." He looked away. "Well, I've been working. All this time I've put in improving my ranch, all the work with the Settlers' Call? It's been me working on *me*. For you!"

"For me?"

"So you could see what I can be," he said.

Annileen's eyes goggled. They had an audience now, bystanders who had drifted away from the city's attempts to trap the Kayven whistlers. Suddenly self-aware, she stepped back. "Are you looking for an answer now?"

"Soon," Orrin said. He looked back up the street in the direction of the town house. "Sure, why not now? I know you like Kerner Plaza. They have weddings there all the time. What do you think?"

"I think you need to take one of your stress pills!"

"No joke, Annie," he said, sinking down on one knee. "I'm for real!"

Shaken, she looked around again. At the landspeeder. At Ben. At the others, and then again at Ben. Her eyes back on Orrin, she spoke a little louder, partly for the benefit of the strangers. "I'll need a little time to think about it," she said.

Smile wilting a little, Orrin rose from the ground and dusted off his trouser leg. He bowed to Annileen and turned back to his vehicle. The loiterers, sensing the moment had ended, drifted away.

Seeing Orrin conferring with his children, Annileen spoke with hers. "Have you ever seen anything like it?"

Kallie shook her head. "If Veeka Gault becomes my sister, I'm going to become one of those B'omarr monks."

"They cut your brains out," Ben said.

"Trust me," Kallie said. "It'd be preferable."

Speaking quietly, Orrin finished the thirty-second summation of events in the town house for Mullen and Veeka.

"We're not going to get out of this by talking," he said. He wiped the sweat from his brow. "It's not unexpected. Always two plans, you know."

"I'm not so sure about Plan Two," Mullen said.

Orrin looked at his son, exhausted. "Great suns, what's wrong with Zedd this time? Surely his ribs have healed by—"

"He called from the clinic. He's been taking the wrong painkillers," Veeka said. "Zedd's addicted to Wookiee meds."

Orrin shook his head. "He is incredibly fired."

"Do we have to go *tonight*?" Mullen asked. "I don't think we can go without him."

"Tonight or nothing," Orrin said. "We need a fourth, and fast. But I think I've found him." Orrin looked at the Calwells, gathered between their LiteVan and Annileen's swanky ride. Jabe nodded back to him, respectfully.

Orrin had been bringing Jabe into his confidence a little at a time, and the boy seemed more than eager to be helpful. "Yeah, that'll actually work pretty well," Orrin said, walking toward the group.

"Jabe," he called out. "You want to ride back to the oasis with us?"

Jabe looked surprised by the offer. Standing by the Gault vehicle, Veeka winked at him. Excited, Jabe looked to his mother.

Annileen was skeptical. "Kallie has to take the LiteVan home now to get the animals fed. I didn't want her going alone—"

"We'll drive along behind as far as my place," Orrin said. "My cook droid will get Jabe fed and I'll drop him at home tonight. Everyone will be safe."

Overwhelmed by the earlier attention, Annileen assented.

"It's settled," Orrin said, waving the boy to his landspeeder. Turning, Orrin saw Ben standing in contemplation, hood shading his eyes. "I thought you had some repair work to pick up," Orrin said, frostily.

"That I do." Ben nodded and turned to Annileen. "I can find my own way home."

"No," she said. "I'll drop you and the cooling unit

back at your place." She looked over at Orrin, who seemed none too happy. "I'm still my own woman— I think."

"Fine," Orrin said, the old smile returning. "Then I'll see you tonight."

CHAPTER THIRTY-FIVE

SO THIS IS HOW A HERMIT LIVES, Annileen thought as she looked around Ben's house. It was cleaner inside than outside, which was what she'd imagined, knowing Ben. But the furnishings were impossibly spare. She could not picture him living here in any kind of comfort at all. Every day must be like camping. Which might not be such a bad way to go, she thought, remembering the clutter of her own life.

Annileen finished washing her hands in the basin and dried them quickly. It wouldn't do to linger here, when she'd just come inside to freshen up—and she'd had to finagle that.

But she had a good excuse. Rooh had found her way home, as Annileen had predicted, but she'd been wrong about how close the animal was to birth. Annileen and Ben had arrived just as the first sun touched the western Jundland mountains—and found mother and son right outside the trough. Annileen's examination of the eopie and her kid found both healthy; the exertions of the morning must have brought on the early labor.

With a last look around, Annileen stepped through the curtain and into the warm evening. Ben knelt beside Rooh, who was happily munching feed. Annileen lingered outside the door, not wanting to disturb the serene moment.

But Ben noticed her presence. "Rooh's quite energetic, given her ordeal," he said, patting the new mother's snout. "How long should she rest?"

"Eopies are made out of elastic bands," Annileen joked. "She's probably ready to race."

Ben marveled. "So soon?"

Annileen laughed. "Believe me, I envy her. Jabe knocked me off my feet for a month."

She walked into the yard. The repaired cooling unit sat amid the other junk outside. Ben had remained mostly quiet during the drive to fetch it and the journey here. He'd added little to his tale about Orrin's absence, apart from a question about the man's finances, which she found oddly timed. Ben hadn't pried further. And he hadn't asked at all about the one thing she most wanted an opinion about.

"Well," Ben said, rising. "I'd better get the equipment inside while there's still light. It was a lovely day. Thanks for the help." With that, he passed her and walked toward the coolant unit. Annileen stood frozen as he knelt beside it.

Finally, she cracked. She marched into his field of view. "Ben," she said. "Should I marry Orrin?"

Ben paused. "Do you *want* to marry Orrin?"

"Not especially," she said. "A lot of people think I should."

Ben heaved the unit from the ground. "I'm sure your other friends would be more qualified to advise. Leelee—"

"No," Annileen said. "Not Leelee." She walked after him and blocked him from the doorway. He looked at her, puzzled, as she tugged the coolant unit from his hands and set it down by the door. "I want to know what *you* want me to do."

Ben shrugged. "It's your life. Every individual decides his or her own fate—"

Annileen groaned. "Everything's an adage with you. Ben, are you telling me you've never had to deal with a real-life situation? Where you had to make a decision about someone else?"

Finally seeming to sense her frustration, Ben looked away. "I'm human," he said. "There was someone, once. It wasn't to be."

"And you gave up and moved to the Jundland Wastes?" She laughed. "I'd say you didn't find the right person."

"Perhaps I did," Ben said, looking back at her from beneath his hood. "But *I* wasn't the right person."

"More double-talk from Crazy Ben," Annileen said. Feeling her confidence grow, she took a step toward him, cutting the space between them in half. "Well, I don't think you're so crazy. I think you've found someone you didn't expect to find. And that's not a bad thing," she said, reaching toward him.

Ben put his hands before him to slow her advance. "Annileen—no. I can't do this."

"Are you sure?" She looked up into his eyes. "I think you can."

"No, I *definitely* can't."

"Everyone loses the reins once in a while."

He gave an uncomfortable half chuckle. "I said that, didn't I?"

"Yep." She clasped his hands and pulled him closer . . .

. . . and he drew back and turned away.

"What is it?" She stared at his back. "Is it because of Orrin? Don't worry about that. I've told you, I don't feel that way about him."

"And I don't think you feel that way about me, either," Ben said, walking toward the eopies.

"You're the expert on what I think?" She smiled

warmly. "Well, that's proof right there that something's happening between us. Orrin's known me my whole life and doesn't know what I think. You've met me a handful of times and you can read my mind." Her eyes sparkled in the evening light. "Often. So either you're superhumanly perceptive, Ben—or I've had your complete attention."

Ben took Rooh's lead and walked her to the corral. Her wobbly child followed. "Annileen, I think you have a good home, a lovely family, and a successful business. And I think you are bored out of your mind."

She looked at him, incredulous. "You think I'm that simple?"

"No," he said, lifting the kid over the fencing. "I think you're that *complicated*."

Annileen crossed her arms. "You think poor little Annie gets bored with Tatooine, and the first time a stranger from offworld comes along, it's off to the races?"

"Others have done it."

"Well, you're wrong."

He looked back at her. "Honestly? You're *not* bored?"

Annileen turned and kicked the coolant unit with a clang. "I'm too *tired* to be bored! I've got a home that's falling apart because I'm dead every evening. Half the time, I fall asleep at the kitchen table. My kids keep trying to find new ways to kill themselves, as if this place weren't dangerous enough. And my *business*—" She sputtered as she stormed toward the corral. "My business is playing mother bantha to a herd of full-grown orphans! People are not flying to the Rim to trade places with old Annileen."

"I know some who would," Ben said, his back leaning on the fence.

She glared at him.

He began to say something and stopped. For a moment, there was only the sound of the baby eopie, nuzzling his mother.

At last, Ben spoke again. "Annileen . . . I think you've learned to live with these things. But you can't pretend anymore that they challenge you. There's too much to you." Turning, he placed both hands on the fence railing and looked out onto the desert. "You've reached your limit, and you're looking for a lifeline. And since you think you can't move, you're desperate for someone to come along and keep you company in that world. Someone who challenges you."

"I don't know," Annileen said, joining him at the fence. "Erbaly Nap'tee is pretty challenging."

"You know what I mean."

She looked down at the eopies and sighed. She did know what he meant. "You're telling me that you don't escape a trap by luring someone else in."

"Every trap has multiple ways out," Ben said. "I saw that just today."

Annileen thought that a strange comment, but he changed the subject. "Besides," he said, "I'd make a terrible shopkeeper."

"You can barely shop right," she said.

They laughed.

Ben started to move from the fence when she touched his arm—less insistently this time. "Wait," she said. "You're not going to get away that easily. This isn't just about me," she said. "This is about you."

He put up his hand again. "I told you, I not looking for a—"

"No," Annileen said. "Not that. I asked you outside the Claim that day if something bad had happened to you. You said it happened to someone else."

"Yes."

She grabbed his wrist. "You're a liar."

"Excuse me?"

"You're lying to yourself. This thing, this bad thing—it may have happened to someone else. Someone you cared about, I'm guessing. And that means it happened to *you*, too."

Ben resisted. "I don't—"

"Yes, you do. Something horrible happened, Ben, and it's ripping you apart. Maybe it's why you're here. But you're trying to go on like you didn't care, like you weren't—"

She paused. His hands back on the railing, he looked up at her.

"You were *there*," Annileen whispered. "Weren't you? When this bad thing happened," she mouthed. *"You were there."*

Ben closed his eyes and nodded. "It didn't just happen," he said, hardly breathing. *"I caused it."*

Annileen's mind raced. Raced and veered into dark imaginings that she wanted to dismiss. But Ben was serious about whatever it was, and she had to be, too. "You . . . you hurt someone?"

"They hurt themselves," Ben said. "I came along at the end—the very end. But I was also there at the beginning. I should have stopped it."

She shook her head. "You're just one man."

"I should have stopped it!" The railing shook. "I failed! It was on me to stop it, and I didn't. And I will have that on my conscience forever."

Annileen's eyes looked left and right. The fence quaked so hard under his hands that she thought the very posts might fly out of the ground. "Ben, you can't blame—"

"You can't know." He turned and clutched at her shoulders, surprising her. "I failed everyone. Do you have any idea how many people have paid for that? Do you know how many people *are* paying, right now?"

"I only know one," she said.

Ben let go of her. His arms wilted.

She had never seen such anguish in anyone's eyes before. What had he been through? What had he done? What did he *think* he had done? So many theories about his past had coalesced and dispersed since she'd known him. Annileen struggled to run through them now. Had there been a domestic tragedy? Had he been a soldier, whose actions had cost his platoon? An executive, whose negligence had wiped out his corporation?

Her thoughts ranged from the small to the improbably large, before determining that it didn't matter. Hurt was hurt. And whether Ben had harmed someone before, she judged him to be no danger now. Except, perhaps to his own happiness.

Every human instinct told her to embrace him. But something else, somewhere, told her to step back.

Which she did.

"Ben, I think I understand. You're out here, I guess, to atone. Maybe more than that—I don't know. But that's part of it. If talking about things would help—"

Ben shook his head. "It won't." He glanced at the setting suns, then took a deep breath. His body straightened. "I'm sorry. I do thank you for the day out, but you should get home while there's still light."

Annileen watched as he turned back to his house. The familiar reserve had returned. She had gotten in for a moment; she could tell that for sure. But she saw she would get no further. Not today.

Hands hanging at her sides, Annileen walked back to her landspeeder, which gleamed crimson in the sunset. At its side, she turned back and looked at Ben. "All right," she said. "I'm not going to hide outside your door, waiting for you to tell me. You can do it in your own time."

He stopped in his path and looked away to the east, melancholy. "Time, I have."

"Well, I have it, too," Annileen said, slipping behind the controls of the vehicle. "I'm not going anywhere."

She started the engine. "Did you hear that, Ben? *I am not going anywhere.* So when you're ready . . . you know what the sign says."

She drove away into the dusk, leaving behind a contemplative Ben. Who, she suspected, remembered very well what she meant.

FIND WHAT YOU NEED AT DANNAR'S CLAIM.

Meditation

Annileen.

This is becoming a problem. For her—and that makes it a problem for me.

No, I know what you're thinking. I've been tested on this score before—and I've seen what it means to get too close to someone. Years ago, with Siri Tachi—you were there for part of that.

And then there was Satine . . . I've vowed never to put anyone else in similar jeopardy.

And that's just it: I'm not some moon-eyed Padawan. Not anymore. I know personal ties can work against us. We endanger them, sometimes, because of the nature of our duties. And worse, they become possessions, to be protected and obsessed over.

I admit, I do wonder sometimes if that sells Jedi short. Not everyone is Anakin. And if the simple act of caring deeply for a person—especially someone as good as Padmé—is destructive in principle, then the Force has a peculiar view of what constitutes good and evil. You told me yourself that the Jedi weren't always against relationships. And consider: families are strong in the Force. Does the Force really understand what it wants?

No matter—I understand myself. I can give up love. I have given up love. But I wasn't prepared to give up the thing that I had instead.

Community.

I've lived my life in the structure of the Jedi Order. Yes, it was an organization with a goal—but it was also a family. I said it myself: Anakin was my brother. I had many brothers and sisters. And fathers and mothers. And even a strange little green uncle.

I don't have that home now. I don't have that family.

Almost every friend I've ever had is dead.

I . . . I've never thought about it in exactly those terms, before. It nearly took my breath away, just now. Almost every friend I've ever had is dead. Most killed by Sith evil.

And I've never lived without the Jedi Order to fall back on, to help me when things went badly. What does it mean to be a Jedi alone?

I think you tried to tell me, more than once. Your stories about other Jedi who lived without the trappings of the Order—but who still followed the Code. Kerra Holt, back in Bane's time, cut off from the Republic. And who was that half Jedi? Zayne something? Zayne Carrick. He wasn't a part of the Jedi Order, and yet he did good deeds anyway, on his own. He relied on his friends and didn't need some official imprimatur to do the right thing.

Maybe I can do that. I can't rebuild the Jedi Order, but I can certainly put together the support system it provided. Emotionally, if not in terms of power to resist the Emperor.

Maybe starting with Annileen and the Claim . . .

No. That would be following the living Force alone—wrapping myself in the present. Not worry-

ing about the future, the longer strands, the bigger issues. A Jedi is responsible for balancing both. I'm responsible—especially now when there's no one else to do it.

Still, Annileen . . .
Wait.
Hold on.
I just realized something.
I'll be back.

PART FOUR

THE RIFT

CHAPTER THIRTY-SIX

THE EYEPIECES OF A TUSKEN narrow and confine the world, but they also bring it into focus. Now, just hours after the suns had set, there was much to be seen on the sprawling ranch southeast of the oasis.

Shining yellow through the lens were the domes of the ranch house, a cluster of bubbles beneath the rising moons. Larger than many of the other homes on the desert, it was further lit by security lights on masts. Sheltered decks atop the sand connected the house to its garages.

The old man stood on one of these porches, bracing against the nighttime chill. The door to his house was open behind him, and light spilled from it—as did the words of his wife, audible all the way to the northern ridge. Old Ulbreck sought peace outside most evenings, and did so again tonight. Puffing on a cigarra forbidden him by his doctor and wife, Ulbreck looked relaxed and confident in his domain. No one here could tell him what to do.

The other person present would have been harder to see, but for his movement. Wrapped against the cold, Langer, the night watch, continued to wear a rut into the ground. Usually, the guard stood motionless, but not when the old man was outside. Langer was reputedly a good shot with his rifle, but he hadn't used it in years; some relation of Ulbreck's wife, he had the easy business of protecting the household. The other sentries were far out in the fields, patrolling the vaporators. Those were what the old man really cared about.

The watchful intruders, who'd studied the ranch on previous nights, knew all this. They knew Ulbreck's habits and defenses, and they knew the timing of the sentry landspeeders' circuits around the ranch. The daylight theft of a vaporator thirty-seven hours earlier had resulted in Ulbreck assigning more sentries to each vehicle, but the routes and timing hadn't yet changed.

The members of the raiding party had arrived separately, from two different directions. On their final approach, the four had converged, running single-file, in the Tusken manner, until they reached their planned stations behind the northern ridge. Through their eyepieces, they all saw the same thing. All was as expected. What remained was to wait for the clouds to pass over the larger moon.

When it happened, they moved. The first pair of raiders charged across the ridge, careful not to stumble over their bulky robes. Behind, the remaining two atop the dune lifted their rifles and fired. Several shots to the security lights left the farm in darkness.

Langer noticed it first. *"Tuskens!"* But the call just brought blasterfire in return. Langer dived to avoid the shots, which paused long enough to allow the advance pair of raiders to strike. The nimbler attacker arrived first, gaderffii raised. The blunt end of the weapon struck Langer across the face, sending him into unconsciousness.

Ulbreck had started to move on the sentry's yell. His rifle sat where it usually did these evenings, just outside the door to his house. But now the shots from the ridge raked the decking, keeping him from reaching his weapon. He slumped behind a post and yelled to the open door. "Magda! Call for help!"

It was too late. With Langer incapacitated, the advance pair easily reached the house. The stockier assailant kicked in the side door and threw something inside. A flash—and seconds later smoke poured from the building.

Coughing, an elderly woman stumbled outside into the waiting gloved hands of the raiders. Terrified, she wailed in their grip. "Wyle! Wyle!"

"I'm coming, Maggie!" Ulbreck yelled. But he could go nowhere with the shots peppering the deck. When they did pause, it was only because the shooters were charging down from the ridge, bellowing a war cry. The old farmer struggled to reach his feet, but the smaller of the attackers was upon him, swinging his rifle like a club. The butt of the weapon struck the old man in the nose. Ulbreck howled in pain and hit the deck hard, his face bleeding.

Magda Ulbreck screamed as the invaders dragged her before the house, in sight of her injured husband. The leader of the foursome set down his rifle and drew a knife from his bandolier. Rusty blade flashing in the moonlight, the robed figure loomed menacingly over Ulbreck.

Magda shrieked again. But even in agony, her husband remained defiant. "You cussed things couldn't kill me at the Claim! I won't beg now!"

The knife wielder nodded. This response was expected. Ulbreck would remain defiant, they all knew, until his wife was threatened. The attackers would turn on Magda, and scare her. They might do some cosmetic harm for effect; it would be worse than that if she fought.

But both Ulbrecks would remain alive, chastened and terrified. And if the harrowing night didn't convince Wyle Ulbreck of the error of his ways, Magda certainly would.

It would go entirely according to plan. It had worked before, elsewhere.

Perfect.

Except for the figure leaping down from the top of the covered porch.

Boots landed squarely on the leader's shoulders, knocking him back off his feet. The knife flew from his hand as he struck the ground, and his night-vision goggles twisted sideways beneath the Tusken head wrappings. For moments, he could see nothing at all; he heard only a struggle, all around.

Shifting the goggles so he could at least see with one eye, the leader tumbled over, desperately trying to reach the rifle on the ground. But the man who had pounced from above was already fighting Magda's former captors. *Former,* because the woman had fallen free when the figure in light tan charged. He stood between her and them now, quickly dodging one lumbering gaderffii swing after another.

He leapt. He ducked. And in one more lightning move, he caught one of the weapons. He flipped backward, taking the gaderffii with him. Touching down, he bounded back into the fray with it. The now-weaponless raider tumbled backward, somehow—it didn't even look like a wrong step, to the leader's only available eye—leaving the other marauder to fight on. Gaderffii clashed loudly, metal sparking in the night.

With energy belying her age, Magda scrambled past. The smallest of the invaders, captivated by the nearby combat, did nothing as she collected her bleeding husband and helped him toward the garages, and escape.

While the Ulbrecks fled, the lead attacker at last found the errant rifle. He tried to draw a bead on the dueling rescuer, but again his facial wrappings were askew, preventing it.

Ahead, the gaderffii duel drew to a close. The Ulbrecks' would-be hero caught his opponent under the arm with the flange of the weapon, producing a high-pitched— and very human—squeal.

Enough! The lead invader ripped off his bandages and night-vision goggles and raised his rifle. Eyes unfettered at last, Orrin Gault looked into the face of the Ulbrecks' savior.

Ben Kenobi.

Orrin stared in the darkness, unbelieving for a second. *"You?"*

Then he fired.

Ben spun, somehow using the gaderffii to deflect the shot. The bolt sizzled past Orrin to strike one of the porch supports, right above the head of the smallest would-be Tusken. Startled, the boy turned to run. "Come on, Orrin!"

Orrin fired again.

Behind Ben, Orrin saw the other two invaders standing, one helping the other. When Ben deflected the second blaster shot, they started to move toward him.

Ben turned to look back. "Don't try it, Mullen," he said. "Masquerade's over."

On the far side of Orrin, a dome opened. The Ulbreck repulsortruck peeled out, Magda at the controls. The vehicle swerved violently away from the house and turned east. The barracks were that way, Orrin knew, and more sentries.

His kids knew it, too. "Dad, go!"

With that, Mullen and Veeka took off, heading behind the house.

Ben looked back with satisfaction—and then stared directly at Orrin. "I noticed something today. You don't do so well alone."

Orrin turned and ran.

In the blackness to the north, Orrin saw two Sand People rocketing away on speeder bikes. A surreal sight, but one that meant that Mullen and Veeka had escaped. His heart pounding, Orrin hastened over the dunes to the west.

Why did I park so far away?

Breathless, he glanced behind him. He'd lost his rifle tumbling over the side of a dune, and he wasn't going back for it. Especially not now, as Ben appeared over the rise. The man dropped Mullen's gaderffii in the sand.

Orrin patted at his chest as he ran. He'd replaced his pistol since the afternoon in the Hutt's abode, but he wasn't about to try to fish for it in the folds of the stupid Tusken garb. Not when his speeder bike was there, its engine already running, thanks to his young assistant.

Mask discarded, Jabe Calwell stood between the bikes, frightened out of his wits. "Orrin, hurry!" he yelled. "He's coming!"

Orrin looked quickly behind him. Ben was still on top of the crest, yelling something. "Orrin, watch out!"

Orrin decided he wasn't falling for that. He reached the speeder bike—

—and, in that instant, four figures arose from the night, lunging at them.

Real Sand People.

Two Tuskens grabbed at Jabe, yanking him down into the darkness. Another charged at Orrin, striking the back of his speeder bike with a gaderffii. The hover-

ing vehicle spiraled on the air toward him. Without another thought, Orrin leapt onto it.

The bike continued to spin with him aboard, and the
world spun in Orrin's mind, too. He saw Kenobi, still
frozen on the hillside. He saw Jabe, clawing at the air in
vain as one captor raised a rock to strike him. And he
saw the fourth Tusken charging him, gaderffii held high.

Plug-eye.

Orrin squeezed the throttle and vanished into the
night.

CHAPTER THIRTY-SEVEN

ANNILEEN WEARILY PACED the floor of the darkened store. Another night, another missing child. What else was new?

She didn't know what was keeping Jabe, but at least this time she knew where he was. Or thought she did. Orrin had driven his kids and Jabe to the Gault ranch; Kallie had continued onward to the Claim, as promised. Annileen's exhausted daughter had shared that much before heading back to the residence to collapse.

But it was nearing midnight, and no one was answering her pages at the Gault place. She'd even tried to reach Orrin on the red comlink, but something must have been wrong with the subspace network. All she heard on the other side were grunts, sounds like the Gamorreans had made in her store. A wrong connection, to be sure. Who knew Gamorreans even carried comlinks?

At least this time she could worry in peace. The store had been empty when Annileen returned from Ben's. Tar Lup had closed the Claim on schedule, which was more than she could do, most nights. The Shistavanen clerk was staying with a friend locally and would drop off the passkeys in the morning. Annileen reminded herself to thank him. As tightly as she ran the Claim, she had to admit Tar would make a decent manager of his own place someday.

The moons shone outside the window behind the counter, casting the interior contours of the Claim into bluish shadow. Annileen sighed. The store always seemed so much friendlier at night. During the days it was either trying to kill her with stress or bore her to death. There was no middle path.

She'd grown accustomed over the years to the fact that nothing was ever going to change. Sure, there would be some trends amid the daily disasters and intermittent doldrums. Jabe and Kallie would present new and different challenges. The customers would become harder to take. And there would continue to be less time for her at the end of each day. But these would be gentle slides, ending only when she could no longer get her hover-chair behind the counter. Then they'd check her into the senior center outside Bestine, where, no doubt, Erbaly Nap'tee would be her roommate. Annileen would spend her remaining years explaining that no, she didn't work for the center.

The slide *had* been gentle—until now. The ride had gotten bumpier. The highs had been higher, filling her with excitement and anticipation. And the slow moments she now found interminable. She'd become more concerned about wasting days than wasting profits. It was as if her life had suddenly gained an importance and a weight it previously didn't have, or that she'd denied. She didn't know the reason.

Well, something *had* changed, of course. There was Ben.

Since that day out on The Rumbles, every hour she'd spent around Ben had seemed full of life. It staggered belief that, in fact, they'd only known each other for a few hours over the course of half a dozen meetings. So much had happened.

The Tuskens had *attacked the oasis*, something they hadn't done in years. She'd ridden into a battle and met a most-wanted Tusken warlord—who turned out to be a matriarch and mother, like herself. She and Orrin had both been hassled by big-city lowlifes. And the man her kids knew as the jovial uncle had suddenly declared his love for her.

And she'd begun to imagine a different life for herself. All this had happened, since Ben's arrival from . . . where? She still didn't know. Unbelievable.

Some people are trouble magnets, her mother had said. And by "people" her mother had meant "men," and by "some," she meant "all." It had taken Dannar four years to pass the Nella Thaney Stress Test. Four years during which he'd had to show that, while he might once have been a sand-spitting rowdy, he could stay in the same place and open the store every day. For Annileen's first two years working the counter, her mother had counted her pay every week, just to see if Dannar was keeping his word. A credit short and he'd have been a no-account dreamer again. But Dannar was Tatooine's greatest salesman, because eventually he sold Nella Thaney on himself.

Nella wouldn't have let Ben Kenobi within rifle range of her daughter.

Her mother's sayings came fresh to her ears. *A man with no past is a man with no future. No one with sense moves to Tatooine. Nothing good comes from the Jundland Wastes.* Annileen remembered them well. She'd caught herself saying them to Kallie a few times, although she had the integrity to curse herself afterward. Ben had no visible means of support, no occupation, no seeming willingness to commit to anything beyond his solitary existence. And despite his efforts, trouble found him everywhere.

But if he was a jinx, why did she feel so much better having him around?

Annileen walked to the counter and closed the hinged flap. She wouldn't need her blaster. She wouldn't take her new landspeeder out in the night to see if the lights were on at Orrin's house. She would imagine that Jabe had gotten caught up in an all-night sabacc game at the Gault place with Mullen and Veeka and their friends, and she would be fine with that.

Because she was going to see Ben again. Sometime. Maybe soon, and everything would be fine. It always was, when he was around.

Annileen walked through the stacked tables and chairs toward the hallway leading to her residence. Down the darkened hall, something moved in the shadows, giving her a terrifying start.

"Kallie, I thought you'd gone to bed!" Annileen said, heart pounding. She squinted down the hallway. "Kallie?"

A shadowy figure slumped in the doorway to the corridor leading to the garages. "It's me, Annie." Orrin's voice was scratchy and unusually high-pitched. "We have to talk."

Orrin sat at the bar stool Annileen had pulled down from the counter. "Don't turn on the lights," he said.

"I never do at this hour," she said, pouring him a drink in the darkness. "The last thing I want is for anyone to think I'm still serving." She withheld the mug from him long enough to survey him. In the moonlight, Orrin looked as gray as she'd ever seen him. His hair was messed, his face dirty. Gone were the spiffy clothes from Mos Eisley that day; he looked as if he'd dressed out of the back of his landspeeder. "You brought Jabe back, I hope?"

Orrin reached past the mug in her hand and grabbed

the bottle instead. "I don't know where to begin," he said, raising it.

"Try at the start," she said, pitching the contents of the mug into the basin.

He looked at her and started to say something. Then he shook his head. "No, no, I can't tell you that part right now. You'll never—"

"Start somewhere!"

He clasped his hands together. They were shaking. Gathering himself, he finally spoke. "I'm out of time. This time tomorrow—" He paused, looking through the darkness at the chrono behind the counter. "No. In about fifteen hours, I have to come up with fifty-six thousand credits."

Annileen laughed. "What crazy scheme is it now?"

"No scheme," Orrin said between gulps. He wiped his face with his sleeve. "Just a plan to save my life. My ranch. Everything."

Annileen gaped at him for a moment before looking at the office door. "Wait. Not the Gossam and the Gamorreans?" She put her hands on the counter and loomed over him. "*That's* what the Mos Eisley thing was about?"

Orrin looked down in silence.

"Of course," Annileen said, wandering half dazed to the end of the counter. "Of course!" She looked back at him. "I called you on the direct link. I got a Gamorrean!"

His head down, Orrin rolled the bottle against his forehead. "I lost the comlink in Jabba's town house."

"*Jabba!*" Annileen exploded.

Orrin didn't move. "They're going to kill me, Annie."

"They'll have to wait in line!" she thundered. She stomped toward him. "Is this about the vaporators? I thought that bank in Mos Eisley loaned you the money to buy the Pretormins!"

"They did," Orrin said. "Six years ago. After Dannar

died. After Liselle left. My land was the collateral. But the harvest I needed never came in. I never could figure out the formula." He stood abruptly and started to pace. "I had to borrow more and more. And they wouldn't loan me any more, and I couldn't make the interest payments."

"So you went to *Jabba*?" Annileen seethed. Nothing her son had ever done, no previous madcap act of Orrin's, had ever angered her so. "The Hutt? The criminal!"

"I went everywhere," Orrin said, looking up at her. In the moon rays from the window, he looked like a wounded animal. "No one helps a farmer! And I didn't go to Jabba. When someone offered money, I took it—"

"No questions asked," Annileen finished.

Orrin hung his head in shame. "Not enough questions, no. And now I need your help." He cast his eyes past her, to where the cashbox and her datapads rested. "I know how you save. You can save me. Save my world—"

Annileen fell back against the sink basin, stunned. "You want my money. To pay the Hutt!"

"No," Orrin said, waving his hand. "I mean yes. But no, it won't be like that. It'll be *our* money, and my fields will be your fields. Once we're married!"

Annileen rubbed her temples. "I think I'm going to have a stroke." She looked over at him. "You're still going on about that?"

"Yes. We belong together!" Orrin put on a smile, but it began to wilt as she watched.

Annileen shook her head. "I don't get it. You're in financial trouble, but you've got enough money to buy me a landspeeder just so you can win me over? It must have cost—"

"Thousands. But thousands won't make any difference to me. My problem's a lot larger. It's going to take your whole cash account to make Jabba go away."

"How do you know he will? He's a Hutt!"

"I don't know," Orrin said. "Maybe he won't. But I know the *bank* won't go away, and I owe them many times as much." He stepped up to the counter again and tried to compose himself. "I also talked to them today," he said more calmly. "They'd be willing to renegotiate—and that's where the store comes in."

Shocked, Annileen looked around in all directions. "I'm not giving them my store!"

"It'll be *our* store," Orrin said. "If the Claim is added to my land as collateral, they'll negotiate a new payment plan. There's enough in your cash account to get out from under Jabba now. Then the store's cash flow will help me service the loan until we get a good harvest." He gestured to the darkened shelves behind him. "They know what it's worth, what it brings in. They *want* it operating!"

Annileen reeled, struggling to register it all.

He folded his hands on the counter, nervous. "They just want an ironclad guarantee that the Claim will always be there as collateral, always operating to service the debt."

"I can't guarantee that," Annileen said. Looking at him, she felt a moment's pity. "You know, if you'd asked like a normal person, I'd have tried to help you. You know that. But even then, I wouldn't be able to just chain myself here for years more—for years, just to help a friend!"

"That's why we have to get married," he said. Orrin walked to the counter and lifted the hinged section. "The bank said—"

"You told the bank before you proposed to me?" Annileen nearly split apart with outrage. "How romantic! Did they give their blessing?"

"They'd be satisfied," Orrin said, walking back behind the counter. He reached for her hand. "They'd know you and I were in it together for the long haul, to make both the farm and the Claim a success." He tried to smile again. "They won't foreclose. And Jabba won't foreclose on me. We'll all be fine."

Annileen tried to draw her hand away. She couldn't go along with this, but she didn't want anything to happen to Orrin, either. For a moment, she wondered whether Jabe knew anything about all this. Had he even returned with Orrin?

And then she thought of something else, and yanked her hand away violently. "Wait," she said, stepping to the cashbox and datapads. "How did you know what's in my accounts? And how would the bank know the value of this place?"

Head drooping in the low light, Orrin sighed. "I made copies of the records this morning after you left."

"You did *what*?" Annileen's mouth fell open.

"And I made some holograms."

Annileen slammed her hands on the back counter. It made sense, now, Orrin getting her out for the day. A family trip to Mos Eisley to get a new landspeeder—that would do it. "Did Tar Lup help you snoop through my files?"

"No, no. But you had lent me the codes so he could work. I logged in before Tar showed up."

"Get out," Annileen ordered.

"Annie—"

"Don't 'Annie' me," she said. She turned her back on him. "I won't help you fix this. Get out."

Orrin approached her. "Annie, they're going to kill me."

Standing at the end of the counter, she said nothing. There weren't words.

"Annie, I'm begging," he said, choking up. "You've got to marry me. The bank says—"

"Just go," Annileen said, tearing up. She felt his presence behind her, could hear his fast breathing. He'd ruined his life and was here, now, invading the one place that was absolutely hers, trying to take it away. "Just go."

"Okay," Orrin said, arms sagging. He turned around and started to walk. But after a second, Annileen heard the footsteps stop. Orrin lingered behind the counter with her, calculating. "Maybe there's another way," he said.

Annileen looked back but said nothing.

"The store's just got to be in the family," Orrin said, stepping toward her, eyes wild. "Maybe the kids—"

Annileen winced. It was almost comical, now. "I really don't think Mullen is marriage material!"

"No," Orrin said. "But I could marry Kallie."

Annileen's eyebrows shot up. *"What?"*

Orrin raised his hands to explain. "She's nearly twenty—"

"In three years!"

Before Orrin could say more, Annileen's right fist struck his jaw. *Krakk!*

Hand on his bleeding mouth, Orrin looked at her, betrayed and bewildered.

"Get out!" Annileen yelled, shoving in an attempt to force him out from behind her bar. But the larger man turned instead, his hands grabbing her shoulders like a vise.

Rage entered his eyes. "I don't care how it happens! But I'm done asking! I've got to save myself, can't you see?"

Annileen struggled. "Let go!"

Orrin wrestled with her in the cramped space. Overturned bottles smashed to the floor. His anger grew, and he shook her. Annileen wailed. "Annie, just listen—"

Kr-chowww!

A blaze of blue light lit the darkness, striking the wall just behind Orrin's shoulder. Annileen still frozen in his clutches, Orrin looked across the bar. There in the moonlight stood Kallie, in her nightshirt, rifle quivering in her hands. "Get away from her!" Kallie yelled.

"Kallie, you wouldn't shoot me—"

"Don't bet on it!" Kallie fired again, shattering a bottle just to his left. "I've never liked you people!" Her face twisted in anger. "You always take advantage of Mom, and now you're trying to ruin Jabe! Now let her go—and tell me what's going on here!"

Orrin released Annileen and shook his head. "Kallie," he said, "you just don't get it. None of you do." He looked up, his face lit by the light from outside. "Jabe is dead."

CHAPTER THIRTY-EIGHT

A'YARK LOOKED DOWN at the exposed face of the unconscious settler in Tusken clothing. Grotesque, as flesh always was. A'Yark was glad it was nighttime. But she could tell the human was not much older than her A'Deen had been. His forehead bled from the rock he had been struck with. He still breathed only because A'Yark wanted to know something. *Why is he here?*

Curiosity had driven A'Yark to the ranch in the first place. The vaporator thieves from the day before were the dregs of the clan, but they'd stumbled on a gap in the area patrolled by the Smiling One's posses. A'Yark had insisted on returning with them after dark, to learn more.

The findings had disappointed. By pilfering the worthless water-making device, the young fools had put the local farmer on alert. His house lacked sufficient defenses, but even so, A'Yark had no faith in her companions' ability to strike it.

But before she could turn her band back to The Pillars, the false Tuskens had arrived. A'Yark's eye was good enough to tell imposters even at a distance through darkness; the worst of her people didn't comport themselves like the costumed bumblers. Then Ben had arrived, galloping past on his eopie. A'Yark had instantly resolved to stay, ordering the others to hollow out a hiding place near the pretenders' parked speeder bikes.

Alone, atop the western ridge, she'd seen an initially weaponless Ben fight the costumed settlers. The fight had confirmed what she'd suspected.

"You are Ben," she said to him now.

"Yes," Ben said. He stood halfway down the rise, looking down at her and her companions, all standing guard over the motionless youth.

A'Yark strained to remember the words K'Sheek had spoken in their exchanges, so long ago. But they came to her now, when needed. "You are . . . a great worrier."

Ben chuckled. "Yes, I suppose I am."

"Great *warrior*," A'Yark repeated, annoyed.

"Wars do not—" he began, still grinning in the moonlight. Seeing that his expression offended her, he changed it. "Never mind."

Ben walked cautiously down into the depression. He looked different now. Dark robe removed, he wore a light tunic giving him more range of movement—and yet he did not shiver in the wind. He gestured to the prisoner, collapsed and guarded at the bottom of the dugout. "This boy, Jabe, is the son of my friend. You met her."

"Ann-uh-*leen*," A'Yark pronounced, without thinking.

"Yes, you did hear me say it," he replied. For some reason, the human's words were easier for A'Yark to understand, and he understood her. Was it his magic, somehow?

"Release Jabe," he said, slowly. "So I can take him to her."

"No," A'Yark said.

Ben raised his hand and waved it before A'Yark. "*You will release him.*"

"No," A'Yark said.

Ben nodded. "All right." He put his hand down. A'Yark watched warily as he began to pace, keeping a generous distance between himself and A'Yark's party.

"All right. You *should* release him, then," Ben said. "It is right. You remember—I brought you your son. The day of the massacre."

"My son was dead," A'Yark said, words dripping with bile. With that, she turned and stepped over Jabe's body. Turning back so Ben could see, she suspended her gaderffii above Jabe's head, ready to plunge the heavy end downward into his skull. "You takes Annileen a dead son," she announced. "It is right."

Her companions fanned out, gaderffii ready. Ben reached for the fold of his tunic. In the dark, A'Yark couldn't see where he carried the weapon, but she was sure it was there. "I hoped we could bargain," he said, calmly. "I guess you're not a transactional people."

A'Yark stood silent, not understanding.

Somehow sensing her confusion, Ben spoke. "*Trade.* Tuskens don't trade."

"No. Tuskens *take*!" A'Yark shouted, raising her gaderffii.

At the sound of her voice, two young warriors charged Ben from either side. Ben swept his hands upward. The fighters went aloft, carried by an unseen windstorm. They landed to either side of the pit—while one of the gaderffii pinwheeled through the air right over A'Yark's head. The other weapon buried itself into the ground to her left.

Ben hadn't even looked at the attackers.

"Wait," she told the others in their language. Theirs was a mad attack, but it told her again how powerful he was. Yet Ben had chosen not to kill her companions. Was it intentional?

Ben looked over his shoulder. "Any forces the Ul-brecks reach will secure the house first, before searching here. There's still time for us all to get what we want, A'Yark. I want the boy."

"No," A'Yark said, bringing her weapon down again to a menacing position over Jabe's body. She poked at the teenager's clothing with the blunt end of the gaderffii. "It is forbidden for Tusken to unmask. But for a settler to wear the mask of a Tusken—"

"—it is indescribably worse," Ben said. "That's your belief, isn't it?"

"It is believed." A'Yark gripped the gaderffii. "Jabe dies."

"Then we are at an impasse," Ben said, pulling out the metal weapon that A'Yark had seen before. He activated it, and a spear of blue energy lit the gully. Sharad Hett had named it once for her. *A lightsaber.*

Ben walked toward the pit. "I won't let you kill Jabe, no matter what he's done."

"We are born to die," A'Yark said.

"Maybe you are," Ben said. "But it is possible to be ready to die—and still prefer to live. And I think you do."

Her gemstone eyepiece glinted purple in the light. "You are wrong!"

"I think not," Ben said, staring at her. "I've heard the settlers talk about you, A'Yark—and seen your actions. You don't strike just for menace. You have *goals.*" He lowered the lightsaber slightly. "Like at the oasis store. You came for Annileen. Why?"

A'Yark stood motionless, astounded. How could a human know anything that motivated a Tusken?

Ben paused for a moment. "Ah," he said. "I see. You thought she was like me. And like Sharad Hett," he said. "If you knew Sharad, you must have known that he was not like the other settlers. He carried a weapon, like this." Ben moved the shining lightsaber to and fro, slicing the air before A'Yark and her captive. "And he could do other things."

"Sharad . . . *wizard*," A'Yark said.

"Wiz—" Ben stopped moving the lightsaber. "Yes. He would have seemed."

"You are his kind," A'Yark said, mesmerized. "You knew him."

"I am of his kind, yes. And I knew him." Ben's eyes narrowed in the light as he searched carefully for words. "Sharad Hett . . . *left* my people. Many years ago. He brought his skills to you—became a Tusken." He looked away, gravely. "He was *not* supposed to do this. But you took him in."

"Yes."

Struck with a notion, Ben looked down at A'Yark, "You weren't his *wife*, were you?"

A'Yark shook her head. "No. K'Sheek lived as my sister, when she lived."

"Ah. I didn't know her name."

The recovered attackers from earlier gave A'Yark long and imploring looks. Of course, they were wondering. It was madness, conversing with so powerful a human—and on settler lands, too! But A'Yark realized this was the moment she'd been working toward since the massacre in the gorge. "Ben will join us," she said, abruptly.

"I—" Ben seemed startled. "Me, join you?"

"Yes. As Sharad did." A'Yark kicked at Jabe's shoulder. "To save Jabe. That would be . . . what you call a trade. A *Tusken* trade."

Ben mused for a moment, as if contemplating a possibility he'd never even considered.

"The Sand People in The Pillars are few," A'Yark said. "Ben joins. Leads war parties."

Ben gestured toward her. "But your people *have* a war leader, A'Yark. A formidable one—in *you*."

A'Yark sneered. Whether he intended to flatter her made no difference. Whatever A'Yark was, Ben was different. Something greater. "You would attract others," she said. "Some lives who remembers Sharad. They would follow. Sand People will thrive."

Never in A'Yark's memory had such an offer been made to an outlander. Even Sharad was made to endure trials. And yet this human actually seemed amused by the invitation. "Well," Ben said, under his breath, "that would certainly be one way for me to stay out of sight."

"What?"

"Nothing," he said, seriousness returning to his face.

A'Yark paused, suddenly apprehensive. Not about the impending return of sentries, but rather, wondering whether to speak the rest. She'd told herself many times she was not as superstitious as the others. But some things handed down had meaning, and having seen Sharad's feats, she was inclined to believe this thing. "They says a warrior will come from the sky to lead us. He will grow mighty. Generations unborn will walk in fear."

For a moment, Ben seemed puzzled. A'Yark wondered if she had spoken the words properly. "This—was a prophecy?" he asked. "A dream someone had?"

"Those are the same thing."

"And you desire this end?"

"Tuskens want. Yes." It was a foolish question for Ben to ask, A'Yark thought. Had he not heard of the destruction wrought years earlier on the Tusken camp, where all present died, regardless of age? Sand People could not live where such threats existed unopposed. If Sharad had not been the arrival of legend, then perhaps Ben was instead.

Yet for reasons that eluded A'Yark, Ben seemed troubled by the prospect of gaining immense power. He bowed slightly.

"I cannot join you," he said. "No offense intended. I,

er . . . recognize what I'm giving up. But it can't happen."

"Then boy dies. And we dies, killing him. And clan ends." She lifted the gaderffii again over Jabe's head. "It is right."

Ben looked down, seemingly disappointed. Readying his lightsaber, he started to close the distance with the Tuskens.

Then he stopped. He looked over at the lone speeder bike. "You saw who was with the boy."

A'Yark nodded. "The settler leader. The Smiling One."

"The Smiling—" Ben's face lit with recognition. "Orrin Gault. You mean Orrin Gault!"

"*Or-rin-gaalt,*" A'Yark sounded out. "I will kill Or-ringault. And all who follows." She spoke aloud the theory that had been forming since seeing the imposters. "By day, he strikes us. By night, he schemes—so to strike us again by day."

Ben lowered his weapon. "You mean Orrin has done something like this before?"

"Settlers have avenged attacks that did not fall," A'Yark said. "I don't knows what settlers do. But I knows what Tuskens do."

Quickly, A'Yark named some locations. Ben's knowledge of the geography of the desert was not the same as hers, and he asked questions in response. She answered them.

At last, he deactivated his lightsaber and returned it to its hiding place. "A'Yark, your people have been wronged. What Orrin has done is forbidden for *my* people. Taboo. And he has led Jabe into it. If you let me take the boy, I will see that no more harm comes from either of them."

A'Yark stood fast. "Vengeance must be *ours.*" She studied Ben. "And you don't speak for the settlers."

Ben scratched his hairy chin. "No, you're right. I don't. This isn't even my responsibility, not anymore. But neither can you get satisfaction alone. You don't have the forces to threaten the oasis, do you?"

A'Yark said nothing.

"I didn't think so." Ben nodded to the warriors he'd let live. "If you'll . . . defer for a day, I will find a way that you can get justice."

A'Yark didn't know what *justice* meant. K'Sheek and Sharad both had been full of nonsense terms. But she caught Ben's drift. "I must *see* this *jus-tiss*," she said, hissing the last syllable. "To know."

Ben nodded. "I think I understand. There may be a way."

"Speak."

"That's what I propose," Ben concluded, a couple of minutes later. "But it requires bringing the settlers to your—er, doorstep."

As A'Yark looked back on her junior warriors, doubts quickly filled her mind. "Plan works," she said. "I would see. But plan risks the clan."

"I understand, but you need not worry," Ben said. "I would not endanger them, nor you. I would be there to protect your people—"

"*Ootman* lies!" A'Yark snapped. "No outlander would care what happens to Tuskens!"

At her feet, Jabe woke up, moaning. Opening his eyes, he saw A'Yark overhead. "Uh-oh," he said, in a tiny voice.

"Hold still, son," Ben advised. "We're at a critical stage." He looked back at A'Yark. "I told you what I would do. Will you free him?"

A'Yark looked back at her feckless companions. Unaware of what had been discussed, they fidgeted at a sound from faraway: landspeeders, heading toward the ranch from the northeast. There wasn't much time to make a decision, and A'Yark was inclined to reject Ben's proposal. It was impossible to think he could succeed. No one could.

She clutched the gaderffii. "I say—"

Another sound came from the south, interrupting her. Movement! The warriors stumbled backward, afraid. "The settlers," one called to A'Yark. "We are surrounded!"

"It's all right," Ben said, walking toward the southern dune. "Just a second."

"Don't leave me!" Jabe screamed.

Ben was gone for just over three seconds when an eopie trotted over the southern crest. Ben followed, carrying a bundle in his arms. "I forgot I parked near here," he called.

The eopie wandered into the middle of the mystified Tuskens. At A'Yark's feet, it began nuzzling at Jabe's cheek with its snout. A'Yark looked back at the bundle Ben was carrying. It was moving. "What is that?"

A bleat came from the shadowy mass, and Ben set it upon the ground. Dark cloth opened. A young eopie, just a few hours old, ambled toward its mother.

"That . . . is not from here," A'Yark said. She knew the old man who lived here kept no livestock.

"Hmm? Ah, yes," Ben said, musing as he watched mother and child together. "When I realized Orrin was targeting this ranch, I had to get here quickly, so I had no choice but to ride. But Rooh had just given birth this morning, and I couldn't leave the child."

A'Yark stared at him. "How—"

Ben picked up the cloth. "I carried him. In my cloak." He shook out the garment and put it on. "He slept pretty well."

A'Yark looked at the eopie with the two children, one

human. She knew how far it was to Ben's home. He had ridden across the desert—with an infant eopie in his lap?

It occurred to her Ben would do anything to return Annileen's child to her—just as he had returned A'Deen. And so he might be capable of anything.

Lights swept over the eastern ridge. "They have come," A'Yark said. She poked Jabe lightly in the shoulder with the point of her weapon. "You must go. I agree to Ben's trade."

Ben looked around. He spied the speeder bike. "I need to get to the oasis fast, but—" He looked apprehensively at the eopies. "I can't ride alongside, and I can't carry us all."

A'Yark gestured, and warriors stepped up to lead the eopies away. At least they were capable of that, she thought. The night was still young, and she had much to prepare, as well.

Helping a confused Jabe toward the speeder bike, Ben looked back with apprehension. "You . . . you won't *eat* them, will you?"

"We do what we want," A'Yark said, offended. The insinuation that they wouldn't was worse than any assumption about their diet. "But no one acts, but I say." That much was true, now.

Ben climbed aboard the vehicle in front of Jabe. "I'll return. And if I fail—the next time you see me, I will do as you ask. I swear."

"I will makes sure of it," A'Yark said. With that, the Tuskens and their animal charges vanished over the dune and into the night.

CHAPTER THIRTY-NINE

IN THE DARKNESS OF THE CLAIM, Annileen staggered against the counter. "What . . . *what did you say?*"

"Jabe is dead," Orrin repeated. He knelt beside the shards of the bottles on the floor at his feet. Down in the darkness, his mind raced. Annileen would have to learn sometime that the Tuskens had taken Jabe, but he'd hoped to put it off until after he settled his financial affairs.

Now he wondered what to say. Could he say Jabba's toughs had struck at him, killing Jabe instead? That would sell Annileen on the danger Orrin was in, but it might solidify her resolve not to pay the criminals. No, he thought as he picked up the pieces, there might be a way instead to ensure that she *did* help him. And it involved the truth.

Starting at a certain point, of course. "The Tuskens killed him," he said, rising with the shards. "I was bringing him back here from my place when I broke down. Plug-eye got him."

"The Tuskens?" Annileen grabbed at him. "Where?"

Orrin dumped the glass into the refuse bin. "Out on the desert. You won't find him. They took him away."

"Then he might not be dead!" Kallie yelled, tears glinting in her eyes.

Annileen shoved past Orrin, finally escaping from behind the counter. "I've got to go," she said, heading toward the gun racks. She looked back at Kallie. "Get dressed."

Kallie handed her rifle to her mother and ran back into the residence. "What are you waiting for, Orrin? Activate the Settlers' Call!"

Orrin stood taller, having formulated his plan. "At first light," he said. "You know there's nothing anyone can do until then." He stepped forward from behind the bar. "But I swear, I'll call out every vehicle we've got until we find him. You need to stay—"

"Not a chance!" Annileen looked back at Orrin. "Trigger the Call, or I will!"

Orrin wiped his hands on a rag from the bar. "No one will come at this hour. You'll just scare the Tuskens farther into the wastes. Or push Plug-eye to do something desperate. You're going to have to trust me, Annie. Nobody knows Pluggy like me. I've been chasing this guy for years!"

Annileen glowered. "Some expert. Plug-eye's a female!"

"Huh?"

"I met her again on the range with Ben that day!" she told him, grabbing a satchel.

Orrin stared, puzzled. He started to ask more—but then returned to the immediate problem. He walked toward her, wary of where her rifle was pointing. "I promise you. Wait, and I'll have the Grand Army of the Oasis out there."

Annileen shook her head. Nothing, it seemed, was going to keep her from searching. Kallie ran back in wearing warm clothes, and her mother passed her a rifle. Annileen looked back at him in anger. "Why didn't you tell me this when you came in?"

"I had to make sure you understood first," Orrin said. "I can't help you find Jabe tomorrow if I've got the

Hutt's goons showing up." He walked to the gun counter and picked up a rifle of his own, figuring a physical show of support would be good now. "Look, I'll ride out with you. We can have a quick look." He turned to face Annileen. "Then we've got to come back here. Forget the business about the store. You'll give me the money to make Jabba go away—"

"*Jabba?*" Kallie repeated, stunned.

"—and I'll devote the rest of my life to finding Jabe." Orrin struggled to look earnest. "And if it's already too late, I'll exterminate the lot of them. You lost Dannar to these monsters. I lost a son. Do it my way, and it'll be—"

At the front of the store, the door clicked open.

Rifle in hand, Orrin looked up. Annileen and Kallie were already moving, dashing up the long aisle through the darkness. Their weapons clattered to the floor. "*Jabe, Jabe!*"

Startled, Orrin followed. There, through the open doorway, Jabe was staggering in. A great brown robe, a bit too large for him, blew in the night wind as he entered. In a second, his mother and sister were at his side.

"You're hurt," Annileen said, looking at the dried gash on his forehead.

"It's okay, Mom," Jabe said weakly. "Ben looked at it."

"*Ben?*" Orrin and the women said it at the same time.

"He brought me home," the boy said, looking tired and bewildered.

Orrin tromped forward, weapon raised. "Is Kenobi here?"

"No," Jabe said. "He saved me from Plug-eye. I don't know how he did it, but he did." He rubbed his bruises. "I guess I was wrong about him."

Annileen embraced her son again. "This is Ben's cloak!" she blurted as she grasped his collar.

"He . . . uh, thought I was cold," Jabe said, pulling away.

Orrin stood, dumbfounded. Kenobi had seen him in Tusken guise at the Ulbreck place, yes. But Orrin had assumed that the real Tuskens had killed both Ben and Jabe. If Ben lived, that changed everything.

As the women turned back into the store for water and a medpac, Orrin sidled up to confer quietly with Jabe. "Where did Kenobi go?"

"You left me out there," Jabe said icily.

"Never mind that! Where did he go?"

"I don't know," Jabe said. "But he was in a hurry." Looking first to make sure his mother and sister were still in the back, he slipped the cloak slightly open so Orrin could see that he still wore the Tusken costume underneath. "He didn't want the locals here to see me in this," he whispered.

"Huh." Orrin wondered at that. Why didn't Ben want to expose Jabe? There could be sinister reasons. Kenobi thought he had something now. *Leverage.* How would he use it? To blackmail Orrin for money? Or maybe to stop him from marrying Annileen?

Orrin decided it didn't matter which. Something had to be done about him. "Don't say anything about tonight," he urged Jabe quietly. "Don't tell—"

"Don't tell me what?" Annileen stood nearby, holding the chair she'd brought for Jabe. She dropped it on the floor. "There's something else, isn't there? Something you've done, to try to pay off your debts?" She looked at Jabe and then back at Orrin. "Was that what tonight was about? What have you done?" she demanded. "What *else* have you done?"

"What I had to do," Orrin said. "And right now, I could be in trouble."

"You're *already* in trouble!"

"A different kind of trouble," Orrin said. "Legal trouble. The kind that will make it difficult for me to walk around freely, even if I get clear of the criminals and the bank."

Annileen raised her hands to the ceiling. "Why not? You've ruined everything else in your life." She took a deep breath and grabbed his sleeve. "Orrin, that's enough," she said, yanking him toward the doorway. "Leave, and don't come back. I'll have the stuff in your office here cleaned out and sent to you!"

"You don't understand," Orrin said. "This trouble. I'm in it, yes. But Jabe's in it, too."

Annileen and Kallie looked at the boy, baffled. "Jabe?"

Standing in the shadows, Jabe looked down and swallowed. "Yes. I'm in it."

His mother gawked. "What? What have you done?"

"It doesn't matter," Orrin said. He pointed his finger in Jabe's face. "What matters is Jabe will go away, too, if it comes out. But it won't come out. Only one other person knows, and I'm going to take care of that."

Overwhelmed and confused, Annileen seemed not to know where to look. Orrin changed that by getting in her face. "Did you hear me? I can make sure Jabe stays free," he said, snarling. There wasn't any reason not to let his anger show. "I've been helping your family for years. Bringing business here, watching over you. It's time you paid me back! So you'd karking well better help me stay alive in the next twenty-four hours." He jabbed his finger in the direction of the cashbox. "That means we pay Jabba off tomorrow. Me—and *you*. You're in this with me whether you want to be or not."

Kallie moved to her mother's side. "Mom, what's going on? What's going to happen?"

"I don't know, sweetie," Annileen said, looking between Jabe and Orrin. "But I think we need help."

Orrin looked up at the chrono. A little over fourteen hours until Jabba's deadline. The hoodlums would be serious, this time. However it had happened—and it was still a mystery to Orrin—Mosep Binneed and his minions had been embarrassed today in the town house. Orrin didn't expect that anyone in Jabba's organization could let that happen twice. Not and continue to draw breath. They'd have to be paid and taken care of.

But he had to deal with Kenobi first. Reenergized, he opened the front door to the night. "I'll be back in time, tomorrow. I'll fix it all. You'll see."

Her arms around her children, Annileen shuddered. "I see a monster," she said.

"I'm a farmer," Orrin replied. "And I'm going to save my farm." Adjusting the settings on his rifle, he called back to Jabe. "Kenobi—did he say where he was going, boy? Did he say *anything*?"

Jabe responded coolly. "He had a message for you."

"For me?" The tall man paused, curious.

"Yes," Jabe said. *"Turn back now."*

Orrin's eyes widened as he weighed the words. Then he stepped out into the night.

Annileen locked another door and barred it. She'd changed the passcodes on all the electronic locks, even from the entryway from the garages. Tar Lup would just have to knock in the morning. She'd thought then about entering Orrin's satellite office in the store, until she remembered Jabe needed tending to back in the house.

Her son sat under the lonely light at her kitchen table. Ben's cloak was off and being folded lovingly by Kallie. Underneath, Jabe wore the rags of a Tusken Raider. He made no move to hide them, but he looked embarrassed and humiliated.

Seeing her mother stare, Kallie spoke to the air. "I think I'm going to have ammunition in every fight from now on."

Jabe shook his head. "It's a long story," he mumbled. "You won't believe it."

Annileen pulled up a chair and sighed tiredly. "Try me."

Jabe started speaking slowly at first, and then gained speed, rambling from one part of his young life to another. His lost father. His hated job. His need to fit in with the Gaults, whom he saw as doing something with their lives. And his desperate desire to please Orrin, a man of stature and independence.

And he spoke of the favor Orrin had asked, in Mos Eisley.

"He said it was a prank," Jabe said. "We were going to dress up and scare the Ulbrecks."

The air went out of Annileen's body. She sagged. "Wyle Ulbreck. My best customer, Wyle Ulbreck."

Kallie brought her mother a warm drink. The mug shook in Annileen's hands. She put it down without tasting it.

"Zedd was supposed to go with them, but he couldn't," Jabe said. "Orrin had a whole trove of the Tusken gear—from the Settlers' Call rescues, I guess. I thought—I don't know, that maybe this was my chance to get on Orrin's lead support team."

"By dressing up like the people who murdered your father and scaring an old man." Annileen was numb as a droid, at this point. "Makes perfect sense to me." She waved aimlessly. "Continue."

"It was just supposed to have been rifles on stun," Jabe said, his voice faltering. "It was to teach Old Wyle a lesson, for showing up Orrin all the time. Nobody likes Ulbreck anyway, Mom. You know that!"

Wraithlike, she rose and found the medpac on the kitchen counter. There was still that raging bruise and cut on Jabe's forehead. She could treat that, even if she had no idea what was going on inside his skull.

Jabe breathed faster, the details of the raid spilling forth as Annileen cleaned the cut. He told of knocking Wyle down, and of Mullen and Veeka's capture of Magda Ulbreck. He told of Ben's arrival and the Gaults' subsequent departure. And he told of the real Tuskens appearing, and the ambush. His words growing quicker and louder, he moved his head against Annileen's efforts to treat him.

"Ow! *Ow!*"

"Do you want me to stop?" Annileen asked, pulling back the applicator.

"No," Jabe said, tears in his eyes. "I want to feel it." Forlorn, he looked up at her. "Do you want *me* to stop?"

She shook her head. "I need to know. You said Ben saved you?"

Jabe nodded. "I woke up and Orrin was gone. And Plug-eye was there. And Ben was talking to them. In Basic," he said, puzzled. "Somehow he was talking to them, bargaining for me!" Every word seeming to remind him of how close he'd come to the end, he struggled to catch his breath. "Mom, they were going to kill me—or worse!" He blinked rapidly, tears finally falling.

Annileen put down the applicator and pulled his head close to her chest. "I know. But Ben was there."

"Yeah," Jabe said, sniffling. "I don't know what he said, but it worked. And he took me out of there." He looked up at her, his eyes red. "But the Gaults just left me. Orrin *ran*—"

"It's okay—"

"—he ran, and the others were already gone," he said, his voice rising with alarm. "And Mullen and Veeka, back with the old woman—they acted like they were really going to hurt her, Mom! And I hit that old man . . ."

"And that's not okay," she said, stroking his blood-matted hair. "But we've all found out a lot tonight."

"I wanted something to do," he said, voice faltering. "I've just been so sick of the store. I wanted some action. But this wasn't like going with the posses. This was wrong."

Anhileen just nodded. *Well, I'm glad to hear that.*

She released him and dried his eyes. "Did you tell all this to Ben?" she asked, placing the bandage.

"All of it."

"And?"

Jabe wiped his eyes. "He said I should follow his advice for Orrin—that I should turn back now. And he said that only a fool follows another fool."

Kallie watched, mystified. "Do you still think he's crazy?"

Jabe smiled weakly. "I'm not one to judge."

CHAPTER FORTY

ANNILEEN HAD SAT with her children until after midnight, comparing notes about what had transpired with Orrin. Now that her exhausted kids had gone to bed, Annileen clutched her pillow against the breeze and tried to sort it out. So much news. So little sense.

What Jabe had done was bad, yes—but she couldn't figure out Orrin's involvement. He'd made the trouble Jabe was in sound darker than a botched prank. But if Orrin needed untraceable money, he wasn't going to get it robbing Wyle Ulbreck, who famously kept most of his fortune in aurodium-plated ingots, buried somewhere underneath his septic system.

So what were they doing out there?

She looked for the seventh time at the chrono by her bed. It was her birthday, now, and had been for three and a half hours. Hours in which she hadn't closed her eyes, except to cry. Her sparely furnished room lay more than a meter underground, with a high window cracked open to the outside; the smells from the livery, as pungent as they sometimes were, reminded her of her childhood home. But after the night's events, she just felt cold. She pulled at the brown fabric she'd been resting under until it was over her head.

"Is my cloak comfortable?"

Annileen looked out from beneath the makeshift cover. Backlit by moonlight, Ben sat perched in the open window. He wore the clothes she'd seen him wearing outside his house, the day of that first visit—and he looked grim.

But she was glad to see him, even here, even now. Given his penchant for sudden appearances, this circumstance seemed almost normal.

"Hello, Ben," she said, sitting up. Belatedly realizing she was lying half dressed under his cloak, she pulled it to her chin and blushed. "Sorry," she said. "I guess you need this back."

"No, no, you hang on to it!" Ben turned his head quickly, nearly hitting it on the ceiling above him.

Annileen chuckled, her first laugh in hours. She had him look outside for a moment while she found her nightshirt. "Crisis averted," she said, passing him his cloak as he slipped down to the floor.

"You must be exhausted," she said, watching his shoulders sag as he sat on the floor against the wall. She had almost forgotten that their day had started in the desert, before Mos Eisley.

"I am tired. I've been very busy," he replied quietly, a respectful distance from her bed. In the hallway, there was only darkness. "I need you to listen," he said, "because I don't have much time." He looked up at her. "I know Orrin was here."

Shifting to sit on her knees, Annileen nodded.

"He told you about the money he owed Jabba?" Ben asked.

"And the bank." Annileen shook her head sadly. "It's so much. I don't get how he came to this."

"It's about water," Ben said. "A magical water, that tasted better than any other. And the vaporators that produced it."

"You mean this," Annileen said, holding up the flask from her bedstand. She handed it to him.

Ben didn't refuse it. He drank, thirstily. Wiping his face, he continued. "You told me Dannar had never developed the formula because of the cost. But that after Dannar died, Orrin invested heavily."

"Six years ago," she said, nodding. "Dannar was gone. Orrin's wife had left. He'd hit bottom. I think Orrin decided it was the way to reclaim his life."

"But success never came," Ben said. "Orrin's debts grew. And he took a loan from someone who really worked for Mosep Binneed, one of Jabba's business managers."

"Orrin told me," Annileen said.

"He started selling things off," Ben said. "I know because I just came from his office at his ranch."

Her eyes widened. "Really?"

Ben nodded. "I figured he kept things there he wouldn't keep in his office here in the store." Then he looked up at her guiltily. "Although I checked there, too."

"But how did you get in?" Annileen squinted. She sighed, impatient. "Never mind. Go on."

Ben stood, still speaking quietly. "Orrin was broke. So he turned to a resource he had control of. A public trust."

Annileen gasped. "The Settlers' Call!"

"You told me there was once enough money in the Fund to defend half the galaxy."

"I wasn't serious," Annileen said, reaching over to nudge the door to the hallway shut. "And he was legitimately using the money to buy weapons and landspeeders. There's that whole arsenal in the garages!"

"But he also uses those speeders for his ranch," Ben said. "And there are loans taken out on all the Fund's vehicles. As for the weapons, they all came from your store. He wasn't exactly paying full price."

"And my new landspeeder?"

"Leased. The dealer wasn't supposed to tell you."

"Figures." Annileen's mouth twisted as she rolled her eyes. "So he's an embezzler. I guess I'm not surprised."

Ben paced back in front of the window, his shadow cast by the moon outside falling across the bed. "I'm afraid that's not all. Orrin could only rely on the Settlers' Call for financing while the Fund was flush. When the Tuskens were on the rampage, that was no problem. But three or so years ago . . . something happened."

"I remember," Annileen said. "After the raid at the Lars place."

"Yes," Ben said, looking mysterious in the moonlight. "I've heard about that. After that attack, something *happened* to the Tuskens—I'm not sure what. But it chilled the Sand People to their bones. And the attacks mostly stopped afterward. Didn't they?"

Annileen sat, wooden, contemplating.

"The attacks stopped," he said. "And within months, the money stopped. The Settlers' Call Fund began to dry up."

"People even stopped buying so many weapons here," she added.

"Orrin couldn't make Jabba's payments. There was nothing left to borrow against. His strategy relied on fear of the Tuskens. So when that fear vanished, he had to create some."

Annileen's eyebrows shot up. "I can't believe this!"

"It's true," Ben said, clasping his hands together. "Orrin and his kids—and probably some hands—staged their own attacks. And your arms business came back, and the Fund came back." He looked out the window. "And they didn't choose random targets. They struck those who wouldn't contribute."

Her mouth dropped open. "How do you know this? Did Jabe tell you?"

Ben shook his head. "The boy seems only to have been brought in now, at the end."

Annileen was glad to hear that.

"No, the first clue I got was from A'Yark, tonight. She said her Tuskens of the Roiya Rift—what they call The Pillars—have been struck by settlers nine times this season." He counted on his fingers. "That matches the Fund's recorded attacks. But A'Yark said the area Tuskens have only raided *four* homes in that time."

Annileen sat fully upright. "You believe her?"

Ben looked directly at her. "Why, exactly, would a Tusken lie?"

"It could have been another band. There are so many!" Looking back at the closed door, she lowered her voice. "A Tusken can't know everything that happens!"

"I think *this* Tusken knows. More than most, anyway," he said. Ben knelt before her. "Orrin targeted the holdouts. His strikes never killed. But they frightened and injured, and drove people to buy in. And to complete the illusion, he sent his vigilantes to wage punitive strikes against the Tuskens—and those *did* kill. Orrin needed a cycle of violence to profit. So he created one." Ben looked away. "I've seen it before," he said, darkly.

She looked at him in anguish. "But there *are* Tusken attacks! We lived through one!"

"Yes. But how often do you think real Tuskens strike isolated farmers and leave them alive?" Ben stroked his beard. "Do you know Lotho Pelhane?"

Of course she did. "Tyla Bezzard's father. He worked for Orrin's ranch, years ago. The Tuskens killed him the day you and I met!"

"Lotho was a holdout. Weeks earlier, he was beaten by night raiders. He moved to his kids' place, where they finally subscribed to the Fund." Ben looked at her. "That's in Orrin's records—along with a notation of *problem solved* from the night Lotho was originally attacked, allegedly by Tuskens." He sighed. "There were others. Orrin wasn't just skimming from the Fund. He made it into something Jabba would understand: a protection racket."

Annileen looked into the blackness. "Then he's betrayed every single person on the oasis."

"And the wastes," Ben said. "Don't forget that. Sand People have been dying, because killing Sand People was the service he sold."

"You're not going to get me to feel sorry for the Tuskens," Annileen said indignantly.

"All life is sacred," Ben said. "Even life that comes in forms that we don't understand." He looked up at her. "You know that, don't you?"

She closed her eyes tightly, caught her breath, and nodded.

"But everything changed today. Mosep wants his money. That's what the Mos Eisley trip was about," he said.

"So you *did* overhear something!"

"Yes." Eyes on her, Ben spoke tactfully. "I . . . fear the marriage proposal is more about money than love. I'm sorry to have to tell you this."

"I found out a couple of hours ago," Annileen said. "I don't care. I just wish you'd told me on the way home today!"

Ben took a deep breath. "I don't like to interfere. But Mosep said something else about Orrin's 'other resources' that put me to thinking about the Settlers' Call, and about Ulbreck, his biggest holdout. On a hunch, I rode there and saw Orrin in his disguise. And he saw me. That changes everything." He spoke gravely. "Right now, if I know his mind, Orrin is planning to have me killed."

"Killed!" She laughed. "Orrin might play dress-up, but he's no killer!"

Ben disagreed. "He won't come for me alone. His kind never does. But I can handle it. I have a plan."

Annileen sat forward on the bed and appealed to him. "Ben, no. Seriously. You said yourself he hadn't killed any settlers. He's not some galactic menace—"

"There are monsters in all walks of life," Ben said. "One doesn't need unlimited power to create victims. One just needs to be desperate."

"There's still good in him," Annileen said, thinking of the smiling man she'd known for years. "I admit he's a lying, cheating, out-of-control scoundrel and that it's hard to see the good—"

"Maybe there *is* good," Ben said, rising from the floor. "There's good in most. But look at what he's done. What he's willing to do. Where do you draw the line?"

The question made Annileen dizzy. "I thought you two were friends."

Ben fixed his gaze on a darkened corner. "I don't know that we were," he said, softly. "But even if we'd been friends for years, things would be no different. When friends go wrong, you don't get a choice about what to do."

"It sounds . . . like you know something about that."

"More than I ever wanted to," he murmured. He looked away.

Annileen stood. Ben had to be reasoned with. Yes, Orrin's crimes would hurt the Calwells if exposed, even if Jabe's role in the Ulbreck attack never became known. The families were linked in the eyes of the whole oasis, and she had been profiting from the Fund's weapons purchases. All might well be lost for her as well as Orrin. But she couldn't risk another life being destroyed.

She reached for him. "You don't have to face him, Ben. This isn't your responsibility."

"No," Ben said, turning his back to her. "It's in motion. He'll call out his allies to silence me, and I'll call on my own." He didn't explain who or what they were. "But no matter what the end, your path is clear."

"My path?" she asked.

Ben turned and placed his hands gently on her shoulders. "Annileen, do you trust me?"

"What?"

"Do you trust me? To know what to do now?"

"Yes," she whispered without pause. "Absolutely." *Like no one since Dannar,* she nearly said.

He looked her in the eye. "What are you prepared to give up, to save your future?"

Annileen inhaled deeply. "A few hours ago, I was ready to give up everything to rescue my son."

"That's what I needed to hear," Ben said. He spoke urgently. "Tomorrow, when Orrin comes for me, I want you to clear out. You, and your family. Take what you need, but also take what you don't want to lose. Because you will never be coming back."

Annileen's heart caught in her throat. "It's that bad?"

His eyes bored into hers. "I think you know it is. I said I could handle Orrin, and I will. But if we do what's right, the lives of you and your children here are collateral damage. I'm sorry." He looked down. "I'd stop it if I could. I know there's nothing worse than losing a home you've known for years. But I can't see any future where that doesn't happen."

Annileen's tears were flowing now. She didn't know what to say, other than that he was right. She survived entirely upon her neighbors' trust. When the truth came out, what had taken twenty years to build would vanish in an instant, no matter how they'd felt about her before.

He dabbed at her cheeks gently with the back of his hand. "It isn't fair, I know. The order in our lives can simply vanish. Sometimes it's because we're not diligent. Sometimes it's no one's fault—"

Sniffling, she looked up at him. "No," she said, wiping her face. "It was my fault. I wasn't diligent." A feeling of resolve came over her. A second wind—or whatever had blown Ben into her world? It didn't matter. She'd had her low moment. Weakness wasn't in her. She straightened her shoulders. "All right," she said, "let's fix this. I'm ready."

Ben brightened. "All right, then." He turned and hoisted himself up to the windowsill. "Start packing. Make the arrangements you need, but tell no one else. Join me again just before the suns set. My work should be done, then."

She handed his cloak to him. "Where will I be going?"

"My house," Ben said. "And that's just the start."

Meditation

I am putting an end to this.

You see where I am, Qui-Gon. Sitting in the cold, alone on a hillside, waiting for the suns to rise. You see what I've been doing, the steps I've taken.

Moreover, you've seen why I've taken them. I hope you don't judge me too harshly, because of it.

"There's still good in him." That's just what Padmé said to me about Anakin. I don't know whether I believed that about him. Maybe if I had been more aware of his smaller transgressions, I might have seen what they were leading toward. I don't know. I do know that Orrin Gault hasn't fallen as the result of a single act; he's had a lifetime of small crimes. He smiles, and lies, and people like him. But the bill has come due. And his fear has driven him to ever-worse acts.

I think there's a chance for Jabe Calwell, if he can get away from Orrin. I know, I know—it wasn't Palpatine alone who corrupted Anakin. Anakin had flaws of his own. Flaws I failed to see, that I didn't prepare him to deal with. But the Emperor played a role. I don't know if it would have been possible to isolate Anakin from his influence. I tried—but too late. Jabe is another story, I think.

Another chance to get it right.

I understand. I am not here to find redemption, saving random youngsters from destruction. I'm not even here to atone, as Annileen suggested earlier. I know I'm here for one reason.

To protect Luke Skywalker.

And to be ready when he—and Bail Organa, or whoever supports hope in the galaxy—needs me. If I achieve absolution in that act, fine. But it's secondary.

And so, I fear, is everything else around me. Annileen. The oasis. These people. It's all got to be secondary. The only way I can act on a galactic scale is by doing nothing locally. Nothing at all.

No matter what my mind or my heart tells me.

You've heard me these last few weeks. At least I hope you have. You haven't talked to me, but I hope you've heard me. You know I'm failing again— this time, at being a hermit. Obi-Wan keeps taking charge of Ben Kenobi's life. We're one and the same, of course. But the Obi-Wan part of me wants to help someone, to do something right. To be a Jedi! Only then will I feel that I am able to live in peace while others are suffering.

I've had such trouble, reconciling it all. How can Ben exist if Obi-Wan won't let him?

But the Force is showing me the way.

It will be difficult, but there is a path I can walk

among all these influences. One that will provide some justice, while giving me the privacy I need to do my job. It depends on many things going right, and making use of that message drop I mentioned a few weeks back.

And then there are my "allies." I can never assume what the Tuskens will do. They are capable of unforgivable things. I know what a group did to Anakin's mother, a few years ago: Padmé told me that much. I always felt there was something more that she wasn't telling me—maybe something that had to do with Anakin's fate. I don't know that I'll find those secrets here. But A'Yark, at least, seems to feel responsible for her people. I will hope that Orrin admits his guilt and turns back—but if he doesn't, I must try to prevent further harm all around.

So many things to consider.

But when the suns rise, I think I can make it all work out. I think.

Well . . . there is one more potential wrinkle.

Annileen. She cares for me—and rightly or wrongly, I've drawn upon that. Just this hour, I've set my plans for her in motion. But what if she doesn't want to go along with them?

What then?

CHAPTER FORTY-ONE

MORNINGS ON TATOOINE HAD never failed Orrin Gault. And this one was better than his wildest dreams.

He hadn't had much time to dream—or sleep—after leaving the Claim the night before. He'd gone home to find an empty house, quiet but for some soft thumping in the office—a sand-mouse behind the shelves, he figured. Mullen and Veeka were out back, burning their Tusken outfits. That had always been the plan, in case of discovery.

Veeka had bandaged her shoulder where Ben had caught her with the gaderffii; Mullen had a bruised tailbone from his fall. Orrin had stood in the cold with them, working out their next moves.

Those moves started at the Claim. The second sun had scarcely been up when Orrin activated the Settlers' Call. After minutes of the screeching siren, the workers of the oasis appeared in front of the garages, waiting to be directed. It hadn't taken long. Many were headed to the Claim for breakfast and were hungry, which was just how he wanted them.

Today they'd be fighting for Orrin's benefit. And someone new.

"You see, Wyle?" Orrin said, looking across the milling throng of vigilantes. "There's my army. *Your* army."

"Yeah," Wyle Ulbreck said. Standing beside Orrin, the old man looked tired beyond measure. His nose was broken and bandaged, and he carried something Orrin had never seen him with before: a small oxygen bottle, which he tapped every few breaths. "We still have to wait for my guys to show up," he muttered. He spat on the ground.

Orrin smirked. Ulbreck had been a surprise, a fabulous bonus. Orrin would have triggered the Call anyway, to execute his next move. But moments after first sunup, a driver had brought Ulbreck to a stop in front of him. The old man had spoken grudgingly then, of how his forces had failed him the night before, and how his Magda had nearly died. Then he'd said the words that Orrin had longed to hear for years: "I want in."

The plan had worked after all. Amazing!

It made sense, Orrin thought. Ulbreck had seen Ben's arrival, but not Orrin's unmasking. And a scout *had* sighted Plug-eye leaving the territory. It had been enough to make Tatooine's tightest miser pay the price for protection. Ulbreck was having the appropriate amount in aurodium-plated ingots trucked in, as soon as someone extricated the filthy things from beneath his refresher station.

It was enough to pay off a large portion of Orrin's debt to Jabba. Orrin was going to throw the retaliatory strike in for free.

And that would take care of yet another matter. Ulbreck's presence meant Ben hadn't gone to him to accuse Orrin. At least not yet, presuming he intended to at all. Orrin's secret could be kept safe. And shortly, the whole chapter would be closed.

Things were going to be okay.

Orrin spied Annileen walking from the store to the garages. He hadn't dared to set foot in the store, but he did note that she must have asked Tar Lup to stay over and work the breakfast shift. That was fine. She probably needed rest, after the night before. He felt bad about that, but he'd make it up to her. Starting now.

Excusing himself from Ulbreck's side, he walked over to Annileen. She wore her heaviest-duty work clothes; her hair was pulled back. She looked at him warily.

"A little bit of good news, Annie," he said. "I won't need as much money as I thought."

"Fine."

"I thought you'd like that."

"Fine." Looking straight ahead, she saw Ulbreck. She stepped forward. "Are you okay, Wyle?"

Orrin watched nervously as she approached the old man. He knew Jabe might have told Annileen about the raid, but that was all the boy knew.

Her words put Orrin at ease. "I'm sorry this happened to you and Magda," she said, clutching the old man's hand. "*Really* sorry." Parting from him, she shot a bitter look at Orrin.

That was fine, Orrin thought. She would protect her son, and she would be set back some money. But she'd get over it.

Annileen stopped to look at the mustering masses. "What's this?" she asked, almost indifferently.

"You heard the Call," Orrin said, knowing well that anyone with eardrums had heard it. "You know how it works. There was an attack. There'll be an answer." He looked at her. "Is Jabe all right?"

"He'll be fine. He's not working today." Spying Gloamer at work in the garages, she excused herself.

"Are you going to wish us luck?" Orrin said, smiling. It was too much, he realized. Annileen simply walked away faster.

Oh, well, he thought. *It's better if she doesn't hear the rest, anyway.*

* * *

"I can't belieeeeve this, mistress," Gloamer said.

"That's the offer," Annileen said, reviewing the document on the datapad. "You've been doing a great job with the garages, and I know you've had your eye on expanding."

With his eyes a tiny feature on his elongated cranium, the Phindian mechanic always looked a little mournful. But now even Annileen could read his surprise. He'd invited her to the garage to tell her that the parts for her old landspeeder had finally arrived. Instead, he'd gotten the deal of a lifetime.

"Running a shop!" he said, long arms in the air. "I don't knoooow. I don't knoooow how—"

"I doubt that," Annileen said, patting him on the back. "You're good with customers. And there's not much to hustling power cells and ale. Talk to Tar. He knows how. And he'd like the chance."

The mechanic hummed contemplatively. Finally, he nodded, stepping back a meter so he could offer his tremendously long limb in a handshake. "I will maaaake the credit transfer," he said, taking the datapad.

"You can't tell anyone," she said. "Not until tonight, after we leave."

Gloamer nodded. The Phindian's head tilted ninety degrees. Yellow eyes studied her sadly. "Wheeeere are you going?"

Annileen smiled gently. "On an adventure."

She turned from him and walked back into the hallway to the Claim. Exhaling, she leaned against the wall with a thump. Had she just done that? *Did I really just sell the store?*

Even more amazing was the fact that her kids were going along with it—so far. She'd learned upon waking that Kallie and Jabe had heard her talking to Ben, after all; they'd heard the last part, anyway. Jabe was still in such a lather over the raid that he was ready to move to the Corporate Sector. And Kallie had been so smitten with Ben since their first meeting that the prospect of him sweeping in to rescue her family from dishonor perfectly fit the myth.

Still, the last hour had been tough. On seeing Ulbreck arrive, Jabe had feared the worst; Annileen had coaxed him from hiding and assigned him the job of getting the house packed up. And Kallie, out in the livery, had realized what leaving really meant. There was no obvious successor to take care of her beloved animals, and Annileen's best idea, letting the people who rented the critters today keep them, wasn't sitting well with Kallie.

It wasn't sitting well with Annileen, either. Walking through the shop, she saw them all there: Bohmer, at his table with his mug; Leelee, hastily addressing another stack of boxes; even Erbaly Nap'tee, counting buttons out loud as she rummaged through a drawer filled with secondhand clothes. How could she leave all this?

She could imagine her mother's voice in her head. What could Annileen be thinking? She cared for Ben, yes. More deeply than she'd imagined possible at this stage. No one else had measured up to Dannar Calwell. But did Ben really expect her to give up everything, just on the prospect of bad times ahead?

Nella Thaney would turn her daughter right back to the garages. She'd have Annileen tell Gloamer it was a joke, and he'd forget it. The mechanic didn't understand humor anyway. Annileen might not even have to protect her family from fallout at all; from the side door, she could see Orrin, a smile on his face as he talked to Ulbreck. Orrin would find a way to fix his troubles. He always did. And Ben faced no danger—Orrin was just a blowhard! Why go through with this?

Annileen already knew why. She knew, and it had

swept all doubts away. All that remained was seeing what Orrin had planned.

She slipped outside the Claim to watch the spectacle. It was easy to hide in the crowd; the mob was the largest she'd seen. It wasn't just the regular vigilantes, now. Wyle Ulbreck's landspeeders sat packed with farmhands, parked along the western dune. Mullen and Veeka were passing weapons to the riders. Annileen wondered how Orrin could even be seen in the crowd, much less make himself heard.

She soon found out.

"Everyone, listen up!" Orrin bellowed. Annileen looked up. Orrin had climbed the service ladder and was clinging to Old Number One. With his free hand, he held to his mouth a loudhailer, a portable amplifier that boomed his voice across the parking area.

"This is a big day," he said. "And a terrible day. One of us has turned *traitor*!"

A buzz went through the armed crowd. *A traitor, here?*

"Well, don't worry. He's not one of *us*," Orrin added. "You're all good people. But you know him: *Ben Kenobi*!"

Annileen gulped for air. The name Kallie had overheard was suddenly on everyone's lips.

"You heard right," Orrin said, speaking through the green metal device. "You may have seen him coming around, may have heard people talk. Crazy Ben, someone called him. Living in the desert, talking to himself. Well, he's crazy all right. He's a Tusken-lover!"

"No!" Annileen heard someone shout.

"I know," Orrin said. "Hard to believe any settler would help those monsters. But here's what we know. Kenobi popped up here right after Plug-eye's day raids started. He ran out of the store after his first visit without even taking what he bought! And the next time we saw him? The Tuskens attacked the Claim!" His voice rose. "He was here when they attacked, but he didn't fight 'em! Then he supposedly saved Annie Calwell from Plug-eye by talking to the Tuskens. *Talking* to them!"

The crowd rumbled with shock. *Talking to Tuskens? Impossible!*

"I hear you," Orrin said, lowering his pitch. "But it makes sense. No barbarian could figure out the Settlers' Call, right? Well, Kenobi helped 'em. He'd heard me talking in the Claim. He knew Ulbreck's ranch was the only place that wasn't covered." He nodded in Ulbreck's direction, below. "Well, the Tuskens stole a vaporator unit from Master Ulbreck a couple of days ago. And then last night, they hit his home. And Kenobi was with them!"

Annileen watched, hypnotized, as a farmhand set out a box for Wyle to stand on. The old man seemed shaky.

"Gault is right," Ulbreck called out to the listeners. "I did see Kenobi. But he was scrapping with the Tuskies, I thought. I'm not sure. My Maggie was in trouble—"

"Because of Kenobi," Orrin quickly interjected. "Because of the Sand People he brought there! I'm willing to bet old Ben was mad at his partners. He was there for Wyle's money, I'll wager—and the Tuskens don't care about money. They started fighting."

Another ripple in the crowd. Everyone knew about Ulbreck's fortune.

Orrin shook his head sadly, so all could see his emotion. "This Kenobi—if that's even his name—I don't know him. He showed me one face, a false one. I don't know if he's a bandit, or if he's gone Tusken, as crazy as that sounds. It doesn't matter. What matters is he's put good folks in jeopardy. And we're gonna stop him *forever*!"

Blasters fired into the air. Annileen cringed. This wasn't what she'd expected at all! Ben had said Orrin would round up some allies, but she'd expected more oafish farmhands of the Zedd sort. This was something different. The force was too large, and Orrin was different, too. He was electric. Telling the vigilantes of Ben's hideout in the Jundland Wastes, a place no decent person would live, Orrin sent a hateful energy through the gathering, rousing the crowd to action.

He'd made the sale, jumping from wheedler to warlord with a few words. She'd never seen anything like it. And certainly not from him.

Orrin hit his crescendo. "We take care of our own. So follow me—and let's ride!"

A raucous, angry cheer went up. Engines started, one after another, as more blasters went off. Annileen nearly dropped to her knees, life drained from her limbs. This couldn't have been what Ben was expecting. Who *could* have expected it?

Orrin shimmied down from the tower and turned. Mullen and Veeka were waiting, holding a spread-open flak jacket. Orrin stuck his arms out, and they dressed him in it like a warrior king.

Stepping toward his USV-5, Orrin spied Annileen. He winked, and was off.

Dust blew against the store as one blaster-bedecked speeder after another whizzed away. Watching helplessly, Annileen flashed for a moment on the retaliatory raid after the oasis strike. That day, she'd grabbed the speeder bike and gone with Ben to follow Jabe. But now it was Ben in danger. Ben, who'd saved Jabe. Ben, who'd told her in the night not to follow, that he could take care of Orrin.

Annileen looked back at the garages, mostly empty now but for her two landspeeders. Staring at the leased luxury vehicle, she suddenly remembered something.

She dashed back into the store. Tar, serving children dropped off by their parents, looked at her from the dining area, startled. Annileen ignored him and rushed behind the counter. Kneeling, she overturned the trash bin and started rummaging.

Amid broken glass, she found the red comlink she'd discarded the night before. She clicked it on and hit the page key.

"Hello? Who is this?" asked the genteel voice on the other end of the link.

"This is Annileen Calwell," she said, speaking urgently. "I'm a neighbor of Orrin Gault's. I know who you are. And you need to know what he's about to do!"

CHAPTER FORTY-TWO

TURN BACK NOW.

Jabe had said the words at the store, supposedly Ben's message to Orrin. Now, as Orrin checked his blaster, the farmer heard the words again. Or thought he did, in the wind whistling past his landspeeder.

Orrin hadn't known what to make of the message. If Ben planned to extort him, there'd have to be a meeting to parley. If he'd simply planned to expose the Gaults, he'd have come to the Claim. Or perhaps he would have gone in search of someone in authority, oblivious to the fact that no such power existed here.

It didn't make sense.

"Fifteen clicks to Kenobi's hut," the goggle-wearing Mullen said, guiding the vehicle.

Orrin nodded. Holstering the blaster, he looked around in awe. His USV-5 rode at the apex of a flying wing of hovercraft, rocketing to the southwest. Every vehicle the Settlers' Call Fund operated was here, plus Ulbreck's teams. Orrin doubted there had ever been so many vehicles traversing the desert at once.

He chuckled in spite of himself. *Yep, Orrin, some pull you've got indeed.* Maybe farming wasn't his calling. Tatooine didn't offer many chances for a career politician, but with that new Empire on the rise, who knew?

Whatever. Ben wouldn't know what hit him. Orrin lifted his macrobinoculars to scan the nothingness ahead.

From the backseat, Veeka pointed ahead, to the left. "There!"

In the middle of the desert, Ben stood brazenly astride a speeder bike. One of *Orrin's* speeder bikes, Orrin saw as he focused in: the one Jabe had ridden to the Ulbrecks'.

Mullen pointed. "Everyone's spotted him. Dad, I think we should turn back now."

Orrin looked up, startled. "What did you say?"

"I said if we turn and double back, the left flank will follow us," his son said. "We'll catch him between and herd him like a bantha."

"Oh, okay," Orrin said, fishing inside the jacket for a handkerchief. He wiped the sweat from his brow. The landspeeder lurched and wheeled, and a dozen-plus repulsorcraft followed.

Orrin trained the viewfinder on Ben again, still almost a kilometer away. The man simply looked back, serenely, as if aware Orrin's eyes were on him. Finally, Ben activated the bike and turned.

"That's right," Orrin said, grinning. "*You* turn back now."

Kenobi was zigzagging across the open sand. West, back to his place, was barred to him by one line of landspeeders; north, and the open range, by the other. Orrin had thought for a moment that the man might make for the great gap in the Jundland, the pathway the Jawas took to reach the Western Dune Sea. But he seemed to be heading instead for the branch of the Jundland highlands farther east.

Orrin figured it out immediately. "Cute," he said. "He's trying to get us into Hanter's Gorge." Annileen had said she and Ben had witnessed the Tusken massacre there. Orrin didn't know whether Ben had a soft spot for Sand People or not, but all the same, he wasn't going to be led into a trap. "Cut him off," he said over the comm system. "Send him into the rift!"

The Roiya Rift had always looked to Orrin like a wall that a child had built out of blocks—and then knocked half of it down. Here, the Jundland Wastes bowed inward, a semicircle of flat desert terrain at the mouth of a half ring of jagged, towering teeth. The wide passageways between the teeth twisted south into the wastes, climbing and subdividing into smaller corridors; the Tuskens loved to hide here. The oasis attackers had been making for the rift when they'd wound up in Hanter's Gorge, kilometers to the east, by mistake. But with the rift, there was no prospect of those on high ground sniping at the posse. The pillars of stone climbed too high, and the paths between rose too gradually, twisting and bending as they went.

The landspeeder lines held, and Ben veered into the gap. Without pause, his speeder bike rocketed for one of the narrower, rubble-strewn ramps. Within seconds, he was gone from sight. Orrin knew then that it was all over for Kenobi. Vigilante vehicles streamed into the semicircle, taking up station in front of all the apertures, not just the one Ben had taken. There was no escape.

Mullen brought the Gault landspeeder to a stop. "Are we going up after him?"

"Not sure we'll have to," Orrin said. "He's a tourist. He'll find out there's Tuskens up there and will turn right back around."

"What if he's pals with the Tuskies, like you said?" Mullen asked.

Orrin rolled his eyes. "That was for the *crowd*, Mullen!" He smirked. "But so what if he is? They'll see we've brought an army and kill him all the same."

Orrin stepped out of the vehicle and straightened his jacket. He nodded for his kids to approach. "Now, remember," he said quietly. "If Kenobi comes out, don't give him a chance to say a word. You cut him down fast and the others will follow."

Veeka looked at her father. "What if he's unarmed?"

"We'll say we saw him draw on us," Orrin said. He glared at his daughter. "Are you that worried about him? You do want to continue living it up on my money, don't you?"

"I don't care," she said, spitting on the ground. "One less beggar in the desert. I just wanted to know what you were gonna say."

"Just follow my lead, as usual." Orrin reached inside the vehicle for the loudhailer. Turning, he walked into the middle of the gathering. Under the noon suns, the stone formations gave Orrin the impression of standing within a giant, natural coliseum. The place had fallen silent except for the *click-clack*s of blaster rifles being adjusted. Armed settlers crouched behind hovering repulsorcraft. Any eyes that weren't on the gaps were on Orrin.

Orrin shouted into the amplifier. "Come on out, Kenobi!"

His voice echoed all around. But no response came.

Watching from cover, Ulbreck looked back, warily. "Don't like this."

"Don't worry," Orrin said, gesturing toward a group of settlers in the rear. "Send up the smoke charges." The mortars were one of the Fund's earlier investments, and they'd never had occasion to use them. But they were designed for exactly this: flushing out the opposition. A few parabolic shots up into the crags and Ben would have nowhere to—

"*Ayooooo-eh-EH-EHH!*"

Orrin froze. The screech came again from the hills. A

krayt dragon call: just like the Settlers' Call siren, only more natural sounding. Rising and trilling, the noise reached every listener in the would-be arena.

Orrin looked back at the others, a canny grin on his face. "Don't be fooled, folks. That's *our* trick."

Some of the settlers shifted nervously, but they all stayed in position. Orrin walked back to his landspeeder and brought the loudhailer to his mouth. "You'd better cut that out, Kenobi, or you'll scare your friends." He waved back to the settlers setting up the mortars. It was time.

Then it happened. The Zeltron, Leelee's husband, noticed it first. "Listen!" Waller Pace said. "Do you feel it?"

Orrin didn't have time for empathic Zeltrons and their feelings. "Stay focused," he said. But now Orrin felt it, too, and heard it. A low rumble, rising slowly to a crescendo. Pebbles on the ground began to roll. Dust rose.

"Groundquake!" Veeka yelled.

Orrin shook his head. No, that wasn't it. It was something else, thundering downward, through the gaps from the Jundland Wastes. And now he saw what it was.

Banthas!

One after another, the enormous beasts charged down the stone chute Ben had ridden his speeder bike up. And not just from there! Several broad pathways wound down from the mountains—and now they were filled, too, disgorging banthas of all sizes. Right at the settlers.

"*Stampede!*" Ulbreck yelled, ducking under his hovering vehicle. The hairy mass coursed across the desert floor like water from a broken dam, sending settlers diving in all directions.

The loudhailer fell from Orrin's hand into the open cab of his landspeeder. He tried to use his vehicle for cover, too, but a giant bantha struck it first, ramming the hovercraft's hood into his midsection. A heartbeat later a second bantha struck the USV-5, sending both Orrin and the vehicle spinning.

All around, the scene repeated. The charging animals smashed into landspeeders and sent them careening like toys. Settlers dived and fell in desperation. In the rear, the beasts upset the mortars, resulting in smoke rounds shrieking over the vigilantes' heads. Two struck the wall of the rift with an ear-shattering clang—and in the next instant smoke filled the air.

Orrin clung to his landspeeder until it bounced into a boulder, knocking him to the dust. Dazed and dizzy, he spent long moments lost in the smoke. Somewhere, a blaster went off. A farmer screamed. Orrin didn't move.

In the fog, a voice came from nearby. It was Ben's.

"Turn back now."

Orrin blinked. Before, he had heard the words only in Jabe's voice, and then later when Mullen had said them. Hearing them now, from Ben himself, he realized the message wasn't a demand. Instead, Ben's voice was calm and consoling, as if giving advice to a friend.

Orrin reached for his blaster, which was still secure in his holster, but there was nowhere to point it.

Finally, as the yellowish smoke settled, he coughed and rubbed his eyes. The landspeeders had been thrown around like sabacc cards in the breeze. Some still hovered, their engines driving them futilely into the nearby walls. Others were upended, or half on top of other vehicles. The settlers were in the dust, gasping for air and grasping for their fallen weapons. At least they were all moving, as far as Orrin could see.

Into this scene, three remaining creatures emerged from the uplands. A bantha calf trotted down—followed, improbably, by an eopie mother and her kid. The trio of laggards tromped heedlessly through the chaotic scene, following the herd into the open desert to the northwest.

Orrin found Mullen and Veeka awkwardly getting to their feet. Mullen had taken a bantha horn to the side of his head; he was bleeding from his temple. "Can you fight?" Orrin asked.

Mullen grunted angrily.

Orrin took it as affirmative. "Kenobi's playing games," he muttered. He turned, blaster in hand.

But something else came screaming down from the stone fissure. A speeder bike and rider, sizzling down the pathway Kenobi had taken up into the mountains. It soared in a straight line, one that would take it over the heads of the vigilantes and to the open desert beyond.

"Blast him! Blast him!"

Quick-witted vigilantes caught the vehicle in a crossfire as it zipped past. Several shots struck true, and the speeder bike flashed with fire, spiraling to the right. Its forward struts struck the ground hard. The vehicle and its passenger flipped end over end, finally smashing into an unoccupied repulsorcraft.

Orrin rushed forward. Wreckage was everywhere. A body burned in the debris. Excitedly, Orrin approached the rider's side.

And saw that it was, in fact, a burlap duffel. Half of the smoking bag had ripped open where it had been tied to the handlebars. Without thinking, Orrin shoved his hand into the smoldering debris and found the fake rider's stuffing: a bundle of Tusken head wrappings.

"It's from your wardrobe, Orrin," Ben said. His voice echoed all around, louder than the krayt call and certainly louder than the phantom whisper Orrin had heard earlier. "I brought it from your place!"

Looking about in surprise, Orrin threw the wrappings away. How Ben was saying it wasn't important. Remembering where he had dropped the loudhailer, Orrin dashed toward his landspeeder, piled up against the rock. He skidded to a stop beside it and reached inside the vehicle, fishing for the amplifier's handle. Finding something, he lifted it—

—and stared, mystified, at the gaderffii in his hand.

"That's also from your stash," Ben called from above.

He's using the loudhailer, Orrin realized. Somehow, the man had returned to the floor of the rift on foot in the smoky chaos and switched the gaderffii for the loudhailer. But there wasn't time for Orrin to contemplate that. Half the posse was staring at him as he held the Tusken weapon.

And wherever Kenobi was, he saw it.

"They're interested in your collection, Orrin. The weapons and clothing you've taken from Tuskens in the past. That you've used—you and your family—in strikes against your neighbors!"

Aware of the stares, Orrin threw the weapon to the ground, repulsed. "What a crazy story," he said, forcing a chuckle. "Dancing with Tuskens is Kenobi's game!"

"You have me wrong," Ben said, his voice coming from everywhere and nowhere. "I only wanted to live here in peace. You're the one who's making war, all to sell your protection service!"

"It's not ours," Veeka yelled, clearly rattled. "Tell them, Dad!"

Orrin looked urgently toward her. *Shut up,* he implored with his eyes. *I have to do the talking!*

"He's wrong," Orrin said, facing the others. "We keep some trophies, sure. Who wouldn't? But he got this stuff from his friends back there, who sent the banthas. And the Settlers' Call Fund isn't ours, either. It's a public trust!"

"Then tell them the balance," Ben said. "Tell them you haven't been stealing from it to pay your debts. Tell them you didn't attack Tyla Bezzard's father when he wouldn't join, leaving the man hobbled and unable to save himself later when the Tuskens attacked for real."

His voice grew louder. "Tell them you didn't attack the Ulbreck place yourself, last night. Tell them you didn't flee, when I happened along!"

Orrin straightened, searching for a friendly face on which to fix his gaze. There weren't many. One settler after another looked angered, agitated, or bewildered. And Wyle Ulbreck looked ready to explode. "Is that true, Gault? Is that true?"

Mullen looked at his father, mortified.

But there was a way out. Orrin fished for his best smile, and found it. "People, people. I'm a farmer," he said, shouting so all could hear. "Like you. I get water out of the air. That man—he gets stories out of it." He shrugged theatrically. "You've enjoyed my generosity. You know I do well enough on my own. I have all the money I would ever need!"

"That's excellent news," came another amplified voice, this one from the desert. Orrin looked back, suddenly aware of the large hoverskiff floating outside the rift. On its deck, flanked by gun-toting thugs, was Mosep Binneed. He wore a neck brace and held a loud-hailer in front of his mouth. "Jabba wants his money, Orrin Gault! And he wants it now!"

CHAPTER FORTY-THREE

A'YARK STOOD FLAT AGAINST one of The Pillars and looked down the rocky incline to the settlers far below.

"The Hutt's people," she said, her voice dripping with disgust. "We can smells them." The Tusken cast her eye across the natural corridor. "You said there would only be settlers."

Ben crouched nearby, holding Orrin's green sound device and surveying the scene below. Beneath his cowl, Ben had wrapped a loose cloth over his lower face in deference to the Tuskens' sensibilities; now he pulled it down and scratched his chin. The human seemed startled by the appearance of the skiff. "This wasn't in my plan."

The war leader's ire boiled. "You told us—"

"I told you I'd bring Orrin Gault to justice. He could choose between his people's justice—or yours." Ben shook his head. "I thought he'd turn back."

A'Yark didn't care what the settlers wanted. Ben had brought the enemy to their gate, as promised, but they'd come in far greater numbers than the clan could oppose. A'Yark had stationed the few warriors she had at the other access points, but if the settlers really wanted to follow Ben up into The Pillars, nothing could stop them. The high camp would be overrun.

Ben had acted quickly then, calling for the Tusken women and children to herd their precious banthas down into the arroyo. Many of the banthas had lost their riders in the gorge massacre, and A'Yark had been pleased to see them getting some small revenge. The animals had bought them precious time. But now the arrival of the Hutt's minions had compounded the danger. The criminals did not fear the Tuskens, as all should.

It was the Hutts that had killed Sharad Hett, years earlier.

A'Yark knew that Ben deserved death for bringing this upon them. She would give it to him, were it in her power.

But in the light of the suns, she had to admit their fall had begun long before he arrived.

"It went wrong," she said, not knowing why she was speaking. "We are so weak—Tuskens are all so weak—because of what happened, more than three cycles ago."

Ben looked at her, curious. "What happened?"

"There was another massacre," she said. "A camp of mighty warriors, wiped away. The women and children, too."

For some reason, her words seemed to strike a target deep within Ben. "The children, all killed?" He swallowed. "A krayt dragon? Some other predator?"

A'Yark shook her head. "A predator, yes. But death came on two legs," she said. "We know."

"But the children," Ben said. "Settlers don't usually kill them, do they?"

"Settlers orphan, settlers abandon," she said. "Predator slaughtered."

Ben paused, as if seeming to piece something together. "I wonder . . ."

A'Yark saw his eyes fix forward, filling with dread. It looked to her as if Ben was in another place, now, imagining—or experiencing—something that filled his mind with horror. "What?" she asked.

Ben regained his composure. "Something I'm going to have to look into at another time," he said. "I'm starting to suspect the Sand People's confidence may not have been the only victim of that event."

"No matter now," she said, withdrawing from the lookout point. "I must hide my people."

"I'll help," Ben said, rising to follow. "Protecting homes is my speciality." With that, he turned back and followed her up the incline.

Mullen gaped at his father. "Jabba's people? It's too soon! We've got five hours yet!"

Orrin stared wordlessly at the new arrivals. More landspeeders laden with lowlifes arrived behind the skiff. But why now? And how did they know to come?

Settlers trained their weapons on the skiff, keeping the criminals at bay. The vigilantes, already made restless by the banthas and Ben's words, looked positively rattled now. Jabba's thugs lived right alongside Tuskens in the settlers' list of enemies. Both lived by a strange code in a world to themselves—until they came out to terrorize the peaceful. Now they'd blocked the settlers' access to the desert, even as they themselves had trapped Ben.

Waller goggled. His crimson eyebrows flared as he looked at Orrin. "Jabba? You dealt with Jabba?"

Before Orrin could think of a response, Mosep spoke again. "I was told you were taking an army—such as it is—back into the hills. Now, why would you do such a thing when a bill is due today?"

Veeka looked at her father, concerned.

"It's an old story," the Nimbanel accountant continued, from the deck of the skiff. "People refuse their obligations and try to run. Some take up arms and try to fight." He snapped his hairy fingers, and Jorrk took up station at the skiff's deck gun. "The afternoon deadline is rescinded, Orrin. You will pay us now."

"What's this about?" Orrin yelled nervously. "Did the *Tusken-lover* bring you here?" Elated to have hit on another tactic, he brightened as he looked around. "I guess Kenobi works with scum, too!"

"I don't know who you mean," Mosep said, growing impatient. Behind the skiff, another vehicle was arriving from the north. "Your *neighbor* called me."

My neighbor? Orrin swallowed, his throat dry. He had rivals among the farmers, here. Did one of them know something? He looked around in shock and surprise, anxious to make a good show of it. "Is one of you here trying to set me up—to embarrass me with this nonsense?"

The landspeeder that had been racing up from behind now passed through the criminals' line of vehicles. Settlers raised rifles against the hovercraft entering their midst—and then lowered them, as they recognized the driver.

Navigating among the overturned landspeeders, Annileen brought the ruby JG-8 to a stop near one of the pathways leading up the rift. She stepped out near the Gaults and held a red comlink high. "*I* called them," she said.

Aboard the skiff, Mosep raised an identical communicator: the one Orrin had dropped in his lair. He smiled toothily. "Good to see you, Mistress Calwell."

Orrin gaped at Annileen. "*Y-you?*"

"Yes." Catching her breath, she turned to the vigilantes. "Ben's innocent. I heard what Orrin said back at the Claim. Now you should hear the real story!"

Mullen started menacingly toward Annileen. "Woman, you'd better not!"

Annileen turned to see Veeka approaching from her

other side. Veeka clutched at Annileen's arm. Her eyes looked wild. "Think about that whelp of yours!" Veeka said.

Orrin could only look at Annileen imploringly.

Annileen pulled her arm free from Veeka's grasp. Staring at Orrin, she spoke with an assurance he'd heard before—the tower of power he'd often described her as. "I'm not going to let you hurt someone whose only crime was to help me," she said. "I *do* care about my family. But what you've done is *wrong*!"

Ulbreck stepped forward, rifle in hand and clearly flustered. "I don't know what in blazes is going on here!"

"I think I do," Waller said. He shook his head at Orrin. "We trusted you." All around, settlers began to turn their weapons away from the skiff and its associated hovercraft and toward the Gaults.

Orrin looked to his right. There was the USV-5, where it had come to rest after the stampede. He started toward it—

—only to see his precious hovercraft explode in a blossom of metal and flame.

Spun around by the shock wave, Orrin saw what had happened. On the skiff, Mosep gestured to the Klatooinian at the smoking deck gun. "Jorrk's an oaf, but with a big enough gun, even he can't miss," the accountant said. "You people can't have Gault until we're finished. He owes us money!"

Ulbreck shot a hateful look at the Nimbanel. "You pirates don't have any say here! This is the range!"

The old farmer's companions raised their rifles. "Our justice comes first!" another settler said.

Mosep glanced up at the suns and mopped sweat from his fuzzy face. "You really are a trying lot," he said. "I told Orrin's handler it was a mistake to offer credit to any of you." He turned the loudhailer to address his thugs. "Try not to kill the human woman who just drove up," Mosep said. "She brought us here. It wouldn't be polite." He tugged at his neck brace and looked back at the settlers. "I'm sorry, but if you insist on making this unpleasant—"

A blaster rifle sounded, followed by a high-pitched crack to Mosep's side. Startled, he twisted his torso to see what had happened. There was Jorrk, staring stupidly at what was left of his exploded and smoking deck gun. Another shot sounded—and the Klatooinian fell backward, dead. Mosep looked toward the settlers.

"I killed me a room full of Tuskens," Ulbreck shouted, rifle sight set on the skiff. "I ain't gonna let you people push me around!"

At the sound of the old man's words, all the settlers reached the same conclusion. As one, they turned and fired at Jabba's thugs. Return fire came in, sending others to dive for cover behind the upturned landspeeders. On the skiff, Mosep screamed and hid behind the nearest Gamorrean, only to be flattened when the green thug took a blaster shot between the eyes.

Stuck in the open, Orrin grabbed at Annileen, pulling her from the crossfire. For a second she looked at him, speechless—until his hand tightened around her arm.

"Kids! Let's go!" Orrin yelled.

Startled, Annileen tried to pull away. But now Mullen grabbed her other arm. With blaster shots from the thugs coming into the rift, Orrin shoved her toward the JG-8, still parked nearby.

Annileen yelled, but in the din, only Waller and two other settlers, crouching in cover, heard.

Waller turned. "Orrin, stop!"

With his free hand, Orrin pulled his pistol and placed it at Annileen's head. "We're getting out of here," he said, pushing her toward the landspeeder.

Veeka threw an armload of weapons into the front of the vehicle and slid behind the controls. "We can't get through all that," she yelled, pointing back at the raging battle.

Orrin had no intention of going that way. He pointed to the sloping corridor leading upward, the rocky path Ben had taken up into the formation. "There! Go!"

Under fire from Mosep's henchmen, Waller could only watch as Orrin's daughter gunned the JG-8 up the impossible terrain. The hovercraft whined in protest, slamming against ground it had never been designed to navigate. Stray blasterfire struck nearby. A steering vane caught against an outcrop and snapped off. Then the landspeeder left the battle behind . . .

A'Yark ran across the high camp, robes flying.

"To the caves!" she yelled, herding elder and animal alike. Children and scaly canine massiffs squealed and ran, leaving chores and meals unfinished near the sacred well.

The clearing was a somewhat level theater surrounded by more of the great towers of stone, half a kilometer up the formation. Most of the day it was in shadows, but now, at mid-suns, all was exposed. To east and west, crumbling blocks piled against the mountains. Normally, those offered shade and shelter; today, they were the hiding place of last resort. A'Yark shoved blaster rifles into the hands of a pair of nurses heading off to hide the children. She had no confidence they would know what to do with the weapons. She had waited too long to teach them.

A mechanical noise came from the gap to the north: the downward passage that had been guarded by A'Yark and Ben. A landspeeder, she instantly realized. The ascent should have been impossible! Desperately, she looked to either side. Their few warriors were still down at their observation posts, watching the firefight. There was no way to call them. Time was up.

She turned to see Ben running with a writhing pair of Tusken toddlers, carrying them to cover. Gaderffii in hand, she dashed toward him.

Handing off the second child to a Tusken woman in hiding, Ben looked to a wide opening between the titanic stones to the south. "That way?" he asked.

"Bad country," A'Yark said. "It is too late. They are here. Quickly!"

A'Yark and Ben slid over a collapsed pile of granite. Looking back over it, they saw the red landspeeder thumping over the rocky entrance in the north.

"Orrin," Ben said quietly. "He just won't turn back."

A'Yark looked out. The Smiling One wasn't alone. His offspring were in the front seats, and he held Annileen in the back, at gunpoint. Seconds later the landspeeder ground to an anguished halt on the rough terrain, eighty meters from their position. Orrin's children stepped out and looked around warily.

The warrior quietly set down her gaderffii. There was a rifle behind her. She reached for it, but Ben touched her gloved hand. "You can't," he said. "They have Annileen!"

"She does not matter," A'Yark whispered to Ben.

"I decide that."

A'Yark shook her head. *Madness.* The humans were arming themselves. Would more follow soon?

Held by Orrin, Annileen called out. "Ben—if you're here, stay away!"

A'Yark couldn't hear what Annileen's captors said to her after that, but it was clear they were doing nothing to keep her from yelling.

"They mean to flush me out," Ben whispered. He felt for the lightsaber beneath his cloak—and then withdrew his hand. "I can't endanger Annileen."

"Then I attacks." A'Yark clutched Ben's wrist. "You, too. You have a duty."

"Don't worry." Ben looked behind, to where three children were cowering beneath an overhang. "I told you, I'll protect your people if Orrin should—"

"Not that." A'Yark looked at Ben, searchingly. *Can he not know what all Tuskens knew?*

She spoke quietly but quickly. "Orringault showed his true face. You kills him now, or he pursues you forever!" She pointed to the suns. "It is the way of sky-brothers."

Ben stared. "This—this is another legend?"

"It is *the* legend."

A'Yark watched Ben, who contemplated the story. After a moment, he shook his head. "I *won't* leave this undone. But I won't risk Annileen, either." He looked to the left, to the forest of monoliths piled against the western mount. "Stay here," he said, crawling away behind cover. "I have an idea!"

CHAPTER FORTY-FOUR

ORRIN SAW NO COLOR in the place, apart from the landspeeder. Even its showroom shine was gone now, buried beneath dust. Veeka knelt beside it, examining an undercarriage battered from the raucous ride up the mountain.

"Will she run?" Orrin asked, still holding Annileen.

Veeka shook her head. "Stabilizers are gone," she said. "You could fly it, if you don't care where it goes."

"There's nowhere *to* go," Mullen said, looking warily around the abandoned camp. "How can anyone live in a place like this?"

"I wouldn't call it living." Orrin sneered contemptuously. He shoved Annileen toward Mullen. "Hold her."

Orrin scanned the bases of the stony pylons around them. Reaching a decision, he checked his flak vest and blaster. "Veeka, forget the speeder and watch for snipers. I'm going to try something."

Cautiously, he walked across the rubble toward the center of the clearing. A sad well sat there, little more than a jagged hole surrounded by dented tin pots. He turned. *"Kenobi!"* he yelled.

Nothing but echoes.

And Annileen. "He's too smart for you," she said.

Orrin looked back and scowled. "Shut up."

He turned his attention back to the perimeter. Something was moving out there, on both sides of the clearing. He could hear it. But as soon as he looked in either direction, the noise stopped, too.

This is no good, Orrin thought. He looked back at the route they'd taken to get here. He wished he had some idea what was happening in the battle below. Could he and the kids bring down Kenobi's body and blame the mess on him? Or did they need to keep moving, perhaps crossing enough of the Jundland to reach freedom? He stalked around the well, kicking a pail.

From behind a boulder, a spiky reptilian half a meter long bounded into the clearing. A massiff! Dark-eyed and big-jawed, it charged straight for Orrin, who quickly drew a bead and shot. Struck by the orange energy, the massiff squawked and fell to the ground.

Orrin looked back at Mullen and Veeka. "Thanks for the assist," he said drily.

"We're watching for the big game," Mullen said. He had Annileen's arm in one hand and his blaster in the other, as his eyes continued to scan their surroundings.

Orrin looked at the smoking creature and got an idea. Checking first that he was covered, he holstered his weapon and stepped toward the oozing massiff. He lifted the carcass. "Let's do some home improvement," he said loudly. Arriving back at the well, he dangled the dripping body theatrically over the hole. "Down you go—"

"Don't!" Ben's voice called out from afar.

Orrin lifted the massiff by its legs and looked around. "What," he called out, "you don't want me to poison your friends' well?"

"I was saying that to A'Yark," Ben's voice boomed. "The one you call Plug-eye. Because she's going to shoot you, and you might accidentally drop the animal in anyway."

Somewhere, Orrin heard a weapon safety clicking on. He nodded. So the Tuskens *were* listening to Kenobi. "Glad to have gotten your attention," he said.

"Turn back now," Ben repeated.

This time, Orrin could tell that the voice was coming from the forest of pillars to the west. "I don't feel like turning back," he said, tossing the creature's limp form down the hole. It bounced twice before hitting bottom with a thud. The well was dry.

Orrin looked around. No one had fired at him. Ben wanted Annileen alive, and the Tuskens were following his lead. But Ben could change his mind at any moment, and Orrin wasn't about to let him call the Sandies down on him.

Pulling his weapon, Orrin made his way carefully to an opening in the western rocks. He shot a look back to Mullen and Veeka and mouthed a command. *Wait for me.*

Orrin stepped amid the megaliths. It was as bizarre a natural formation as he'd seen on Tatooine—almost designed by nature to form a labyrinth. Mountain wind whistled between the towers, which rose high enough to blot out even the midday suns. He certainly didn't lack for cover here. Getting a clean shot would be another matter.

"I know you're there, Kenobi!" he bellowed.

"Turn back now." Ben's voice resounded through the rocks, closer than before.

Orrin spun and fired. The shot hit the base of a tower, leaving a smoking pit in the surface.

He kept walking. There was more movement. Footsteps, fast and light. Orrin fired again, down a long corridor.

Nothing. Somewhere, he heard a Tusken child crying. Orrin growled impatiently. "Enough games, Kenobi!"

"Agreed," Ben said, his voice coming from a different side now. "So turn back."

"No!" Orrin felt his eyes burning. With his left hand, he pulled out his second blaster; he raised both weapons and fired. Again and again, turning in all directions. He could see movement and dust rising. He only needed one lucky shot. Just one!

Blasterfire from the labyrinth resounded across the clearing.

"Ben, watch out!" Annileen yelled again.

Unrestrained by his father's presence, Mullen shoved her forward. Annileen stumbled across the shattered stones and fell. Sprawled across the rocks, she turned around to see the young man aiming his blaster at her.

"I've never been able to stand these snotty Calwells," he said, one eyelid twitching as he stalked toward her.

Rifle in hand, Veeka looked at her brother. "Dad didn't say to kill her."

"Do we need her now?" Mullen asked.

"I don't know that we ever needed her," his sister responded.

"Do you care?"

"Not really," Veeka said.

Orrin continued to fire as he marched forward. He parted his hands and shot in either direction down the stony aisles—and then ahead and behind. He heard screaming from multiple quarters: the pathetic wails of frightened Tusken younglings. A bonus. All the frustration of the past months, all the worry of the last days fed through his body and the blasters in his hands.

Show yourself!

A cracking sound emanated from above. Reflexively,

Orrin pointed his blasters upward. He'd been pounced on by Kenobi before—but the man wouldn't get the drop on him again.

Except the rock pillars were too tall for any man to scale, he saw. Then, suddenly, he heard another sickening snap, and a knife-shaped slab that had balanced for eons slid off the formation, plummeting toward him.

Orrin leapt forward just before the massive chunk of stone stabbed the ground where he'd stood. Above, a fissure appeared in another stone tower. And another. Orrin cast his terrified eyes up and across the long rows of stone columns. This wasn't a groundquake-by-bantha. This was something unreal—as if something invisible was pushing against the stones!

He ran forward, blasters still clutched in his hands but his arms bent to shield his face from the rain of dust. Pebbles came down, and then chunks sheared off, striking all around.

Orrin coughed as nuggets pelted his back. Another huge shard struck just ahead, and then another, behind. He screamed. *"What's going on?"*

Orrin looked up as a shadow fell over him.

Thunder sounded in the rocks to the west. Mullen glared at his sister. "What in the blazes is going on over—"

Before he could finish his sentence, Annileen threw a fistful of sand in his face. Blinded, he staggered, and Annileen grabbed his ankle, pulled it toward her, and bit down hard.

Hearing her brother's howl, Veeka pointed her rifle at Annileen. She fired once, but her injured shoulder jerked her arm to the left and the shot missed. With animal instinct, Annileen dived for Mullen's legs, knocking him backward. She tried to wrestle with him to keep Veeka from drawing another clear shot, but Mullen was too strong. Pinning her, he pointed his blaster in her face.

That was when Veeka screamed.

A'Yark charged in from the cover to the west, howling a Tusken war cry. Before Veeka could bring her rifle around, A'Yark's gaderffii smashed it from her hands. A return stroke sent the point of the gaderffii ripping through Veeka's side.

In agony, Veeka clutched her wound and fell away, scrambling to escape. A'Yark sprang over her toward Annileen and Mullen. Startled, Mullen pulled the blaster from Annileen's face to take aim at the Tusken warrior.

With all her might, Annileen heaved, forcing the burly man off to the side. His blaster sent a bolt just past A'Yark's head, but the Tusken war leader did not stop. Swinging, A'Yark stabbed her gaderffii point deep in his abdomen. Annileen launched herself clear as A'Yark brought the weapon down again and again on Mullen's body.

"Posse kills," A'Yark said in Basic. "Posse dies!"

In a fog of dust, Orrin tried to crawl out from beneath the pile of rubble. Every move was painful. When he heard Veeka's scream, he jolted upright—and felt the bones shift in his left leg.

He fell to the ground at Ben's feet.

In the shadows, the cloaked figure knelt over Orrin. "I *did* tell you to turn back," Ben said.

Mullen howled from beyond. Ben looked up for a moment—and shook his head sadly. Whatever was happening, Orrin thought, Ben seemed satisfied that Annileen was safe. The man was in no hurry to leave.

Orrin spat bitter dust from his mouth. "Couldn't . . . turn back. Jabba's people there . . ."

Ben shook his head. "That's not what I meant. Your

fear led to this—all of it. Fear of losing what you had. It put you on a path to suffering."

Ben looked back. From his position on the ground, Orrin saw a cowering Tusken youngling emerge from behind one of the stone pillars to stare at the two humans. Ben smiled reassuringly at the tiny masked figure before looking back to Orrin.

"I know how the path ends for you," the cloaked man said. "But there is still time, if you turn back now. Accept responsibility for what you've done. That won't square you with the Tuskens, but it will be a start toward redemption."

Orrin sat up. He blinked the sand from his eyes. "I'll lose everything,"

Ben inhaled deeply. "Sometimes it takes losing everything to find your true path."

Ben started to stand—but then he looked up, alert. To the west, a monolith with a triangular slab balanced above it suddenly gave way, unable to support its own enormous weight. Huge rocks tumbled down. The little Tusken rushed to Ben's side for protection. More stones snapped loose and slammed to the ground.

Orrin could hear more Tusken children yowling in the maze as the debris landed. But he was more interested in Ben's reaction. The man had seemed completely unafraid of the earlier phenomenon—almost as if he'd orchestrated the whole thing. But now, one hand on the clinging Tusken youngling, Ben looked worried.

"Something's wrong," Ben said, his voice barely audible. *"I didn't do that . . ."*

A'Yark brought the gaderffii down again and again. Trying to reach her feet, Annileen saw Veeka crouching nearby. Limp and ashen-faced, Orrin's daughter watched as her brother struggled, clawed, and finally ceased to move under A'Yark's attack. Then she turned and fled for the northern gap, and the trail leading downhill.

A'Yark lifted her bloodied weapon and glanced back at the departing Veeka. But before she could give chase, the Tusken younglings, frightened by the clamor in the stone forest, poured from their hiding places to the west and clustered around A'Yark, separating her from Annileen.

Annileen turned to follow—but A'Yark surprised her by calling out, *"Ben!"*

Annileen stopped and looked back. As the crowd of children clutched at her robes, A'Yark lowered her weapon and looked to the west. A cloud of gray dust was rising into the air above the standing stones. A'Yark, who moments before had been in a blood rage, seemed spellbound. She spoke to the children in her own language—before looking at Annileen and repeating her words in Basic. "See it, Ann-uh-leen," A'Yark said. "See Ben."

Annileen stared, uncomprehending, at the rising dust. She knew she was in the heart of Tusken territory, and that she should follow Veeka to the safety of the posse. But Ben was still here, and so was Orrin—and something big had happened. "Was it an avalanche?" she asked as the dust climbed. "Is Ben in trouble?"

"No trouble," A'Yark said softly. She nodded, watching again to the west. "No avalanche. I was right."

Annileen prepared to move again. But now the Tusken children began chattering and tugging at A'Yark's garment. The warrior spoke to them hurriedly, clearly concerned about whatever information the excited younglings were providing. Then another deafening boom from the west followed—one that shook the pillars all around.

"Is *that* trouble?" Annileen asked A'Yark. The warrior somehow seemed less fearsome now, surrounded by frantic younglings.

"Is trouble," A'Yark replied.

The next sound from the west chilled Annileen's spine. *"Ayooooo-eh-EH-EHH!"*

She had heard the sound many times before—and she instantly knew this was no recording. "Krayt dragon," she whispered.

"Awakened by the sounds," A'Yark said. Hastily, she tried to hoist a pair of children while still holding the bloody gaderffii. More younglings fled into the clearing from the western pillars. "I must hide the *uli-ah*," the warrior said.

On impulse, Annileen stepped forward and reached for a young Tusken's gloved hand. "I'll help."

CHAPTER FORTY-FIVE

ORRIN STARED, STUPEFIED, as a monster stormed through the stone pillars toward him. Too large by far to fit into the corridor between the megaliths, the great reptile simply forced its way through like a battle tank, shattering them as it went. Hefty boulders bounced harmlessly off the quadruped's greenish hide.

It was a canyon krayt, bigger than any Orrin had ever heard of. Fifty meters long? Sixty? He wasn't about to measure it. Terrified, he scanned the debris for his blasters. One was there, smashed beneath a rock. Where was the other? Could it do any good?

"Kenobi!" Orrin yelled. "Help me up!"

Clearly startled by the new arrival, Ben looked back at Orrin. But more squealing Tusken brats ran past, shocked out of hiding, and his attention turned to them. "Quickly!" Ben yelled, pointing to the east. "Go!"

"Forget them!" Orrin tried to get Ben's attention again, but saw that it was too late. The krayt had seen them through the dust cloud. Golden eyes glowing, it bounded forward, its clawed feet scrambling easily over the stones.

It went for Ben and the Tusken child first, lashing out with its mighty tail. Orrin threw his arm in front of his face, petrified. He looked out to see Ben duck quickly,

pushing the child to the ground as he did. The pillar the
tail struck shattered, its pieces plummeting toward the
man and child at its base. Ben started to move again. To
grab the youngling, Orrin thought—

—but instead, Ben thrust his arms high. The rubble
halted in midair, as if collected in an invisible basin.
Orrin looked at it in awe. And then looked back at Ben,
mesmerized. Ben's face strained from the effort, but he
gritted his teeth and gave a shove to the air. Half a ton
of collapsing stone tipped harmlessly away from the
prone Tusken child.

Orrin gawked. The krayt lunged.

So did Ben, now wielding a weapon of gleaming blue
light. *A lightsaber!*

Leaping directly into the creature's path, he sliced out
with his weapon. The ripping movement caught the
krayt in the face, severing a number of its already-jagged
teeth. Startled, the dragon reared back. Behind Ben, the
Tusken child scrambled to Orrin's side—but the farmer
was too fearful to shoo it away. Ben was moving again:
this time, hopping lithely up a rock to the creature's left,
attracting its attention away from Orrin and the little
Tusken.

Mighty rocks grinding to powder beneath its feet,
the behemoth wrenched violently. It pounded its horned
head against the broken pillar Ben had perched on top
of. But Ben was no longer there, Orrin saw. A backflip
put the man on the krayt's hind side, with an interven-
ing lightsaber slash at one of its tough backfins.

The act seemed only to infuriate the dragon. It charged
away from Ben, pulverizing more columns as it did.
From behind a teetering formation, a Tusken elder appeared, carrying an infant. The figure froze in panic before the rushing creature's advance.

Ben was running, too. His free hand whisked through
the air in a purposeful wave—and up ahead of the krayt,

the Tusken pair suddenly went aloft, flying harmlessly out of the monster's path. Startled, the dragon slid to a halt—and screeched to the sky.

It was a sound they'd hear in the oasis, Orrin thought. The Tusken child cowered, burying its head against Orrin's shoulder. This time, Orrin pushed it away. Ben, the madman, had reached the dragon in the newly created clearing. Any thought of escape had passed: Orrin had to see this.

Aware now of the danger Ben's weapon posed, the krayt turned on all fours and lashed out with its massive barbed tail. Ben leapt over it the first time it passed, ducked it the second, and slashed at it on the third. There was no fourth stroke. The krayt howled, recoiling.

Orrin looked on with amazement. The surrounding stone pillars framed the combatants like some impromptu arena—only one far too narrow, and that would surely become Ben's undoing, Orrin thought. The krayt seemed to realize it, too. Hampered by its injured tail, the krayt chose a new tactic—crushing Ben with its immense weight. Pointing toward Ben and tilting its head, the dragon threw its body into a roll. With nowhere to leap, Ben disappeared beneath the mass of tumbling fury. Another megalith was struck, and then another—tipping and shattering like ale bottles knocked over on a bar. Shards pummeled the krayt. And still it rolled, vanishing in the rising cloud of dust, Ben nowhere in sight.

A second later the dragon appeared again, racing from the haze on all fours toward Orrin and the Tusken child. Orrin yelled—but then the krayt did, too, stopping meters short of them. Its head turned, its pointed beaklike mouth snapping in the direction of its shoulders—and now Orrin saw why. Ben was there, clinging to the creature's jagged back, his tunic dirtied and torn. Somehow he had survived the roll and wound up on top. And he was no passive rider. He raked the creature's haunches repeatedly with the lightsaber. That was what had stopped its advance, Orrin realized.

And stopping, for the krayt, was deadly. Hopping from scale to stony scale, Ben landed astride the monster's neck. Finding a weak plate in its carapace, Ben plunged his blue blade in. The krayt screamed, louder than any of Orrin's sirens ever had. It shuddered, and Ben had to fight to stay atop the beast. But he did, and his lightsaber found a home again in the animal—this time, inside its primitive brain.

The dragon died, its head thudding to rest meters from Orrin and the child.

Mesmerized, Orrin looked at the massive carcass. A nasty black tongue slipped from its mouth. Beside Orrin, the youngling glanced back once at the dragon—and then at his savior—before scampering away without a word.

Ben slipped off the creature's back and stared silently at it. To Orrin, Ben seemed satisfied in the first moment—and then crestfallen in the next, as he seemed to realize what he'd just done in front of his witness.

"You . . . *you're a Jedi*!" Orrin exclaimed.

Ben said nothing. His arms hung at his sides, the lightsaber limply pointing toward the ground.

Orrin's mind raced. He thought back to the holonews he'd seen in Anchorhead a while back. There'd been some kind of coup, waged against the Republic by the Jedi, he thought. Orrin didn't know much about Jedi. It had never made sense to him why the Republic would put its faith in a group it neither controlled nor understood. It wasn't smart business. Something must have gone wrong, because the Jedi had been purged, giving rise to the Empire.

"That's why you're here," Orrin said, clawing at one

of the rocky walls in an attempt to stand. "That's why you're hiding. They're looking for you. Everyone!"

Ben just looked at the krayt corpse. But he had not deactivated his weapon, and at once, Orrin realized the danger he was in. Ben had just killed a krayt dragon—and now his secret was out.

Orrin winced as he tried to move, supporting himself against the stone towers. "You're going to kill me!"

Ben looked back at him. "I haven't decided about that."

"You haven't *decided*?"

A weak smile came over Ben's face. "I'm not inclined to kill to silence people. That's something you'd do."

Orrin staggered from one stone surface to another, trying to make his way to the clearing. Behind, Ben sighed and turned to follow. But he walked slowly—and as he did, he switched off his lightsaber and returned it to its hiding place beneath his robe.

He's not going to kill me, Orrin thought, forging ahead against the pain. That led to his next thought. *I've got a card to play.*

Orrin would go offworld and visit this Empire, and become something again. He had something to sell again: Ben Kenobi's hide. To blazes with Tatooine, with all of it! Struggling, he stepped out into the light of the suns.

Annileen was nowhere to be seen, nor Veeka. But Mullen was there, on the ground near the JG-8. A lone massiff stood over his body, feasting.

Heart in his throat, Orrin dragged his broken leg across the clearing. The massiff, done gorging, wandered away. Orrin reached his son's side and collapsed onto the ground beside him, wailing. Mullen was dead at the hands of a Tusken, just like his beloved younger son, Veeka's twin.

Where was Veeka? Squinting, he saw footprints and a light trail of blood heading off to the northern exit. Was it Veeka's blood, or Annileen's? Would Veeka really have fled back to the posse? If so, there was no helping her now, any more than if the Tuskens had gotten her.

Ben approached, staying a respectful distance away. Orrin looked up from the mess that had been Mullen. Did Ben expect him to repent now? After all this?

He snarled hatefully. "I'm going to tell them. The Empire! And they'll *destroy* you!"

Ben folded his hands together and looked at the ground.

Orrin struggled to stand again. "Did you hear me, Jedi? The Empire will destroy you—and everything you love."

Ben shook his head. "They've already done that."

The farmer ignored him. He staggered toward the damaged landspeeder. "You'd better kill me now, because I mean it!" He heaved himself into the vehicle. "I'll do it, Kenobi!"

"No, you won't," Ben said. "I've seen your future. I don't think you're going to live much longer."

"Because of *you!*"

"Because of you. Because you didn't turn back." With that, Ben pivoted and started walking away.

Orrin gawked at the man, but only for a moment. He activated the JG-8, which groaned in protest. There was no going back, not with the posse and the crooks down there. No, there was only forward, through the opening to the south, and whatever lay that way. If Veeka lived, he'd find her again—somehow.

Ben simply stood and watched as the vehicle lurched forward a few meters at a time, starting and stopping fitfully. Orrin fought with the controls, pounding at the dashboard with his fist. "Blast you, move!"

* * *

The younglings hidden, Annileen reentered the clearing from a narrow opening to the east. Visiting Tuskens in their place of last resort was unnerving on its own, but she nearly turned right back around when she saw Orrin hovering toward her in the battered JG-8.

Then she realized he wasn't heading for her at all, but rather making for the exit to the south. Orrin looked even more beat up than the vehicle, his hair covered with dust and his mouth bloodied. He seemed to be paying her no mind. Looking back, she saw Ben standing, fifty meters away, making no effort to pursue.

Orrin seemed to notice her at last when the reluctant landspeeder came to another sudden stop. Annileen could barely recognize the man she knew—but for the wicked smile that came over his face when he saw her. His words dripped with delightful venom. "Ben's been lying to you," he said.

Annileen shrugged. "*You* did it all the time."

Orrin sneered. But before he could say anything else, the Tusken he knew as Plug-eye emerged, gaderffii in hand, from the western labyrinth near the southern opening. The adversaries saw each other. Orrin took aim and crushed the accelerator.

The JG-8 seemed to forget its reservations, gunning forward. A'Yark stood stoically as Orrin raced to ram her—until the moment she hurled her gaderffii. The heavy implement spun through the air, striking the windshield with terrible force.

A spray of glass showered Orrin, his windshield smashed for the second time by someone he'd angered. But the landspeeder surged forward anyway, striking the Tusken warrior with full force and carrying her with it toward the southern exit.

Annileen pursued the landspeeder. Orrin couldn't see anything through the fractured windshield, she realized—but he was accelerating nonetheless. She skidded to a stop in time to watch the hovercraft miss the narrow bantha path that led down the side of the cliff. The vehicle sailed freely for seconds until, lacking anything for the antigrav units to repel against, it tumbled downward, end over end. It vanished in the bad country.

Meters behind Annileen, Ben ran up. "A'Yark!" he yelled.

Annileen looked down. Off the edge of the sheer drop from the bantha trail, A'Yark clung to a jutting rock. Annileen scrambled to the side and reached down for the raider's hand. Dazed, the Tusken stared up at her, jeweled eye gleaming in the suns. Then the Tusken murmured something, and Annileen felt A'Yark's grip loosening.

Reaching Annileen's side, Ben leaned over her shoulder and looked down at A'Yark. "You want to live," he said. "Remember?"

For a moment, A'Yark didn't move, but then her hand tightened around Annileen's. The settler and the stranger hauled the warlord up.

Bowed but unbroken, A'Yark knelt and gazed at the smoke rising from the canyon hills below. The Jundland was unforgiving.

"You have what you wanted," Ben said.

"Not all." A'Yark turned back. Straightening, she pushed past Ben and Annileen and climbed back onto the plateau. "But deal is done. You go."

Annileen nodded. She could hear the sounds of pounding boots; the Tuskens would be returning at any minute. But with Ben there, she felt no fear at all.

"I thank you," he said to A'Yark, bowing.

Standing before a passageway into the labyrinth, A'Yark looked back coolly. "You remembers, Ben," she said. "You knows what you can be."

With that, she slipped back into the shadows.

Annileen and Ben walked swiftly across the clearing,

stopping only at Mullen's corpse. Annileen blanched then—and turned to gaze back in the direction of Orrin's departure.

Ben looked at her. "I'm sorry," he said.

"I'm not," Annileen replied. Turning, she embraced him.

It was not a passionate hug, but the exhausted collapse of someone who had had a very long day—and night, and day. This embrace, Ben did not refuse. She looked up at him and started to speak.

He spoke first. "Not here," he said. He smiled. "My place. Tonight."

Then he nudged her in the direction of the trail leading down.

CHAPTER FORTY-SIX

BEN HAD FOUND HIS OWN WAY HOME. So had Annileen, and it began the hardest afternoon of her life.

She'd emerged from the hills to find a muted victory celebration. The farmers who'd come to the Jundland after a would-be traitor had found instead a battle with a perennial enemy, the gangsters of Mos Eisley. And the country folk had absolutely routed the city folk. Mosep Binneed, mathematician enough to calculate odds on the fly, had decided to cut his losses in the Gault affair and withdraw with only the tail of his skiff on fire.

Ulbreck and the others were relieved to see Annileen, but unhappy to hear that they'd been robbed of their chance to settle with Orrin. Nearby, Annileen found Veeka, under treatment from Doc Mell. In shock, the injured woman didn't respond at all when Annileen told her of her father's demise.

Questions came at Annileen from all directions. Thankfully, Leelee's husband saw her situation and offered to drive her back to the Claim alone. He dropped her off and departed without a word. Home, the famished Annileen ate as she packed, explaining to her puzzled children between bites what had happened. What she understood of it, anyway.

In late afternoon, Leelee arrived at the back door of

the residence, her face an ashen pink. She stayed outside as she recounted to Annileen what was being said at her home—and at others across the oasis.

In a moment in which every hidden resentment against the Gaults suddenly found voice, most had been quick to find Ben faultless. It was so like Orrin, they said, to deflect blame to a hapless newcomer—and someone would have had to be terrified to seek shelter in a known Tusken nest. Or crazy. But while all appreciated Ben's revelation, it rankled many that he'd evidently learned truths in days that had evaded people who worked around Orrin for years. Blameless or not, Ben was a strange character, and few were in any hurry to see him again.

Under the settlers' questioning, once-tough Veeka had melted into a pathetic, simpering thing, describing in detail Orrin's embezzlement from the Fund and his attacks against those who wouldn't subscribe to it. Then, fearing for her life, she'd lashed out at the Calwells, claiming Jabe had been along not just on the staged Ulbreck raid, but all the ones before. And in Veeka's story, Annileen had known all about it, had profited from the sales of guns and ale.

No one was overly inclined to believe Veeka—nor the oafish Zedd, who echoed her story when confronted for his role. But the financial records found in Orrin's home—which he had failed to erase, through lack of time or overconfidence—held damaging facts. They detailed tens of thousands of credits paid from the Fund to the Claim over the years for ale, weapons, and garaging, all the way back to Dannar Calwell's time.

All quite legitimate, from Annileen's point of view; but the sums boggled the minds of many poor prospectors, who saw conspiracy. Several old-timers recalled Jabba trumping up a Tusken war, years earlier, to sell shoddy weapons. Was this like that? Annileen had seemed beyond corruption, sure—but hadn't they seen Orrin walking behind the counter many times, plucking money from the cashbox with Annileen's indulgence? And what about all her private financial records, sitting in the datapad right on his desk? How separate *were* the families, really?

Annileen already knew: not very separate at all. There were just too many ties to disentangle, ties that Annileen had let grow over the years because it was easier not to argue with Orrin. But where the links between the two families had brought them to a position of respect and relative wealth, it now made them the focus of envy and suspicion.

It had all transpired just as Ben had said it would; Annileen now counted fortune telling among his other talents. She had already noted that no one had arrived at the Claim for dinner. Her position was untenable. Given time, she might sort it out—if she were on Coruscant, with a lawyer. But this was Tatooine, where rumor and bad feeling spread like sand on the wind, and where minds, once made up, never changed.

She and Leelee hugged tearfully, Annileen unable to begin to explain to her friend what had transpired, or what her plans were. She simply promised to contact her again.

And then she shut the door, ready to walk the Claim one last time.

Light returned to Orrin slowly. When it arrived, it was piercing—and so was the pain.

The sky shimmered for some reason, a brilliant whorl at the end of a tunnel. He could not feel his legs. They were there, he could tell; his hands were resting against them. But there was no feeling in his feet or toes at all.

It's the crash, he thought. *I've been burned.* He'd been

through this before. As a child, he'd stayed out on a
midsummer day with no hat or skin protection—and
had come back with a face so raw and parched that even
smiling hurt. His parents had kept him inside for a day,
his face bandaged to keep him from picking at it. The
fabric on his face now felt like that, only rougher.

Yes, that was it. He'd been bandaged and taken to
Bestine. Doc Mell was probably there, conferring with
the local doctors about his case. Orrin breathed in relief.

And then he heard his breath.

Something was over his mouth, something metallic,
clacking against his broken teeth when he opened wide.

Another sense memory flooded back, from his one
offworld trip. He'd picked up a bacterial infection that
had left his limbs raw and scabbing; it had earned him
an hour in a bacta tank, something uncommon on Tatooine. He'd worn a breather mask then. He wore something like that now—only tinny, and cold to his lips.

The light above disappeared. Slowly, the face of a
Tusken came into view and vanished.

No.

He pushed down with his hands, lifting his torso. He
saw his legs, now, bandaged. He felt the gloves on his
fingertips. He felt the shroud on his face, and the metallic eyepieces against his eyelids.

Merciful universe, no.

Another Tusken stepped into view. "Orringault."

Orrin heard it as an animal grunt. But it was his name,
and it was definitely the one-eyed Tusken he'd tried to
ram. Plug-eye.

"I am A'Yark," the Tusken warlord said. "You lives,
Orringault."

He clutched at the bumpy surface beneath his body.
He realized he was lying some distance off the ground,
atop a rectangular pile of stones.

"This is my son's burial platform," A'Yark said.

Orrin simply shook his head, his eyes too dry for tears. He had seen the things before.

A'Yark grabbed at his shoulders. "You have work." She turned him. Orrin saw the familiar stone pillars go past—until, finally, he faced a shorter, metallic cylinder.

It was a vaporator.

He knew the model by sight. It was the vaporator the Tuskens had stolen from Wyle Ulbreck. But instead of gutting it for metals, the warrior and her companions had placed it upright. Now, heaving, they brought it closer. As it approached, he realized the funereal bier had been expanded to become something else.

It wasn't to be Orrin's grave. It was his work platform.

"You gives us water," A'Yark said. "And you will be fed."

Orrin struggled. The parts of his body that could still move were suffocating, they were so tightly wound beneath the wrappings.

"You will be fed. And we moves you when we move. And you will live—while we have water."

Orrin heard his breath rasping louder and louder.

No. No. No.

Orrin thought it, but didn't say it. For *no* was a word, and hearing his voice through the mouthpiece would confirm what he knew: that he was now one of *them*.

A Sand Person.

He resolved never to speak again.

The first sun was slipping behind the cliffs to the west when two hovercraft arrived at the foot of Ben's hill. Gloamer had kept Annileen's battered old landspeeder and the LiteVan, which Tar would need to run the store. In exchange, he'd provided her with two of his souped-up sports speeders, which she figured would come in handy in the desert—or wherever they and Ben ended up.

She chuckled to herself as she parked. She'd seen Ben on a hoverbike, but had no idea if he drove a land-speeder. Well, she'd have time to find out—and teach him, if he didn't. She stepped out of the vehicle, its back-seat packed to overflowing with hastily packed luggage and goods. Across from her, Jabe and Kallie emerged from their similarly loaded repulsorcraft.

So much stuff—but so little, too, worth taking away from a lifetime. It was sad, Annileen thought. But also refreshing.

Jabe's face fell as he looked up at the hut. "This is *it*?"

"He still doesn't have a door," Kallie noted. Anni-leen's daughter had been quiet since closing the livery. But seeing Ben emerge from the home cheered her up. As it did Annileen.

"Welcome," Ben said, walking down the slope. In-stead of his cloak, he wore a white shirt with long cuffs and light gray trousers, an ensemble she hadn't seen him in before. He looked refreshed, as if he'd somehow got-ten some sleep in the few hours since she'd seen him. He carried a small beige backpack over his shoulder.

Annileen stepped toward him, glowing. But before she could reach him, Ben's eopies trotted from inside the house, bleating to him. "Ah," he said, setting down the backpack. "I found them on the way home."

"The gang's all here," Annileen said affectionately.

Ben looked up. "Are your affairs settled?"

"As much as they'll ever be," she said.

In the vehicle, she had hard currency from her stash. And Gloamer's payment to her electronic account could be accessed in Bestine or Mos Eisley. It was enough to live on for a long time, especially out here. She didn't know if that was Ben's plan: he had only told her to pack for time away. Wherever it was, though, she felt safe in assuming they'd be together.

As Kallie knelt to nuzzle Rooh and the baby, Ben studied Jabe. "Are you all right, son?" he asked.

"Yeah. I—I want to thank you for helping us. And for saving me last night." Jabe looked down, shamefaced. "I didn't deserve it—"

Ben shook the boy's hand. "You were only a few steps down the wrong path." He looked Jabe in the eye. "You were desperate for something to do. But someone I respect once told me that wise people never make desperate decisions." He reflected for a moment, then smiled. "Actually, he phrased it a lot differently from what I just said. But the advice is sound."

Jabe smiled. Annileen beamed.

She looked back at the landspeeders. "It'll be dark soon. Should we unload?"

"No," Ben said, turning toward the pouch on the ground. "That can wait until Mos Eisley."

Kallie's eyes widened. "Mos Eisley?"

"I know we were just there yesterday," he said, lifting the backpack. "It certainly doesn't seem like yesterday. But there's a transport preparing to leave from Docking Bay Fifty-Six the day after tomorrow, and passage is booked."

Annileen gawked. "How is that possible?"

Before Ben could answer, Kallie hugged him—just hard enough to cause him to drop the pouch again. He laughed. "Don't you want to hear the destination?"

"Not really!" Jabe said, stepping back and slapping hands triumphantly with his sister.

"The first stop is Bestine," Ben said. "The planet, not the city."

"*First* stop?" Annileen echoed.

"That's right." Ben smiled and looked over at the single sun that remained. "It should be safe going to Mos

Eisley, tonight of all nights. With all the posse activity out there today, Tuskens will be avoiding the north for weeks." He gestured to the second landspeeder. "If you would, kids, please wait at the bottom of the hill. I need to talk to your mother for a moment."

Dazzled, Kallie looked back at her mother. "You never said we'd be leaving Tatooine!"

"I didn't know," Annileen said, mind still reeling. It seemed to fit, though: just one more impulsive act in a day of them. She felt as if gravity would give way next.

Jabe was already behind the controls of the second landspeeder, waving. "Kallie, come on!"

Kallie leapt up, kissing Ben on the cheek. "We'll see you soon!" She spun and dashed to the vehicle, dust flying beneath her feet. In a moment, the siblings were driving to the foot of the hill, cheering audibly over the engine.

Annileen looked at Ben and marveled. "You don't give a woman a chance to catch her breath, do you?"

Ben smiled wanly for a moment before turning away to his eopies. "I want you to know something," he said, reaching for Rooh's lead. "I . . . would have liked to have saved Orrin."

"He wasn't your responsibility," she countered, watching him place the animals in their pen. "You didn't live around him for years, not knowing what he'd turned into."

Ben smiled back. "But once you knew, you did something. And you didn't wait."

"You're giving me too much credit. The only reason I did anything was because of you."

"No, I think you deserve quite a bit of credit. And a new start," he said. He walked to the backpack. Opening it, he drew out a datapad.

Annileen recognized it in the dimming light. "Hey, that's my old one. The one I gave you!"

Ben activated it. "I had to take the speeder bike to a village to get a signal offworld this morning. And I rode on Rooh this afternoon to get a response. But it's official," he said, passing the device to her. "You're in."

Annileen's eyes scanned the words. She staggered backward, as if struck by a great weight. "You sent my application?" She gawked at him. "But that was twenty years old!"

"Alderaan still exists, right? So does the university system." Ben stepped beside her and pointed to an entry on the screen. "They're still doing the exobiology expeditions, launching from their branch on Naboo."

Annileen remembered the advertisement by heart. Ten worlds in two years, studying a thousand species, most little understood by science. She looked at it again. "Accepted? How is that possible?"

Ben crossed his arms. "That's one of those things I can't let you ask me about. Let's just say you had strong references on Alderaan."

She wasn't sure whether to believe it—or him. The whole thing seemed impossible, incomprehensible. "Going to university at my age! I just can't believe it. It doesn't make any sense!"

"It makes more sense than someone of your abilities serving caf and shelving feed," he said. "There's a slot for Kallie to get in this season, too. And there will surely be more opportunity out there for your son than there is here."

Annileen looked at the screen and laughed, in spite of herself. "I see you couldn't get me into a school on Coruscant."

"My powers are indeed limited." Ben took the datapad back from her and walked with it to her landspeeder.

She glided after him, barely feeling the ground under her feet. He placed the datapad safely inside the vehicle.

Almost giddy, she cracked a joke. "Are you sure you're going to be happy being the traveling companion of a middle-aged student?"

"I can't deny I miss the stars," he said, his hands resting on the door of the landspeeder. "And in another life?" He nodded gently, his mouth crinkling into the tiniest smile. Then he looked up at her, solemn. "But I'm afraid I can't go."

Annileen froze. "What do you mean?"

"I have responsibilities here. Things to look after."

"What kind of responsibilities?" Annileen looked back at the house. She spied Rooh in the pen. "If it's the eopies, we can drop them at a ranch on the way!"

"That's not it." Ben shook his head and started walking away from the landspeeder.

"Wait. You did all this. You saved us. You led us all here!" She stepped after him. "*We're* who you're looking after!"

"You don't need looking after, Annileen," Ben said, his back to her as he walked up the hill. "You're quite capable. *Extremely* capable."

Annileen stood in the swiftly falling night, bewildered. Since her talk with Ben in the bedroom, momentum had carried her through the events of the day. That, and the knowledge that he was part of the next chapter. "I don't *want* you to stay," she implored. "I want you with me!"

"Annileen—"

"Annie! I told you, everyone calls me Annie!"

"—you know that's not possible. It's not even sensible—"

"Sensible? What's *sensible*?" She kicked at the sand. "Working with someone for twenty years only to find out they've been defrauding half the oasis?"

"This is just a fantasy—"

"Like Tusken Raiders you can reason with?" She

grabbed at his shoulder and spun him around. "Or a man who arrives out of nowhere, who risks his neck to help people he's never met, like he's some kind of . . ." She stopped, searching vainly for the next word.

Ben took a step back. It was a small step, almost imperceptible. But to Annileen, totally aware of him, it seemed like a light-year, and she lost her train of thought.

It made her take a breath.

"I'm sorry," she said, struggling to control her emotions. "But we want you with us." She reached for his hand. "*I* want you with us. With *me*. Now just—"

"I *have* a family already," Ben said, abruptly pulling his hand back.

His eyes shone at her in the fading light.

"You—you have . . ."

"You once asked me if I had a family to look after," he said. "I do. It's why I am here."

Annileen looked around, laughing nervously. "Not the eopies?" she asked in a small voice.

"No. There's a child," he said, looking as if he'd given her his most secret truth. "It's my responsibility."

Annileen shook her head, tears finally arriving. Yes, she'd imagined this possibility once, but had put it out of her head. It didn't make sense that it would trap him here forever. "You can make provisions," she said. "Families do it all the time. You can look after the child and still—"

"No, I can't," Ben said, firmly. "I must be here." He turned to leave.

She looked about at the shadows. "Then *we'll* stay! We don't have to go offworld!"

"You have your destiny, Annileen. I have mine."

Annileen looked back at the landspeeder. "That's what this was all about? The university? You're sending me away?"

"I can't have you here," Ben said, walking back to his house. "And you can't stay."

Annileen stared blankly at him as he opened the curtain that covered the front doorway. None of it made sense. Since before dawn, it had been the vision of a life with Ben in the picture that had gotten her through the craziness. Events had been so extreme that the lifeline he represented had taken on the feeling of a long-held dream.

And that made it all the worse.

"You lied to me," she said, her words barely audible.

Ben turned in the doorway. "What's that?"

"You lied to me," she said, feeling numb. "You lied to me. It may have been for fifteen hours rather than for years, like Orrin—but you lied to me. Like Orrin said."

Ben's eyes widened. "I never—" he started to say, before stopping. After a moment, he spoke again. "Yes, I guess I have been lying to you." He looked off to the side. "And not just about tonight, or the child. I've been lying to you about other things. A *lot* of other things. From the beginning."

Annileen closed her eyes. "Well," she said quietly, "I think we can both agree on one thing." She opened her eyes and looked directly at him. "I don't need that. Not anymore." She turned and started walking. "I feel sad for you, Ben. Good-bye."

Stiffly, she climbed into the landspeeder. She paused only for a single look back to see Ben, alone and watching from the doorway.

Then she drove down to where her children awaited and beckoned for them to follow. Together, they sped across a desert already covered with stars.

CHAPTER FORTY-SEVEN

THE YOUNG WARRIOR SWUNG his gaderffii, impaling the Jawa. The little beast squealed and shook, and life left his body.

A'Yark looked on the carnage with approval. The change was working. Two days earlier, settlers had been threatening to overrun The Pillars. Now, attacking at sunset rather than dawn, her little band had conducted its first raid in the Western Dune Sea, south of the Jundland. The region was sparsely populated, and tonight's catch was nothing more than a caravan of Jawas late for a rendezvous with their sandcrawler. The clan of Yark and Sharad Hett would never have bothered with such rodents. But tonight, they'd made excellent prey for a people robbed of confidence.

A day at a time had always been the only path forward for the Tuskens; there seemed no other way for those who lived under a curse. Something, however, had changed, and it had changed in A'Yark. The war leader wanted her whole clan to reach the future. That meant selecting targets in the proper order. Attrition was unacceptable. Strikes had to be more than an expression of Tusken hate and dominance. They had to be useful. They had to teach the warriors something.

And her desire to survive had required something else.

The one called Orrin had taken to mewling weakly at all hours. They had tied a guard massiff to him, to make sure he didn't try to drag himself away, but there seemed no danger of that. A'Yark doubted he would live much longer. But he'd gotten the vaporator working in his hours on the bier, and that was all that was important. Alone among clans this season, A'Yark's people would drink and grow mightier.

Taking water from the sky was forbidden, yes. But A'Yark had paid little mind to other superstitions in the past. Neither skybrother was worthy of respect. Why should their sky be protected? A metal knife to the clouds was no less than they deserved.

The water began transforming the remnants of the tribe within hours. It was sweet to the taste; magical, the elders said. Little children on the edge of death began to revive. Banthas were working longer. Even the few remaining warriors seemed readier to fight. A'Yark would take any improvement. Sometimes, a little sacrilege came in handy.

They would live. And they had to live, because for the first time, her people were daring to care about tomorrow.

The other Tuskens had seen Ben's defense—had seen the monstrous cloud he raised in The Pillars, had seen the corpse of the krayt. There had to be some reason these powerful figures kept arriving amid the Sand People. Some role their clan was intended to play, in the next cycle of the story of the suns. More vocally than ever, her people spoke their longings for a powerful outsider to help them destroy their enemies.

Ben would never be that person. A'Yark would warn the other Tuskens away from his home; he had nothing to take, and there was little value in irritating a wizard. It didn't matter, the believers said: someone would come. But while A'Yark welcomed any hope that encouraged her people to strive once more, she herself now looked to a different day.

A day when the clan would realize that it didn't need a mystical outsider, after all—that it already had the leader it needed.

With that thought, A'Yark plunged her gaderffii again into the Jawa leader's back. Existence *was* a curse. But it was not without its pleasures.

The *Lady of Bestine* hung in orbit over the glistening golden crescent of Tatooine. Annileen stood at the giant observation window in her cabin and looked down. It seemed so strange to see her world like this for the first time. Tatooine had more clouds from this angle than she had ever seen from the ground.

Ben's Alderaanian patron, whoever he or she was, had come through not only with the university fellowship, but with first-class accommodations. *Lady* had not been expected to launch until early that morning, and Annileen had figured on taking the kids to the Twin Shadows Inn. But *Lady*'s compartment dwarfed any room to be had on Kerner Plaza, and so, after dropping off their cargo, the family had simply stayed aboard.

They'd left only to close her bank account and to dispose of Gloamer's snazzy landspeeders. One, they'd abandoned with a note of apology in Garn Delroix's lot. The JG-8 he'd leased to Orrin wouldn't be coming back, after all. The other, they'd sold to a dealership close to the spaceport. They'd deposited the proceeds, along with what extra she could afford, in a parcel addressed to Leelee at the Claim, for distribution to the Settlers' Fund members.

It wasn't enough. But it was necessary.

Annileen had barely felt the ship's launch, refusing to stand glued to the window as her children had. She'd wandered the inner halls for hours as the vessel orbited, awaiting rendezvous with a shuttle bearing more passengers. Annileen *looked* like she belonged, in the fancy Chandrilan gown her husband had bought her; she finally had a place to wear it. But she didn't feel as though she'd gone anywhere yet.

No, her thoughts had remained on the ground, still back at the little hut on the edge of the mountains. Kallie had been devastated by Ben's refusal to join them; Jabe, simply confused. Annileen had been both. She had walked and wondered, replaying every short moment she'd spent with him. Trying to see how she'd misunderstood.

She didn't know if she believed Ben's family story at all, and she wondered again and again if she'd left too abruptly. Orrin's deception had stung her, and Ben's words had struck her hard. But clearly the man was genuinely committed to something that kept him there, and that was what mattered.

In the end, she'd been left with a puzzle as impenetrable as the Jundland Wastes themselves. And now, in her cabin at last, she could see that rugged land as it began to slip behind the terminator into night.

Down there, the suns would be setting on Mos Eisley, with the scoundrels freer to work their mischief. Dewbacks on the ranches would settle down and snooze. Sand People in the hills would be on the move, preying on the helpless. And patrons of the Claim would come to terms with the new ownership and drink to forget their workdays. She hoped someone was keeping Bohmer's carafe full.

Her children joined her at the window. "We'll be going into hyperspace soon," Kallie said. She looked at her mother. "Thinking about Ben?"

Annileen shook her head. "The store," she said. "When your father died, I swore to myself I wouldn't let the store go under, if it was the last thing I did. It was all I could do for him, to remember him."

"You did fine, Mom," Jabe said.

She looked at him, so handsome in his dress clothes. He looked just like his father. "I *did* do fine," she said, putting her arm around him. "And I pushed you to help me, and I'm sorry. That wasn't your dream." She smiled weakly. "It wasn't mine, either. But I felt like I had to stay for it."

Kallie moved closer, and Annileen embraced them both.

"I think . . . I think maybe Ben's doing the same thing," Annileen said. "He's not staying on Tatooine because he wants to. I think he thinks he *has* to. Maybe somebody entrusted him with something, something he feels he has no right to abandon. Someone else's dream, maybe—like Dannar and the store."

Sniffling, Kallie looked up. "But you're leaving."

Eyes glistening, Annileen gave a crumpled smile. "I did my time," she said. "Ben hasn't, yet. But who knows? Maybe in five or ten or twenty years, he'll have done his time, too."

Her children at her side, she looked down from space as the ship's engines revved up. "Good-bye, Ben," Annileen whispered. *And thank you.*

Outside, the world blurred and vanished.

Meditation

It has been a long couple of days. But I don't feel tired.

This was another test, Qui-Gon, wasn't it? When you finally answer, you must tell me what you thought of my solution.

I know where I am now. I'm in the rain shadow. Being near all the big events in the galaxy—I was on the mountaintop for many years. Now I'm on the back, on the lee side. It's supposed to be dry here.

But I'll leave the shadow one day.

I've been keeping watch tonight over the Lars farmhouse—and looking to see something else. Up there, over the horizon—I think that must have been the passenger ship. Stars don't disappear.

They're safe, above. Luke is safe, below.

And I will be . . . okay.

It's a long way back to the house, Qui-Gon. May the Force be with you.

It's time for me to go home.

INCOGNITO

JOHN JACKSON MILLER

"YOU, THERE! LEAVE HER ALONE!"

Dewell Bronk's entreaty was barely more than a whisper, and it was no surprise that the toughs didn't hear him. He looked urgently across the aisle of the transport at the delinquents, a pair of young, horn-headed Devaronians. They'd been hassling the poor old Twi'lek woman since she'd boarded. When they had first yanked at her satchel, she had resisted briefly, but now she looked on meekly as the youths pawed through her belongings.

Dewell wanted to tell them to stop. Louder, this time.

He could: he had an authoritative voice, one he was famous for. But that was in a different world, one where his small stature meant very little. No one was going to listen to a meter-tall, pudgy Kedorzhan in the lower hold of a passenger transport.

He looked around in desperation. The Tallaan Clipper had no security personnel on this level, just the frightening-looking first officer that Dewell never wanted to talk to again. He missed his bodyguards, who could have sorted this out in an instant. But he hadn't seen them since he hurriedly left his apartment on Coruscant. He expected he would never see them—or the apartment—again.

No, for the first time in ages, Dewell Bronk was alone and without help. And worst of all, he was unable to help—a new experience for the three-time recipient of the Coruscant Benevolent Society's Good Neighbor of the Year award.

Life had changed. And he already hated it.

One of the Devaronians looked directly at him: an angry stare. Feeling his public-spiritness flee with his courage, Dewell instantly looked away. His whiskered jowls sagged, and he sank low in his seat. He was being foolish. How could he be anyone's rescuer now, when he was trying to avoid attention?

Worried, he felt again for the weight by his feet. Everything he owned was in a sack, tied with a small rope that he had looped around his ankle. Since leaving on the first leg of his odyssey, he had kept the bag mashed between his heels; he didn't want to wake from sleep to find it stolen. Not that there was anything much to take. The credits he'd planned to use in his escape were already gone; spent, to pay for his seat on this transport and the next one, and for the single meal a day that was supposed to come with the fares.

It was a sad predicament for someone who had lived his life close to the bright spots of the galaxy, traveling at will and, occasionally, in style. That moment had passed—and might never return again. Now Dewell, someone who had fought for justice his whole career, was reduced to doing nothing as thieves harassed an elderly fellow being. He could hear it: they were pulling rudely at her head-tendrils now. Dewell's heart ached. There was nothing he could do.

"You don't want to disturb that woman," a nearby voice said. Its tones were warm and confident. A human voice, Dewell thought, but he didn't dare to look up. Some poor hero was about to be thrashed.

"We don't want to disturb this woman," a gruff Devaronian voice responded.

Puzzled, Dewell leaned over and peeked across the aisle. The two hoodlums had dropped the Twi'lek's pouch and were walking to the ladder leading to the upper level. The person who had spoken first was the human who had boarded at the previous stop—the one Dewell had mentally labeled "the Young Father."

Dewell didn't know if the human was father to the child. Nor did he really know how young the man was. Kedorzhan eyes were sharp in the dark, but most other species lived in the light. Kedorzhans seldom opened their eyes beyond a crack in daylight. Dewell had always refused to wear a visor, feeling it better to be able to look directly into the eyes of his listeners, even if it meant he often had trouble telling one person from another. To Dewell, people tended to become shapes, happy and sad, cruel and innocent. In the harshly lit cabin, the Young Father was a kindly blur, his face obscured by a brown hood as he cradled the bundled infant.

Dewell looked left and right. No one else had seen or heard what had happened with the Devaronians; everyone else had moved away, fearful to get involved. And now the Twi'lek moved, too, grabbing her bag and rushing off to the rear compartment. The Young Father sighed and sat in her vacated seat.

"That's telling those punks," Dewell said reflexively.

He knew it was a mistake for a fugitive to speak to a stranger—even a chivalrous one. Who knew how many people were searching for him, and what tactics their agents might use?

But the human barely turned. Beneath the man's cowl, the Kedorzhan made out two shining blue-gray dots in a hairy face.

"Just some high-spirited kids," the human said.

"I know young spirits," Dewell said. His broad nose twitched disdainfully. "Those were criminals." He cleared his throat.

"You should report them to the captain."

"It's really not necessary."

Dewell sighed, embarrassed. So brave, volunteering someone else to do the right thing. The Young Father had taken one risk but would go no further. Seeing the child fussing in the man's arms, Dewell couldn't blame him.

The human checked and rechecked the child's wrappings. Even with his poor eyesight, Dewell could tell the man was puzzled.

"Your child is hungry," Dewell said.

"He just ate a little while ago," the Young Father replied.

"I didn't think it was time again."

"The child decides when it is time again," Dewell said, feeling a little more comfortable. He grinned as the human went fishing in his backpack for a bottle. New parents were amusing. Dewell had only had time for seven children in his life; not many for a Kedorzhan, but there had been so many more important things to do. Now, squinting at the infant, Dewell found himself wishing that he'd spent more time with his own children—and wondering where all of them were today.

Well, he knew where one was. Poor Tyloor was dead, his body lost somewhere out on the battlefield. Dead, like so many other children of the Republic, in a conflict that had never made any sense to Dewell. And while the Clone Wars were thankfully—and suddenly—over, the main battle of the Kedorzhan's career seemed lost, too.

The Kedorzhans were a small people in height, power, and numbers. Short-legged with four fat fingers on each hand, they had migrated everywhere underground work was to be found. Most worlds had welcomed the pleasant, plump-faced people; they kept to themselves and caused few problems. When the Kedorzhans had finally obtained Republic representation and a Senate seat, many had assumed that the diminutive beings would conduct themselves just as Dewell was now. Certainly, they would mind their own business, taking the lead of other species while trying not to be noticed.

But Dewell and his illustrious predecessors had defied expectations, using their newfound power to fight for the weakest of the galaxy. They had lived underfoot; that experience had driven them to help others.

That fact—and Tyloor's death, among so many others—was why he had signed the Petition of the 2000 without question. Supreme Chancellor Palpatine had overstepped his bounds, clawing for government rights that had been reserved for the people. And not simply important powers of use in an emergency. No, many of the new measures were simply arbitrary, undoing protections for the weak for no reason at all.

His advisers had told him not to sign the petition. Now, with the Jedi gone and the Empire declared, many of his colleagues had already withdrawn their names. Dewell would not. But he feared that would be the last act of bravery he would ever—

The wretched first officer appeared in the doorway, as drunk as he had been before. "Station stop," he called into the hold. "Cross over to Pad 560 to reach our line's connector flight for the Outer Rim. Everyone else, thanks for . . ." Dewell didn't hear the rest, reaching down for the bag of belongings at his feet. It was time to move again.

Dewell didn't know what planet he was on, except that the sky was a bright green, and that again he was having trouble seeing. He was glad to get off the Space Slug, in any event.

He had waited for the Devaronians to disembark first. He hadn't seen where the Young Father had gone. That was too bad; the human had seemed a decent sort. This was how it was going to be, Dewell realized. Going from one place to another, never forming a relationship that lasted more than five minutes, never mind a friendship. It was hardly a life worth living, much less fighting for.

Slouching as he walked across the grungy spaceport, his bag tightly in hand, he looked around at the crowd. He felt eyes on him, and while he couldn't see any faces clearly, he imagined the rest. He spotted a lonely passageway leading between two of the maintenance buildings, and headed toward it. That way he could get to the landing pad while avoiding most of the foot traffic.

Walking down the tiled alley, he heard a bleating cry from around a corner. Instinctively, he stepped forward and looked.

A long-trunked Ortolan janitor, still clutching his mop, was being shaken by two figures in white armor. Clone troopers, from the so-called Grand Army of the Republic. Dewell couldn't hear what they were saying, but the stubby blue figure howled as they shook him.

That was enough! Forgetting his size—and everything else that concerned him—Dewell charged into the secluded area. "Stop that!" he yelled. The troopers paid him no mind. The rope wrapped tightly around his paw, Dewell slung his bag of belongings forward. It struck the trooper holding the janitor on the shin.

He had their attention now, whether he wanted it or not.

The trooper dropped the Ortolan, who ran off through one of the side passages, abandoning his cleaning cart and bucket. Pulling a blaster rifle from over his shoulder, the trooper looked directly at the Kedorzhan. "Dewell Bronk?"

Dewell looked up, startled. "That is my name."

"Senator Bronk, you are under arrest."

"On whose authority?"

"Emperor Palpatine." The second trooper held up a datapad with Dewell's image.

Dewell's eyes opened to their full, enormous width. Of course, there was no Imperial interest in hassling janitors. At least, not yet. It was a trap, and he had walked right into it. His arms fell to his sides. "I guess I knew this was—"

Before he could finish, something astonishing happened. The janitor's bucket landed over the helmet of the first clone trooper with a loud clang, spilling sudsy water and completely obscuring the soldier's vision. The second trooper turned, raising his rifle; surely, it would have taken someone a Wookiee's height to shove the bucket over his partner's head. But there was no one behind him at all. Instead, there was someone to the side— wielding, of all things, a large spray can. As Dewell dove for the ground, he heard the loud spritzing noise and smelled the high-pressure cleanser foam.

Looking up, he saw the comical sight of the trooper, his eye ports and air intakes clogged with the thick goo, moving his rifle in an attempt to fire randomly. But his assailant was on him now, wresting away the weapon. The secluded area was shaded enough that Dewell could make out his rescuer's identity.

The Young Father!

In one swift move, the human smashed the trooper in the head with the butt of his own rifle. The armored figure stumbled backwards, bumping into his bucket-headed partner. The Young Father shoved at them both now—exactly how, Dewell could not see—pushing them into one of the side doorways. It was a maintenance pit, he realized. He heard the colossal clamor as the armored men tumbled down a staircase.

The Young Father walked over and closed the door, locking it. "They won't be bothering you again, Senator."

Dewell looked around. "But where . . ."

The Young Father nodded toward a spot behind him. Stepping forward, Dewell made out the shape of the baby, cradled and resting comfortably atop the Ortolan's janitorial cart. The man lifted the child.

"I believe they've been following you since the Space Slug," the Young Father said. "The Emperor has agents everywhere."

Bronk didn't ask how the man knew. "I don't understand. There are plenty of Kedorzhans—and we mostly look alike. My documents were perfectly forged. Was it the first officer?"

"The Devaronians, I think. Forgeries can get you far— but they knew your reputation for protecting the weak. I suspect they knew you were on the run, and were using that to smoke you out. There, and here." He nodded toward the locked door. "But it's early days for Palpatine's Empire. Next time, it might well be the victim— the Twi'lek woman or the Ortolan janitor—who's the informant."

Dewell shook his head. "It's not in my nature not to trust."

"Mine either," the Young Father said, pulling the child close.

He turned and began walking away. "Your next flight is over here," he said. "I'll see you get there."

Bronk followed the short distance across to Pad 560, glad that no one seemed to have noticed the earlier commotion. The starship was little better than the Space Slug, but it was outgassing and ready to go, and that made it look heavenly.

Dewell stood near the landing ramp and looked back to the Young Father. "Thank you."

The man simply nodded and started to turn away.

"This is what it's going to be like, isn't it?" Dewell asked, looking down at the ground.

The Young Father paused. "How do you mean?"

"Life in hiding. In exile. I'll need to fear every stranger, every comm connection. I won't be able to touch a datapad without fear that Palpatine's cronies are looking in." Dewell looked up. "I'm exaggerating, right?"

"I'm afraid not," the man said. He nodded sympathetically. "It will be that way and worse. Things that are basic to your being, things that brought you joy and fulfillment, may become liabilities. Even the thing that defines you—the very desire to help others."

Dewell looked back at the starship, and then out at the milling blur of passengers, heading this way and that. Gesturing to them, the Young Father continued, keeping his head down. "You'll think crowds will offer security—but that only works as long as you offer nothing of yourself to anyone. And that's not the worst thing. Kind acts by others will have to be evaluated with skepticism, and suspicion." He smiled gently. "Present company excepted."

Dewell looked down. The man didn't look familiar—he saw so few human faces clearly that he remembered none of them. But he knew a companion in crisis when he heard one. "It sounds like you're in the same situation."

"Not exactly," the man said. "You have more choices available than I do."

Dewell stared at the ground for a moment, until he realized what the man meant. "I can't live in hiding." Taking a breath, the little Kedorzhan straightened. "I guess I go back."

The human nodded somberly.

"I'll have to recant, to declare support for Palpatine." The words made him feel nauseous as he stepped away from the ramp.

"You'll be in a better position to help people," the Young Father said. "That may be the place to be, until people of your strength are called for."

"Strength!" Dewell laughed. "I'm afraid of every bright light and loud noise."

"Your strength may surprise you," the Young Father said, squeezing the bundle he was holding. "Even the smallest among us could change the galaxy."

"Even your child."

The Young Father looked down and smiled. "Even he."

"I hope we don't have to wait that long," Dewell said.

"Agreed." The Young Father nodded. "But I'm prepared to."

He looked over his shoulder. Across the tarmac, another transport was readying to lift off. "That's my ride."

Dewell watched as the man turned. "I'm sorry," he called.

"I don't think I caught your name."

"Who I am is no longer important," the Young Father said, not looking back.

Dewell nodded. "Maybe. But what you do is." He waved. "Keep doing it . . . if you can."

A long time ago, in a galaxy far, far away . . .
a new era begins

Read on for an excerpt from

A NEW DAWN

by
JOHN JACKSON MILLER

CHAPTER ONE

"SOUND COLLISION!"

Only a moment earlier, the Star Destroyer had emerged from hyperspace; now, a cargo ship careened straight toward its bridge. Before *Ultimatum*'s shields could be raised or cannons could be brought to bear, the approaching vessel abruptly veered upward.

Rae Sloane watched, incredulous, as the wayward freighter hurtled above her bridge's viewport and out of sight. But not out of hearing: a tiny scraping *ka-thump* signaled it had just clipped the top of the giant ship's hull. The new captain looked back at her first officer. "Damage?"

"None, Captain."

No surprise, she thought. It was surely worse for the other guy. "These yokels act as if they haven't seen a Star Destroyer before!"

"I'm sure they haven't," Commander Chamas said.

"They'd better get used to it." Sloane observed the cloud of transports ahead of *Ultimatum*. Her enormous *Imperial*-class starship had arrived from hyperspace on the edge of the appointed safe-approach lane, bringing it perilously close to what had to be the biggest traffic jam in the Inner Rim. She addressed the dozens of crewmembers at their stations. "Stay alert. *Ultimatum*'s too new to bring back with a scratched finish." Thinking again, she narrowed her eyes. "Send a message on the Mining Guild channel. The next moron that comes within a kilometer of us gets a turbolaser haircut."

"Aye, Captain."

Of course, Sloane had never been to this system either, having just attained her captaincy in time for *Ultimatum*'s shakedown cruise. Tall, muscular, dark-skinned, and black-haired, Sloane had performed exceptionally from the start and ascended swiftly through the ranks. True, she was only substituting on *Ultimatum*, whose intended captain was serving on assignment to the construction committee—but how many others had helmed capital ships at thirty? She didn't know: the Imperial Navy had only been in existence by that name for less than a decade, since Chancellor Palpatine put down the traitorous Jedi and transformed the Republic into the Galactic Empire. Sloane just knew the days ahead would decide whether she got a ship of her own.

This system, she'd been briefed, was home to something rare: a true astronomical odd couple. Gorse, out the forward viewport, lived up to its reputation as perhaps the ugliest planet in the galaxy. Tidally locked to its parent star, the steaming mudball had one side that forever baked. Only the permanently dark side was habitable, home to an enormous industrial city amid a landscape of strip mines. Sloane couldn't imagine living on a world that never saw a sunrise—if you could call sweating through an endless muggy summer night *living*. Looking off to the right, she saw the real jewel: Cynda, Gorse's sole moon. Almost large enough to be counted in Imperial record keeping as a double planet with Gorse, Cynda had a glorious silver shine—as charming as its parent was bleak.

But Sloane wasn't interested in the sights, or the travails of the lives of all the losers on Gorse. She started to turn from the window. "Inform Count Vidian we have—"

"*You're doing it wrong,*" snapped a low baritone voice.

The harshly intoned words startled everyone on the bridge, for they had all heard them before—just seldom from this source. It was their famous passenger's catchphrase, quoted on many a business program during the Republic days and still used to introduce his successful series of management aids now that he had moved on to government service.

So delightful, then, to have it used on her. "Count Vidian," Sloane stated, her eyes searching from doorway to doorway.

Denetrius Vidian appeared in the entryway farthest from Sloane. "I said, you're doing it wrong," he repeated, although there was no doubting everyone had heard him the first time. "I heard you transmit the order for mining traffic to avoid you. It would be more efficient for *you* to back away from their transit lanes."

Sloane straightened. "The Imperial Navy does not back away from *commercial traffic.*"

Vidian stamped his metal heel on the deck. "Spare me your institutional pride. If it weren't for the thorilide this system produces, you'd only have a shuttle to captain!"

Sloane scowled, hating to be talked down to on her own bridge. This needed to seem like her decision. "It's the Empire's thorilide. Give them a wide berth. Chamas, back us a kilometer from the convoy lanes—and monitor all traffic."

"Aye, Captain."

"Aye is right," Vidian said. Each syllable was crisply pronounced and mechanically modulated, as if recorded in a studio, and amplified so all could hear. But Sloane would never get over the strangest part, which she'd noticed when he boarded: the man's mouth never moved. Vidian's words came from a special vocal prosthetic, a computer attached to a speaker embedded in the silvery plating that ringed his neck.

She'd once heard the voice of Darth Vader, the Emperor's principal emissary; while mechanically amplified, the Dark Lord's much deeper voice still retained some natural trace of whatever was inside that black armor. In contrast, Count Vidian had reportedly chosen his artificial voice based on opinion research, in a quest to own the most motivational voice in the business sector.

And since he had boarded her ship with his aides a week earlier, Vidian had shown no qualms about speaking as loudly as he felt necessary. About *Ultimatum*, her crew—and her.

Vidian strode mechanically onto the bridge. It was the only way to describe it. He was as human as she was, but much of his body had been replaced. His arms and legs were armor-plated, rather than false-flesh prosthetics; everyone knew because he made little effort to hide them. His regal burgundy tunic and knee-length black kilt were his only nods to normal attire for a fiftyish lord of industry.

But it was Vidian's face that attracted the most awkward notice. His flesh lost to the same malady that had once consumed his limbs and vocal cords, Vidian covered his features with a synthskin coating. And then there were his eyes: artificial constructs, glowing yellow irises sitting in seas of red. The eyes appeared meant for some other species besides humans; Vidian had chosen them solely for what they could do. She could tell that now as he walked, glanced outside from convoy to convoy, ship to ship, mentally analyzing the whole picture.

"We've already met some of the locals," she said. "You probably heard the bump. The people here are—"

"Disorganized. It's why I'm here." He turned and walked along the line of terminal operators until he arrived at the tactical station depicting all the ships in the area. He pushed past Cauley, the young human ensign, and tapped a command key. Then Vidian stepped back from the console and froze, seeming to stare blankly into space.

"My lord?" Cauley asked, unnerved.

"I have fed the output from your screen to my optical implants," Vidian said. "You may return to your work while I read."

The tactical officer did so—no doubt relieved, Sloane thought, not to have the cyborg hanging over his shoulder. Vidian's ways were strange, to be sure, but effective, and that was why he was on her ship. The onetime industrialist was now the Emperor's favorite efficiency expert.

Gorse's factories produced refined thorilide, a rare strategic substance needed in massive quantities for a variety of Imperial projects. But the raw material these days came from Cynda, its moon: hence the traffic jam of cargo ships crisscrossing the void between the two globes. The Emperor had dispatched Vidian to improve production—a job he was uniquely qualified for.

Vidian was known for squeezing the very last erg of energy, the very last kilogram of raw material, the very last unit of factory production from one world after another. He was not in the Emperor's closest circle of advisors—not yet. But it was clear to Sloane he soon would be, provided there was no relapse of whatever ailment it was that had brought him low years earlier. Vidian's billions had bought him extra life—and he seemed determined that neither he nor anyone else waste a moment of it.

Since he'd boarded, she hadn't had a conversation

with him where he hadn't interrupted at least a dozen times.

"We've alerted the local mining firms to your arrival, Count. The thorilide production totals—"

"—are already coming in," Vidian said, and with that, he marched to another data terminal in the aft section of the bridge.

Commander Chamas joined her far forward, many meters away from the count. In his late forties, Chamas had been leapfrogged in rank by several younger officers. The man loved gossip too much.

"You know," Chamas said quietly, "I heard he bought the title."

"Are you surprised? Everything else about him is artificial," Sloane whispered. "Ship's doctor even thinks some of his parts were voluntarily—"

"You waste time wondering," Vidian said, not looking up from where he was studying.

Sloane's dark eyes widened. "I'm sorry, my lord—"

"Forget the formality—and the apology. There is little point for either. But it is well for your crew to know someone is always listening—and may have better ears than yours."

Even if they had to buy them in a store, Sloane thought. The ragged fleshy lobes that had once been Vidian's ears held special hearing aids. They could obviously hear her words—and more. She approached him.

"This is exactly what I'd expected," Vidian said, staring at whatever unseen thing was before his eyes. "I told the Emperor it would be worth sending me here." A number of underproducing worlds that manufactured items critical to the security of the Empire had been removed from their local governors' jurisdictions and placed under Vidian's authority: Gorse was the latest. "Messy work might have been good enough for the Republic—but the Empire is order from chaos. What we do here—and in thousands of systems just like this one—brings us closer to our ultimate goal."

Sloane thought for a moment. "Perfection?"

"Whatever the Emperor wants."

Sloane nodded.

A tinny squawk came from Vidian's neck-speaker—an unnerving sound she'd learned to interpret as his equivalent of an angry sigh. "There's a laggard holding up the moonward convoy," he said, staring into nothingness. Looking at her tactician's screen, Sloane saw it was the cargo vessel that had bumped them earlier. She ordered *Ultimatum* turned to face it.

A shower of sparks flew from the freighter's underside. Other vessels hung back, fearful it might explode. "Hail the freighter," she said.

A quavering nonhuman voice was piped onto the bridge. "This is *Cynda Dreaming*. Sorry about that scrape earlier. We weren't expecting—"

Sloane cut to the point. "What's your payload?"

"Nothing, yet. We were heading to pick up a load of thorilide on the moon for refining at Calladan Chemworks down on Gorse."

"Can you haul in your condition?"

"We need to get to the repair shop to know. I'm not sure how bad it is. Could be a couple of months—"

Vidian spoke up. "Captain, target that vessel and fire."

It was almost idly stated, to the extent that Vidian's intonations ever conveyed any genuine emotion. The directive nonetheless startled Chamas. Standing before the gunnery crew, he turned to the captain for guidance.

The freighter pilot, having heard the new voice, sounded no less surprised. "I'm sorry—I didn't get that. Did you just—"

Sloane looked for an instant at Vidian, and then at her first officer. "Fire."

The freighter captain sounded stunned. "What? You can't be—"

This time, *Ultimatum*'s turbolasers provided the interruption. Orange energy ripped through space, turning *Cynda Dreaming* into a confusion of fire and flak.

Sloane watched as the other ships of the convoy quickly rerouted. Her gunners had done their jobs, targeting the ship in a way that resulted in minimal hazard for the nearby ships. All the freighters were moving faster.

"You understand," Vidian said, turning toward her. "Replacement time for one freighter and crew in this sector is—"

"—three weeks," Sloane said, "which is less than two months." *See, I've read your reports, too.*

This was the way to handle this assignment, she realized. So what if Vidian was strange? Figuring out what the Emperor—and those who spoke for him—wanted and then providing it was the path to success. Debating his directives only wasted time and made her look bad. It was the secret of advancement in the service: always be on the side of what is going to happen anyway.

Sloane clasped her arms behind her back. "We'll see that the convoys make double time—and challenge any ship that refuses."

"It isn't just transit," Vidian said. "There are problems on the ground, too—on planet and moon. Surveillance speaks of unruly labor, of safety and environmental protests. And there's always the unexpected."

Sloane clasped her arms behind her back. "*Ultimatum* stands at your service, my lord. This system will do what you—what the Emperor—requires of it."

"So it will," Vidian said, bloodred eyes narrowing. "So it will."

* * *

Hera Syndulla watched from afar as the scattered remains of the freighter burned silently in space. No recovery vehicles were in sight. As unlikely a prospect as survivors were, no one looked for any. There were only the shipping convoys, quickly rerouting around the wreckage.

Obeying the master's whip.

This was mercy in the time of the Empire, she thought. The Imperials had none; now, to all appearances, their lack of care was infecting the people.

The green-skinned Twi'lek in her stealth-rigged starship didn't believe that was true. People were basically decent, and would one day rise up against their unjust government. But it wouldn't happen now, and certainly not here. It was too soon, and Gorse was barely awake politically. This wasn't a recruitment trip. No, these days were for seeing what the Empire could do—a project that suited the ever-curious Hera perfectly. And Count Vidian, the Emperor's miracle man, practically begged investigation.

In previous weeks, the Imperial fixer had cut a swath through the sector, "improving efficiency." On three previous worlds, like-minded acquaintances of Hera's on the HoloNet had reported misery levels skyrocketing under Vidian's electronic eyes. Then her contacts had simply vanished. That had piqued Hera's interest—and learning of Vidian's visit to the Gorse system brought her the rest of the way.

She had another contact on Gorse, one who had promised much information on the regime. She wanted that information—but first she wanted to check out Vidian, and the system's notoriously anarchic mining trade offered her a variety of chances to get close. Industrial confusion, the perfect lure for Vidian, would provide excellent cover for her to study his methods.

Emperor Palpatine had too many minions with great power and influence. It was worth finding out whether Count Vidian had real magic before he rose any higher.

It was time to move. She picked out the identifying transponder signal of a ship in the convoy. One button-push later, her ship *was* that vessel, as far as anyone trying to watch traffic was concerned. With practiced ease, she weaved her freighter into the chaotic flood of cargo ships heading to the moon.

None of these guys can fly worth a flip, she thought. It was just as well it wasn't a recruiting trip. She probably wouldn't have found anyone worth her time.